AMERICAN BOMBSHELL

DAVID KING

POOLBEG

Published 2023
by Poolbeg Press Ltd
123 Grange Hill, Baldoyle
Dublin 13, Ireland
E-mail: poolbeg@poolbeg.com
www.poolbeg.com

The moral right of the author has been asserted.
A catalogue record for this book is available from the British Library.

ISBN 978-1-78199-708-6

About the Author

David King is originally from England but now lives in Kenmare, County Kerry, Ireland. When he isn't reading or writing, David loves walking along the coast with the family Labrador, watching the sea during a storm, and enjoying the occasional glass of wine. He got his first degree in Classics and Archaeology from the University of Warwick, spent much of his career protecting the environment, and now lives with dog and flock of sheep on a rocky small holding on Kerry's wild and windy Atlantic coast.

To the World War Two Generation.
You were stronger than we will ever be.

Acknowledgements

I would like to thank the women who have made this book what it is.
They are (in no particular order) Paula Campbell at Poolbeg Press, for
seeing something worthwhile in what was an admittedly rough
manuscript, my editor Gaye Shortland, the ever patient Sarah King
and the Honourable Mary Montagu.

I would also like to thank the staff at the Imperial War Museum,
including the Archive and Research Room; the Shuttleworth Collection
at Biggleswade; the Kent Battle of Britain Museum at Hawkinge; the
American Air Museum in Britain (online archive); Time Ghost World
War Two YouTube Channel; Queenmary.com; Bromley Historical
Times for the recipe for Woolton Pie.

Thanks also to Wing Commander Robert Foster, DFC, Flight
Lieutenant Jimmy 'Binder' Corbin, DFC, and Edith Kupp for their
wartime memories and for answering my foolish questions.

And, finally, my mother and father for living the wartime lives they
did and Graham and Allison Huxter for their unflagging encouragement.

PROLOGUE

RMS *Queen Mary*

White Star Line
Southampton
February, 1947

My Dear Friend,

Just minutes ago, I was standing at the rail of this famous liner, this Castle of Steel as Mr. Churchill called it. I could feel the shuddering of the engines through my feet, and behind smoke was rising from the three tall, red funnels. Far below, I could make out the dockers, scurrying around like beetles, releasing the ropes and getting the Queen Mary ready to brave the great, grey Atlantic.

In the blurry, bulging crowd, flashbulbs were popping, and on a platform I could see a newsreel man and his camera. Somehow I had become part of something enormous, an event that would be remembered as a moment in time, and in history. And it was crazy. I'm just an ordinary factory girl. A nobody. Yet there I was, standing where film stars and kings had stood. It was like a moving picture, more than real life.

1

You wouldn't believe the size of the crowd that came to see us off, all waving, crying, calling out goodbyes. I had never seen so many people in one place, ten times the number that worked at Morelli's. Around me too, pressing against the rail, were hundreds of women and children, packed tightly together onto one noisy, pregnant ship. The sound of the voices was a roaring, like a storm at sea must be, or a cup final. But high above it you could still make out ships' horns blaring, anchor chains rattling and gulls mewing. It was far, far louder than the factory line ever was.

But the excitement meant little to me. It flowed around and beyond me, barely touching what you might call my soul. My thoughts were elsewhere. I was thinking that back along those snow-stained roads, beyond Southampton dock, hundreds of miles inland, was everything I'd ever seen or heard. It struck me that I was leaving behind both the good and the bad, the living and those now dead. I knew I'd never see poor old bombed-out England again. Nor you, my love.

Luck's so important in war, and in life, isn't it? It was pure luck I survived the flying bomb the Germans sent to blot out my life, and the same for the one that nearly ended yours. Without luck I wouldn't have met you. Or the American. Without luck I wouldn't be here to see the victory and all of this wonderful madness. Despite the orphanage, and the things that happened there, despite Hitler and his Luftwaffe, despite surprises, disappointment and deaths all around, I've survived. It seems very much against the odds.

It's strange to lie here, in this great mahogany cabin, writing a letter that will need an American stamp. I can't imagine one without the King's head, can you? In five short days I'll know what the Yanks have on theirs. Yes. America. Home of film stars, Coca-Cola and jazz. The way some people talk you'd think it was the Promised Land. But is it? It seems an enormous place to someone not even out of their teens. I don't show it, but deep down the prospect of setting foot there, and meeting Him, makes me feel shiver.

But, I have to succeed, not just for me but for those who didn't make it, for my dad's memory and even perhaps for you.

So like this ship, I'm pointing myself forward, into the wind. Wish me luck (though you can't wave me goodbye). I've no idea what happens now, but I shall never forget you, or that cold, wet, loving summer of nineteen forty-four.

Three Years Earlier

CHAPTER 1

February 1944

The seventeen-year-old girl hesitated at the low garden gate, the familiar blue paint of which had now begun to peel with age. Her childhood home, with its rough red-brick façade, crooked windows and temperamental, ill-fitting doors, seemed smaller and grubbier than memory had suggested. Her body was tall and slim, yet with curves that were pronounced enough to have attracted unwanted attention on her long train journey. She had more than the usual pallor of the typical ration-fed civilian, her undernourished pale skin looking more like that of a recently released prisoner, or a perhaps a refugee. The impoverished impression was strengthened by her home-cut, mousey-blonde hair, a set of much-repaired clothes, and the cheap, battered suitcase she had placed beside her on the pavement. But the young woman held her body upright, her striking slate-blue eyes regarding the humble Midlands terrace with determination as much as wariness.

At the end of the path was a kneeling female figure, scrubbing the step ferociously with a stiff brush, dipping it every so often into a bucket of grey sudsy water, and cursing softly to herself.

For a second Rosie hesitated. It had been a long time since the mother she now saw had sent her away and, although the cottage held happy memories of childhood, it was also the place of accusation, humiliation and death. Rosie picked up the case and paused for one last second, building strength for the confrontation that she knew must follow.

The old house, she thought, as she walked slowly down the slippery brick path, was as ramshackle as she remembered, from the gap-toothed picket fence to the bubbling paint on the old front door. She knew the windows would whistle creepily when the wind blew from the east, just as the slates would slip and clatter when it came from the north. There would still be a damp patch on the ceiling of the bedroom she'd once called her own, and in the winter the Parkray would fail to heat either house or water to much above freezing.

Next-door's pink chintz curtains twitched, and the young woman wondered what her mother had said to the neighbours by way of explanation for her daughter's absence. Among the flood of evacuees of 1940, her departure might have gone unnoticed. But Rosie was no evacuee, and her brother, now in the Navy, had remained. She drew in her breath, reminded herself that her stay would be temporary, and slowly pushed open the gate.

'That you, Rosie?'

A scarfed head bobbed suddenly upwards. It was attached to a tiny, thrifty-faced woman. Her voice was hoarse from cheap, unfiltered cigarettes and even cheaper whisky. She turned, greeting her daughter with a cursory nod and a pair of empty grey eyes. She'd aged, Rosie thought as she drew level.

'Supper's on the table, Rosie,' said her mother, turning away. ''Tis cold but there it is, I've work to do.' She spoke in short, dry bursts, quickly replacing the cigarette that hung, dribbling grey fumes, from her mouth.

The obsessive swishing of the brush resumed and Rosie noticed the gnarled hands were stained yellow-brown by dirt and nicotine.

'I'll go in then.' The words came out haltingly.

'Suit yourself.'

The daughter hesitated. After the years apart, the gap between them was as wide and unbridgeable as it had always been.

The front door swung open. His hair had greyed and the soulful brown eyes had acquired the faint pearly opacity of age, but the dog's thumping tail still beat strongly. The animal leapt, delighted to see his friend back after her unexplained odyssey, as though only a few days had passed. Here was a welcome worth the name.

'*Peter!*' Rosie embraced him.

The dog had survived against the odds, his tendency towards domestic burglary having always put him at risk. The incorrigible black Labrador grinned, a floppy pink tongue protruding from his mouth, like a thick slice of ham. The dog overflowed with affection and suddenly Rosie realised how much she'd missed him. She closed the door and the dog sniffed her suitcase curiously, as if to ask where his long-lost friend had been.

Inside the dim, low-ceilinged living room, a dinner plate covered with a tea towel had been left on the table. As the dog watched, not without self-interest, the young woman wolfed down the cold spam and mash that waited there. The potato was lumpy and the meat seared black, proving her mother's cooking to be as grim as ever. But Rosie was starving, and she ate rapidly, as though someone might take the meal from her at any moment, her gaze flicking rapidly around. The tick of the mantelpiece Napoleon still filled the air and a lonely tongue of flame darted deep inside the Parkray. On the mantelpiece next to the clock stood a framed photograph of her brother, now almost unrecognisable. Impossibly adult in his naval uniform. The Welsh dresser was there, decked with willow-pattern plates, and the Chinese rug, though worn, had also endured.

Suddenly Rosie paused, her fork frozen midway between plate and mouth. The wall where her father's bookcase had stood was blank, marks on the wallpaper indicating where the shelves had blocked the light. All of the books, pamphlets, encyclopaedias and atlases, the six-penny novels and the scientific magazines had gone. She put down the fork. It was as if the heart of the house had been torn out and she had no doubt who had done it. For a few moments she focused silently back on the plate. Then, gathering her strength, she excavated another blob of nubby potato.

Rosie finished the meal, and knelt before the stove, holding out her thin, pale hands to catch the feeble warmth bleeding slowly through the glass, before she stood and moved to the kitchen where she put on her mother's apron and began to wash up, clanking the dishes together in the cold water as she stood at the stained Belfast sink.

In the yard outside the window lay the few feet of gritty earth that formed the tiny vegetable garden her father had planted, but now, from within a cage on the path, a pair of curious, balding chickens blinked. Impulsively she shook the water from her hands, grabbed a scrap of dry bread from the breadbin, pushed open the still-stubborn door and went out into the yard.

'Hello,' she said, introducing herself. 'What's this?'

The chickens jabbed and jostled eagerly. They were keen-eyed, clucking and pushing one another to get to the unexpected treat. Like Rosie herself, they looked half starved.

The backyard, she noted, was the same. The black, sherd-strewn dirt looked set to yield only its usual harvest of grotesque carrots, perforated cabbages and wormy potatoes. The cinder path crunched familiarly beneath her feet and led down to the handmade wooden gate, with its perennially squeaky hinges, behind which, she knew, ran the dank, unsavoury alley. The paint on the timbers felt rough under her fingers, crumbling easily in sharp, brittle flakes. For a moment she was a young girl again, standing in the summer sun, watching her father daub the bright blue with a sad, balding brush. She felt his large hands once more gripping hers as he painstakingly demonstrated: dipping in the pot, then using quick-spreading strokes to apply the paint, mopping up the drips as they formed.

Rosie returned indoors, grabbed her suitcase and climbed the steep and narrow stairs. The latch to her old room was rusty and stiff, opening after some effort with a metallic clunk, and inside the familiar wallpaper, though yellowed, clung defiantly to the crazily sloped ceiling of the tiny attic room. The pin-up images of movie stars were gone, but her eiderdown still sagged on the old wooden bed.

She began to transfer her few belongings into the chest of drawers, finding in one an old copy of *Movie Star*, and a faded school exercise book. '*Rosemary Haskell, Form 2B.*' Nothing more of her earlier, almost forgotten life seemed to have survived.

Thrusting her suitcase under the bed, Rosie met unexpected resistance. She peered under the frame and was greeted by the sight of a large, dusty cardboard box. Curious, she tugged the dog-eared container out and as she opened the lid was delighted to find it crammed with books.

Eagerly she opened the first, a large blue volume: *Pears World Atlas*. Wonderingly, she turned the pages of the heavy, dusty volume. Her father had bought it when she was eight and, despite its bulk, she'd taken it on their first trip to the seaside in his gleaming red-and-black motorcycle combination, that summer of 1935, convinced of its necessity on such a long voyage.

Rosie closed her eyes. She could almost hear the thumping of the engine, and thought for a second she caught the faintest whiff of its oily, petroley smell.

***

It had been hot, that day, with her and her brother Roger jammed into the sidecar's two tiny seats, the dog curled awkwardly on the floor, while buckets, spades, a football and a picnic basket sat on laps or stuck haphazardly out into the slipstream. It had been a blustery journey alright, cool despite the English summer sun, and it was the wind as much as the sunlight that had reddened their faces. Along seemingly endless highways they'd roared, their capped and goggled father hunched forward over the handlebars as their sensitive young noses filled with the scent of hot oil, the earthiness of the passing fields and the aromatic tang of blistering-hot tarmac.

No sooner had they arrived at the prom than the children extruded themselves from their cramped travelling space, tumbled carelessly over the low sea wall and careered down the beach to the sea, accompanied by the madly barking dog. After the cramped side-car, the briny water flowed deliciously around their legs, cooling their flesh until they hopped and squealed. Beneath the water pale feet sank gently into the yielding sand, which squidged sensually between their hot wriggling toes.

Peter had been young and full of bounce then, barking furiously at the restless waves which seemed to have such an unreasonable life of their own. He'd become obsessed with digging holes, and several times her father had to apologise when the animal stole a towel, a pair of trunks and shoes from prostrate holiday-makers.

'He's full of life, you see!' her father had explained, in his eccentric way. 'Aware of the enormous possibilities of the day! Of the Great and Wonderful, the What and Where!'

Mostly people nodded politely and looked away. A few, the nicer ones, grinned and fussed over the incorrigible Labrador.

Rosie and Roger sat on the sea wall, kicking legs absently against the warm concrete, watching their father remove the checked tea towel covering the picnic basket. They fell on the sandwiches he produced, as though they hadn't eaten in days.

Their father talked, as he usually did on such occasions, about sailing ships and seashells and quoted the poem about the walrus and the carpenter. He pointed out in the atlas where they were, and Rosie had been disappointed to find they were, after such an epic journey, still in England.

For one unhappy moment she remembered her mother had prepared the picnic, Edith's absence suddenly apparent, like a cloud drifting over the sun.

She'd heard them arguing before they left and, clambering from the loaded sidecar, had walked apprehensively to the still-open front door. Her mother hadn't seen her, and continued, wandering distractedly to and fro. Every so often she would stop and pick something up, only to put it down again.

'I know they've been in here,' she'd said, preoccupied. 'Those people from the shop. They've been in here and taken my hat.'

Her father had approached the distracted woman and taken her hand. But despite his gentleness, Rosie could tell from his body that he wanted to leave.

'Come on, lass, let's be going,' he cajoled.

Suddenly she sat down and, to Rosie's alarm, burst into tears.

'Those people!' Her mother was sobbing. 'They've been in and taken my hat. They hate me! They all do!'

Rosie's eyes had opened wide. Her father sighed and put an arm around his wife's shoulders.

'You know that's not true, Edie. Let's be going, *eh*? The kids are aboard already.'

But her mother had shaken off her father's comforting hand and sat silently, dabbing her nose with the handkerchief she kept tucked into the sleeve of her dress.

Rosie tiptoed quietly back to the sidecar, feeling oddly guilty. It was an ominous start, and she began to fret. Back inside the house she could hear her father making tea, his voice low and reassuring. But the sun was getting higher and the day warmer, and she could almost feel the pull of the sea. She shifted uncomfortably. Roger meanwhile had gathered a number of revolting earthworms from the garden and was trying to frighten her with them. She frowned at him, sighed and longed to get moving. Just when she'd almost given up hope, the door slammed and she saw her father walking briskly down the path. He swung his leg stiffly astride and kicked the motorcycle roughly into life.

'*You're mother's not well!*' he shouted, pulling down his goggles. '*So we're off! Hands In, and Hang On!*'

On the seawall, they finished the picnic. Her father took his children's hands and wandered down to the sea, brother and sister hanging from his arms like fruit clinging to a tree. Roger took his spade and with it they buried their dad in the yellow sand, then ran away screaming when he arose, growling like a sea monster. They paddled in the rock pools, where Roger caught a crab, a few darting shrimps and a funny squidgy thing no one knew the name of. He wanted to take his collection home in a jam-jar but was dissuaded.

At the end of the afternoon, with Roger dragging sandalled feet in fractious exhaustion, they finally arrived back at the wall.

'Come on, children, lend me a hand!'

Reluctantly they'd packed the sidecar, an action that seemed to set off an exodus, for within minutes an evacuation of day-trippers began across the beach: deckchairs were folded, sand shaken off rugs. Fathers began to struggle up the beach, overloaded with windbreaks, picnic baskets and fishing rods, and here and there a few disobedient offspring clung stubbornly to the sand in lingering last-minute games of cricket.

As Rosie watched, the beach took on the pinks and yellows of the evening, while overhead piratical gulls swooped, dive-bombing any tempting leftovers. By the water's edge, grown-ups clung to each other, hand in hand, and gazed lingeringly in each other's eyes, as if by such strength of feeling they could prolong the day. But the light was bleeding into the horizon, and she knew that soon the sun would slip off the edge of the world and fall away into the darkness.

She peered at her father. He had the faraway look he'd had when they first arrived and seemed, if not sad, then deep in thought. He leant against the bike and closed his eyes, relishing the evening breeze.

'Faeries,' he said at last, turning to his children, 'come take me out of this dull world, For I would ride with you upon the wind, Run on the top of the dishevelled tide, And dance upon the mountains like a flame!'

His love of words spilled from him as easily as water from a spring and made Rosie laugh.

She reached into the sidecar and fished out an old pullover. She was determined not to endure the return journey in the same space as her fractious brother, and climbed firmly onto the seat behind her father, entwining her arms around his waist. His body contracted with a short laugh, she felt the vibration as the bike revved, and then they were off.

As they hit the highway, the thump of the engine and burbling of exhaust melded with the rush of the slipstream into a lullaby so effective that Roger was soon asleep, slumped low in the sidecar. Peter sat upright, leaning so far out, his face to the wind, eyes closed, that it was a miracle he didn't fall. Rosie rested against her father's back, smiling at the dog's carefree happiness, and hung on. She resisted sleep and instead entered a part-dream world where passing shapes merged into a stream of fluid thoughts and meanings. The passing trees became friendly giants waving them on their way, the regular lampposts stern policemen, while the sunbeams took on the gleaming faces of fair-haired, golden angels.

Rosie sniffed the air and looked around her tiny, dimly lit room. Reluctantly she put the book carefully back in the box. The air in the attic was chilly and stale, redolent of mothballs, a world away from the warmth and joy of that summer. She cast her threadbare coat, its collar still stamped with her number from the institution, to the floor and crawled gratefully beneath the bedclothes. The room, for all its failings, was at the top of the house and a sanctuary of sorts from her mother. And she was well beyond the terrifyingly arbitrary authority of the orphanage too. Yet she felt little relief, only the fragile triumph of an absconding prisoner: broken out and on the run perhaps, but not yet truly free.

Rosie shivered as her slender body warmed, pulling the comfortingly heavy eiderdown over her head until only her nose protruded into the cold, and sighed. She would be staying only as long as it took for her plan to work. Three years had been more than long enough to think of her future. She sighed again.

She was more tired than she had thought. And soon her eyes fluttered, opened and closed. Awareness of the room began to fade, the blood-red light filtering through her eyelids began to form into abstract shapes as, step by step, her mind began to descend from the hardness of reality into the warm embrace of dreams.

CHAPTER 2

Antony Morelli's complexion was Mediterranean and his dark, slicked-back hair shone with Brylcreem as he sat behind his desk. He wore an expensive-looking suit and from a beaming face a pair of black, glinting eyes looked her lingeringly. He was, she guessed, quite old – in his thirties perhaps, and although he had an easy, confident charm, there was something about him that was as slippery as his hair.

Rosie shifted uncomfortably in the capacious leather chair and glanced quickly around the modern wood-panelled office. In the corner stood a gleaming teak Morelli Radiogram, the floor was richly carpeted, and gold-framed prints of scientific instruments decorated the walls. On the desk was a wood and brass plaque with the words *'A. Morelli, Jnr. Managing Director.'*

Without a school certificate she'd been lucky to get an interview in a place like the radio factory. But she'd answered a barrage of questions, and had been relieved when the matter of her education featured only marginally.

When he wasn't staring at her, the manager, rather oddly she thought, spent most of his time doodling on the blotter. Without warning Morelli glanced at his watch, stood abruptly and held out his hand, which she found herself shaking dumbly.

'Good, good,' he was saying, a smile playing around his thin lips. 'I'm happy to say you have the job of assembly worker. Can you begin today?'

Rosie's mood soared. Perhaps it her keenness or good manners that had impressed him.

'Thank you! I—"

'Just one thing.' He looked her casually up and down. 'Your vital statistics.'

'I beg your pardon?'

His gaze was oddly piercing, and she felt herself blushing.

'Bust, waist, hips. For the uniform.' He gestured to her to stand in a manner that suggested he was used to being obeyed.

'Thirty-four, twenty-six, thirty-four, I think,' she said, getting hesitantly to her feet, and feeling strangely humiliated.

Morelli looked her over with what seemed like a practised eye while Rosie regarded him warily.

'Height?'

'Five foot six.'

'Very good,' he said at last, like a doctor having completed an examination.

He escorted her to the door, pointed to the end of the long corridor and told her to go down the stairs to the shop floor. She turned to thank him, but he was already walking away, humming a contented-sounding tune to himself.

Downstairs, she opened a pair of double doors and gulped, staring wonderingly around.

The vast whirring factory looked like a set from *Journey to the Centre of the Earth*, a cavern hidden from the outside, yet inside humming

16

with electric light and strange, subterranean activity. The room was as tall as a cathedral, and perhaps twice as wide, the whole width of the floor divided into rows of benches, between which ran slithering conveyors which filled the background with the continuous hum. At each station on the line women wielded tools, and every so often one would set a gadget on the belt which was immediately carried away. Rather oddly, as if it had been an afterthought, dance music played in the background over unseen speakers.

A tall, long-limbed girl in dungarees with short bobbed blonde hair, appeared. A beam of sunshine, descending from a roof-light, formed a coincidental pool in which she stood, making her clear skin glow. Despite her pretty face, with its upturned nose and pert smile, there was an almost masculine vitality about her, a nimbleness and confidence of movement that implied strength. Lively green eyes sparkled and she bore a welcoming smile, which Rosie saw with some relief. She looked to be about twenty-one or two.

'How-do!' said the woman in a strange northern accent. 'Tha must be Rosemary. Them upstairs said tha would be comin' this mornin'.'

Her voice was as smooth as English butter toffee, but with an underlying depth that was strangely attractive. On the lapel of her overall was a small enamel brooch featuring a gold hammer-and-sickle against a red background. The impressively confident girl held out a hand which Rosie shook.

'My name's Hazel and I'll show thee round, Rosemary.'

'Rosie. Please.'

'Aye, alright. Rosie. Come with me.'

The girl's poise and confidence in the alien, technical world was impressive, but her grin was warm, and her eyes twinkled with what looked like mischief. Like Morelli, she seemed to be appraising the new arrival.

Hazel led Rosie down a long row, pointing out aspects of the factory as they went. Rosie couldn't help but notice that, despite the masculine attire and a strong-looking pair of shoulders which implied an almost Amazonian strength, Hazel's body was not without feminine curves. She looked as though she would be experienced in the ways of the world, and of men.

At last they reached a gang of overalled workers gathered round a table, industriously stuffing odd-looking electrical gadgets into boxes.

Hazel grabbed an overall from a hook and threw it to Rosie, who put it on, wondering to herself why she'd had to be measured for a uniform if they were provided so literally 'off the peg'.

'First, tha takes one of these boxes,' Hazel was saying. 'Then tha takes one of these 'ere thingumabobs ...'

With surprising delicacy her new friend picked up one of the strange metal devices covered in wires. 'Tha pops him in, and then tha fills the space in the box with wood shavings.' She scooped a handful from a large metal hopper to demonstrate, grinning. 'And then tha tapes the box shut with this new Sellotape stuff!'

Hazel placed the box in a wheeled metal trolley basket, already filled to the brim with completed packages.

'Clarence!' Hazel called to a young man.

The boy grinned and nodded at them with an odd kind of childishness as he walked over. He saluted, giggled and began to push the loaded trolley away.

'Two sandwiches short of a picnic,' said Hazel, noting Rosie's quizzical expression. 'But the lad has a heart of gold, and 'ee's well liked. Some of the girls here treat 'im like a baby brother like they've left back at 'ome.'

'Oh.' Rosie watched the beaming young man as he made his way across the factory, nodding and smiling at everyone as he passed. Like her, perhaps, he'd been an outsider, underestimated and discarded. But someone had given him a job here in the factory and now he was earning a living and 'doing his bit' for the war effort, just like any man. It seemed a good sign, an omen perhaps of a world that was changing.

Hazel interrupted her thoughts.

'Now it's thy turn.'

Rosie picked up one of the frail items gingerly, dropped it heavily into a box and scooped in some shavings, which despite her efforts scattered everywhere.

A dark-haired, pretty, long-nosed brunette laughed. 'Hey, girls, we've got a right daft one here!' she remarked sneeringly.

'I'm sorry,' Rosie mumbled, glowing with embarrassment.

'Take no notice of starchy knickers over there,' cut in Hazel stiffly. 'Tha'll be alright. Our Clara's as mardy as a moo-cow cos her boyfriend been playin' away from home.'

The other girls laughed loudly, while Clara's eyes narrowed.

It was clear Hazel could take care of herself, but Clara was taller than many men and looked like what her mother would have called a right 'sort'.

The women continued packing until they'd reached the end of their supplies, at which point Hazel took charge again.

'Follow me, duck.' She took Rosie's hand and pulled her along towards the far end of the building where tall shelves stood, loaded with materials.

Rosie was above average height, but still she struggled to keep up with Hazel's confident, long-legged gait.

She ventured a question. 'Does everyone know everyone else's business here?'

'About boyfriends?' replied Hazel. 'Aye, especially as how her new boyfriend's the owner's son!' She indicated Morelli who, dressed in a white shop coat, was chatting in a surprisingly familiar manner with a group of girls further down the line.

'She's going out with him?' asked Rosie, astonished. He seemed very old for Clara.

'It's a right strange arrangement,' agreed Hazel, with a disgruntled expression on her face, 'but she's got her heart set on being Mrs. Morelli. Besides, Clara's got no morals at all.'

'Oh.'

'Aye,' Hazel continued, brightening considerably, 'but Morelli can't keep his equipment inside 'is trousers. And that keeps Clara moody alright!'

Rosie, who suddenly felt very inexperienced in such matters, thought a reply was called for but didn't know quite what to say. 'Isn't Morelli an Italian name?' she managed at last.

'Aye, but he was naturalised before the war.' Hazel paused before adding conspiratorially in a stage whisper, 'Most of us girls say he should have been sterilised!' She grinned at the joke but, seeing Rosie's blank expression, continued, ''e's alright, but don't let 'im creep up behind you. 'as wandering hands, does that feller.'

Rosie worked at the packing table for an hour before being taken to a bench where a formidable cockney woman named Beryl demonstrated the art of soldering. Beryl wore a man's boiler suit and her hair was up in a red Paisley scarf. Her pitted and plain face was permanently furrowed and on her upper lip one could make out a faint black moustache. But, despite the fact that her hands were the size of plates, the oversized woman nevertheless proved surprisingly adept at melting strips of metallic solder using a smoking hot iron and transferring just the right amount to bond two components. As Rosie soon found for herself, it was harder than it looked.

After the soldering, there were several more moves and new jobs in the day, broken only by lunch in the steam-filled canteen.

So occupied was Rosie that it seemed impossible when the wailing of the factory siren signalled the end of the day and her first ever shift.

Looking at her hands, she found that the price of her first day had been two broken nails and a few livid blisters, but they seemed a small price to pay. From somewhere above there came a whirring, like a hundred fairground cars slowing at the same time, and on the shop floor over a vast area she could see the slithering conveyors come finally to a halt.

The room filled instantly with chatter as the girls began putting tools away, before heading off to the changing rooms in small clacking knots.

'Going into town?' Hazel asked as they walked.

'Yes,' replied Rosie – if only her new friend knew how glad she was of company.

'Is tha walkin'?' Hazel enquired solicitously.

'Well –' Rosie halted. Her feet were aching. 'I'd like to take the bus.'

'But tha hasn't been paid yet?' said Hazel, grinning.

Rosie nodded, embarrassed.

'I'll pay and yer can pay me back on payday,' Hazel announced.

They passed off the shop floor through the double doors where Rosie had come in and through another set into a long, narrow changing room. It was crammed with undressing women, some removing scarves and letting down their hair, others wriggling out of overalls and hanging them onto the hooks that lined each wall, almost all of them talking carelessly to each other so that the space was filled with a murmuring of voices.

''Tis a long day, isn't it?' said Hazel, indicating a spot next to her own for Rosie to hang her overall.

Glad to have someone to talk to, Rosie grinned and nodded.

'Yes, but it's good to be busy. It all went past so quickly.'

'Tha liked it then? The work?' Her new friend seemed to be regarding her with a flattering amount of interest and seemed pleasantly relieved when Rosie confirmed she had.

They passed out again through the double doors into the foyer and spontaneously Hazel linked arms, an unconscious gesture, yet it had been so long since Rosie had felt affection she felt tears well suddenly in her eyes. She blinked them away, but glowed with quiet gratitude for her new, tactile friend.

A draught of cool evening air, scented with woodsmoke and cigarettes, swept by as they walked through the factory doors and out into the gathering dusk beyond.

They'd not walked more than a couple of dozen yards outside the gates when they passed a pair of grinning G.I.s next to a jeep. Every so often one stepped forward and pressed something into the hands a passing female.

'Ladies!'

Rosie realised with a shock that the soldier was talking to them. It was the closest she'd ever been to an American and was impressed that close up they seemed almost as much like film stars as she'd imagined, with broad smiles and well-fed faces.

'Yeah, you two lovely ladies! Today is your lucky day!'

The accent was out of place, the glamour of Hollywood come to a small English town. But the beaming soldier seemed really friendly, and passed them a leaflet with a theatrical flourish and confidential wink.

'Champion!' Hazel exclaimed, reading keenly as they walked on. 'Been ages since they had a dance.' She touched her hair thoughtfully. 'I can fettle my hair, but I've nothing to sodding wear.' She handed the leaflet to Rosie and called back to the soldiers, 'Thank you, boys!'

She was rewarded with an embarrassingly loud wolf whistle.

Rosie read the leaflet. The Americans were promising not only dancing but a ballroom, a full bar and something intriguingly calling itself the 'Kings of Swing Show Band'. It sounded both dangerous and wonderful.

'Does tha dance, Rosie?'

Rosie hesitated. She'd dreamed of dancing, but now that the chance had come she seemed paralysed.

'I can't,' she confessed quietly. 'Dance, I mean.'

The orphanage had been strict in its insistence on what the overbearing Matron called 'physical and moral cleanliness'. It had never been clear how dancing could be unclean, but it had certainly been branded immoral, on a par with such terrible sins as swearing and smoking. Now she was free, Rosie had a good mind to take up all three, but the dancing would require time, and lessons.

By the time they reached the town square, Rosie had learnt Hazel's father died in a mining accident when she was 'just a bairn', that she was saving for a motorcycle, couldn't abide steak-and-kidney pie, smoked Woodbines, hoped for a labour government after the war and considered herself a socialist. She was not on speaking terms with her mother. The last fact seemed to bind them even closer together and soon they were holding hands, wandering on past understocked shops and untidy houses, the pavements thickening rapidly around them with the evening's migratory foot traffic.

The bus stop passed unnoticed.

'How come tha can't dance? Has tha never tried?' Hazel asked.

Rosie shook her head, unwilling to disclose the reason. 'Haven't you got a feller to go with?' she mumbled hurriedly.

'Nay!' Hazel laughed. 'Footloose and fancy free, that's me!'

Rosie grinned. Hazel's speech was like something from a past age, she thought, the sentences full of things that belonged in the Bible: thee's, tha's and thou's. She found she rather liked it but couldn't stop a small laugh.

'What?' said Hazel.

'Sorry,' Rosie said hurriedly. 'It's your accent. Where are you from?'

'Yorkshire born and bred,' Hazel answered proudly.

'Oh, I see.'

'I were conscripted down here, along with half the others. From all over, they are.' She waved a hand at the hordes of women on both sides of the road, who Rosie suddenly realised must have all been released from various factories, including Morelli's, at the same time. Thanks to the war, the entire town had become a huge machine regulated by the clocks of its new factories.

They were drawing close to Rosie's turning.

'Perhaps I could just come along and watch – the dancing, I mean,' she ventured.

'Tha's a funny one and no mistake!' Hazel grinned. 'I can show thee. We'll have a practice. There's a gramophone where I'm lodgin'.' She turned a few dance steps along the pavement. '*Ta-rah!* Tha see, it's not hard!'

Rosie laughed. She had the feeling that Hazel wasn't going to take no for an answer.

'Well, alright,' she found herself saying, wondering where she would get a dress that hadn't been darned, or shoes that weren't repaired with cardboard.

Hazel beamed. 'Tha should dance, tha's got the figure for it,' she said encouragingly, her eyes glinting.

CHAPTER 3

'You in there? I shall 'ave breakfast on the table in five minutes!'

There was a short, martial knock on Rosie's bedroom door before a muttering voice receded down the stairs.

Rosie could hear the piercing shriek of the kettle and the bright, brittle clinking of china. She wouldn't put it past her mother to tip her breakfast in the dustbin if she lingered, so she hastily pulled on her childhood dressing gown, scooped cold water from the nightstand and tried, and failed, to do something with her hair.

Downstairs a thin morning meal of tea and burnt, frugally margarined toast was waiting.

Her mother was seated at the table, an opened letter and magnifying glass before her.

'I expect you enjoyed yourself while you were away,' she said suddenly, though without looking up.

Enjoyed? The orphanage? Rosie glanced disbelievingly at her mother.

Edith looked up and beamed over her teacup. Her mood was bright yet brittle and her mind seemed to be skipping about. She wasn't all there. 'A lovely time, I expect,' she was saying, 'gambolling around!'

Rosie stared. Even by her mother's dotty standards this was something.

'No, Mother,' she replied determinedly. 'As a matter of fact, it was completely horrible.'

Her mother paused, a faint flicker of displeasure on her face as if a guest had passed wind in the presence of the vicar. She resumed her blithe manner.

'I knew it would be the making of you, that place. Would you like some more toast?'

It was hard to tell if she was listening at all. Rosie had things she would say about the orphanage, but she was not yet ready. She'd been just a child when she'd been banished from the house, but to the growing self-awareness of approaching adulthood, the separation from her home had nurtured a strong sense of independence, as well as more muted, yet building anger.

'We've had a letter,' her mother announced, picking up the sheet of notepaper and waving it vaguely at Rosie. There was an uncharacteristic springiness in her voice. 'Roger has got some leave.' She beamed as if she'd just announced the Second Coming.

An image of her brother flashed into Rosie's mind. They were children again, playing Tarzan in the trees. Her brother had insisted on being Tarzan and had relegated his sister to the role of chimpanzee. It was not a dignified position and consisted mostly of making monkey noises and doing whatever he told her. In the end she'd climbed the tallest tree she could find and he'd fallen to the ground trying to follow.

She smiled politely at her mother.

Edith peered at the letter through the magnifying glass. Finally she put it down and looked with what seemed like renewed interest at the living room.

Rosie watched her carefully, with a wearied eye.

'I'll have to give the place a complete turn-out,' Edith announced, apparently to herself.

She rose, removing the letter and magnifying glass, fetched a cloth from the kitchen and commenced a vigorous wiping.

Rosie sat dumbly, finishing her toast, as her mother worked around her.

Fetching a balding feather duster from a cupboard, and standing on a chair to reach the cobwebs, Edith was soon at work, evicting their eight-legged creators as she sang cheerfully to herself. Rosie watched, draining her tea as her mother completed the murderous task.

There seemed to be no stopping her, and a few minutes later she came bustling past, lugging one of the settee cushions. On her way, no doubt, to give it a merciless whacking outside with the carpet-beater.

All in all, it seemed safer to be out. Rosie grabbed her old school coat and slipped the lead on the dog. She left the dim and now dusty cottage without saying goodbye and together the pair headed for town. It wasn't much of a walk, and on arrival a few minutes later, she found the shop windows even barer than she'd imagined. She stopped at Bentham's, the newsagent's, and tendered the necessary coupons for her sweet ration: a quarter of some nameless boiled sweets in muted colours. Clutching the white paper bag, she left the untidy little shop and turned into the High Street. There she stopped, as her mother often did, at Merridew's.

The mahogany shopfront might have been tatty and the heavy plate-glass window uncleaned, but they still made Merridew's one of the grandest retail establishments in the small town. There would probably be a queue of women outside if anything new arrived, but today Rosie stood alone and, raising a hand against the glare, she peered inside. As well as providing clothes 'on the ration', a notice informed her that the shop was surviving the war by tailoring, presumably for those who wanted to escape the poor quality British uniforms and had the means to do so. She'd already heard they did a side-line in under-the-counter wedding dresses fashioned illegally from parachute silk, but there was nothing so glamorous in the windows, just a series of mannequins draped in the tweedy gloom of the all-too-sensible 'Austerity'. Coupon values were displayed alongside prices, but Rosie had neither the coupons nor the money.

'Rosie, isn't it?'

Startled, she turned, feeling a simultaneous tug on the dog's lead.

'Mrs. B.!'

Rosie recognised the old lady at once. On her childhood map, Mrs. Barton's house had been a place of refuge from her mother's temper; and somewhere their ragged little gang congregated – to play in her yard, 'test' her home-baked cakes, or try to teach Cyril the budgie to talk, occasionally with alarmingly rude results.

Peter pulled on the lead, sniffing the old woman approvingly.

Rosie knew that Mrs. B.'s own children had long flown the nest. They'd scattered over the empire; a son in sugarcane in the West Indies, another sheep-farming in Australia, and the daughter married to a check-shirted lumbermill manager somewhere in the wilds of Canada.

'My, you've grown!' Mrs. Barton peered at the young woman, her face cracking into a craggy smile. She came forward and, they embraced, a tad awkwardly.

'It's lovely to see you,' Mrs. B. continued. 'Will you come in for a cup of tea?'

They walked back to Mrs. B.'s end-of-terrace home and soon Rosie was in the parlour, with its eternal scents of baking, beeswax and lavender. She took in the framed photographs on the walls, floral wallpaper and familiar gleaming brass ornaments by the fireplace. The house seemed unchanged, as if it had been frozen since her last visit.

The old lady had been a schoolteacher and, so it was rumoured, a published author. Not that anyone knew much about the books – some kind of romances. She remembered something about a 'friendship' with a French officer, something clearly untoward as it had always been discussed in hushed tones accompanied by raised eyebrows and knowing looks. Her mother had once said something about her being a nurse in France during the First War and Rosie had got the impression this was meant to explain Mrs. B.'s well-known displays of emotion when hearing a certain piece of music, the wonderful accordion piece she so often played on her gramophone, the one that had always made the young Rosie want to spring up and dance. *Chanson* … something or other.

'Sweets?' The old lady was peering at the crumpled paper bag Rosie was carrying.

Rosie nodded.

Mrs. B. sighed and pointed to a huge apothecary's jar which stood empty on the dark-oak sideboard. 'Not so easy to keep it filled these days,' she intoned sadly.

'No.' Rosie could recall the jar full of clumped-together boiled sweets like bull's-eyes, clove rocks and humbugs, a lure for grubby young fingers and eager mouths. She remembered how Mrs. B. would reward a song on her doorstep with a sweet and had given pennies for odd jobs that didn't really need doing,

'I'll put the kettle on,' the old lady said, leaving the room.

For a moment Rosie gazed at the jar. On an impulse she rose quickly and emptied her own paper bag into it, replacing the lid as quietly as she could, and sitting down before the old woman re-entered.

Mrs. B. called her through into the separate dining room, where Rosie found her setting the table, shaking the linen tablecloth, laying out her best china and the gleaming silver apostle spoons Rosie recalled from memory. The Spode porcelain rattled now in more mottled and less steady hands. The set, she remembered, was valuable. Something her mother would kill for, probably literally.

Soon the red-gold liquid was swirling into the delicate pink-and-gold cups and the old lady's tremulous hand added a splash of milk before a spoon clinked and the mixture became the familiar warm tan of English tea.

'It's been an exciting time here, as you may know.' Mrs. B. wriggled visibly in her seat as she settled down, seemingly looking forward to a good gossip. 'Smarts – the jam people – were bombed. Can you imagine, a bomb in a jam factory? A fire like hell, they said – you could smell the sugar for miles. On Bull Hill it ran in a river of caramel and people were collecting it in jars!' She paused for breath. 'And Mrs. Jones, her with the twitchy curtains and son that never gets the call-up, she was hauled before the magistrate for opening curtains in the blackout – fined five whole pounds!'

Rosie listened patiently, smiling politely, nodding or raising eyebrows as appropriate, as the old lady unburdened herself of the pent-up news she'd accumulated over the lonely months.

'And now the Americans,' Mrs. B. continued. 'Hundreds of them at the new airbase at Bosworth's Field. They've upset some of the local boys, what with having more money and taking all the girls. They've landed on us like a bit of a bombshell!' Mrs. B. looked shrewdly at Rosie and leant forward in her chair, speaking in a theatrically lowered voice. 'Personally, I don't think there's anything wrong with a man just because he comes from somewhere else, or speaks with a different accent.'

Rosie nodded eagerly. 'I'm going to their base tonight – for a dance,' she found herself blurting out. But it was good to tell someone. And it strengthened her decision to go.

Mrs. B.'s eyes widened. 'Wonderful!' She glanced at a picture on the wall. Faded, it showed two people in quaint, old-fashioned clothes. 'You must be excited.'

Rosie squirmed slightly and nodded.

'But what are you going to wear?' Mrs. B. asked. 'I was always late because I couldn't decide! Oh yes, even for my wedding! In the end I came in wearing half of one outfit and half of another. You should have seen the looks!'

Rosie laughed politely, and glanced uncomfortably down at her own plain blue dress.

'It's not easy for you young people nowadays, what with the rationing and everything,' said Mrs. B. more soberly.

'No.'

'Do you have a gown?'

Rosie coughed. 'No, I – no, I don't have anything except ...' Embarrassed, she indicated her dress.

For a moment Mrs. B. looked surprised, then she pulled herself upright.

'Just a minute,' she said. 'I'll be right back.'

While she was gone, Rosie looked at the picture on the wall again and realised that the young woman in it must be Mrs. Barton. She'd been beautiful back then, hauntingly so, with high cheekbones, long dark hair, intelligent eyes and an enigmatic smile.

'Here!' Mrs. B. came in, carrying two boxes, the larger of which bore florid French writing. She set them on the floor and flopped back into her armchair.

'Well, go on! Open them!'

Rosie bent forward. The larger lid opened to reveal a blue velvet off-the-shoulder evening dress.

She lifted it up. The material was thick and heavy. It was one of the most beautiful things she'd ever seen.

Mrs. B. beamed a smile. 'It was bought for me. A bit old-fashioned now, but quality never ages. It will look wonderful on you.'

'But ...' Rosie stammered. 'But, it might have to be altered ...'

'It's not to borrow, silly girl. It's yours. A gift. Like the shoes.' She indicated the smaller box.

Rosie found it contained a pair of black evening shoes. She pulled them out and laid them alongside her own. They were only a tiny bit longer, and she could pad that out.

Rosie's eyes began to fill and the room became hazy. She tried to slow her breathing.

Mrs B. was standing and had her hand on her arm.

'Just a moment. I've thought of something else.' She seemed to be enjoying herself and almost scampered from the room.

Rosie pulled the dress up to the correct height. It would be a generous but viable fit.

Mrs. B. returned and handed Rosie a silver evening bag. On the front a silver tulip was emblazoned, surrounded by imitation pearls.

'I'd like you to have that too. And – these.' Mrs. Barton's fingers fumbled for a moment with a velvet-lined jewel case.

Glinting on the cushioned surface were a pair of silver-and-pearl earrings and a silver necklace with a pendant like a flower. The Art Nouveau style looked old-fashioned but elegant, but the Tiffany label looked impossibly posh.

'Oh.' Rosie didn't know what to say. It was the greatest gift she'd received in her life.

'Come, come!' The old lady was leading her to the mirror over the mantelpiece.

With shaking hands Rosie clipped on the earrings and necklace.

Silently they surveyed the result.

'I want you to have them. Since my Arthur passed away they haven't been out much. They need to see the light. Like you.'

Spontaneously Rosie turned and embraced her. For a moment the old woman's hand caressed her hair. Then, hurriedly, they parted and sat back down, both a little pinker in complexion.

'It's so very generous of you, Mrs. B.,' Rosie gulped.

The old woman smiled. 'It's my pleasure. Perhaps you could tell me what it was like afterwards – the dance?'

'Oh, yes. I will, I will.'

Rosie smiled dizzily and held the purse to the light.

Mrs. B. coughed. 'And how is your mother?' A steely note had crept into her voice, and with it the spell was broken.

'She's, well, you know – Mother.' Rosie was embarrassed. She felt safe with Mrs. B., but the subject of her mother was difficult.

'Well, I have to tell you, my dear, we are worried about her. She's got worse since your father passed.' She caught sight of Rosie's expression. 'I expect you still miss him.'

Rosie nodded.

'A lovely man.'

There was an uncomfortable silence. They tried to restart the conversation but the mood had imperceptibly shifted.

After a few minutes of chatter, Rosie stood. She gathered the jewellery and dress carefully.

'I don't think I can ever properly thank you.'

'Nonsense. The look on your face was thanks enough. You'll be the belle of the ball! And remember, I shall expect a report!'

The door closed behind the young woman and the old lady turned. Her eye caught the sweet jar and she stopped. Moving closer, she peered at it again, before giving a short, dry cackle of laughter.

'Bless you, dear girl, bless you!' she said, holding the ancient vessel up to the light.

CHAPTER 4

Captain Eugene Flynn of the American Eighth Air Force raised the glass and examined the golden liquid through which streams of tiny bubbles were rising, swelling the ranks of a creamy head on top of the imported American beer. He ran a hand through his dark wavy hair in an unconscious, oddly nervous gesture that was instantly recognisable to all but himself.

Around him at the table in the noisy Air Force bar sat the chattering members of his crew, the scrubbed-pink choirboy faces of the younger ones belying the adult boasting of their green and olive uniforms.

Eugene sighed. He was barely five years older than they, yet it might as well have been a lifetime. He smiled wryly as Tony, the loud, Bronx waist-gunner, a self-proclaimed wise guy, teased Babyface, their shy, bespectacled navigator. Big Hank, the only one older than himself and his respected co-pilot, had yet to arrive for the pre-dance drinks, but the others were there, from Billy, one of the waist-gunners, a quiet tin-whistle-playing cowboy, to Meatball, the chubby food-obsessed tail-gunner. Despite their macho banter, the crew had gathered like

35

children around the feet of a father and, though he'd reluctantly come to understand how necessary this was for their peace of mind, and perhaps his own, it was a role he hadn't asked for.

Eugene watched as Wyatt and Joe – two tall, plank-thin hillbilly cousins from Tennessee – continued their efforts to improve the English curse-word vocabulary of Karl, their Polish-American bombardier, his serious, bushy-eyebrowed, basset-hound face occasionally cracking into a grin when they explained the meaning of a particularly crude English gem.

They relied on Eugene, as the pilot, to get them all home, and that was fine. He could do his job with his eyes shut. It was the other stuff. The personal problems they brought to him, or the advice they sought, from how to romance a dame to how to write a letter home. He couldn't tell them that he knew little more about life than they did, nor could he share the growing sense of fear that had begun to settle like a cold hard ball in his stomach hours before every mission. It was just as well they knew nothing about the little blue pills he got from the doc to keep him awake on long trips, nor the shots provided by an over-friendly and obliging base nurse to bring him down afterwards.

He'd begun to hate the hero worship. To be the polestar for their young lives, and to have the responsibility for bringing them safely home, was hard to bear. He envied the fighter jocks, who only had themselves to think of. As captain of the boys' 'ship' he was expected to be mom, pop, and brother to all of them. They held him to be the card ace of the mess hall, an expert with the fairer sex based on his supposed Irish-American charm, and to all of them he was the baseball legend of many an inter-squadron game. The latter at least was true. Somehow, in their young minds, it all seemed to add up to something worth following.

At first, in the blissful days when their missions were 'milk runs' to easy targets, he'd almost enjoyed the adulation. But the more he learned about himself, the further from their heroic, all-knowing ideal he seemed, and the harder it was to play the role with conviction. He knew it was plain stupid to be living a lie, and that one day he would get caught out.

'What you think, Cap?'

Eugene snapped back into the conversation. Wyatt was holding out something, his thin, cadaverous face breaking in a bucktoothed smile that betrayed the ill-fed and erratic childhood he'd suffered in the small wooden cabin he'd shared with nine siblings. It was some kind of small paper manual, and on the cover was the picture of a motorcycle.

'Got it from some darn limey fella,' Joe chipped in, chewing on the battered corncob pipe he habitually used as a prop to make himself look older. He gestured with the stem. 'Darn fine machine – three gears and a ton o' guts.'

Sensing the eagerness with which his approval was sought, Eugene whistled and raised his eyebrows approvingly.

He could hear himself chatting, but his voice seemed distant. He continued on autopilot. During training in the States and on the voyage over, he'd always been able to lose himself in a book, usually a humorous fantasy like White's *Sword in the Stone*, Gibbons' *Cold Comfort Farm* or perhaps the mind-bending but wickedly funny modern poetry of e.e. cummings. But the power of the written word to take him out of himself was waning. Beer didn't cut it anymore, nor the company of the guys. Only sex, or perhaps sex and dancing, the faster the better, and the drugs remained. Any combination of these things could hold his mind at some kind of equilibrium, away from the nightmares that were starting to appear now as sudden flashes during the day – a new torment to add to the others.

Suddenly he was standing, the adolescent faces of his crew peering up at his six-foot frame curiously, their drinks frozen midway to waiting mouths. He needed to walk, to burn off some adrenaline. He affected his customary nonchalance, promised them he would see them later inside the hanger that was to serve as the night's dance hall, and left.

He wandered out into the dark, relieved by the sudden release from responsibility and the comforting anonymity of the night. At the edge of the field he found the wire perimeter mesh glinting like a geometric spider's web in the starlight, and began to walk along its length. He'd learnt he could keep the sudden splinters of unbidden memory out of his mind as long as he was busy, or his body in motion.

After a hundred yards, he stopped, felt in his pocket and drew out a battered brass hipflask. The whiskey tasted smoky-hot and burned slightly as it met the churning acid of his stomach. Halfway round his second circuit, he exchanged words with the sentries. They glanced respectfully at his pilot's insignia, saluting smartly, which only made him feel worse.

But the whiskey soon began to work, re-inflating his sagging ego. Draining the last of his flask, he checked his hands. They'd almost stopped shaking, which meant it was time to dance.

His mind cleared as he strode to the hanger. The Benzedrine he'd taken the day before to keep him sharp was taking a time to flush out. It had made him jumpy all afternoon, but the booze was bringing him down, and some fresh female company would get him off. It was time to forget everything, and everyone, and live only in the moment.

CHAPTER 5

Rosie stood checking her outfit for the fifth time. Her heart was a hammer, beating madly, and it seemed to have taken up a new place of residence in her throat. She would have to walk past her mother. It didn't help that she'd never taken to the sewing and knitting classes at the orphanage and grimaced at the thought that the adjustments she'd made to Mrs. B.'s dress were all too visible. A sudden wave of nausea gripped her and she stumbled forward, vomiting into the nightstand.

Rosie swayed and steadied herself and soon felt calmer. Dabbing her mouth with a handkerchief, she picked up her evening bag and made her way gingerly down the narrow stairs, trying to avoid the one that creaked, and conscious her mother might hear the rustling of the gown against the narrow wooden stairwell.

She paused on the bottom tread and pressed her ear against the thin panelled door to the front room. There were two voices, one belonging to Mrs. Soames, the stick-faced washerwoman from across the alley, an on-off friend of her mother's who consumed Woodbines like a smouldering two-legged bonfire.

Steeling herself, Rosie walked in.

There was the sound of falling teacups and spoons and a look of astonishment on her mother's face. Mrs. Soames gawped as she took in the dress, and the borrowed make-up.

Rosie had made it halfway to the door when her mother finally spoke.

'And where do you think you are going, dressed like a common tart?'

There was a time when the same ominous intonation had filled Rosie with fear. But now it irritated. She turned.

'*Out!*' She said the word forcefully yet couldn't make herself meet her mother's eye. She hadn't yet found the right time for the discussion she was determined to have, but it would come.

'Well, I never!'

Mrs. Soames' words echoed behind Rosie as she stepped out into the cool of the night and closed the door firmly behind her. She breathed a sigh of relief and hurried off into the merciful embrace of the darkness.

At the end of their street Rosie met one of the big green-painted buses laid on by the Yanks, exhaling again as she took her seat. They pulled away into the night, the clattering diesel competing with the excited voices of the thirty or so women aboard. Through the darkening, anonymous streets, grimly forbidding at the best of times, but far gloomier in the blackout, the coach growled, pausing here and there to pick up passengers, before lurching away again into the gloom.

Eventually they arrived at the tall, metal gates of the base, where, as the passengers competed with each other to catch a glimpse of the normally off-limit surroundings, they were briskly waved through by a pair of glum-faced sentries. Finally, one among many in the noisy rubbernecking crowd around her, Rosie trooped down the slippery metal steps of the coach onto the tarmac.

The women were all looked around, gawping at the unfamiliar sights, giggling and murmuring, until eventually they were directed to a vast steel building by a tall, and Rosie noticed, far from disinterested, white-helmeted soldier.

A wave of light and sound reached Rosie as she walked uncertainly into the glowing interior of the hangar. A sea of bodies and faces took up much of the huge space, except for tables along one side, a stage far away at one end and a dance floor in the centre.

At last she glimpsed Hazel, half-hidden behind a group of other laughing young women. She was wearing a blue-and-white floral dress, and at the end of her now stockinged legs were a pair of eye-catching red shoes that made Rosie think of Dorothy in *The Wizard of Oz*.

'Hey, lass!' Hazel said, and coming over. 'Happen us looks like a pair of pork sandwiches with everything on!'

Rosie laughed, Hazel wasn't a bit like Dorothy. Her friend's eyes ran up and down the ball gown and locked like magnets onto the silver earrings and pendant, which were flashing shamelessly in the light.

'By heck,' Hazel said, casting a lingering glance at her friend's new adornments, 'tha's a dark horse. Where did tha get these?' She fingered one of the earrings curiously.

Rosie felt suddenly awkward. The earrings far outshone the now familiar hammer-and-sickle enamel brooch Hazel had fastened to her own outfit.

Rosie mumbled a reply and turned and tried to take it all in. The hangar was cavernous, great beams of steel stretching upwards from the floor like the vaulting of a futuristic cathedral. On the walls hung swags of tinsel and a few familiar war posters, while over the centre flew the flags of the allies; the Stars and Stripes, the Union Jack,

France's Tricolour and Russia's Hammer and Sickle. A space had been cleared in the centre, and a shiny floor laid. Over this, spinning on a wire, a magnificent mirror-ball hung, its multifaceted surface spangling a rainbow of moving colours repeatedly through the haze.

'Oh!' Rosie breathed, her nervousness fading.

At the far end, illuminated by searchlights, the band were playing: a twelve-piece in matching outfits, churning out a passable version of 'Moonlight Serenade,' with a gravelly-voiced blonde vocalist. In front of the band, metal seats and tables formed the shoreline of an enthusiastic crowd of uniformed men and well-dressed girls, convecting slowly around the shimmering pool of light that was the dance floor.

Rosie stared. There had been times she'd thought she'd never see such a thing, but now that it was here, she experienced an unexpected but crippling awkwardness.

Perhaps Hazel was also struck, for they just stood for a while time, watching girls being led out by grinning partners. Part of Rosie wanted to be chosen but, something inside her dreaded it too. For a second she wished she hadn't agreed to come.

'Would you care to dance?'

Rosie jumped, then looked up. Realising that the stranger was speaking to Hazel and embarrassed by her mistake, she looked away. She watched as the short, fat American sergeant bore her waving friend away, into the thickening pool of dresses and uniforms.

Alone again, Rosie allayed the panic by looking around as casually as possible. The dulcet tunes and finely tailored green and beige Army Air Force uniforms, glittering with brass and medal ribbons, were matched by the dresses of the women, creating a cocoon of glamour a world away from the orphanage, or the wartime bleakness of the town. Alone for a few moments, she found herself closing her eyes and pretending she was the star of a glamorous movie: Ginger Rogers, perhaps, just waiting for Fred Astaire to ask her to dance.

Rosie was smiling vacantly to herself at this happy daydream when she heard the voice that would change her life.

'Miss?'

The question reverberated in a rich American baritone.

Rosie turned and found herself looking into the face of a tall, smiling airman. The well-tailored jacket, with two bars on the shoulder and wings on the breast, suggested he was a pilot. Far older than her, in his late twenties at least. He looked so impossibly fit for the part, like someone who had just stepped from a film set, that she almost laughed. A sharp female cough brought her back to earth and she found, of all people, Clara standing next to her.

The tall girl had appeared silently, like a shark that had swum deftly through a group of swimmers. She was wearing a red evening gown, with evening gloves, her long dark hair up in an elaborate style. She placed a hand softly on the airman's sleeve.

'I'll dance,' she said, in a husky voice that Rosie realised with a start was faked.

The airman looked helplessly from one to the other. 'Well, I ...' he began, considering his sudden embarrassment of riches.

Rosie pushed her way forward with a determination that surprised even herself. 'He asked me, I believe.' She held his eye and raised an eyebrow.

Suddenly the band launched into Glen Miller's 'American Patrol'. 'Shall we?'

For a second the American hesitated. Then holding his hand out to Rosie, he led her out into the throng.

Rosie felt giddily triumphant as they sailed around the floor. She'd surprised herself by her boldness and, when she could spare a moment from glancing down at her feet, she gazed up at the airman as he whirled her around. His skin was a healthy, ruddy hue and his hair dark and silky. He was tall, almost as handsome as Tyrone Power, and his embrace sent small electric shocks up and down her spine as their bodies moved in time to the music. He was so close she could smell his cologne. What would her mother say? She no longer cared and restrained a laugh at the thought.

'Oh, I'm sorry!' She'd stepped on his toes and realised ruefully that, despite Hazel's coaching, as dancers went he was a lot closer to Fred Astaire than she was to Ginger Rogers. Fortunately, at that moment the number ended with a flourish and a round of applause before she could bruise him again.

She blushed. 'I'm all left feet tonight.' She tried to say it as if she danced every evening, but inwardly she cursed her own lack of experience.

'No, you're just fine.' He smiled broadly and seemed to be examining her. His mouth revealed a set of pearly teeth and a pair of amber-brown eyes shone from a face that looked like it enjoyed smiling. 'I think you're a fine dancer.'

She laughed at his noble lie and found herself blushing again. He seemed more relaxed after the dance, as if he were genuinely enjoying it. His laughter came easily and so, she noticed, did a twinkle in his eye.

Behind them, the band struck up again, the tempo faster. The crowd parted and two or three couples began to whirl. It was an astonishing display – primitive, athletic, almost rude. Rosie found her pulse responding as her feet began to tap by themselves. She'd never heard anything like it before. There was no stopping the penetration of the music however, which had begun to ride up through her, making her sway in time and sending her inhibitions fleeing.

'I don't know this one –' she began.

But was too late. They'd already begun to move, the airman steering her firmly into the centre of the floor. To one side she could see the tall slender figure of Clara standing alone, tugging off her evening gloves with a menacing vigour and glaring into the crowd. Before Rosie could think any more of the potential consequences, her attention was grabbed by a laughing blonde next to her. The girl seemed to know what she was doing, swinging wildly in time, and for want of better Rosie began to copy her. The airman, who had been holding her at arm's length, nodded encouragingly before suddenly pulling her towards him. She felt herself whirl like a top and, returning, collided with his chest and laughed. Every so often the men would lift their partners and flip them over, showing their underwear. It was crazy, and outrageous, but fun. She heard herself scream as it happened to her.

It was the maddest fairground ride, wild, scandalous and forbidden, but Rosie's eyes were gleaming as her body synchronised with the beat.

It was all over far too soon and, as the music ended, she saw the airman glance over at the bar. He looked as if he was about to speak but at that moment the band struck up again, and it was a tune she knew, an old one: 'Painting the Clouds with Sunshine!'

He looked at her quizzically but, as the jaunty tune began, she found herself grabbing him and pulling him back onto the floor. Dancing, she thought, was addictive, immoral or not.

Several dances later the band itself finally paused, their blonde singer blowing kisses into the audience and walking offstage to an enthusiastic round of applause, whistles and cries of appreciation. Rosie noticed that although the airman still had the same infectious grin, he was perspiring. Perhaps she should let him stop? But she needn't have worried for, as if at a hidden signal, a surge for the bar began in which they were inextricably caught up. Arriving at the bar, they found themselves pressed together against the wooden countertop. The space was filled with smoking, flirting and loud talking. Everywhere dollar bills were waving, orders were shouted. An intriguing cocktail of smells drifted past over the tang of smoke. Most were new to her although she could make out the large, upside-down bottles behind the bar: whiskey, rum, gin, as well as steel barrels from which a light-coloured beer was being poured. She recognised the nose-tingling floral effervescence of cool tonic, one of her mother's favourites, and of course the much-longed-for nutty sweetness of Coca-Cola that had been an occasional childhood treat but was hard to get in wartime.

'What's your poison?' He bent down so she could hear the words among the babble.

She looked over the bar. Apart from a secret shandy beer given her once by her father when they'd stopped on his motorcycle at a country pub, it would be her first alcoholic drink. She hesitated.

The barman was pouring a dark liquid into two tall glasses of bubbling cola. 'Rum and Coca-Cola!' He handed the order over to a happy sergeant, and even happier local woman, and took the money.

'I'll have a rum and Coca-Cola, please,' Rosie said, crossing her fingers and hoping it sounded like a regular thing.

He smiled. 'Make it two,' he said to the barman.

Gripping the drinks, the airman headed from the bar through the swirling human sea, Rosie following as best she could in his wake. A few people smiled at her and she smiled back, her confidence growing. It felt an impossibly grown-up place to be, yet no one seemed to think she didn't belong. No one asked her to leave. They found a table at the far side. Everywhere around them couples were talking, drinking and smoking. It was all so grown up.

'Eugene Flynn,' he said, holding out a hand.

The flesh was warm. He wore no ring and his shirt was fixed with cufflinks shaped like planes.

'Rosie Haskell.' She sipped the drink, which tasted strange, almost medicinal. 'Delicious.'

'Rosie Haskell is delicious,' he replied, laughing.

'I meant the drink.' She smiled, embarrassed.

'I know. But you're pretty delicious yourself.'

Rosie blushed at the American's forwardness. His gaze was running over her dress, lingering for a moment where the neckline plunged and the material was pushed outward by her breasts.

'You live close to the base?' he asked, dragging his eyes upward.

'Yes, in the town, at Potter's Lane.' She paused, suddenly aware she'd told him her address on the first meeting. She thought of a question. 'And where do you come from?'

She half-expected him to say 'Mars' or perhaps 'Hollywood'.

'Well, my folks are from New England, near Boston.'

'Oh.' He might as well have said Mars after all.

A parade of noisy airmen and local girls passed their table, jabbering and laughing. Eugene looked up and nodded to one or two of the men.

Rosie thought rapidly of something else to say.

'Flynn – but that's an Irish name, isn't it?'

The airman nodded. 'Yes, miss. And the name of a certain actor, before you say it!'

She smiled. He didn't look anything like the famous blonde-haired Errol. Not that he wasn't, in his own way, glamorous, but his dark, earthy looks were a million miles from the flamboyant matinee idol.

'My great-grandfather came over from County Kerry sometime in the last century. Times were hard, and there was no choice for anyone young – they had to leave if they wanted a life.' He took a swig of his drink. 'I thought of flying over there, to Ireland, that is, but it turns out it's the opposite direction to the missions we run from here.'

Rosie nodded. 'Yes, it's to the west of us.'

'So it is.' He smiled at her grasp of geography. 'I had no idea that it was even close to England before I enlisted. It was,' he suddenly adopted a thick stage Irish accent, 'just a mythical island of one t'ousand shades o' green, somewhere in dur vastness of dur sea.'

Rosie laughed. He was so confident and entertaining, she felt herself relax.

'And your family settled in … New England?' she queried.

Seeing her quizzical expression, he reached into his pocket and retrieved a small pencil.

'Here,' he said, producing a scrap of paper, 'this one I do know.'

She leant forward as he drew a passable map of North America. He sketched confidently, adding place names and cartoon-like palm trees over on the west side, then skyscrapers for New York and Boston on the east.

'About here,' he said, indicating a spot north of New York. 'I guess around three thousand miles away as the crow, or bomber flies.'

He chuckled and folded out the paper, expanding the drawing to include a more shakily drawn British Isles.

At that moment a rotund, sequin-clad woman in a dress far too small for her tried to squeeze past, swayed, lost her balance and sat heavily on their table. Eugene, with remarkable reflexes, removed the drinks just in time.

'Oh, I am sorry,' the intruder slurred, smiled and rose unsteadily before veering away into the crowd. '*Danny, Danny*' she called, '*where are you?*' in a distressed, high falsetto.

Eugene grinned and restored the drinks to the table.

Rosie pointed to his wings. 'You're a pilot, aren't you?'

'Yes, I sure am.'

He looked proud, but at the same time there was just a flicker of something else, a line formed on his brow, appearing for a second and then vanishing as fast.

'It must be something to fly and see all the country below you, like a bird sees it,' said Rosie thoughtfully.

'Yes, it is pretty up there.' He smiled. 'Especially when we come home and fly over your English green fields. It's a welcome sight.'

'Hey, Eugene!'

A diminutive sergeant with a stiff crop of strawberry-blonde hair appeared from the crowd.

'How 'bout a beer, Cap?'

He spoke with an inebriated grin.

'Rosie, this is Rick.' Eugene smiled wryly. 'He's a gunner on our ship.'

The young man stood to attention, not without difficulty, and saluted.

'Worst ball-turret gunner in the Eighth Air Force, absolutely no kills! Pleasure to meet you, miss.'

He was short, with freckles that joined up over his nose, and was as lean as a greyhound.

'You want a beer, Cap?' the young man repeated.

Eugene shook his head. 'No, you go ahead, Rick. I'll see you later.'

The young airman nodded and turned to go.

'And Rick?'

The sergeant turned.

'Cap?'

'Go easy on the beer.'

There seemed to be a great deal of casualness between the officers and men, Rosie thought, not at all like the British officers and men she'd seen in town. Perhaps it was part of being American. Nevertheless, for a moment she'd seen the odd strain appear again on Eugene's otherwise calm face.

'Sorry about that.' He nodded at the receding gunner. 'I let them have as much slack as I can. Given what they have to do, I figure it's only fair.' He smiled. 'OK, what do you do when you're not impersonating Ginger Rogers?'

Rosie laughed. It was funny he should have thought of that particular dancer. 'It's alright, I'm an awful dancer. You don't have to pretend. I work at Morelli's. We make radios. For the war.'

'I know it,' he said, taking a swig of his drink. 'We fly right over it.'

'Yes, and make the whole building shake!' She put her hand to her mouth. She hadn't meant to sound critical. 'I mean …' Hurriedly she improvised. 'Did the Air Force teach you to fly?'

Eugene shook his head.

'I flew before the war,' he said. 'Crop-dusting mainly, that and delivering the mail.'

Her eyebrows rose. Mail was brought by old men on bicycles. It seemed impossible for it to be flown through the air. Rosie's tummy was feeling warm from the drink. Suddenly she wanted to sit and listen to him all night.

The airman sipped his drink slowly, and she noticed that his deep-brown eyes didn't deviate from her. She hadn't realised she was staring back.

He coughed. 'And then,' he continued, 'after college, a friend of mine had a casino. But it didn't work out.'

She could feel the effects of the drink more fully now, a delightful light-headedness and a tendency for the room to take a second to catch up when she turned her head. A casino sounded exotically glamorous. Rosie pictured him in a white tuxedo, standing at the door like Humphrey Bogart in *Casablanca*.

'It sounds wonderful.'

He shook his head. 'There are some bad people in that business. My friend he got, *uh*, hurt.'

She raised her eyebrows.

He leant back in his chair. Sometimes there was the hint of a wry smile, then his expression would become suddenly serious.

Rosie felt herself being pulled into his world, as though she were an iron nail and he a magnet. She must avoid a silence. She racked her brains for something else to say. What about his first flight?

'Oh, that was a long time ago,' he said, his eyes distant again, remembering. 'I was just a kid. I went to a fair. There were cows and a rodeo. But the thing that drew me was the flying circus. You know? A group of stunt-planes – acrobatics, looping the loop that kinda stuff. Ten bucks for a flight, and my dad paid for me to go up.'

Her eyes grew wider. To actually fly, among the clouds, to see what before their century only birds had seen.

'I'd like to take you up and show the world to you,' he was saying, 'just like a bird sees it – as I've seen it, as no one before us has seen it.'

It was almost as if he could read her thoughts.

'I'd like to fly.' She said it dreamily. There was something about him, about all of them, that made them different from ordinary men. They were American, and foreigners, and that made them exotic; kin to heroes, or movie stars. But there was something else. It was as though, by learning to fly, they'd become a different species, not bound to the earth but free to soar like angels, as her mood seemed to be doing now.

The glasses were empty.

'Would you like a top-up?' he asked solicitously.

She found herself nodding. Another one would be wonderful.

While he was away from the table Rosie looked around as casually as possible. Her head was spinning, but it felt wonderful – even the coloured dresses of the other girls seemed brighter and the voices of the crowd were melding into one happy mumbling, like the sea. He returned quickly with two more rum and Coca-Colas.

'And after the war?' he continued as though he'd not been away.

'Oh, I have dreams.' She said it hesitantly, afraid at once she'd bore him.

'Of fame and fortune?'

'No!' She laughed. 'Nothing like that. I want to learn. About things and the world.'

It sounded lame, but he nodded as though he understood perfectly.

'I liked college,' he said wistfully.

'Really? I love reading, and poems.'

He took a draught of the cool drink and cast a look around before replying. Suddenly his eyes were on her again.

'Poems?' He seemed genuinely curious. 'What's your favourite?' Seeing her pause, he nudged her and grinned. 'Care to give us a rendition?'

'Oh,' she blushed, 'I couldn't. I mean …'

But his smile was persuasive, his eyes seemed locked on hers. He raised his eyebrows and smiled expectantly. There was nothing for it. She scanned her memory and, finding something suitable, cleared her throat.

'"High Flight" – John Gillespie Magee, Junior.' She began, hoping she'd remember all of the words.

'Up, up the long, delirious, burning blue
I've topped the wind-swept heights with easy grace.
Where never lark, or even eagle flew –
And, while with silent, lifting mind I've trod
The high untrespassed sanctity of space,
Put out my hand, and touched the face of God.'

52

His glass had stopped, halfway to his mouth and he seemed to be re-assessing her. For a few moments, there was silence. The conversation resumed and, though it might have been her imagination, they seemed to be moving closer together, in mind as well as space.

They talked a while longer, and she was hardly surprised when it turned out he knew one of her favourite stories, Jack London's *Call of the Wild*. She told him about her father and brother and he related stories of his time at college before the war. She grew unaware of their surroundings, seeing only his face and hearing only his voice. He too seemed to be responding, leaning forward in his chair and holding her gaze.

A crazy thought ran through her mind. That here tonight, in this strange place, in a war and not months out of the orphanage, she'd met her future husband. A vestige of sanity swiftly contradicted the ridiculous notion and, struggling through the alcohol, she managed to calm her over-active imagination. Somewhere inside herself she knew her own, pent-up need for affirmation and love, would lead her astray if she let it. And yet she wanted to believe.

Soon, the conversation shifted back to flying. He became animated, and her mind was carried along with his thoughts, past the towering cumulonimbus he described and on into the great blue limitless sunlit vault of the sky.

'Come on,' he said suddenly, smiling and standing unsteadily.

'What?'

She rose uncertainly, but it was too late to change her mind. Her seat had been promptly taken by another girl.

'Excuse me,' the invader said, sitting down firmly and motioning to a male companion to join her.

Bridges apparently burned, Rosie followed Eugene unsteadily across the hanger. The vast steel doors they opened to let the aircraft in and out were closed but at the smaller entrance they'd come through earlier stood a barrel-chested, uniformed GI with a face like a bloodhound. On his helmet were the letters 'MP' in white and he carried an impressively lethal-looking pistol in a leather holster. The MP held up a hand as they approached but seemed to relax when he recognised Rosie's partner. After a brief discussion with Eugene he glanced around before gesturing discreetly to the door.

Rosie collected her coat from the rack behind the MP and they passed on through, out into goodness knew where. In the cool darkness she felt the airman's hand silently slide around her own.

CHAPTER 6

'Don't go getting ideas about them, my girl!'

'Them?'

There'd been an article about the American Air Force in the radio news, and Rosie's face must have given her away. Her mother's nose for gossip was sharper than a shark's scent for blood.

'Aye,' her mother continued. 'Yanks. There's many a girl has regretted getting involved with them. A dance is bad enough but, at your age, don't go a-courting any of that lot!'

Rosie bridled at her mother's all too predictable prejudice. There'd been a time when she wouldn't have answered back, but the under-the-counter joint of lamb they'd just eaten had been paid for out of her own wage packet.

'There're just boys, Mother,' she replied, as calmly as she could. 'No worse than English ones.'

'No worse?' her mother sat up in her armchair, incredulous, peering at her daughter as if she had just escaped from an asylum. 'Of course they're worse. They got no morals, them lot! All that dancing and loud music, and –' she leaned forward and whispered, 'and they brought niggers with them too. Imagine! Blackies!'

Rosie shook her head in disbelief. 'I've heard some have actually married English girls.'

Her mother snorted. 'Aye, and how fair is that to our boys?'

'It's not about being fair. If two people love each other –'

'*Love?*' Edith laughed caustically. 'What do you know about love? Stick to girls is my advice, ones of your own age!'

Rosie's face flushed. Her mother's attitude to Americans, especially the coloured ones, was bad enough, but what made it infuriating was that the jibe about lack of experience was uncomfortably close to the mark.

The BBC news had finished and the Sunday service came on.

Tight-lipped, Rosie braced herself for her mother's inevitable accompaniment. She didn't have to wait long.

'*When other helpers fail and comforts flee, Help of the helpless, O abide with me!*' duly warbled her mother, as simultaneously she clutched the shapeless knitting she kept in the carpet bag by her chair.

Rosie sighed, but made no comment on the irony of 'Abide with Me' as a hymn choice. Instead she flicked idly through the paper. It had been over a week since the dance and she'd begun to wonder if the airman would write. Meanwhile her mother was rising to full choral mode, and Rosie shuddered, not so much at the tunelessness, but at what her mother would say if she knew what she'd been doing with one Yank in particular, alone and in the darkness of an airbase.

'We're not supposed to be here, are we?' she'd said, craning her neck to gaze at the night sky.

The stars had glinted brightly above the hangar, like diamonds spilt over a velvet cloth and they stood close together, feeling the sudden cool of the night. Rosie felt light-headed from the drink, and almost deliriously happy, even perhaps poetic. Part of her wanted to dance madly across the runway, and she was restrained only by the thought that she'd look foolish. Instead she stood solemnly and followed his gaze upwards. The pale fog of the Milky Way reclined diagonally over them like a thin cobweb, and in deep, intergalactic space stars winked and sparked without a boastful moon to outshine them. She'd gazed at the stars many times, but tonight the universe seemed different, less indifferent and in some indefinable way less hostile.

'Come,' he whispered.

It was too dark to see her feet as he pulled urgently on her arm, and she began to follow him away from the hangar and towards a shadowy row of Quonset huts. She dimly sensed a latent, unspecified danger, but it seemed insignificant.

'Where are ...' Her words slid into silence as she saw the view.

They were suddenly beyond the row of huts and facing the open grass field, having emerged by a narrow path. Running at right angles to left and right of them were a row of parked aircraft, which stood silently, their dark outlines mute but menacing, as they towered over them. She found herself holding her breath, as though the gigantic beasts were really alive and any sound she made might wake them.

She found that Eugene had walked away, and briskly she hurried after him, past several of the planes, the tails of which stuck up like the black fins of gigantic whales. He'd stopped and was looking up, apparently deep in thought.

'Here she is,' he said softly.

He pointed and on the side of one of the enormous planes Rosie saw a cartoon – a leggy woman with horns and tail holding a hand of cards. Underneath was written '*Luck of The Devil*,' in bright, lurid red.

Reaching underneath, Eugene fumbled and a metal hatch swung down. Quietly lifting a set of steps that had lain nearby, he positioned them carefully underneath th dark hole that had appeared.

'You want to see inside?' he whispered hoarsely.

His demeanour was friendly though she sensed an odd sense of urgency. But the drink gave her courage and she nodded.

'I'll go first. OK?' he said.

'OK,' Rosie whispered back, suddenly wondering what would happen if they were caught.

She looked up and after a moment a pair of pale hands materialised from inside the gloomy aircraft.

'Come on up,' he said quietly, the suppressed tone emphasising the illicit nature of their venture.

Rosie swallowed, glanced around and began to climb, finally grabbing his hands as she made it into the fuselage. Immediately she was struck by the smell of rubber and metal – an industrial smell, like a factory or a garage. In the dim light she saw the walls and roof were indeed of metal, but the floor, oddly, seemed to be plywood. At the front of the plane, a bubble of glass faced forward and just before that, a complicated-looking machine was bolted firmly to the floor.

He caught her wide-eyed expression. 'It's OK,' he said, grinning. 'You're with me.' The grin implied their visit was permitted, but the tone of his voice indicated otherwise. 'I'll take you to the cockpit. But first you have to come backwards to go forwards and into the fuselage. Here, take my hand.'

Rosie grabbed his hand and clambered through another hatchway up onto a high deck. She'd expected the inside to be smooth and shiny like a spaceship, and was disappointed to find it resembled a long, cluttered shed, strewn with sagging cables, mysterious pipes and bulbous metal cylinders. Halfway towards the back were two gaping rectangular holes to the outside. She turned and went forward, squeezing after him through a surprisingly narrow gap, to sit at last in the right-hand one of two identical seats.

In front of her the plane's windscreen was covered in condensation, but through the blur she could still make out the field and the glistening thread of the runway trailing off into the darkness. On either side stood the stilled propellers, much bigger than she'd imagined.

It was fascinating to see the place where the pilots sat, and she thought briefly of how her father would have envied her the view.

'Make yourself at home!' Eugene said with a grin, wiping away some of the fog with a glove.

The space was surprisingly cramped, or perhaps 'cosy' was the word for she noticed how everything seemed to be close to hand. The ceiling was very low while a couple of feet in front of them were metal panels covered in dials, switches and numerous levers, and between her legs a column rose up from the floor, topped with a half-wheel bearing the word 'BOEING' in large white letters. Cautiously she placed her hand on the wheel and gripped it like the steering wheel in a car.

'*Wow!*' she breathed, unable to supress a giggle.

Everywhere in front of her and even to the side were more levers, dials, switches and knobs, and fixed to the walls were some yellow metal bottle-like things.

'Oxygen bottles,' he said, following her gaze. 'Above ten thousand feet we need them to breathe.'

Mechanically Rosie nodded, still taking in the alien but intriguing world, the secret world, of a pilot. Ten thousand feet seemed impossibly high. She did a few mental calculations and realised that would be about two miles. She wondered what it would be like to start the huge engines, and feel the aircraft tremble and shake as they roared into life. It must be deafening, but thrilling too. She had a mad impulse to press a button and find out.

Eugene had donned an oversized steel helmet. Perhaps it was the drink, but she couldn't suppress a laugh, and he joined in.

'It's OK.' He laughed. 'I don't really wear this. It's just a spare – the guys on the waist-guns have them and sometimes the bombardier wears one – if things get a bit hairy.'

It seemed an odd expression – 'hairy' – but she knew instinctively what he meant and her smile vanished. He went on calmly, and she thought, a little proudly, describing the plane in detail.

He seemed surprised when she interrupted him with questions.

'How many men are there in a crew?'

'Ten. We have two pilots, a radio operator, a bomb-aimer and guys to work the twelve guns.'

'Twelve guns?' she asked, surprised. It seemed a lot.

'Yup. Everything about a fort is big: hundred-and-five-foot wingspan, twelve guns, four engines. Can make almost three hundred miles an hour if she wants to.'

'Three hundred?' Rosie put her hands thoughtfully on the half-wheel again.

'That's the control column,' he said quietly. 'It makes the plane climb or dive, and we can bank with it too.' He indicated with his hand a leaning, sideways movement.

She nodded and touched the throttles, reading the names painted neatly onto the control panel 'The accelerators?' she asked.

He nodded and raised his eyebrows. 'You could call it that, yes. We say throttles.'

She nodded again, looking over the array of instruments. 'Throttles. Altimeter, engine revs, fuel, switches, one set for each engine I suppose,' she mused.

'You seem to know a lot about planes, for a girl,' he said, amazed but at the same time amused.

She laughed nervously. 'Oh, Not really. I just like mechanical things. My father used to have a motorcycle and I would help him with, you know, the maintenance. A bit odd for a girl, I know.'

'You did?'

She nodded. 'Yes. Why are there two pilots?'

He sat upright and looked out through the screen..

'In case one of us is hit.'

'Oh.' Once again she was reminded of the plane's purpose.

But the all-enclosing body of the plane reminded her of Jonah's whale. Metal ribs, spaced at regular intervals, receded down to a tail, while a thin outer skin was wrapped over the outside, creating a strong, rigid enclosure. Rosie keenly felt the sense of separation from the outside world. He'd called it a 'fuselage' and mentally she filed the name away. How wonderful it would be to know all about aeroplanes, what made them fly, and how they were made!

Eugene was suddenly close, looking at her intently, and it occurred her that he might kiss her. But something in her wasn't ready, and belatedly the dim alarm bell sounded again. She smiled and hurriedly asked him a question and, deflected, he answered, making a show of checking the instruments, flicking a switch here and there, but stealing sideways glances.

'We'd better get back,' she said last and he sighed heavily, but nodded, taking her hand.

His grip was strong, comforting, and part of her asked whether perhaps she should have interrupted him after all.

But he moved fast and was already dropping down behind the seats.

'Come on,' he said, his voice muffled.

Soon they were heading back to the hanger. He walked close, but when he came closer still she edged gently away, as though flying in her own unique formation.

'Can I write to you?' He asked the question suddenly as they emerged into the relative light of the apron in front of the hangar.

61

At that moment the small door in the hanger they'd come out of earlier swung open and a chattering stream of young women burst out, indicating that the dance was over.

'Sure.' She tried to say it carelessly. She'd thought the evening had gone well but had nothing to compare it to. Now her optimism was confirmed and she beamed in relief. Thoughts of her mother's likely response if she gave the American her home address ran briefly through her mind. Fumbling in her evening bag she found the crumpled plain postcard she'd received inviting her for an interview at the factory and held it out to him. 'Send it to Rosie Haskell, Assembly Shop, Morelli's.'

He nodded and tipped his hat, hesitated for a second and then bent forward.

She was as surprised by the kiss as much as she was by his sudden departure afterwards, for he tipped his hat again and strode rapidly away.

'Goodbye, Eugene,' she said quietly, the unfamiliar name sounding curious, even exotic.

Around her, most of the departing women flowed straight to the coaches that, as if at some hidden signal, had pulled up. But some, she noticed with a twinge of jealousy, lingered – shadowy figures clinging to a last kiss, an embrace or a few urgently whispered words in the darkness. Some couples were laughing and joking, some were holding hands, while some hurried off on foot to goodness knew where.

Rosie peered towards the hangar. The coaches were beginning to leave but she could just make Eugene out in the gloom. He'd halted outside the huge doors where he was being spoken to with apparent urgency by one of the sergeants she'd seen earlier. The stream of departing women suddenly surged, and in the melee she finally lost sight of him. Thoughtfully, she turned and made her way to the last remaining bus.

Four Years Earlier

CHAPTER 7

August 31st–Sept 5th, 1940

'Dad!' The young voice rang clearly through the small cottage.

Leonard stooped under the lintel to enter their home, his GWR overalls stained black with coal, the marks matching similar greasy smears on his cheeks.

'Rosie!'

The man greeted his thirteen-year-old daughter with the usual smile, but seemed more tired than usual. He bent briefly to fuss over the dog, dropped his gas-mask case, and sat down heavily at the table on which Rosie had spread her drawing paper, a box of paints and jar of cloudy water.

Exhaling, Leonard mopped his brow with a handkerchief. 'Any chance of a pot, Edie?' he called back into the kitchen and Rosie's mother appeared.

'You're late again! I hope they're going to pay you for all this extra work. You went in an hour early as it is.' She was resentful of his job and the hold it had over him.

'There's a war on, Edie. More trains running, and more trains mean more coal.'

Edith tutted to herself, mumbled about her husband's reluctance to turn down overtime and disappeared into the kitchen, from whence came the dinging of the kettle and the machine-gun rattle of teaspoons.

Rosie glanced at her father, who seemed curiously subdued.

'What's the picture?' Leonard leant over to look at what she'd been painting.

Shyly she turned it round and he saw a portrait of a swallow, the bird sitting neatly on a wire against a blue sky. He picked up the sheet.

'I'm afraid it's not very good,' Rosie said modestly.

'Never worry about mistakes,' her father replied, smiling, "'*A life spent making mistakes is not only more honourable, but more useful than a life spent doing nothing.*" Who said that?'

She shook her head.

'A very clever man named George Bernard ...'

'Shaw!'

He smiled. 'Your painting is wonderful.' He looked at it again. He seemed to be making some kind of calculation.

'It's almost time, Dad!' Roger's head, with its shock of red hair, popped into the room from the kitchen. 'Better get the radio on.'

'Hello, Roger.' Leonard smiled. 'What're you up to?'

But his son had returned to the kitchen.

Rosie switched on the radio. Through the slots in the front she counted the glowing valves until, amid the burbling static, music began to seep through the speaker. She twiddled the Bakelite knob and the signal became clear, a melodious sound filling the room.

Edith arrived with tea. It had become a nightly ritual to listen to the news. With a German invasion imminent, knowing what was happening seemed important.

The announcer began, carefully giving his name before reading the headlines.

'They do that so you know it's not the Germans,' said Edith.

'*We know!*' chorused her children.

She said it every day and it had become a standing joke.

'*Today more raids took place over the South of England, where the invading aircraft were met with heavy resistance. Damage was inflicted on a number of targets, including the bases of RAF fighter command. The enemy lost over thirty aircraft.*'

'*Cor!*' exclaimed Roger, almost choking on his tea. 'Ole Hitler's going to lose at this rate.'

His father nodded. 'What's more important is that most of those planes were bombers, with several men in a crew. Our planes have only the pilot, so the German losses in men will be higher.'

'Is that important?' Rosie asked. She could guess the answer but loved to hear her father talk, and would ask questions just to keep him going, so the sound of his voice wouldn't stop.

He smiled at her, knowing her trick. 'They can replace planes quickly but a man takes years to train. And, if their men bale out, they're out of the fight. If our men bale out, they live to fight again. Some are back in the air the same day. It's like playing a match on your home ground.'

'*Over* your home ground.' Roger interjected.

'Yes, quite right. Over it.'

Eventually the programme ended.

Rosie watched as her mother retreated into her domestic domain where the scraping of pots foretold a weighty and, if they were lucky, edible supper. Roger went out to play with his gang of grubby waifs and strays. But, for a while, father and daughter sat, Rosie brooding over the war news, something that now permeated every aspect of her time at school.

'I hate Hitler,' she announced.

Her father's daily explanations of the newspapers had begun to develop a capacity for critical thought in her, and she understood clearly that the Nazi leader was not simply a bad man, but was intrinsically an enemy of peace, of England and perhaps even of reason. In all these things he seemed the precise opposite of her father.

Leonard smiled benignly. 'I noticed you did,' he replied, remembering the increasingly harsh punishments his daughter advocated daily for the German *Führer*. 'But beware of hatred in your heart, my girl. It's a poison that does no one any good. Still,' he ruffled her hair, 'perhaps you're right about that one.'

He rose, wandered to the window and stood there, fumbling with his pipe.

'What do you say about trying for the scholarship before you leave school?' he asked suddenly, before drawing air through the mixture while applying a Swan Vesta. He had no idea of how they would afford it – uniform, books and all – but the girl was becoming more obviously bright by the day.

'Do you think I might?' Rosie asked, surprised. She enjoyed lessons and had secretly been hoping her education would not have to end at fourteen along with the others of her class.

'I do. You'll be smarter than all of us one day.'

She ran, throwing her arms around him.

'Oh Dad! That would be wonderful!'

She looked at the bookcase behind them, so much a part of her world. He'd made it one rainy bank holiday, and now it was groaning under the weight of fraying and friendly paper. On the lower levels were the ominously heavy volumes, the encyclopaedias, the atlases of the earth and stars, the books on foreign travel and *Old Moore's Almanack*. Further up was what her father called 'Philosophy', complicated works by George Bernard Shaw, Orwell, Russel and

Wolfe, that he seemed to love, eccentrically mixed with a few optimistic titles on cookery and some practical ones on household and motorcycle maintenance. There was science too, great tomes like *Engineering Wonders of the World*, and Lasser's *Conquest of Space* with its cover showing a roaring rocket.

Her favourite shelf was the one of stories and poems. Some, like *Winnie the Pooh* and *The Sword in the Stone*, were for children, others for grown-up reading by her father, penned by Forster, Huxley and H. G. Wells, which nevertheless she had peered into. She'd never dared to reach the forbidden top shelf though she could make out some of the tiles: The *Diary of Samuel Pepys, Tropic of Cancer* and something called *Lady's Chatterley's Lover* by someone brave enough to put his first name last, D.H. Lawrence.

Most of the books were six-penny Penguins from Woolworth's, while others were hardbacks, an expense that frequently drew her mother's wrath.

Rosie was fascinated by the knowledge the volumes contained and, already from dipping in and out, absorbing as much as she could in bite-sized pieces, she'd begun to amass sufficient knowledge to pull her clear of the rest of her class. More subconsciously she'd begun to understand her father's thinking. She knew he was interested in everyone, thought women as intelligent as men. He valued the mind, but thought its rightful keeper was the heart. He was wise, knew when to sow seeds or harvest potatoes and was often more accurate than the weather forecast. He'd said there would be war, and there was one.

'I love you, Rosie-child, always remember that.'

He smiled and ruffled her hair, bringing his face close to hers so that she could feel his breath on her cheek. He looked at her soft pink hands, small inside his own, large, rough ones. She knew he was going to do poetry again. It was as much a part of him as good morning or goodnight. But this time his eyes seemed to have an urgency as though he wanted her to remember.

He began: *'I do not know what it is about you that closes ...'*

It was that one by the man with the name in small letters – e.e. cummings.

'and opens; only something in me understands
the voice of your eyes is deeper than all roses)
nobody, not even the rain, has such small hands.'

Neither of them heard her mother enter the room.

'What on earth is going on?'

Father and daughter separated.

For some reason she did not understand Rosie felt strangely guilty.

'What are you two doing?'

The accused looked at each other, nonplussed.

'Don't come the innocent with me!' Edith continued, her temper rising. *'I know what's going on! No sooner than my back is turned!'*

Rosie could never remember the exact words of the argument that followed, only that her mother was shrieking and that her father was trying, calmly at first but with increasing anger, to defend himself.

'Upstairs!'

Her mother's barked command to her daughter left no room for argument, and Rosie retreated, confused, to her room. The booming argument below lasted a full half-hour, alternately receding, then blazing forth. Eventually the backdoor slammed as her mother left the house.

Tiptoeing down the stairs, Rosie saw her father, face pale and drawn, sitting in an armchair. There was hopelessness on his face and he shook his head glumly. She sensed she shouldn't approach and retreated back up the narrow stairs.

Years later, she would remember returning to find him sitting on the edge of the settee, gazing out of the window, her mother moving about in the kitchen. His broad shoulders were hunched and, as she entered the room, he looked up but instead of a smile she saw him wince in pain. He looked pale as he rose unsteadily to his feet.

Rosie knew something was terribly wrong. Reaching out, she tried to support her father, but he fell, a collapse she was only partly able to break.

'*Mother!*' she found herself shouting, a surge of panic rising in her chest.

Her father lay blinking slowly on the floor.

'What's the matter, Len?'

Edith pulled her daughter out of the way and knelt by her husband. Her face was tense, draining of colour.

'I'll be alright in a minute.' He sounded breathless. 'Only I've got this terrible pain in my arm.' He gasped. 'It's going all the way up to my jaw.' He grimaced again.

'Go and get the doctor,' Edith said in an odd, clipped voice. She did not look up.

'Rosie!' Leonard waved his wife's hand away. 'Rosie. Remember I love you.'

Edith turned, but Rosie was already flying out of the door, wondering why her father had felt it necessary to tell her he loved her when she already knew.

They laid him out, the pine coffin across the dining table, its lid propped disrespectfully against the wall. The adults – her mother, the vicar and her cousins – parted silently as Rosie approached. Her young mind was running in slow motion, an overwhelming numbness separating her from everyone.

She was afraid, but when she looked was surprised to see her father's face clean-shaven and as ruddy as if he had just dressed to go out. His eyes were closed and he looked peaceful, sleeping. For a moment she waited for him to wake, and felt a sense of bewilderment when he did not. Unable to tear herself away, she remained, gripping the coffin, wanting to touch him, yet not daring. Eventually, she heard a dry cough behind her.

'Come, my dear.'

It was one of the cousins. With a wan but kindly smile, he took her hand and led her away.

'Did you see that?' her mother was saying. 'Not a tear. Not a hint of grief. For her own father! I will never understand that child as long as I live.'

Rosie lost track of the time between the laying out and the funeral, though it must have been no more than a day or two. She forgot to eat and her bowels had stopped working. It was hard to differentiate between sleeping and waking for both were dream-like and unreal. The dog was similarly affected, spending most of his time under the table, beneath the coffin, which place he would not yield to anyone, not even Rosie, but growled at all who approached. With uncharacteristic wisdom Edith let him be.

The dreadful day dared to begin clear and warm, dazzling sunlight piercing the leaves, slots of brightness illuminating the riot of wildflowers on the otherwise shady banks next to the church gate. It was wrong, Rosie thought, for the world to be so bright, and apparently happy. The innocent white clouds and intense blue sky seemed mockingly cheerful, while the blooms of the flowers were just insulting in their show-off beauty.

Slowly the assembled crowd, a blur of featureless putty-faces and hats, dark suits and walking sticks, shuffled into the small, cold church.

Rosie walked like an automaton, while her brother sat close to his mother. Rosie hardly saw them, her mind as blank as a wall, stunned as if she had suffered a physical blow. Such thoughts as flicked through her mind were random and strayed readily from a coherent path. She sat limply down. Behind, the shuffling of mourners and the scraping of chairs continued. Her father's life must have touched many. Someone was speaking and Rosie's eyes came to rest on the pulpit, where the vicar stood in his robe with a solemn face. She was grateful that he, at least, was taking things seriously.

Suddenly, like a film that had abruptly jumped scene, she found herself standing again, the organ bleating out a ragged tune. People were singing, or trying to, and someone pushed an open hymnbook into her hands. She couldn't hold it and watched with odd fascination as it tumbled to the floor, pages awry. She stood silently while the vicar mumbled through prayers, but when her Uncle Todd began to read something from the pulpit she recognised it as words she'd thought her father's own.

'Love suffers long and is kind, love does not envy, love does not boast. Love does not behave rudely, does not seek its own, it is not provoked, love thinks no evil. Love does not rejoice in badness, but rejoices in the truth. Love bears all things, believes all things, hopes all things, endures all things. Love never fails.'

It was an unpolished but sincere performance, drawing tears from the women and nose-blowing even from the men.

The scene changed abruptly and they were outside again. It was raining and they were standing by a deep gash in the ground, its borders stained rusty-orange by the local clay. Men were lowering the coffin into the darkness on ropes, then adults threw in handfuls of the reddish earth. She would remember distinctly the precise sound of the thud as, one by one, the fistfuls of dirt hit the lid. She would remember too the vicar leading the mourners away, and a kindly female voice trying to persuade her to go with them. But she remained stubbornly rooted to the ground, staying in the hush of the softly falling rain, no more able to tear herself away than a dog haunting the last resting place of its master.

Of the 'do' that followed at the Church Hall, she would recall only the ritualistic motions of out-of-the-woodwork relatives: the unknown woman who absorbed her into a suffocating bosom, and the banal mutterings of black-suited men who shuffled silently around like awkward and apologetic crows. There was food and drink on a long table, around which a murmuring crowd gathered, though she couldn't understand how anyone could want to eat.

Her mother however had settled easily into the role of Queen of the Dead, surrounded by mourners, apparently relishing her place as the epicentre of attention and weeping conspicuously into a floral handkerchief.

Rosie huddled in a corner, watching, not thinking but her young mind recording. She wanted to cry, she was supposed to. Yet tears wouldn't come. From time to time a stranger would glance curiously at her, and she began to feel a sense of guilt that she was unable to do what was expected. She sensed she didn't belong, and soon slipped like a ghost from the hall, making her way silently back along the soft, mossy graveyard path. She halted before she reached the grave, watching from behind a tombstone as the gravedigger cast a final spade of earth onto the mound. The digger, an old man in a collarless shirt and waistcoat, wiped his brow and stood respectfully for a second with sagged shoulders. Then he tugged a pocket watch from his jacket hanging on a gravestone, sighed, and oblivious to his lone female watcher wrenched the spade from the reluctant earth before ambling slowly away.

Rosie approached and stood in the rain, staring. Minutes passed until on impulse she stooped, cupping a handful of cold clay. It was red and glutinous, small rivulets of water coursing over it, and it clung to her skin. Without knowing why, she dipped a finger into the shiny mass and slowly anointed her face, like an Indian brave applying war paint.

Then Mrs. Barton arrived. Unlike all the others, she seemed to know when to speak and when to be quiet.

It was Rosie who spoke first, without looking up.

'Why did he have to die?'

Mrs. B. gazed thoughtfully down at her.

'You mean, why of all people did your dad have to die, and why so young?'

'Yes.' Her childish voice was plaintive. 'It's unfair. Everyone loved him.'

'I felt the same,' the old lady replied, 'when my husband passed. It seemed unjust.'

'Yes. It is.'

'The ancient Greeks had a saying: "*Whom the gods love, dies young.*"'

Rosie considered this. 'Why? What do gods want with my daddy?'

'I don't know, my lovely.' Mrs. B. ruffled Rosie's blonde hair. 'But you're not alone in wondering. It just seems as though it's the best of us that die young, while the worst live on into old age.'

Rosie had no answer to this, though she felt a rising sense of injustice against the gods, whoever they were, against fate, against whoever decided that this should be so.

'Well, I hate it,' she said firmly, her cheeks flushing with anger.

Then blindly she ran, out of the churchyard, down the street, on and on through the slippery cobbled streets and dark tarmacked roads, on towards home.

For Rosie, the weeks that followed were empty, with even familiar sensations muted, as though she were experiencing the world through glass. Her favourite foods lost their taste and her appetite dwindled, something that caused her mother to growl with impatience. The girl glared sullenly back, and refused to co-operate. Yet, sitting silently and closed-mouthed at meals, she would steal down in bare feet in the night to raid the larder. Sometimes, for reasons she did not understand, she'd wet the bed.

Her mother reacted harshly, firstly with frustration, then with ridicule and occasionally with a firm slap. But her daughter would not respond. She lacked the vocabulary to say what was happening to her, or how she felt, and since words seemed inadequate remained dumb. Sometimes she thought her stomach or perhaps her whole insides had been removed, and she had been left hollow and empty.

For months she hovered, outside of life as most people lived it – a bane, as her mother wasn't slow to tell her, to everyone. Even the doctor, unsympathetic despite the size of his fees, could not understand it, though he left some foul medicine in a bottle, which to her mother's fury Rosie poured away down the sink. She could not think clearly any more, as though the mechanism of her mind had stopped, like a clock frozen at the moment of her father's death. While the world rushed madly on, she remained stuck and unable to engage.

It must have been months later, the day she woke from a dream of her father, to find him still absent, that the tears finally came. Then they poured out, a hot salty flood, stinging her cheeks, reddening her eyes, soaking pillow and sheets, and not completely subsiding until the dawn light grew strong and the grim shadows of the night withdrew to their hiding places.

After the tears, while a ghost of the emptiness remained, Rosie began to feel the tug of life again: the colours, and tastes and smells returned, the world seemed less distant, and she slipped imperceptibly back into the groove of living.

CHAPTER 8

March 1944

The crowd of women shuffled toward the gawping factory doors, keen to clock in and start earning. Rosie had walked there with Hazel as she'd taken to doing over the last few weeks, past a snaking trail of American army lorries moving slowly through the town. The cheery-faced G.I.s in them had whistled and thrown chocolate bars. They were around her own age or not much older, but Rosie couldn't help thinking how young they looked, to be going off to war. Despite their uniforms, there was something hopeful and innocent in their faces that suggested they hadn't yet seen the enemy. To her surprise she felt an odd, almost maternal, instinct stir inside her. How many of the whistling, bright-faced boys, she wondered, would not be coming back? Her father had been right about Hitler. He *was* a monster.

At the factory, the two friends finally entered the inner world of brightly lit benches and whirring conveyors, a man-made cave redolent of wood, the new Bakelite and harsh, metallic solder. The machines were humming and Morelli was talking to a man in a grey pinstripe.

Rosie arrived at her station on the line. Ahead of her, Hazel had picked up a scrap of paper. Big Beryl was peering over Hazel's overalled shoulder, her brow furrowed.

'And you know who put that there,' Beryl was saying.

'Bloody sauce!' Hazel replied grimly, and together they gazed over at Clara.

The tall, dark-haired girl was waving, a sneery, sarcastic expression on her face.

'I found this pinned to my machine,' Hazel said, handing the note to Rosie but not dropping her gaze from Clara.

'*Leave this line clean and not in a mess! Thank you, darling!*' read Rosie. 'Oh dear, that's a bit rude.' She paused. 'Why does it say "darling"?'

But Hazel wasn't listening. 'I'll show her what rude is,' she muttered. 'Now she's snared Morelli, she thinks she's the queen of the place. Always lookin' for better, that one.'

Rosie turned to her work station and was surprised to see a brown envelope bearing her name. She tore it open and inhaled sharply.

'*Dear Delicious*,' it began in a flamboyant but careful script. Her heart skipped a beat. '*I hope you don't mind my writing to you. I asked the guy on the gate to give this to you because you said you worked at the factory. I hope it finds you. I want you to know that I enjoyed our dance. I want to thank you for a couple of hours when I could forget the war and why we are 'Over Here'. I would really like to see you again. They tell me that there is a village nearby called Much Haddam (hope I spelled that right). Anyway, there's a tearoom there, so folks say. Tony has a bicycle I can borrow and if you have one we could meet there one Sunday if I'm not flying. Let them know at the base – leave a note at the gate and mark for Captain Eugene Flynn.*'

Hurriedly she tucked the letter in a pocket.

The first sub-assemblies arrived on the line, and Rosie began adding the components required as each one passed. But her mind had been shunted out of the present by the letter and she felt herself withdrawing. She couldn't forget being with the airman inside the huge bomber. There had been a sense of specialness, of being chosen, that was attractive. A small voice at the back of her consciousness reminded her she hardly knew him, that her growing dreams had no substance. Yet whenever she thought of him it was with a fondness that held a comforting warmth, driving away the darker shadows and memories of unhappiness, and alleviating boredom. It became like a drug, an uplift of mood that could be summoned just by imagining his face, or saying his name silently to herself.

She looked up as Hazel, who seemed to have forgotten about the earlier note, moved past. She was a fast worker, outpacing the others, and had such confidence – a woman who'd seen something of the world. And she was well-informed too. She might have left school at fourteen but she'd educated herself through reading and the Self-Improvement evening classes she went to in town. Rosie screwed together the sub-assembly desultorily. She glanced at the other girls but all were too busy to acknowledge her, or to smile back. She reverted to the task, trying to focus. Why was everything so difficult this morning? The screws didn't want to line up with the holes and the circuit board didn't fit the once-perfect sub-compartment.

'*Stop the line!*'

It was MacKay, their irascible shop steward, and one of the few men in the building. His ruddy pockmarked face grimaced as he raised an imperious hand.

Immediately a bell sounded, and Rosie's line came to a halt.

She snapped back to reality, finding him suddenly confronting her.

'Miss Haskell,' he said, his precise yet somehow irritating Scottish accent cutting the air like a blade, 'just what the devil d'ye call this?'

To Rosie's horror, a pile of components had built up at the incoming part of her position, causing all stations further down the line to stop. In the background she could hear a mumble of conversation.

'*Idiot!*' called Clara, flicking a V-sign.

Rosie coloured but stayed silent.

'*Be quiet, Miss Clampitt!*' MacKay silenced Clara without even looking.

It was Clara's turn to blush. She glared fiercely, and Rosie noticed Hazel glowering coldly back.

A round of whispering began.

'*Silence!*' bellowed MacKay, his voice echoing around the workshop like a headmaster in an assembly hall.

His eyes flashed angrily and Rosie felt a chill run down her spine. It was like being back in the orphanage and she felt her heart-beat quicken.

'This is precision equipment! *Precision*, do ye get it?' the man was saying. 'If it dunnae work then one of our pilots will end up deed!'

Except for the heating fans, the workshop was deathly silent. MacKay was closer now and Rosie could smell his tobacco-laden breath.

Suddenly he whirled around, addressing the whole room.

'*You're all stupid wee lassies!*' he bellowed, '*Nothing between yer ears but bloody cobwebs!*'

Rosie reached forward onto the line and began to clear the blockage.

'I'm sorry, Mr. MacKay,' she managed.

He turned sharply and tapped her menacingly on the arm with a ruler.

'Aye. I've got my eyes on you, young lady. Comin' in here and takin' a man's job.' He growled. 'One more mistake and I'll report ye.' And with that he withdrew to the small cubicle that with some exaggeration he referred to as his 'office'.

The line restarted almost instantly with the usual whirr and slid on uneventfully for half an hour and, although MacKay's words had stung, Rosie began to settle into the day. She was feeling calmer when a small metal object flew past, narrowly missing her head. Shocked, she turned to see Clara grinning. The missile, some kind of screwdriver, had passed its intended target, but had instead hit Hazel in the back.

A gasp came from the other girls nearby as the victim turned. Slowly, deliberately, Hazel reached out and hit the emergency stop. She threw back her shoulders, drew her hands in front of her and flexed her interlaced fingers, an action that caused an audible crack. She rolled up her sleeves and glared in the direction the screwdriver had come from.

Girls next to Clara began to edge slowly away.

Back at orphanage Rosie had seen girls fight before, but this was at work, in front of everyone.

'Catfight!' said someone quietly.

Hazel crossed the floor, her pace deliberate and calculated.

'You wouldn't think,' said Beryl, now standing at Rosie's elbow, 'they used to be friends.'

'Friends?' Rosie asked, surprised.

'Yeah. They knew each other from up north, before the war. When they got here they were close. *Too* close, some said. That was before Morelli and Clara became an item, of course.'

Rosie was about to ask how you could be too close to someone, but on the other side of the line Hazel had reached Clara.

The words of her raised voice carried despite the background noise.

'I've had all I'm gonna take, from thee. Nothin's ever enough, is it, not fer thee?' Hazel stepped forwards until she and Clara were almost touching. 'Tha screws the boss and still tha wants more. Nothin's nor no one's good enough!'

Rosie gaped at the scene as the women glared at each other from point-blank range. Clara, an inch or so taller than Hazel's five foot eight, spluttered like a firework, her eyes glowing dangerously as she glared at her opponent. But her voice was remained surprisingly cool and disdainful.

'Hazel! I see you are as incoherent as usual.' She forced a patronising smile. 'And you're sober too.' She bent her head until their faces were almost touching. 'To what miracle do we owe this?'

'*Bitch!*' Hazel hissed, not dropping her gaze for a second.

Clara laughed. 'Bitch? I don't look at all like your mother, Hazel.'

'Tha's a bitch, a gold-digger and as vain as a tart,' replied Hazel steadily, adding, with a glance around the room that amounted to a flourish, 'An' thy arse is bigger than a bus.'

A wave of laughter erupted and this was too much for Clara.

'*Cow!*' she shrieked, all pretence at moral superiority abandoned. Her first slap was so hard it almost knocked Hazel over.

The two women locked together and staggered out into the space between the lines, colliding with a cart full of parts, sending them ricocheting. Glass valves spilled in a glassy cascade from a trolley onto the floor, breaking with a series of flashbulb-like pops.

Clarence, who'd been anxiously watching, rushed forward with a dustpan and brush and began obsessively sweeping. He seemed to be upset by the sudden disorder and was chattering in an oddly agitated way to himself.

MacKay meanwhile had emerged from his cubbyhole, and made as if to move forward but found his path blocked by the towering shape of East-ender 'Bermondsey' Beryl. He gulped nervously, mopped his brow and wisely went back to his cubbyhole and the racing results.

The combatants were each attempting to tear the other's hair out, staggering across the floor, the dark and light-coloured locks mixing as they fought.

'*Baggage!*' shrieked Clara as they tumbled to the floor.

'*I'll do you!*' came Hazel's scream from somewhere underneath.

Rosie's eyes widened. She'd seen fights before, but this was different. There was an odd hatred to it, a passion. Soon there would be real injuries. With a decisiveness that surprised her, she walked towards the end of the line.

'*Hazel!*' Rosie caught her friend's fist just as it rose into the air.

Hazel looked up, her eyes were wild, a thin white trail of saliva dribbling from her mouth. For a second Rosie froze, astonished. But when she spoke her voice was stronger than she expected. It almost sounded like someone else.

'*Hazel! No!*'

There was something primitive in the violence of her friend's assault that was not just odd, it was disturbing.

Rosie looked down. '*You too, Clara.*'

Clara, her dark hair disarrayed, sat grimly on the floor. Silently she glared up at Rosie, as if she couldn't believe the cheek of the newcomer and wiped a stream of blood running from her nose. There was something odd about Clara's eyes, Rosie thought. They glinted with malice but were cold and empty, like a shark's. No wonder she and the affable Hazel didn't like each other.

Beryl's deep voice boomed suddenly across the room. '*Break it up, girls! Morelli's comin'!*'

Hazel clambered hastily to her feet, drew a handkerchief from her pocket and began to mop the sweat from her face. She bent over Clara.

'*Mess with me again, tha bloody bitch, and I'll finish thee proper!*'

Clara made no reply, but her hate-filled gaze spoke of resentment dormant, but not yet spent.

CHAPTER 9

Rosie frowned. She'd received his note in reply to hers, confirming he would come, and the time, but she'd been waiting for what seemed like hours and there was still no sign. She had no watch but had timed her journey to the tearoom for midday as she'd cheekily arranged on the works telephone. And it must be at least three by now. An ache in her stomach intensified as she propped the bicycle in front of the tearoom. The building was long, thatched and timber-framed, washed crumbly white with lime. A sign quietly creaking in the wind announced it as *The Copper Kettle,* and over the door curled a rose that had known better days.

She scolded herself. I knew I shouldn't have come, she thought fretfully. She ran a hand though her shoulder-length hair, the carefully set curls since flattened by the spring shower that had caught her as she'd left town. She'd let her dreams run away with her. It had been foolish to think someone as glamorous as Eugene could be interested in someone so ordinary. Rosie reached into the gas-mask case which she'd taken to using as a handbag, and drew out a powder compact. In its stained and cracked glass she glimpsed the disaster of wet hair, smudged lipstick and streaked mascara. To cap it all, there was chain oil from the bike on her socks. God, what a state!

Frustrated, Rosie stared grimly over the surrounding farmland. As if to emphasise her gloom, from the clouds whose blue-grey bellies were still full of rain drifted a gruff rumble of thunder.

As she stood miserably wondering what do next, an old man carrying a crumpled bag over his shoulder went by in. Despite his obvious poverty, he was whistling a tune that seemed annoyingly cheerful and out of place. His figure was stooped and he wore a threadbare jacket and cap. He was what her father would have called 'a gentleman of the road'. His trousers, she noticed, were held up with a piece of thick, knotted string and a dirty toe protruded from the side of an ancient boot.

He smiled when she asked him the time.

'"Tis just after two, miss,' he replied toothlessly. 'I passed th' church a while back, and so it said on th' tower.'

She had the odd feeling he was secretly laughing as he went on his way.

Against her will, Rosie felt the hot stab of tears welling in her eyes. But self-pity quickly turned to anger. She began to tremble with emotion, every second adding to the humiliation, the torment straining as taut as a wire. She forced herself to wait, clinging on as the minutes passed painfully by, until she couldn't stand it anymore. She'd wait no longer.

Snorting with frustration, she grabbed the bicycle, rolled it to the road and mounted. She punished the pedals with hard, downward kicks, and the machine slowly gathered speed as she left the village, until the rough tarmac began to fly past, the wind cutting her eyes. She pedalled harder until the hedgerows either side became no more than a smear of retreating green.

Rounding the bend, a bleary shape whizzed past in the opposite direction and Rosie had a vague sense of narrowly missed collision. Somewhere, far off, could be heard the frantic ringing of a bell. Was it him? No, it couldn't be – it was far too late. A wave of anger washed through her and she pedalled harder, driving the spinning wire wheels faster. It was becoming hard to catch her breath, but still she didn't stop. The speeding bike had reached the long, upward incline of Mote's Hill, the dull grey surface running over the wooded ridge at the top down into the valley beyond, its route hacked from primordial forest by woolly-tunicked Romans, two millennia before.

Standing on the pedals, Rosie pushed still more roughly, muscles and sinews straining in a defiance of gravity, driving the bike up the steep hill, her young body swaying side to side under the strain. Her brow furrowed and her eyes down, she was possessed by a terrible will, a fury she did not know her body could create. She strove harder and harder, wanting to escape her shame, but the incline was steep, and despite the lung-tearing exertion, the bike's speed began to bleed slowly away.

When Rosie finally reached the crest, she was labouring; her face flushed and streaked with sweat. Just beyond the top a violent cramp suddenly seized her leg and, thrown off balance, she braked, hard. The bike skidded on the loose surface, swerved onto the verge and, as the front wheel dug in a rut, pitched her up and over the handlebars. She landed in a hedgerow thick with hawthorn, nettles, and tangly briars.

Rosie rolled onto the ground and stared upward, gazing up at the sky. The thunderclouds were rolling away and widening patches of blue, the colour of a robin's egg, peered curiously down. She was glad to have crashed, glad the madness was over. Glad too she could lie invisible and untormented. The grass beneath her was damp but her mind was clearing, the maddening adrenaline fading. She glanced at the neighbouring field, where the wind was sending shadows scudding across the ground. A pair of horses careened wildly. Overhead the trees flexed and creaked gently. The madness of released tension gone, she lay still, alone among the crushed stems of flowers and barbed purple tentacles of briar, smelling the earth and listening to her own breathing.

'Are you alright?'

The voice came from the road.

Rosie sat up.

Eugene, wearing slacks and a flying jacket, came to stand towering above her, concern on his face. He was breathing heavily and behind him she glimpsed a green bicycle. A rivulet of sweat ran from his temple, staining the collar of his beige shirt.

'I saw you fly past, going like a bat outta hell, and I came right after you but, boy, you were really movin'.' He frowned. 'Say, are you hurt?' He bent down to help her up.

Unsteadily she rose, brushing off the leaves and tendrils.

Oh God, she thought, what must he think?

Blushing, she stammered, 'I'm – I'm quite alright, thank you.'

She was not alright. She must look awful – her hands were scratched and her face must be too – and she had behaved like a mad person.

'Let me.'

With a surprising delicacy he began to extricate the bicycle from the undergrowth, eventually pulling it, festooned with leaves and grass, from the hedge.

'It seems OK.' He ran a hand over the front wheel, adding without looking up her, 'I'm sorry I was late – something came up and I had to deal with it. We had a funeral.'

Rosie couldn't look him in the eye, so she began to remove burrs from her cardigan.

'It's quite alright,' she said.

'*Your knee!*' he exclaimed.

She looked down. A crimson trickle ran down her pale leg and a flap of skin hung free, revealing a small but gory tear on the kneecap. 'Oh.'

Eugene fumbled in his pocket and produced a handkerchief. Swiftly he tore the fabric and fashioned a bandage.

'This may sting a little,' he said, applying the makeshift dressing.

Involuntarily she flexed, grabbing his shoulder. For such a large man he could be oddly gentle with his hands, the movements of which were subtle and light.

She felt ashamed. 'I was running away,' she blurted, 'I thought you had forgotten.'

He stood, facing her, close.

'I know,' he said solemnly.

A grin broke across his face and he laughed.

Suddenly relieved, if embarrassed, she found she couldn't stop herself laughing with him.

She smiled shyly and gazed up at his warm brown eyes.

He embraced her slender body, drawing her against himself.

'I'm sorry I was late, Rosie.'

His body felt hard – she could feel his muscularity and strength and could smell the faint scent of sweat mixed with the tang of cologne. Then, to her surprise, he kissed her. Although part of her wanted it, another part of her cringed back in alarm. For several seconds she writhed in indecision. It was very soon. She hardly knew him. Any decent girl would make him wait. She submitted, finding herself impulsively clasping his back and returning the warmth of the kiss.

Almost Two Years Earlier

CHAPTER 10

10th June 1943

Around her in the moonlit orphanage dormitory the other girls slept, while on the ground floor below the hall clock struck two, a muffled percussion that caused one inmate to murmur, twisting restlessly in unknown dreams. The whispering of the breeze as it stirred the tops of the sweet-smelling limes reached into the room, filling the space with scent and a gentle rustling.

The summer warmth made Rosie think of the lake, a glimmering ornament set perfectly in the institution's landscaped grounds. It would be lying there still, reflecting the moon like a mirror. The night air would be mad with bats, and the hedgerows teeming with the unearthly, green lanterns of glow-worms.

It was the day before her fourteenth birthday when Rosie first saw the orphanage they called 'Cloverly Fields'. And when she saw the horse and cart that had brought her and her suitcase receding up the drive, the depth of abandonment and the building's purpose was clear. She'd looked timorously up at the huge three-storey structure that towered above and swallowed hard.

Even to her young eye, she could see the orphanage was neglected.

The tall octagonal redbrick chimneys, home to chattering starlings, were riven with cracks, sprouting moss and wild, prehistoric ferns. They leaned dangerously outward. Cast-iron gutters, rotten with rust, had long since failed, allowing seasons of rain to fall down the building's flanks. Two of the windows at the front were boarded up, giving the house an odd face, that of a blind man.

Rosie propped herself restlessly on her pillow and glanced across the shadowy dorm. The other girls were strewn around on the beds like seals basking on rocks. Oblivious to the distress she was feeling, their warm bodies rose and fell softly in perfect ignorance. Some of them, she knew, found relief from the orphanage's loveless existence in each other, in some kind of intimacy as yet unknown to her. But her only friend had been Knightly, and now she was gone.

Rosie stood. She walked slowly between the rows of beds and their dreaming occupants, trailing her hand over the cool metal frames. There was no warmth at all left in the world, it seemed, no connection to be made, just the relentless emptiness of being alone. She arrived at the window and surveyed the silvery grounds. Beyond the dark orchard, the lake was shining. The water had begun to silt, willows and rushes conquering the shallows with their leafy canopies and stiff, green spears. But the deeper parts, where lurked carp and the lone old pike that preyed on them, were strewn with lilies and irises. On secret summer days, she'd sit alone and gaze at the water's portrait of the sky, its surface unmarked save for the vee's of swallows drinking on the wing, or the dimple of a lazy fish breaking surface.

Rosie returned restlessly to her bed, slumped down and remembered Knightley, floating alone in the same water, barely a week before. They said she'd been quite dead when the gardener found her, the child's white regulation nightdress splayed out around her pale body like the distended petals of a pale flower. She'd been tiny, probably no more than five feet tall and would often make you jump, arriving unheard in a room, appearing suddenly as though she'd flown in on tiny, concealed wings.

Observed by a dozen pairs of unseen eyes, they – the swarthy matron and the leery nicotine-stained overseer – had heaved the dead girl clumsily in through the kitchen door, like a sack of potatoes. She'd waited after lights-out before padding silently down in the worn old slippers through which her toes protruded. The kitchen was always locked to prevent the underfed residents from breaking in, but it would be possible to see in through the outside window. She unbolted the scullery door, and went outside, and shielding the glass against the moon's light, peered through. The body lay motionless on a huge steel table, rigid as though made of wax. The spirit, the thing that had actually *been* Knightly, was gone. All that was left behind was this cold thing.

Rosie sighed. She was tired beyond tiredness, empty with no understanding of how to fill the void. Lately she'd begun to hide from the present by retreating into a world of stories and daydreams. The old attic library was packed with musty-smelling books and she'd escape by immersing herself in them. She would actively become the protagonist, seeing life as they did, speaking as they did, completely dissolving herself into the plot until it became real. Hers grew into a private world of desperate heroines, noble heroes – a place of reason, where good and sanity triumphed over madness and evil. The everyday world in the dorms and corridors she merely passed through as an observer. But it was different in the orphanage's classroom. There and beyond she threw herself into study, reading encyclopaedias from cover to cover and absorbing as much as she could, scanning difficult and dusty poems by Coleridge and Blake, as well as lighter modern novels and essays, as if by forcing in knowledge she could push out the situation that was unacknowledgeable.

Of living human relationships Rosie at first starved herself, an instinct for self-preservation, or at least the prevention of further harm, holding her back. But later, sensing the absence, she recognised it as a possible trap of her own making, something that could make a bleak situation even worse and so, hesitantly at first, she'd reached out to Knightly. The younger girl had often followed her to the attic library, and there she'd read to her from *One Thousand and One Nights*, or *Grimms' Fairy Tales*, as she sat, cross-legged and wide-eyed, silent, her thumb in her mouth. They would talk during break times and share what meagre treats either happened to come by. But now it seemed that fate, unsatisfied with taking only her father, had seized even this last friend, and the ache of loneliness returned with sheer, overwhelming power until the simple act of living, of rising every day, became like the dragging of a stone.

Rosie's breathing quickened. She got out of bed. A floorboard creaked as she moved to the window. By the pale moonlight, she saw across the grey lawns, ragged hedges and dark herbaceous borders below out to the shimmering lake. A thought came slyly, uninvited, tiptoeing into her mind. What if there really was no point? What if the future was an unending stream of loneliness? Ending the torment was the one thing within her power. With relief, she realised she could die.

'I want to die.' She said it impulsively. Then whispered the words again. '*I want to die.*' She liked their sound, as if it were a prayer and repeated it again. A wave of tiredness coursed through her, as though someone had put a tap into her side and drained away the lifeblood. Perhaps death was like sleep, she thought, something to sink into, something comforting, not to be afraid of, but to be welcomed as a friend. Within the long sleep of death, there could be no pain. But perhaps there was a better existence beyond, perhaps Knightly would be there.

She padded softly on naked feet from the dorm, leaving the heavy door ajar, crossing the narrow uncarpeted hall and stepping slowly and deliberately up the steep stairs to the second-floor library. She passed through the narrow corridors of shelves, her fingers caressing the spines of the slumbering volumes and went to the window, opened the sash and climbed onto the sill. The air was cool, fragrant with the smell of cut grass and warm, damp earth, while behind her the house was so silent you could almost hear it.

Rosie's legs dangled carelessly in the cooler outside air. The path she could dimly see below was hard, and she remembered the texture of its sharp and flinty gravel. Her body would make a mess. Her flesh would be crushed and split by the weight and speed of the fall, and bright-red blood would leak onto the pale stone, splashing up and along the wall. Something in the disorder of such a death was undignified and her mind rebelled. For a moment she paused. And then the thought came. *The lake.* She could walk calmly into the water and let it do the work. It would be quick, peaceful. Even poetic. It would be just as sure as jumping, because she couldn't swim.

Rosie went downstairs. Leaving the dining room's French window open behind her, she walked barefoot down the soft, earthy path to the orchard, where late summer apples were strewn, her nightdress catching in the breeze. The night was close, the air alive with sounds, crackling with electricity. In the shadows, small movements caught the corner of the eye, resolving into dark, mysterious shapes. She felt she were being watched by a hundred tiny eyes. Her senses were working with sharpened acuity, the silvery ground glowed beneath her and, as she entered the garden, she felt the wetness of long grass and the sharp, dagger-stabs of twigs under her feet, each sensation strikingly rich in detail. She walked quietly along the hedge, its foliage decked with a sprinkling of glow-worms, their yellow lights swinging in the darkness.

She stood for a moment, then pulled her nightdress up, over her head, standing naked for a moment at the water's edge. The lake was full, almost to the top of its bank, and rested, enigmatic and dark, the barest whisper of mist hanging like a veil close to the surface. The moon, which was riding a raft of wispy clouds, peered curiously down, its reflection like a silver shilling floating serenely on the unrippled surface. A moth landed softly on Rosie's shoulder. For a while the creature lingered, opening and closing its wings, until a breeze rustled the reeds, sending it fluttering erratically away in a panic.

There was no more time for thinking. The pain was crushing and she longed to be free. Drawing in her breath, Rosie walked into the water, the slippery clay of the lake-bottom sliding under bare feet. The cold was more intense than she expected, and her breathing accelerated, becoming rapid and shallow. Goosebumps appeared on her arms and then she stepped into the abyss, and was gone. At first, surprise prevented her from reacting. She watched with detachment as the silvery surface receded, shiny buttons of quivering air rising upward as she fell slowly away into the dark. The moon, so bright at the surface, dwindled to a flimsy green disc. Only when she touched bottom did she snap back into awareness. Panicking, she pulled hard for the surface, breaching after what felt like an age in a fit of coughing and spluttering. Before she could get her breath, the lake pulled her down again. Rosie's chest strained and she thrashed again, kicking hard for the surface. Deep in her mind a switch had been thrown: suddenly she'd changed her mind. She didn't want to die. She reached the air once more, gasping, this time a little further from shore. But she could feel herself slipping back and for a third time descended. To the silent scream of panic was added the conscious terror that she would die when she wanted to live. The lake, it seemed, wanted to keep her, and was testing the strength of her will as well as her body.

Rosie gulped helplessly, and this time a gulp of water passed into her stomach. She lashed out with her legs, before suddenly connecting with a firm object. Her shoulders rose inexplicably above water. She looked around, astonished, and breathed. She must be standing on something, perhaps a a rock or some kind of ridge rising from the lake floor. She coughed, gasped again for air and swayed dangerously before gaining a precarious balance. Through bleary eyes, she saw the bank. It was remote, at least thirty feet away. She shivered, her body cold, limbs stiff and heavy as iron. It was becoming harder to breathe.

Instinctively she knew she must quell the panic, must slow her chaotic breathing and allow the air to penetrate deep into her gasping lungs. To survive she must gain control. With clenched fists Rosie forced herself to inhale. She held each breath for several agonising seconds before releasing it slowly, jerkily at first, through cold pursed lips. Imperceptibly, then with increasing certainty, the ragged heaving of her chest slowed and deepened until finally a steady rhythm returned.

Rosie pushed her matted hair up and out of her eyes and peered into the darkness. The shilling-moon had vanished, leaving the lakeside dark and indistinct, but her mind had taken on a new clarity. She wouldn't die. She would live, and by living, endure. The orphanage wouldn't be forever and if she could only hang on, one day she would be free. The young woman's eyes narrowed and her jaw took on a firmer set. She would make a plan, and somehow find a better life where she was wanted, and loved, and where she could love freely in return. She would build her own more hopeful world, and build it on solid foundations that would not betray her. In this world there would be no more pain, no more poverty or loneliness, or hunger, or pain, only deliverance from the past and some kind, any kind, of happiness.

She shivered. Perhaps, if she could not swim, she could walk. She looked again at the bank. It was not as far as she'd first thought.

Gathering her courage and taking a deep breath, she stepped off whatever she was standing on. For a few seconds she allowed herself to sink, watching as the air bubbles rose lazily past her through the murky water, until at last her bare feet touched down on the muddy lake bottom. The clay-rich sediment squirmed between her toes as, leaning forward, she pushed one leg in front of the other, half-slipping, half-falling, half-swimming, as she forced herself slowly forward against the heavy resistance of the water.

Then her breath almost spent, she erupted from the lake and found herself standing, head and shoulders completely clear, a ring of ripples spreading out from her body. The mud beneath her feet felt slippery but wonderfully solid. For a few seconds she paused, greedily drawing in life-giving air. But a cramp was beginning in her legs, and grimly she pushed on for the last three yards until, grunting and panting she found herself at last on the bank.

Rosie staggered, stood unsteadily, and was immediately sick. The sober heaviness of gravity tugged remorselessly at her body and she fell, exhausted but very much alive, onto the sweet-smelling grass.

CHAPTER 11

April 1944

It was Charlotte, one of Hazel's housemates, who opened the door to the digs. Her lower half was in pyjamas, and she was trying to pull a blouse over her head while eating toast. Inaudible through her breakfast, she waved Rosie down the corridor to where she could see Hazel in a man's green pullover and denim trousers, filling a kettle.

Rosie walked into the kitchen, nodding acknowledgments. Three other girls were in stages of dress or undress, chattering, eating, cleaning up after breakfast. A thin one was arguing vociferously with the one called Doris. A clothesline had been strung from one side of the kitchen to the other, and the hurrying inhabitants of the shared house navigated the stockings that hung stalactite-like as they ducked beneath.

'How do!' Hazel smiled, setting the kettle on a gas ring, and then nodding her head towards the back garden.

The two of them escaped the pandemonium and sat outside on rain-bleached wooden chairs at an improvised table.

Hazel, her large green eyes fixed on Rosie, began to eat the

95

crumpet she'd brought with her. 'Tha looks knackered,' she said, in her usual matter-of-fact way.

Rosie paused, not wanting to be one of those people who always complained. 'My mother,' she admitted. 'We had another argument. My brother Roger is home, so she's full of, "Rog, would you like some cake?" "Rog, would you like something nice for tea?" "Don't get up, Roger, it's no trouble." I just had to get out of the house.'

Hazel nodded sympathetically.

Rosie looked around the garden, a suburban rectangle of scruffy grass enclosed by a tarred fence, a mossy pear tree at the back and a jungley path up the middle. It had been allowed to go wild and, although at some time in the past an attempt had been made to scrape a vegetable patch, most of it was a thicket of weeds and briars, through which ran the dark tunnels of hedgehogs interspersed with the roosts of birds.

A robin fluttered on the table and hopped about expectantly. He sang a few notes, clear and silvery in the morning air, and put his head on one side.

'Cheeky bugger.' Hazel broke off a tiny piece of crumpet. The bright-eyed bird promptly pounced. She smiled and, taking the remainder, held it out to Rosie.

'For me? But that's your breakfast.'

''Tis my third! Open wide!'

Rosie laughed and took the buttered morsel.

Hazel grinned, her eyes twinkling in the low morning light. She stood. 'Just a mo'.'

She returned a couple of minutes later with two slopping mugs of tea. The drink was blisteringly hot, but the morning was cool and Rosie clutched the mug for warmth, shivering.

'I ken get thee a sweater if tha likes?' Hazel offered.

Rosie nodded gratefully. She'd rushed out, driven by anger at her mother and the anxiety of knowing Eugene was flying.

'Here – have this.' Hazel began to take off her green woollen pully.

'But you'll get cold!'

'Nay, lass. I run hot, tha knows!'

Rosie laughed. 'Is that right?'

'Aye.'

Rosie put on the pullover, still warm from Hazel's body. It was an intimate thing to be wearing someone else's clothes, and felt illicit, even oddly dangerous.

Her friend grinned. 'Tha's got a fine figure. Tha fills it alright.'

Rosie grinned, but felt a twinge of embarrassment. Whether it was the better food she was getting or whether she was still developing, she'd begun to put on weight and had noticed her body starting to fill out. Hazel really was plain-speaking.

'Where did you get it?' Rosie asked, looking at the knitwear, which was wonderfully soft, and looked new. It had to be pre-war.

Hazel slurped her tea. 'Chap whose house it were went into t'army and left a few things. So I nabbed all I could.' She grinned with evident satisfaction.

Hazel was a survivor, Rosie thought. And yet, despite her outer toughness, and down-to earth nature, there was something about her that was still essentially feminine. There was a boyish beauty in her face, with its high cheekbones, short-cut blonde hair and intense green eyes and she had a lad-like charm, almost roguish. But prettiness, from her captivating eyes to her pert mouth, was there too. It was odd she hadn't yet made a conquest among the town's young men, although admittedly there weren't many. Other than soldiers passing through. Or airmen. She was so confident, although perhaps some men might find that off-putting in a woman.

'Missing yer feller?' Hazel asked suddenly, her eyes sharpening.

Rosie nodded. 'I suppose I am. When I'm with him life is fun, and when he's with me I know he's safe. It's the in-between times I worry about.'

Hazel nodded, her face darkening. 'Aye. Them boys is in harm's way alright. Still,' she made an effort to be upbeat, 'tha 'as that course tha enrolled in at t'Town 'all – don't that tek thy mind off worrying?'

Rosie tried to grin gamely, but it came out more like a grimace. 'A bit.'

She'd signed up for the free classes in Creative English and history. Getting a qualification without a school certificate seemed a bit like locking the stable door after the horse had bolted, but it was a path upwards from the shop floor. The classes were on Tuesday evenings which was coincidentally when most of the political talks Hazel went to were held, so they provided a readymade excuse without hurting Hazel's feelings.

'What about you?' Rosie glanced at her friend. 'Got your eyes on anyone?'

Hazel peered into her cup. She seemed to struggle for words.

'I could have,' she said at last.

'What's he like?' Rosie asked, intrigued. It would be fascinating to know what kind of man Hazel might be attracted to. She leant forward, expectantly.

Hazel drew her hand slowly through her short blonde hair, and didn't immediately reply. She seemed to be choosing her words carefully.

'Oh, nice-lookin', clever and ... decent ... but ...'

'But?'

'Vulnerable. Needs lookin' after. Young and don't know much about the world.' She shot her friend a shy glance.

Rosie giggled. She wanted to know more. 'You're going to mother him then? Old Mother Hazel?' She laughed out loud. Anything less motherly than Hazel was hard to imagine.

Hazel glanced away. 'That wasn't what I had in mind.'

'Who is it? Come on, Hazel, tell us!' Rosie prodded her friend playfully.

Hazel stared across the garden. It was clear she wouldn't be rushed.

The robin was singing brightly from the pear tree and the sun was climbing higher, burning off the moisture that had collected in the deep grass and was hanging as droplets on the spiders' webs among the briars.

For a moment Hazel looked as if she was going to speak but then changed her mind. She glanced back at Rosie.

'Just someone – who's with someone else as it happens. But I want to change that. Have the person all for myself.'

'Hazel!' Rosie pretended to be shocked.

Hazel gave a dry laugh and it suddenly dawned on Rosie that, behind her friend's bluff exterior, there was a pool of sadness and perhaps desire.

CHAPTER 12

It was weeks later that Rosie realised her life was settling into a pattern. When Eugene wasn't flying she spent as much time with him as his off-base passes would allow, their manner easing slowly into greater intimacy as they grew to know each other. But in the long and anxious periods when the war drew him away, she increasingly sought the comfort of Hazel's warmth, and here too she had grown closer. Her friend's humour, plain speaking, energy and charm were hard to resist. They'd embrace when they'd meet and sometimes, when walking and putting to rest Rosie's fears in endless conversations, would hold hands. When at work Hazel was far more business-like, but even so hardly a shift passed without them catching other's eye, stopping for a brief chat if the supervisor wasn't looking and walking home from work together, unless they could afford the bus in which case Hazel simply got off at her turning.

Today, Rosie thought, as she watched her friend leaning her red tandem against the Air Force chain-link fence, they were combining her two worlds. Hazel was wearing a pair of men's blue canvas jeans and a check lumberjack-style shirt, one of her typically rebellious outfits that still drew attention, despite the number of women in uniform, and even trousers, around nowadays.

It had been typical of Hazel's generosity to insist they visit the base together, in the hope they might catch sight of Eugene, or his plane.

They'd approached the tall metal gates, but the soldier on duty seemed to have no intention of letting them pass, despite Hazel's persuasion and outrageous offer of a bribe. Yet he'd taken the note Rosie had prepared for Eugene and she hoped that, like the others, it would reach him.

The girls wandered away from the gate, through the thick grass along the perimeter fence, peering through the mesh at intervals to the mile-long runways beyond, their pink concrete surfaces shimmering in the sun.

Some hundred yards from the gate and fifty yards in stood the control tower, and dotted around the field, looking like gigantic molehills, were the grass roofs of what looked like air-raid shelters.

'Tha walks like a cat,' said Hazel, playfully.

Rosie turned. 'A cat?'

'Aye. Like a pussycat.'

Hazel did a passable imitation of an exaggeratedly delicate feline walk.

'I don't!'

'Aye, tha does. Tha behind wiggles as tha goes along but tha feet land right in the line of the last step. Right delicate, like.'

'What about you then?' Rosie asked, observing her friend.

'What about me?' Hazel threw her head back in mock defiance.

'You walk like a great strutting bird!' Rosie said, imitating an easy, long-legged gait. 'Or a man, a soldier on parade!'

'Bugger off!' the other replied, feigning hurt, but laughing all the same.

Hazel drew two cigarettes from a pocket in her trousers, put them in her mouth and cracked open her lighter, passing one of the glowing sticks to Rosie.

Well beyond the fence were the distant hangars, and around them a few planes in states of disassembly.

'Look at all them blokes – there's hundreds of the buggers,' Hazel said, drawing on her fag and looking at the teams of mechanics and uniformed personnel that seemed to be just about everywhere. 'For every one up there, there must be four or five down here. Still, I'd rather be up there flyin' than fartin' about on t'ground.'

Rosie giggled at Hazel's rude language. 'What, bombing Germans? You wouldn't!'

'Aye, I would an' all.' She flicked her cigarette, her face deadly serious.

Perhaps, thought Rosie, she would.

The field was busy despite most of the squadron being somewhere over Germany, probably finishing what the RAF had started the night before. The thought caused her stomach to clench and she hurriedly forced herself to focus on what was happening around them. Vehicles – trucks, tankers and jeeps were moving everywhere she looked, and near her, a group of soldiers were drilling at a sandbagged Anti-Aircraft position, the shouts of the sergeant carrying on the still air.

Rosie trailed her hand along the chain-link as they walked.

'Why do you dress like that, almost always trousers and not a skirt?' she asked suddenly. 'Is it just because they're practical?' It was something she'd been mulling for a while. It seemed odd that a woman as beautiful as Hazel wouldn't want the best of clothes to show herself off in. Their money from the factory was more than they could spend.

Her friend snorted. 'Ha, now there's a story.'

For a while she fell silent.

A twin-engined passenger plane flew low over the field, perhaps in training, for it did not land.

'There were six of us kids,' she said then. 'Five gert strappin' brothers, and then me.'

She shot Rosie a glance that was, for her, oddly doleful. Rosie sensed that there was much she didn't yet know.

'When my father died, we hardly had a brass farthin' between us an' all me clothes were hand-me-downs. And o'course they were boys' stuff. I just had ter get used ter it, like. Besides,' she added, brightening a little, 'I soon preferred 'em anyhow. I were always climbing trees, or ferritn' fer coal along t'railway or running out of a shop after pinchin' summat. It were better ter have shorts, or trousers.'

'But you don't have to do that anymore.' Rosie was feeling she was not much the wiser.

'Nay, but ...' Hazel hesitated, 'it just suits me nature, I suppose. An' it's, like, a statement. Tha knows, a *political* statement.'

'Politics?' Rosie admired Hazel's hard-won self-education from books, newspapers and Labour party pamphlets, but she knew her own understanding was still way behind her friend's.

'Aye, a statement of equality like, of being as good as them.' She nodded towards a group of men gathered around a fire truck that was parked near the closest runway. 'Either that or just confuse 'em, rile 'em up like.' She grinned.

'Ah.' Rosie nodded. From what she knew about her friend, that at least made some sense, although instinctively she felt there was more.

It was almost midday by the time they completed the circuit and Hazel slipped away into town on her bike, returning cheerfully half an hour later with an impromptu picnic of sausage rolls, apples and beer. They sat on a felled tree and Rosie smiled at her friend's appetite.

She didn't feel like eating but, when she started to, found she was hungrier than she'd supposed.

They munched in silence until Hazel passed her a half-gallon flagon.

'Beer at lunchtime? Hazel, you are a wicked woman.' Rosie took the heavy vessel carefully.

Hazel winked. 'Aye, but it'll do thee good.' She patted her friend on the leg. 'Tha feller. He'll come home. I'm sure he will.'

Rosie took a sip of beer but did not reply. To do so would seem like tempting fate. She had almost not come but, when Hazel had suggested it, she'd been drawn to the base as the next best thing to seeing Eugene.

It was getting warmer and the runways were shimmering in the haze.

Rosie spread her mac and they lay together on it. Idly she picked a buttercup and held it up at the sky.

'So, have you plans then, with this feller? Tha scarcely stops talking about him.'

Hazel's voice was close and Rosie felt a hand steal into her own.

'Oh, I don't, do I? I am sorry.'

'I'm jus' kiddin'.' Hazel was chewing thoughtfully on a stem of grass. 'Well, has tha plans?'

It was easier not to answer the question. Too early to share the thoughts that had begun to steal into her mind.

'You know how things have gone so far,' Rosie said, wondering how much she should reveal.

'Aye. But I want to know more. The details!"

'Well … there is one thing I never told you …' This would be embarrassing but Rosie wanted to deflect Hazel from her probing.

'Oh?' Hazel's expression was suddenly serious.

'Oh, it's nothing serious – in fact, you must promise you won't laugh.'

'I promise,' said Hazel, raising two fingers in a mock salute.

'Well, on that first day, I crashed my bike in a hedge and he had to fish me out.'

Hazel howled with laughter, almost swallowed the stem of grass and began to cough.

'You said you wouldn't laugh,' Rosie complained wryly.

Hazel rolled onto her side. 'Aye, I'm sorry. It's the beer, happen as like. Tha didn't tell us that before!' She spat loudly, the phlegm landing on a thistle where is hung glistening in the sun. She rolled back, grinning.

'He was very nice about it,' Rosie said cautiously. 'The crash. I cut my knee, and he …' She paused, remembering the unexpected gentleness with which he'd dressed the tiny wound. 'He provided first aid.'

Hazel laughed. 'I've never heard it called that before!'

'No, he did really. He was very kind. I expect they get trained to do that.'

'Trained? You're a funny one!'

There was a pause.

'Aye? Is that all?' Hazel nudged her friend. 'Didn't he, you know, try anything that first day – as part of his first aid?'

Rosie prevaricated. 'Not really.' She thought of their first kiss and a fizzle of excitement passed through her stomach.

'Not really? What does that mean?

'Well, he kissed me.'

'Fast mover.'

There was a pause.

'And is he any good, like?' Hazel asked slowly. 'As a kisser?'

105

'I wouldn't know, I've not got much to compare it with.'

Hazel chewed on the stem of grass and looked away.

'Most of 'em can't kiss for toffee,' she said, 'Girls … we girls, we're the best kissers. A girl wants a kiss to last, but a feller is too hard, too short.'

For a while they lay there in silence. Rosie's mind was far away, thinking of Eugene. Their first kiss hadn't been short but had lingered. It had been delicious. Absently she'd began to make a daisy chain. The kiss had been a more sensual thing than she'd dared to hope for. And there had been more of them since.

'Be careful with the Yanks,' Hazel said suddenly.

Rosie turned to her. 'Don't you start – my mother's on about that all the time.'

Hazel frowned. 'Well, for once the silly old cow … oh, I'm sorry …'

'No,' replied Rosie resignedly, 'She is. A silly cow. Go on.'

'Well, she might be right. They're only over here for so long and, if they get you in trouble, they can just bugger off. And you're … I mean, you've no experience.'

Rosie considered. 'Well, perhaps I need some.'

Hazel looked as though she was going to say something but didn't.

Rosie continued. 'And we're at war. No one knows what's going to happen. We could all be dead tomorrow.'

She got up and walked to the wire.

She looked back at Hazel. 'Eugene's so – different. He's kind and honest and I feel safe with him.'

Hazel propped herself on one elbow and shaded her eyes, peering at her friend.

'Tha doesn't know much about his past though, does tha?'

'His past?'

'Aye, his family and what he was doing before he got over here.'

Rosie shook her head. She felt suddenly irritated at her friend for picking holes in her dream. She remembered how handsome he looked in the uniform, and how far older women turned to stare when they were out, whether queuing for the cinema or drinking tea in one the town's tearooms. Most of the time, part of her was elated, while another was oddly restless, as though something inside her doubted the dream was real.

'When we walk,' she continued, 'I can hardly believe it – that he is with me.'

'Tha's not so bad tha'self. Why should he not be with thee?'

'I mean, he's so tall and so …'

'American?'

They laughed.

'Yes, so glamorously, wonderfully American.' She was suddenly serious. 'But he's kind. I mean he lets me rabbit on for ages and is interested. He makes me feel I am somebody.'

'Tha needs no man to be somebody. Tha's fine by tha'self.'

'Perhaps I do.' Rosie paused. 'Perhaps I do need someone. I need to find something, some meaning in all of it. I can't bear emptiness, or loneliness. I don't want that ever again.'

Hazel nodded. She got up and came to stand beside her.

'Now't wrong with wanting to love and be loved. Perhaps the only meanin' there is.'

Rosie nodded and looked out over the field.

'In life?'

'Aye.'

About an hour or so later a group of men began to gather near the tower. Officers appeared on the balcony, one drawing rapidly on a pipe, another scanning the sky with binoculars. Some trucks pulled onto the grass and, ominously, were joined by three ambulances and two red fire trucks. The ground crews gave up their desultory game of baseball and began strolling restlessly around, stopping to chat in small groups.

'I reckon this is what them Yanks call "sweating the mission",' said Hazel, observing through a pair of old ivory opera glasses she had 'liberated' from somewhere.

Rosie, who had begun to feel a gripping pain in her stomach, absently tried to extract a final swig from the flagon which had run dry an hour earlier.

The planes would be back soon. Those that did come back. She closed her eyes and not for the first time whispered the words of a prayer, or a spell.

The sound drifted through the air so faintly they couldn't be sure that they'd heard it at all. Then it was a definite faint humming from the east, like the buzzing of a great insect. It grew slowly louder, eventually discernible as the droning of propellers. They strained their eyes and caught sight of a single four-engined bomber approaching. From the hangars a yellow flare arced into the sky, followed rapidly by a red. They exchanged glances and Rose moved to the fence, gripping the mesh anxiously with both hands. Several hundred yards away the black rubber tyres touched down, with a puff of smoke and a faint screech. The plane's speed bled away until it reached taxying speed. It turned off the runway and came to a lurching halt in a dispersal point some distance away.

'Try these.' Hazel held out the glasses.

Rosie snatched them gratefully.

'*Bouncing B–E– Betty*,' she said at last, heaving a sigh. 'Not his.'

The ambulance, emblazoned with a red cross on a white circle, had been tearing its way over the grass, a cloud of dust thrown up in its wake. A door opened in the plane and blanketed shapes were transferred to a stretcher. Fully laden, the ambulance departed rapidly.

'*Here they come!*'

Rosie's voice was strained as she peered through the grazed old lenses. Hazel shielded her eyes and peered at the sky, where three dots were approaching. Gradually materialising into aircraft, they peeled off gracefully to circle the field. More flares popped and in minutes the planes were down, taxying along the runway, the last one trailing oily smoke.

'*Dynamite Duck,*' Rosie intoned without removing the glasses. '*Come and Get It…* and *Country Gal.* Don't they have such funny names?'

For the next ten minutes there was a lull.

Then without warning, the two fire trucks started up and began to move rapidly over the grass. Yet another flare shot skyward and a wounded B17 appeared through the cloudbase near the end of the runway. It was coming in faster than the others, thought Rosie, who was standing on tiptoe. She couldn't see the name. Suddenly a wing dipped and touched the grass, sending up a spurt of rich brown earth. For a second the plane slid but, in a moment that seemed unreal, the tip dug into the soft ground, pitched up, flipping end over end, cartwheeling in flames before smashing onto its back and exploding in a grotesque orange-and-black fireball.

The girls gasped, unable to believe what their eyes were telling them. Rosie dropped the glasses and stood open-mouthed as a wave of heat, scented with aviation spirit, rolled toward them.

Rosie stared at Hazel in fear.

'I couldn't see,' she said at last. 'I couldn't see whose it was.'

Her face had drained of colour, frozen in disbelief. She felt her hands tremble and had a sudden impulse to try to get to the fire.

Hazel bent and picked up the glasses.

The aircraft was engulfed in flames, a cracking amplified by the detonation of ammunition. The fire crews had arrived, subduing the flames with foam. But no one emerged from within the furnace, the searing heat forcing the rescuers back.

The air was suddenly full of returning planes, the air vibrating with the hum of the great radial engines.

'Hey, up! Four more comin' in!' Hazel announced.

They strained to see the returning aircraft.

This time there were no flares and one by one the planes circled before landing normally, Hazel calling out the names as they passed down the runway. '*Bucking Bronco, Take This!* and ... *Luck of the Devil!* It's there!'

Rosie grabbed the glasses. '*Luck of the Devil?* Really?'

It was true. The plane seemed undamaged and taxied normally before coming to a halt.

'Hazel! Oh, thank God! Not a scratch!'

Rosie embraced her friend, the spasm of joy quickly fading to be replaced by a wave of guilt. She pulled away and looked at the edge of the field. There the wreck of the other plane still smouldered. The fire was all but out and grim shapes wrapped in tarpaulins were being loaded onto a waiting ambulance. Who or what decided whether one should make it and the other not? It seemed so random. An empathy began to grow within her, not just for Eugene but for all the Americans who'd come such a long way from home. Her mother's prejudice, still ringing in her memory, seemed suddenly disgusting.

CHAPTER 13

Eugene sat rigidly in his seat. Now he knew what Hell was like. He gazed out of the cockpit at the airfield with all its reminders of reality: the mechanics by the hangars engrossed in their tasks, the solid, welcoming buildings, and the grey lanes of hard concrete runways. Yet it did not seem real. The ground crews were arriving at the other ships in front of his by the jeep-load, but he could barely hear their shouts or the squealing of their brakes. Somewhere in the distance, clinging to the perimeter fence, he vaguely noted a couple of the usual waiting British women.

Yet no one approached *Luck of the Devil*. And they seemed to be enveloped in an odd silence too. Eugene slumped back in the pilot's seat, and wondered whether they had somehow died, back there over Germany, in the chaos that claimed two planes from their own flight of twenty. Perhaps this is what happened when you bought it, you came back home as a ghost plane, that no one else could see. What would be next? Would Death himself come out over the grass to lead them away? It would no longer have surprised him.

Eugene drew a breath and looked sideways at his reassuringly solid, and apparently very much alive crewmate. Hank must have been sitting silently too, but now he seemed to come to, busying himself with the shut-down checklist. Not for the first time Eugene was glad of the steadiness of the older man.

'Thanks, buddy,' he said with feeling.

Hank looked up and they exchanged glances. Eugene knew his friend wouldn't tell what had transpired and was glad he'd had the presence of mind to switch off his intercom. It was embarrassing to have lost control like that, to have shouted in rage, in frustration, and fear. But the fortress crashing in front of them on their final approach had been just too much to take. It could so easily have been them, and having bottled the feeling he'd had to let it out.

'No problem, Gene.' Hank regarded his captain soberly, making his own private assessment. 'Get some rest. And see you later for a beer?'

Eugene nodded numbly. 'Yeah, maybe later.'

He felt ashamed and instinctively deepened his voice, trying to carry more authority. But they both knew that real command had passed from one man to the other long before.

Eugene glanced back along the fuselage. If the others had been affected too, they weren't showing it, so perhaps it was just him. His own personal weakness. What did the British call it ... LMF? Yeah. Lack of Moral Fibre. Perhaps that was it. Perhaps he had no fibre left. Hank left the cockpit but, not wanting to talk with anyone else, Eugene stayed. He looked down and found he was gripping the wheel. Unwanted memories had already started to flash back into his conscious mind.

There had been no trouble until they were well past the enemy coast, which was something, and even then the few enemy fighters that rose to meet them had been quickly swatted away by their own escort of 'little friends', the glittering aluminium Mustangs. How the bomber crews loved those fighter boys! He'd just kept flying, doing his job, checking the instruments, keeping the crew focused over the intercom, trying not to think too far ahead. He'd begun to believe it might be an easy trip, when, over the smoke-covered target, the fortress next to them was hit. It was *Aims to Please*, a rookie crew on their third trip out. He'd been chatting with her raw young captain just before take-off and the guy had proudly shown him a picture of his girl.

An exploding flack shell, probably an 88, had caught the neighbouring plane square, severing the chin turret and, in a ghastly twist of fate, ejecting the bombardier out into the slipstream. It was sickening to see the airman, without a chute, tumbling head over heels, his arms flapping like a cartoon character trying to fly.

Eugene glanced back at the stricken bomber. A bright fire was blazing in its cockpit, rapidly filling the inside with smoke that flowed further down, exiting through the waist-gunners' positions in the sides. With an odd, almost poetical grace, the doomed bomber fell away, like a tired bird gently moving down and back, out of formation. Just before she flipped over, he caught sight of a gloved hand, inside the Plexiglass of the doomed ship, raised in a pathetic gesture.

Aims to Please plummeted through the formation of B17s like a sheet of burning newsprint, shedding large, ashy flakes as it corkscrewed down, but miraculously it didn't collide with any other planes stacked in echelons below. With an odd detachment, Eugene thought of the empty places in the mess hall that evening, and of the standard letters that would be written home by the C.O. Suddenly a blossom of white caught his eye. Two chutes had opened clear of the wreck, their canopies brilliant white against the darkness of the ground. Whoops and shouts erupted over the radio, but they stopped abruptly as first tumbling figure began to spin, winding the trailing white sheet up on itself, and the other canopy caught fire, its passenger spinning down like a hideous human flare. He looked away.

The memory ended, and Eugene exhaled. Somehow, after all that madness, they'd gotten home. With unsteady hands he began unclipping the radio wire and oxygen line, mechanically checking the bottle was off. These things he could do by some inbuilt autopilot and he was glad at least for that small mercy. But the status conferred by his uniform was becoming an embarrassment, the gold bars and wings writing a check that was far too big for him to cash, and for the first time he admitted openly what he'd known for weeks – he was afraid.

Eugene left the cockpit, glancing momentarily along the fuselage. Here and there were a few more holes in the aluminium skin, and about halfway down in the light flooding through the open gun ports, he glimpsed Tony and Billy embracing in the waist-gunners' position.

He called, as cheerfully as he could. 'Well done, guys! I think you got that one-oh-nine, Tony!'

Tony looked up and gave a thumbs-up.

'I'll be claiming it! Thanks for bringing us home, boss!'

Eugene smiled thinly and headed hastily for the hatch. His own margin of sanity, even the small quantity necessary to maintain the banter, was wearing thin. God alone knew how long it would be before it wore through completely, exposing him for the fraud he was.

He dropped from the belly hatch, exiting the aircraft and landing rather ungracefully on the ground. He kicked the dirt with his boot, as if to test its solidity and suddenly caught sight of Rick kneeling by the left wheel. The kid was throwing up. He patted him on the shoulder. Selfishly, part of him felt a kind of joy he was not alone in

114

his fear. If you wanted to see someone really on the edge, there was always the small Missourian.

'It's OK, Rick,' he said, as authoritatively as he could manage. 'I guess we all feel shook up.' It was as close to an admission to the truth as he dared make. The youngster nodded gratefully.

Eugene turned and headed for the main building. He walked as steadily as he could after the mission, kicking the grass to dispel the lingering adrenaline that made his limbs unpleasantly light and shaky. Each of the bombers that fell seemed to shorten the odds, bringing their own demise closer. And today the entire squadron's price for the raid had been a total of six. Six of the giant four-engined bombers, each with a ten-man crew. He could hardly believe he'd been naïve enough to brag of doing more than the required one tour. Now he only wanted to go home.

He wished in vain they'd get some superficial damage, even injuries, just so long as they were enough to placate the gods who played with their lives. Then perhaps they'd have a reason to quit, an excuse that would pass for honour. Would a broken wing do it, or would they have to crash and come out on stretchers? Perhaps it would be worth losing a leg, or even an eye. Perhaps he should sabotage the ship himself? It didn't matter, so long as he and his boys stayed alive. He knew now how much he wanted to live, how precious every hour of it was, and he longed to never have to go back 'upstairs' into the sky, and 'over there'.

Eugene was nearing the building, longing for the sagging sanctuary of his bunk and the coarse grey wool blankets thick enough to shut out the world. He craved darkness, and even more than that, oblivion, a complete release from the whole crazy universe. He paused, and sighed. Sleep wouldn't come unassisted anymore. Furtively he glanced around before swiftly changing course and heading for the M.O.'s office. Ten minutes later he had the yellow chit in his hand, and was bound somewhere that had become a regular if shameful port of call.

He entered the building and walked briskly down the linoleumed corridor to the far red door, his rubber-soled flying boots squeaking intermittently on the shiny surface.

The portal opened and the freckled, elfin face of Ginger the nurse broke at once into a smile of recognition.

'Well, hullo, honey!' Her voice was husky and slow, her smile sly and with just a hint of smugness. Her expression was welcoming, but as a spider might welcome a fly.

He had no words, and instead stared blankly back. The nurse ushered him quickly in and closed the door behind them, pushing into place the sliding panel that would read **'Closed. Do Not Enter'** on the outside. She cupped his face gently before taking from him the doctor's chit, which she tore up and threw into a wastepaper basket.

Lingeringly she looked him up and down. Squeezing his bicep, she giggled softly, as though in anticipation. Eugene sat resignedly on the sickbay couch, mechanically rolling up his sleeve. The redhead smiled again, and he looked away. His eyes came to rest on the hypodermic she was holding in her pale, familiar hand. He knew the syringe didn't contain the sedative the doctor had prescribed. And he was sure that eventually Ginger would want paying, after a fashion, for the morphine she'd replaced it with. But his nerves were screeching like fingernails scraping a blackboard and he felt suddenly sick. He nodded and braced himself. He needed what she had.

She was good with a needle, and he didn't even feel it touch his arm. The effect was instantaneous, and magical. He found himself lying on his back, a sense of peace washing over him like warm and lazy wave, while from somewhere nearby came the warbling music of birdsong. The old cracked plaster ceiling was rippling like water, falling upwards, transforming into a beautiful blue summer sky.

He was floating, or perhaps flying, and the world he'd known had grown distant, the girl far away like a distant ship's sail on the horizon. Around him stood the sun-kissed tops of towering cumulus, majestic and upright, like pillars in the House of God. A bumble-bee throb of engines swelled in the background and the airman watched detached, as birds, or angels, chased each other pell-mell across the bright, shimmering heavens.

CHAPTER 14

She'd waited a grey, empty week before he was off duty again, throwing herself into work at the factory, taking extra shifts to keep occupied and prevent her mind dwelling on the missions that kept them apart. But every so often a group of planes from the field would fly over, the thunderous vibration of their low passing audible even over the hum of the conveyors. Some girls – those on breaks, or not working on the line – would run outside to see the graceful green birds going over, shouting if they made out the names painted onto the aircrafts' noses. But to Rosie it seemed like bad luck to look, and she kept herself glued to the work station, methodically carrying out the task and trying hard to think of nothing else. The technique worked up to a point, but when her attention wandered she'd find herself cursing the war, and the stop-start romances it forced on them all.

When the call finally came through to Morelli's switchboard she was on lunch break and mercifully able to respond to the message over the Tannoy before the call was cut off. Breathlessly she took the receiver from the grinning receptionist. Eugene's voice on the rather crackly line was rapid and clipped. He sounded oddly excited, but the words had a brittle edge that suggested tension, or some other change in him.

Embarrassed to talk in front of the receptionist, she arranged to meet. Clocking out and snatching her coat and hat from the locker, she caught the first bus into town.

She spotted the tall, elegantly uniformed American easily among the restless, migratory crowd of rough British soldiers and dowdy grey civilians at the Depot. He was shifting uneasily from foot to foot and smoking a cigarette in an absent sort of way that suggested a time-passing habit rather than real enjoyment.

But, as she approached, his smile seemed as warm as ever and she felt herself relax slightly. She was relieved to see no outward signs of wounds or injury, yet as they left the station he talked in the same rapid-fire way he had on the telephone, like a record played too fast.

Rosie looked around and was gratified to see that she and her glamorous companion were attracting some attention. She linked arms with him and found herself laughing when he paused to look at her and addressed her with one of his movie-like Americanisms.

'Say, what's up, Toots?'

She grinned. 'It's nothing – you look smart today,' was all she could manage. It had only been a few weeks and a few trips out together, but somehow it felt much longer.

They infiltrated the velvety gloom of the *Roxy* quietly and no one looked up as they entered. They'd come in near the end of the B picture. It was one they'd both seen before; an improbable story of a Frenchman captured by Nazis, only to escape, kill his captors, and rescue his true love in the final reel. But it didn't matter. Like many people, they came not just to be hear a tall tale, but to sit in the warm and dark, and be transported away from the unpleasant reality of the war outside. As their eyes grew accustomed to the gloom, Rosie could see the plush red stalls were less than half full: a few soldiers, a sprinkling of middle-aged women and some school-dodging kids making up the audience.

The couple bowed low, squeezing along the narrow channel between the worn velvet seats, trying to keep below the silvery beams of the projector cutting crisply through the blue fug of cigarette smoke. The film was ending as they settled down in a deserted patch of seats. After a few moments she reached out to touch his hand and was surprised when he visibly jumped. He recovered quickly and she felt his much larger hand squeeze hers reassuringly.

'Are you OK?' she whispered.

Eugene smiled with what seemed nonchalance, flicked his hair back and grinned an affirmative. Rosie wondered. Perhaps he'd seen something on his last trip. Perhaps it had been close. She was learning to read his expressions and moods and was becoming aware that there was perhaps more to him and his world than met the eye, or ear. He was watching the movie and, as she looked at his the profile, suddenly lit for a moment by a bright flicker from the screen she noticed the beginnings of what her father would have called 'worry lines'. His eyelid seemed to have developed a tremor too. Something about his general demeanour and posture was different, as though body was there but soul absent. Rosie felt a sudden wave of disgust at the war and what is subjected young men to, and wove her arm around his, snuggling closer, wishing she could do something to help him.

Suddenly the theatre erupted in a fanfare of trumpets, the beams of overhead light flickering as the *Pathé* newsreel began. They'd already seen it several times before: four thousand tons of bombs dropped on Germany in a day, fierce fighting in Burma around somewhere called Kohima, and a new system of taxation known as Pay As You Earn. Bored, she looked at Eugene, his face profiled against the glowing silvery light. It was hard to square the presence of such a handsome man next to her with the all-too-recent ignominy of the orphanage. The reversal of fortune had been so abrupt, she often found herself doubting its reality. As she looked he turned towards her and for a moment she thought they would kiss.

The newsreel ended and, after a stutter of disjointed frames, the opening music of the main feature began. It was the second time she'd seen *Tunisia*, a picture famous for its style, snappy dialogue, cool hero and beautiful heroine. She was relieved when Eugene finally put his arm around her and she snuggling gratefully into his embrace, resting against his broad shoulder, the fine material of his uniform on her cheek. Half of her consciousness was on the screen, but part of her analysed the still-novel experience of being with a man, every feeling, sound and smell. She breathed in and caught a whiff of his cologne.

The familiar opening scene of Moorish minarets and rooftops, stark and tropical against a foreign sky was showing, the camera panning slowly. The view cut to a narrow, twisting side street crammed with noisy and exotically costumed foreigners over the sound of some Middle Eastern street music, before resolving abruptly to a police station where an officer in Italian uniform began to speak urgently into a wall-telephone: '*Attenzione! Attenzione! All polizia! Two spies carrying stolen documents escaped jail and are believed to be heading for the border! Armed and dangerous! Arrest all usual suspects at once!*'

Rosie felt the story with its exotic language and glamorous location softly seducing her, drawing her into the make-believe world. It was several minutes before she became fully aware of the movement one row ahead and just across the aisle, whose nagging persistence eventually pulled her back. Peering through the dim, flickering haze, she could see a couple she'd first glimpsed as they came in. He was a young American soldier, and she a young girl, probably a kid pretending to be older, Rosie thought, and skipping class from school. But they were clinched in a most adult way, lips clamped together in a penetrating kiss that seemed to go on forever. It was so brazen that Rosie found her first reaction one of stiff, English disapproval. And, then, her heart somehow went out to them, snatching as they were a moment of happiness in a world that was so grim. It occurred to her that her mother would have been scandalised by the scene, and at once she decided she was on the side of the lovers. Stifling a laugh, she nudged Eugene.

'*Look!*'

'*I know, I know!*' he whispered back, clearly amused, '*They'll have to come up for air soon.*'

The dialogue in the film paused and exactly at that moment there came an audible moan from the two lovers, provoking variously sniggers, murmurs of disapproval and harrumphs from the audience.

Behind the amorous duo, a stout older woman could be seen fidgeting in her seat. Jerkily, as though unable to bear the distraction any longer, she finally leant forward. The transatlantic soldier broke surface and an exchange of inaudible but clearly unfriendly words took place. Rosie could tell that the audience was gradually transferring attention to the off-screen action, and had to crane her neck to see around the suddenly raised heads. She found she positively admired the couple's cheek, and couldn't help but dwell on the sheer intensity of their rapture. Many things, she thought, things that had been previously forbidden, were coming out into the open under cover of the war, and it seemed a good thing, as though the Young were replacing the Old, with new hopes and new, fresh ideas, and freedoms.

But the large woman was clearly of the rule-bound past, and was not to be trifled with. Like a whale emerging from the sea, she rose abruptly, raised a hitherto unseen umbrella and struck the young soldier smartly on the head, triggering an immediate eruption of laughs, catcalls and raucous objections from the audience. From somewhere behind them there was even a faint smattering of applause.

Rosie turned and glanced back towards the bespectacled projectionist, peering anxiously through his window in the rear wall and polishing his glasses. She wondered if he would call the police, but he remained fixed in apparent indecision. Either that or he found the new entertainment better than a film he must have seen so many times before.

Meanwhile, up front, the young man had turned and was energetically fending off the assault.

'Holy Cow, lady!' he was saying, loudly, in a twanging Yankee drawl. 'Cool it, why dontcha?'

Some of the audience clearly preferred the new entertainment and were egging the combatants on, a few of them standing to get a better view. Others were complaining, loudly, the combined noise drowning out the onscreen dialogue.

'My money's on her,' said Eugene, who seemed to be regaining some of his normal humour. Rosie nodded, laughing.

A torch-beam sliced suddenly through the gloom. It was the usherette, a formidable woman, striding down the red carpet, the suspended floor alternately bowing and releasing under her considerable weight.

'*You are under arrest!*' boomed the onscreen dialogue, as a suspicious-looking character was arrested by a *poliziotto,* to an outburst of laughter from the audience. In the theatre the soldier, who had been summarily yanked from his seat, was being propelled up the aisle, with his loudly complaining girlfriend in tow. Meanwhile on screen the arrested man and the hero were exchanging words.

'*Johnny! Stop them! Stop them! I don't want to go!*'

'I wouldn't raise a finger if I were you!'

The audience laughed again, uproariously, while back in the movie a volley of shots rang out, and the audience's attention was pulled back to the screen.

The hero was speaking: *'I have no intention of being on the receiving end of that pistol, capitano.'*

'Very well,' said the onscreen policeman. *'Ladies and gentlemen, the entertainment is over. There's nothing more to see. Please enjoy your evening.'*

As if by magic, soothing piano music and a bubbling background of onscreen voices filled the air and, as quickly as they had been distracted, the audience went back to the film.

Rosie and Eugene emerged much later from the black-and-white dream-world, having seen the programme through twice, blinking like rabbits emerging from a burrow into the sunshine. It was a familiar sensation, yet one Rosie hated, like being dragged unwillingly from the womb, eyes and ears assaulted by the bright, explosive brashness of the universe. Part of her wanted to turn around and go back inside. On the worn pavements, pedestrians went about their business, unaware of the beauty within, and part of her resented their ignorance as well as their boring everydayness. She longed to stay forever in the onscreen universe, be always deceived by its lies and escape permanently from the humdrum, the irritating, and the dangerous.

The two of them strolled, the feeling of otherness, of being apart from everyone, ebbing only slowly. He seemed to be coming down too, not just from the film, but from some inner tension. His glance was more focused on her, his manner more personal. She led them to the Lower Park, and was aware of his eyes, watching her from behind as she walked. She turned and caught him, finding herself pleased when, hurriedly, he looked away. Despite his film-star-like status, there was something oddly boyish about him, and she caught it occasionally

124

in a guilty smile or fleeting moment of doubt. She felt her understanding of him, and perhaps of herself growing.

In the park, there was an ornamental garden laid out a generation or more before the war. Some of the beds had recently been replanted with rows of cheerful but untidy *Dig For Victory* vegetables, but most of the ancient Japanese design, including the hump-backed iron bridge over the stream, remained. It felt good to be walking in a familiar place, but with someone, to no longer be alone against the world. A brief thrill of triumph ran through her. This part of her plan, so long dreamed of while in captivity, had succeeded and she reckoned it not only as a victory for herself but as a defeat for her mother, the orphanage and everyone who'd written her off without a thought.

Suddenly she wondered what it would be like to be wanted by the American, as the two lovers in the cinema had wanted each other. So far their embraces had been restrained and the kisses far more circumspect. She'd managed to hold back the yearning she felt for affection. Going further, becoming more intimate would strengthen whatever it was they had and make it grow, perhaps even into love. Here and there in the park others wandered, a few couples, some children and a few older folks. They were not really alone and it could not go too far, not here in public.

They reached the bridge and stopped atop its steep oriental arc, gazing down into the slow-moving pellucid stream. Beneath them the swathes of weed waved like heads of long green hair. Mermaid's hair, her father had called it. At the edges of the water were lily pads, and beneath she could see slow-moving orange and yellow carp, lucky survivors in a war where most things that could be eaten usually were. Some of the gentle behemoths, heavy with scales and mouths the size of golf balls were over a foot long and, so it was said, were over thirty years old. Perhaps, she thought, they'd become wise in their old age, clever enough to avoid capture and see out this war as they'd seen out the last. Perhaps they watched the world above with detachment, or even scornful amusement at the antics of the tall but foolish beings they saw there.

'*Kiss me.*' She said it suddenly, afraid her courage might desert her.

For a second she thought her forwardness had disarmed the airman, for he unexpectedly hesitated.

'Here?' said Eugene, grinning but glancing around. He seemed to be wrestling with some inner thoughts.

But Rosie persisted, holding his gaze and nodding. She wanted to experience the intensity of emotion that she'd seen and a peck on the cheek wouldn't do. Slowly, he bent his head, kissing her gently on the lips. She didn't pull away as he raised his face to look at her. He seemed to be searching her eyes for something, some sign or prompting. She sensed his breathing had become more rapid, and there was a glint of something wild, even manic in his eyes.

He grabbed her so suddenly that for a moment the breath went out of her, his powerful arms encircling her tightly. His lips were on hers, not a gentle brush this time, but more urgent, even desperate, pushing and holding her to him. She felt his mouth opening and was startled when his tongue began to gently penetrate her mouth. A spasm, like a chill, ran through her tummy. The kiss had the same forbidden sensuality as the darkness of the cinema world, the same passion and force, but it was also engulfing, overwhelming. Part of her wanted to submit, to go with the sensation but another was suffocating, or drowning. He seemed out of control, suddenly not even perhaps the same man. She wasn't as ready as she'd thought and she'd mistaken his good manners for cool blood. But now it was all too clear he'd been caging a pent-up force, perhaps for her sake, knowing what would happen if it were unleashed.

She pushed against his chest. '*Eugene, no!*'

At last he pulled back, his face a mixture of sudden shame and still untamed energy.

She exhaled and gathered her wits. They were both breathless.

'It's too much,' she said, her heart thumping.

'*Excuse me!*'

A tall man in a dark pinstripe suit, a giggling child hanging from each hand, was trying to get by.

The pair parted guiltily, flattening themselves against the bridge rail, staring down. As he passed the man gave Eugene a knowing look, which he met an awkward smile.

Rosie looked at Eugene, who glanced back sheepishly.

'I'm sorry,' she said, managing a shy smile. 'It was so …'

He shook his head. 'No, it's me. I'm the one who should be sorry. I am. Truly sorry.'

He went quiet, seemingly lost for words, yet she sensed there was much he yearned to say but could not. She guessed that the surge of raw need in him was in some way related to the stress and horror of what he must have seen and experienced, a kind of outlet or antidote perhaps, but words had deserted her too. As much confused by her own reaction as by his sudden passion, she slipped her hand in his.

They walked off the bridge and down along the crunching gravel of the gently winding path. The gardens had been laid out before she'd been born, not long after the Great War, when oriental themes were in vogue. Here and there clay lanterns and statues stood poignantly amid cultivated fronds of tropical plants and the geometric leaves of dazzling red-and-green maples in landscape carefully designed for effect.

The path led away, under the gloomy canopy of a wood, towards a distant Japanese temple. They entered the dimness of the trees and

Rosie shivered, clinging tightly to Eugene's hand. She hated forests. In her childhood imagination they'd been full of wolves that slinked in sinister shadows, a deep and elemental fear she had not managed to shake. The pair strolled, feet shuffling through the leaf mould, the earthy scent sweetened by the enveloping tang of aromatic cedar and yew. The path was surrounded by dense foliage and above, lost in the shifting green madness of the canopy, came the agitated chirping of a wren. Here and there, shafts of sunlight penetrated, spilling puddles of dizzy, shimmering light onto the ground. She became aware of the silence between them. It seemed to grow, accusingly. Had she, by refusing his kiss so emphatically, repelled him? She did want him, she was sure of it now, and yet she was somehow afraid at the same time. It was maddeningly confusing.

Rosie walked closer, to make their bodies brush lightly against one another. But, although he glanced at her and smiled, still he said nothing and she thought he was drifting away from her. She searched hurriedly for something to say, something that would pull them back together.

'I had a letter from Frank, my brother,' he said suddenly. 'He's in the Pacific.'

'Is he alright?' she asked, relieved.

Eugene halted and shielded his eyes, looking for the wren.

'He was at the time the letter was written,' he said, his words suddenly sorrowful. 'But it's taken two months to get here. He was about to take part in an invasion.'

'Oh.' Invasions had already been tried several times in the war, and everyone knew how hungry they were for human lives.

'Frank's a great guy. I sure hope nothing happens to him. He's the better of the two of us.' He said it as though unburdening himself, like a confession.

The depth of emotion and sudden revelation of another part of his life made her pause. Really, she still knew so little about him.

They strolled through a small glade, in the centre an opening in the canopy let sunlight flood down onto the thick carpet of desiccated needles, in the middle of which was a stone figure. The heat was enough to raise a faint mist from the earth.

'Once,' he confessed, turning to her, 'I got into trouble – I was still at High School and I borrowed a car. I'd had a few drinks, got into a race and, to cut a long story short, I had a crash.'

She was listening, eyes wide open.

'Frank didn't want to be in the car, but he'd driven us out to this old forest road, then I took over. He told me not to drive fast, but this guy came up on us and I just put my foot down.' He shook his head. 'Complete jerk. I lost it on a bend and the car was totalled. Before the cops could get there, Frank swapped seats with me and took the rap.'

'Oh no!'

He nodded. 'Yeah. My dad thinks to this day it was Frank.' He paused. 'Frank was a big guy, but it didn't stop him from getting a beating.' His eyes seemed to have gone a darker shade of brown, almost black. 'He took that for me.' He smiled ruefully. 'And it didn't end there. Dad stopped him from going to college – kept him home to run the business. All these years, Frank's never said a word.'

'But …'

'I should have confessed.' He swallowed. 'But I didn't and so it was me that went to college.' He looked down at his uniform. 'And became an officer.'

'Oh.'

They'd reached the temple – a half-sized ornamental pagoda built from tropical woods, its oddly sloping roof tipped up at the ends, clad in neat oak shingles. They squatted on a seat of mossy stone.

'When the war came,' Eugene continued, 'Frank found he couldn't take working for the old man, so he up and quit and joined the Marines. As a private.'

'Ah …'

'So you see, if anything happens to him, I'm to blame.'

He clenched his hands together, then stuck them in his pockets. He looked up at the temple.

'I wonder why the roof curves up and out like that,' he mused suddenly.

'To let in the winter light.' She said it automatically. 'The sun is low in the winter in Japan, so they curve the roof to let it in.'

'How did you know that?' he turned, raising his eyebrows quizzically.

Rosie smiled. Offhandedly she said, 'Oh, it was a place my father loved, and he knew all the history. He was keen on it, history, and the Park.'

'Yeah?' His expression suggested a re-assessment of her.

'It's all wrong though,' she continued, gaining confidence as she looked at the temple. 'It has two storeys, two roofs, but it should have an odd number, either one or three.'

He laughed. 'Thanks for the history lesson, Teach!'

She shrugged and grinned. 'My father taught me so much. We often walked here.' She didn't add that for both of them it had often been an escape from her mother's acid-tongued moods and violent temper.

They stood and began walking again. She thought the sharing of past lives had brought them a little closer.

'Your brother,' she asked, her curiosity pricked. 'What does he do?'

'As a Marine? He's a medic.'

'Well,' she said, guessing wildly, 'don't they go at the back? I mean they don't carry guns, do they?'

'I think they aren't usually in the first wave,' he said, thinking about it.

'So he's a smart guy who's not at the front. More likely to make it than others.'

She knew it was a hopeless gesture but it was the best she could do for him. She squeezed his hand and looked into his eyes, as if by force of argument, or will, she could stop him worrying.

Later they parted at the town square, a pick-up point for the rumbling green Air Force coaches that ran back and forth to the airfield. Just before he boarded, Rosie reached into her pocket, pulled out a small book she'd found in the town's second-hand bookshop and pushed it into his large hands. He was surprised and, for a second, she worried if it had been a mawkish or childish gesture. But she had wanted to give him something, something of herself, to help him if she could.

He was sitting down and looking at the cover. And as the bus pulled away, just for a second she thought she saw him smile.

CHAPTER 15

The young women walked cautiously down the street in the darkness of blackout, guided only by the faint rays of starlight. Peering uncertainly down, they could barely see the white lines that had been painted optimistically on the kerbs, and gripped each other's hands as they turned at last into Hazel's road. The extra hours tacked on to the shift had made Rosie cold, tired and hungry but at last they made it to her friend's digs.

Hazel nudged the door open. Once inside and the door carefully closed behind them, she switched on the hallway's single bulb.

'No one home?' Rosie asked, peering into the gloom beyond the light.

'Nay. Them's all out, slappers that they are, putting it about in t' Town 'all.'

'Didn't you want to go?' Rosie asked, surprised. When it came to 'putting it about' Hazel was usually all too keen.

'I'm knackered, girl.'

Hazel didn't look tired, Rosie thought. In fact, she was moving with a jerkiness of motion that spoke of excitement, and she'd almost insisted they go back to her place.

Once in the kitchen they shed their coats and, too tired to hang them, threw them over the chair backs. Hazel pushed aside the clotheshorse on which was drying a tatty assortment of female underwear. She reached into a cupboard and pulled out two dark-green bottles. Unscrewing the hard rubber bungs, she poured the frothing beer into enamel mugs where the red-brown liquid gleamed invitingly in the dingy light.

'I am glad to be here,' Rosie confessed with feeling. 'I couldn't bear to go home and face my mother. She's getting worse.' She pushed away the memory of their last argument.

The bungalow that was Hazel's shared digs had become a welcome haven in the last few weeks. Only just pre-war, the kitchen always struck her as very modern, with smart painted cupboards, and the technical marvel of an electric cooker. As workers' digs went, it was positively palatial.

'Sure tha don't mind cooking?' Hazel asked, nodding at the battered old wicker basket her friend had carried from town. In it were some vegetables, potatoes, a familiar rectangular tin, a jar of Marmite, some flour and a bag of oats.

'Sorry it's just Woolton Pie. But there's the corned beef to go with it.'

'It sounds great to me, lass.' Hazel pulled off the flat cap she wore and sat down. Running a hand through her short hair, she leant back in her chair. She looked like a farmer's lad in her checked man's shirt.

Rosie went to the counter and began to peel the potatoes, dropping the peelings carefully into the earthenware pot to go to the street's 'pig club'. After years of being cooked for, either by her mother or the orphanage, it felt oddly empowering to be in charge of a meal.

'I like this place,' she said. 'You really landed on your feet here. And you get on alright with your ...' she searched for the right word.

'Housemates?' Hazel wiped the foam from her lip where it had formed a thin, white moustache. 'Ah, we manage.'

'Charlotte's quite pretty, isn't she? Then there's Doris, the round one with a squint, poor thing, and one other … the thin one …'

'Droopy,' said Hazel with a smile.

Rosie laughed. 'Droopy? No!'

'Aye. 'er real name is Doreen, but she has such a long face we calls 'er Droopy. She's not an easy one to please. Always complainin' if anyone talks about summat she don't approve of.'

'Such as?'

'Such as men, the war, drink, swearin', smokin', men, I'll say that again, and most especially sex.'

'She sounds charming. The long winter nights must have flown by.'

'Oh, aye!'

They laughed.

Putting some potatoes aside to be diced, Rosie put a pan on one of the spiral rings of the cooker to boil. She watched, fascinated, as she turned the knob and saw the thick coil of the element glow red-hot. It was a far cry from her mother's old coal range which took a good hour to get going.

She was peeling the other vegetables when Hazel suddenly said, 'Was that true what tha' said about the orphanage?'

Startled, Rosie glanced over her shoulder. 'What about it?'

'Tha mother really sent thee there?'

Rosie nodded. In front of anyone else she would have felt ashamed.

'And she said it was because she couldn't afford to keep thee?'

'Yes. But … '

'But what?'

Rosie hesitated. 'But I think differently now.'

'Aye?'

'Aye. I mean, yes. I think she was jealous. I was the apple of my father's eye and it was as though she took it ... took it like ... she'd been displaced by me.'

Hazel swivelled in her chair and regarded Rosie's back as she chopped the vegetables with short, aggressive cuts.

'He died, as you know,' Rosie went on. 'They'd been having an almighty argument, over me of course, and he had a heart attack. I got the blame and the orphanage was the revenge.'

Hazel's eyebrows rose. 'Bloody 'ell. I didn't know it were like that. No wonder tha's like dog and cat, the pair o' thee.'

For a few moments there was silence. Then Rosie heard her friend's chair scrape.

A pair of long hands appeared as Hazel slipped her strong arms around Rosie's waist and a second later her head touched her shoulder. It felt a bit odd, and Rosie shrugged her off.

'It's OK, Hazel, I'm alright.' Hazel was always so direct, so quick to show how she felt, and so tactile.

Rebuffed, Hazel sat back at the table, helping herself to some more beer.

'Something's up with thee. Tha's tight as a duck's arse on a December pond,' she observed.

Rosie couldn't help but laugh at the fruity choice of words. She tipped the vegetables into a pot, added enough water to cover them, added a dollop of Marmite and a big spoon of oatmeal and put it on to cook.

She turned to Hazel. 'I dreamt they were shot down and captured,' she confessed.

Hazel shook her head. 'Nay, lass. Eugene captured? By the Jerrys? Tha's not heard owt ter mek thee worry though?'

Rosie sighed as she drained the potatoes. 'No, it was just a silly dream. But do you know they actually give them an escape kit? He showed it me. It's got chocolate, foreign money, a phrase book, and photographs of himself – for fake documents.'

'He ain't, you know, Jewish, is he?' Hazel said thoughtfully. Everyone knew how the Germans would treat a Jew – if they found out somebody was one.

'No. He can't be. I know for sure.'

Hazel looked at her, startled. 'How does tha know?'

'Eats ham.'

They both laughed.

The conversation became easier and the laughter louder as the level of the beer in the bottles fell. Rosie gulped hers down as she mashed the potato and began to make the potato pastry topping, while Hazel put the veg in a baking tin. The aroma wasn't beef or chicken, but it made Rosie's stomach rumble and reminded her of how hungry she was. Soon the pie, covered with the potato pastry, was in the oven.

Hazel brought another pair of bottles from the cupboard and poured them into the mugs, where a bubbling head of foam formed, spilling down onto the table-top.

They sat down and drank.

'I hope the American treats thee right,' Hazel said. 'Anyone would be proud to be with thee.'

'Me?' Rosie laughed. 'I don't think so, but it's kind of you to say so!'

She felt a surge of affection for her friend, and, reaching out, patted her hand. It was good to have someone on your side, another woman. Hazel's forwardness meant she was never in doubt as to how much she was liked.

To her surprise Hazel took her hand in her own.

'I'd be proud,' she said, then coloured slightly and let go of her hand. 'I mean, if I were a man an' all.'

Rosie grinned. 'You'd make a good boy.' She laughed, looking at Hazel's short cropped hair and strong shoulders, adding hastily, 'Not that you're not feminine.'

To her surprise, Hazel beamed.

'I'd be quite happy being a boy,' she said, and coughed, her voice having taken on an odd, husky note.

'You are funny!'

Somewhere in the mid-distance came the unmistakable rumble of anti-aircraft fire. Hazel's mug of beer froze halfway to her mouth.

'There's been no warning,' Rosie said, concerned. There was no shelter in the bungalow.

Hazel stood quietly and switched off the light. They moved to the sink and, guessing her friend's intention, Rosie drew back the heavy blackout curtain. A couple of weeks earlier they'd watched a thunderstorm together from the bungalow's front room, Hazel seemingly oblivious to the danger, evidently thrilled by the peals of thunder and bright veins of lightning that had arced across the night sky.

Together they wiped two circles on the fogged glass of the steel-framed windows and peered out into the night's blackness. Over to the east, a faint glow and half a dozen flailing searchlight beams seemed to indicate the target of the raid.

'Them buggers are 'itting Coveringham again,' Hazel muttered, leaning forward to get a better view. She grabbed the handle and the window flew open, letting in a blast of frigid air.

Rosie shivered, and not just from the cold. Despite the lack of an air-raid warning, the sounds seemed to be getting closer. Perhaps it was not the city, but their own industrial estate that was the target. Hazel, glancing at her friend, grabbed her coat from the chair and, put it comfortingly around Rosie's shoulders.

Together they watched anxiously. From the ARP station at the end of the road, they heard the rising moan of the hand-cranked air-raid siren and exchanged glances. A sudden premonition came to Rosie – the image of a crater where the bungalow had been and a pair of crumpled bodies thrown high on the rubble. Her heart began to beat faster. The electric cooker suddenly went off with a loud click and somewhere outside the AA Batteries on the Common began to fire. After a few seconds, vivid orange flashes above the town indicated the detonation of their shells, the rumble of the explosions reaching them a couple of seconds later. She's spent so much time worrying about what might happen to Eugene, she'd forgotten about herself or Hazel. There were fewer raids these days.

Hazel seemed untroubled. In fact she was smiling, leaning forward, watching. Far from being afraid, she was clearly enjoying it. Suddenly there was a whistling sound.

'Hazel, I'm afraid.' The words came out almost as a whisper and Rosie realised her throat had gone dry.

Hazel's arm tightened around her waist, and Rosie anxiously gripped her friend in a return embrace.

'*One.*' Hazel's eyes were on the sky and she was leaning towards the window, ears cocked. Immediately there came a second whistle. '*Two.*'

Rosie's eyes widened.

A third. '*Three.*'

'Hazel!' Rosie looked around. There was no under-stairs cupboard in the hall, because there were no stairs. Her eyes fixed on the kitchen table. 'Hazel!'

'*Four!*'

At last Hazel grabbed her arm and they threw themselves headlong beneath the table's flimsy shelter.

A bright yellow glow suddenly lit the room as though a searchlight had been turned on the bungalow. They were lying, faces inches from each other. Rosie could feel Hazel's beery breath on her face. Then Hazel reached out and covered Rosie's ears. She was still smiling.

The explosion when it came shook the ground beneath them. Amid the deafening *whump!* was an abrupt lack of air, and for a second Rosie struggled to breathe. Low overhead, as though the aircraft was about to crash into them, came the sound of the departing raider's engines. There followed a few dull thuds from the direction of the roof, and in the garden outside, a brief rain of timbers, bricks and plaster began.

'*Oh, Hazel!*' Rosie opened her eyes and gazed at her friend.

Hazel still had her own eyes closed. A faint smile played about her lips. Incredulous at Hazel's coolness, Rosie found herself laughing. A hand gently caressed the top of her head.

'It's all over, lass,' said Hazel soothingly. ''appen the last bomb went over us. They say they allus drops in sticks of five.'

For a few moments they hugged each other, then got up.

While Hazel went to check on the damage in the street, Rosie closed the window and sat limply at the table. When Hazel returned to tell her a bomb had fallen either side of their street, she nodded mechanically, having already worked as out as much. She'd realised at the same time that if the bomb-aimer had pressed the release a second earlier or later, they would both be dead.

Hazel sat down, and outside the long single note of the all-clear sounded. Soon the ARP would be out, followed by the Fire Brigade or Heavy Rescue Squad if anyone was trapped. Part of her wanted to go and help, but word was out that the Germans had begun to mix their loads with delayed-action mines, and by now everyone in the town had received leaflets telling civilians to leave rescue to the professionals.

The power was still out and, when by candlelight Rosie discovered her Woolton Pie barely half-cooked, she was almost relived. She no longer felt like eating. Under protest she swallowed a slice of corned beef while she watched Hazel consume the rest of the tin with relish.

'Let's get out of the kitchen and into somewhere warmer,' her friend suggested, wiping the inside of the can clean with her finger and licking it with obvious enjoyment.

Rosie expected them to move to the front room and light a fire. There was no gas main in the street, so there seemed little risk, even after a raid. She didn't want Hazel to think she was shivering out of fear, and a cheering fire would surely help. But Hazel picked up the candle and took her firmly by the hand and led her into a small room. Like the rest of the house, it was unheated, but in the centre stood a large bed covered in a thick pink chenille-jacketed eiderdown. On one side stood a dressing table, on the other a bedside cabinet. There was a dark veneered wardrobe that reflected the flickering candle which Hazel had placed on the cabinet.

Hazel drew back the covers on the bed and promptly jumped in.

'Come on! 'Tis warmer under than out!'

Rosie grinned and gratefully climbed in after her. They lay close and she could soon feel the comforting heat of Hazel's body. For a while they talked, but for some reason Rosie felt suddenly very tired and, during a lull, she slipped into a snooze.

It must have been over an hour later that the front door crashed violently open, waking Rosie with a start. The bungalow resounded with the sound of loud female voices. Someone was commenting on the fact the house was still standing, another began demanding loudly how many would like tea and yet another queried the smell of cooking. There were a series of thuds: shoes kicked off, something heavy thrown down.

Hazel was sitting bolt upright, looking at the door in alarm. '*Shit an' shoe-polish!*' she muttered.

Rosie sat up. 'It's just your friends, isn't it?' She rubbed her eyes and yawned sleepily, then flopped back into the warmth of the bed and yawned.

'*Shit!*' Hazel shook Rosie roughly. 'Get thee up, an' be dead quiet, mind. Sneak out t'front door when I say.'

Rosie paused for a moment, trying to take it all in. 'But why? I've met your friends before ...'

'If owd Droopy sees thee in 'ere, in my room, she'll ...'

'She'll what?' Rosie was sitting up again, trying to feel awake.

Hazel bit her lip. 'She'll say we're a pair of lesbians, which is another thing she hates by t'way. She can mek a lot of trouble if she wants. Now get thee goin'!'

'But my coat's in the kitchen!' said Rosie.

'*Buggeration!* Tha'll have ter take me old brown one. 'Tis in t'hall.'

Rosie struggled to pull on her shoes.

A moment later Hazel peeked round the door, then motioned to Rosie to hurry. At the last minute, she reached forward and pecked her on the cheek. 'Go! Get thee gone!'

Rosie emerged from the bedroom, still in the fug of sleep. The house was in something approaching darkness save from a glimmer of candlelight from the kitchen, but she could just make out Hazel's old coat on one of the hooks. The other girls must either be in the kitchen or perhaps the bathroom.

'*Out! Go on!*' Hazel hissed urgently from her hiding place.

Bemused, Rosie opened the door and stepped out into the blackness, wondering to herself what on earth a lesbian was.

CHAPTER 16

Rosie reclined in the canvas chair Eugene had snapped open by the river. She watched as he scrummaged in the car, at last fetching the hamper, kettle and primus and setting them out near the small metal table he'd brought for the picnic. The sense of relief when he'd unexpectedly knocked at her door had surprised her with its intensity, a sensation only reinforced by her mother's detracting comments. It was more than a week since she'd last seen him and she'd been on edge until he finally appeared, trying every day not to think the unthinkable.

Now she could watch him at her ease as he moved around, resplendent in a pair of beige Air Force trousers and a plain white shirt. The edgy, frenetic energy he'd shown before had gone, but she sensed she was seeing a slowing down born of exhaustion rather than relaxation. The bags under his eyes had grown darker and the wisp of grey that had appeared at his temple was expanding. And although they were alone and together, he seemed somehow disconnected from her and even their surroundings. In vain she'd tried to talk to him about his flying, but he gave only general answers. It was clear he wouldn't, or couldn't, talk about it, which frustratingly left her guessing.

Rosie glanced around their spot. In front of them the smooth, glassy river chuckled on over well-rounded pebbles, while in the green depths clumps of weed waved in the current like the skirts of hula-hula dancers. A moorhen darted among the rushes at the water's edge, while a slender breeze played in the treetops, rippling the leaves and invoking a rash of goosebumps on Rosie's freckled arms.

'Music?'

Eugene's enquiring voice seemed ridden with unnecessary emphasis, jerky and falsely cheerful. He came rather comically over the grass, lugging a weighty gramophone with a huge brass trumpet and setting it gently on the table. She'd laughed when she'd first spotted the bulbous contraption in the car, a joke he didn't seem to get, for he looked almost offended at her unexpected mirth. She'd had to hastily hide her smile and reassure him that, after all, it was a brilliant idea, as though having music at a picnic was perfectly normal in England.

She looked around. It was one of those false summer days that occur so often in May, warm in the sun, but cool in the shade – a day when thick white dollops of cloud chased each other across the intense blue sky and the novelty of sunlight, so scarce in the long grey winter, made you squint. The hedgerows were bushing out after their skinny winter months, and underneath blossoms drifted, covering the undergrowth of nettle and cuckoo pint with pink confetti.

Eugene pumped the primus, filled the kettle and set it to boil. He seemed happiest when occupied and went to and from the car what seemed to Rosie an unnecessary number of times.

'For you, honey.' He passed her a plate of sandwiches.

Eugene had only recently taken to calling her 'honey'. She smiled. To her English ears it sounded sophisticated and exotic, like something from an American movie.

Eugene pulled a record from the gramophone's tray, blew away a thin film of dust, and gently lowered the needle. Crackly notes wafted through the air, and at last the restless American halted, dropping back into a canvas chair, his eyes closing. The music was magical. It was impressive he'd chosen something classical, she thought, rather than a few songs from the hit parade. Assuming he had chosen it and the discs had not come randomly with the machine.

In the background, an orchestra played a supporting role, but the lone voice of the soprano soared above, rising and falling, grabbing Rosie's attention. The song, she thought, was full of drama, hauntingly tragic in its tone.

Rosie was stunned. Never in her life had she realised music could be this powerful.

'It's beautiful,' she breathed as the record finally ended and the disc rotated with a repeating click.

Eugene rose. 'It's one of my favourites,' he said expansively, though she thought his voice perhaps lacked the conviction of truth. 'I have a whole stack of them back home, at my place.'

'You have your own place?' It would be wonderful, she thought, to have your own flat – no one to tell you when to come in or go out, no nagging about chores, and space for a gramophone with your own choice of music to play.

'Sure have. It's just an apartment, but it is in town.'

'In London?'

'No, no.' He grinned. 'Manhattan. On the Upper East Side.' He saw her bemused expression. 'New York.'

'You have an apartment in New York?'

She was surprised he'd not mentioned something so significant before.

She lay back, mulling over the idea of an apartment in the most glamorous city in the world.

'What was that called?' she asked at last, referring to the music. 'I didn't know anything could be sad and beautiful at the same time. I thought they were opposites.'

He glanced, a touch surreptitiously, at the record.

'It's by … Puccini,' he said slowly, 'and the name of the song is … "*O Mio Bambino Caro*".'

'Oh. Tell me more. What's it about?'

He turned the cover. 'It's about a young woman called Loretta. She begs her father to help her marry her true love … She says that if he won't then she'll throw herself into the River Arno from the Ponte Vecchio bridge.'

'That's some love.' Rosie couldn't keep a wistful tone from her voice.

'Sure is.'

'If you were to leave, to go home,' she said, provocatively, 'I might throw myself into the river and drown.' She was half teasing, half dreaming, her mind still emerging from the beauty of the song.

'You'd have a job,' he said, peering at the water. 'It's only a couple of feet deep.'

'Some romantic you are!' She threw a piece of cucumber at him, in mock offence.

He dodged the damp missile and laughed, the first time that day.

When they'd finished eating, they sat sipping tea.

'I wonder how people write music like that,' mused Rosie. 'Do they have stuff like that rolling around in their heads all the time? I think I'd just explode if I had something like that bottled up in me.'

He seemed to be searching for something profound to say. 'Beats me,' he said eventually.

She ignored the prosaic reply. 'Perhaps,' she continued, caught up in her own idea, 'they have an idea, then when they sit with the paper

145

it comes pouring out, as if they were just the carrier, and it came from somewhere else.'

He glanced at her, raised his eyebrows but made no comment.

'It's magical,' she continued. 'There's something more than human about it. It makes the hairs stand up on the back of my neck.'

Eugene shook his head as if in incomprehension but, seeing the effect it had had on her, reached for another record.

'Want to hear some more?'

He rose and sorted through the pile of seventy-eights, winding the handle and placing one of the heavy, liquorice-black circles on the turntable.

She wondered idly what he would be doing if he were in the States. Would he be sitting by an American river playing music to some American girl? It was surprising he wasn't already married.

'Something different,' he said, peering at the table. '"*Chanson Bohemien*", by someone called C. Pop.'

'"*Chanson Bohemien*?" That was the name of Mrs. Barton's song. The one Rosie had heard as a child.

He nodded and sat down, as though it were familiar to him too. She'd noticed it before in him on their earlier trips. He liked to impress, to create the image of himself as knowledgeable, and in charge, like telling her how the projector worked at the cinema. And it was true, he was knowledgeable, in comparison with herself. Yet Rosie sensed an odd vulnerability in the behaviour, and a surprising need for acceptance, or approval.

The needle hit the record with a bump, crackled briefly and the tune began. It started with a faint drum, a beat that repeated over and over. Then an accordion joined in, the swirling notes of the music beginning simply but growing into a whirling wave of sound. In the background she could make out what might have been a tambourine

146

and perhaps a flute. It was simple music, peasant music, not grand and majestic like Puccini, but warm, intimate, suggestive of casual, joyful pleasure. There was a repeating theme embedded in it, perhaps a chorus, and closing her eyes she wondered, not for the first time, whether the tune might have once had words. But the simple joy of it, the sense of youth and romance it so clearly suggested needed no words, but swept her along, as though the tune itself had reached out and pulled her onto an imaginary dance floor. She'd wanted to dance to it as a child, but had always been restrained by some mysterious sensitivity that suggested she ought not to. But it must be a dance, the beat was so infectious, so catchy, and she felt the urge to move again, more powerfully. Her head began to sway side to side in time and her feet soon followed.

The music was building, its swirling notes swelling gently towards a climax. It was enchanting. How did any musician manage to impart such feeling, such emotion from an instrument?

'You like it?' Eugene asked suddenly, his tone suggesting surprise at the effect it was having on her.

But Rosie didn't reply. She was thinking of the photograph she'd seen of Mrs. B. when she was young, and the picture in the silver frame of the handsome officer in the foreign uniform with his medals and smart cap. She imagined the woman dressed as a gypsy, clad in a loose-fitting calico dress. She was in a dim room, lit by candlelight and the flicker of the flames from a fire. The yellowed plaster walls were lined with men, among them a handsome Frenchman, whose dark eyes followed her obsessively. The gypsy was swaying as she danced, around and around in the open space they'd cleared for her, twisting and turning slowly, but getting faster as the music grew in intensity. At last she was dancing close to the officer, and for him alone, her body writhing in a fluidity of motion. The crescendo continued to build, the drumbeat louder. And suddenly, with a blaring flourish, it was all over.

Rosie sat, eyes closed, her breathing suddenly rapid and shallow. Strange, half-seen thoughts and sensations flickered through her. It had been transformative, primitively connecting her with parts of herself that she still did not fully know or understand. It was the same old song, but now its effect was different, and enhanced.

'You gotta hand it to those Italians – they sure know how to pull the old heartstrings,' Eugene said baldly.

He rose and began to clear the plates.

Rosie stared at him. The comment seemed so crass, so throwaway. Was that all he could say? And how could he just get up and start clearing away like that? After that perfection? His thoughtless words came as an invasion of the mood she thought they were sharing. She felt a burst of anger.

'I think you'll find,' she said, rising abruptly, 'it was French. And C. Pop. is French for *"Chant Populaire"* – meaning something like "folksong".' The patchy but enforced French lessons at the orphanage had been half-hearted and had probably only taken place because one of the overseers' wives came from France, but at last they had found a use. 'It means there is no composer. It's traditional.'

Eugene recoiled but did not speak. He seemed, she thought with a rather shameful spark of pleasure, to be reappraising his assessment of her upwards.

For weeks, Rosie had been searching for similarities between the two of them, noting them down, adding them together. The things she and he liked and hated, knitting a million mundane things into a shared world for them both. But his reaction had broken the spell. The music had moved her more than him and for reasons she didn't understand this seemed significant. A gap opened in the unity she had been trying to create and she resented it, the contradiction threatening to bring down the edifice.

She rose abruptly and walked to the river. The spot they'd chosen was at the bend of the stream, a natural bay where the current had carelessly deposited unwanted pebbles, freshwater mussel shells and a small beach of soft, pale sand. Slipping off her shoes, she dropped them lackadaisically onto the bank and walked noisily into the cold water. The sand sank sensuously around her feet, the chill water climbing higher up her long freckled limbs. She hitched her dress into the waistband, revealing her slender, pale thighs. On the upstream side the current piled up, created thin, wobbling walls of water, while on the downstream side patches of calm formed like the eddies beneath the supports of a bridge, spanning an intimate world of very small things.

The stream shimmered and fractured the early summer light. Bending, she caught a glimpse of a group of winnowing fry, drawn up in semicircle, investigating the inexplicable intrusion of the white feet. Then, in the depths, a flash of silver amongst the bottle-green suggested the alarm of something larger.

There was a splash behind.

Rosie turned. Eugene was standing behind her in the water, his trousers rolled up. He looked concerned.

'You OK?' he asked. 'Did I say something wrong?'

'It's alright,' she murmured, suddenly repentant. She turned to him and they kissed, the warmth of it and of his taut hard body a contrast to the icy water lapping her chilled flesh. She felt herself responding, and wanting him to understand that her caution did not signal disinterest. She let him explore her lips and mouth with his tongue. Feeling him tremble, she sensed a barely contained desire within him and experienced an answering sensation in her tummy.

But there was something else, an audible vibration external to themselves, and it was growing stronger, tingly in her ears and detectable even in her chest. Surprised, she pulled away and looked around. Above them in the blue spring sky, she found the source of the sound.

'*Look!*' She waded out of the stream onto the bank, Eugene following.

They shielded their eyes against the glare of the open sky. From the western horizon, something dark like a gigantic swarm of bees was approaching. Waves of sound, a dark mechanical throbbing, were growing, and slowly the cloud materialised into lines of aircraft, stacked up and out in a vast, geometric formation several layers deep, all heading east, towards the continent. There were so many, hundreds, perhaps even a thousand, of the glittering metal birds. It was an astonishing display of mechanical beauty and apparently limitless Allied air power.

'There they go.' Eugene said it almost to himself without looking at her.

The roar grew in intensity, and the first craft sailed overhead, very low and thunderously loud.

Rosie raised her voice.

'*You knew this was coming?*' she shouted, having noted his expression.

'*Yeah, I knew!*' he yelled back. '*I knew it was today.*'

'*Is this the Invasion?*' she shouted, suddenly lightheaded, almost delirious. Was this history she was seeing, was the end of the horrible war coming?

He paused. '*Soon!*' He was nodding. '*Not today, but soon.*'

He gazed back up, and she saw he was no longer smiling.

The sound was booming, filling the air and reverberating in their chests as the great metal ships passed over, Plexiglass screens and turrets glinting menacingly in the sun. There were so many of them that, below the great air fleet, a chequerboard of light and dark was projected downward onto the fields. Only slowly did the formation thin, finally receding to the east like a gigantic cloud of insects.

They looked at each other, but the earlier mood had gone. The magic had been sucked out of the day, destroyed by a war they thought they'd outrun, at least for one afternoon. They went back to the picnic table, sat quietly and drank more tea.

Rosie got to her feet first, a cue Eugene seemed to accept gladly judging by the speed with which he followed. Perhaps he had some duty to attend to. Perhaps, instead of bringing them closer together as she'd hoped, the afternoon had somehow pushed them apart.

Wordlessly they packed the car and clambered aboard. The starter whirred, and the Packard's engine shook itself, growling obediently into life. Then with a whine of transmission they were moving, the vehicle lurching out into the lane and onto the road home in a cloud of grey exhaust.

Inside, the leather seats were warm from the sun, and the cabin smelled faintly of warm wood and metal. Hedges, trees and winding lanes rolled by. Rosie soon fell into a doze, a half-dream into which echoes of a more distant childhood day out mingled with the passing landscape and her still-malleable memories of the present day. Bumps in the road brought her abruptly into and out of consciousness, a restless half-sleep in which she dreamed that Eugene didn't love her, but instead ran off with Puccini, who was wearing a dress and threatening to throw himself in a pond while Hazel stood by shouting, '*I told you so!*'

CHAPTER 17

The glowing flecks of condensation clung to the outside of the glass like shimmering jewels and the subdued lights of the Air Force club made the amber liquid glint enticingly. The glass of beer was a thing of beauty but, Eugene, who had once enjoyed the anticipation of just such a moment, found himself staring at the drink cynically. The crews called it 'forgetting juice', but for him it had long since failed to live up to that particular label. It didn't make him forget, didn't stop the irritating tick that had been plaguing his left eye, and didn't even get him high any more. A glass of beer had become just a prop, a visible aid for the role he was playing, its possession at the bar body-language shorthand for 'one of us'.

The club they stood in was one of their colonel's better deeds. By bending the rules, he'd turned the huge prefab shed into somewhere everyone could socialise. The 'Ka-Boom Club' as it had been christened, was the focal point of off-duty life, suiting the natural tendency of the crews to party together, regardless of rank, effectively by-passing the out-dated segregation of the formal mess halls. It even looked passable, with an interior that was, supposedly, taken from a plush but bombed-out hotel somewhere in London.

'I ain't gonna kid ya,' said Hank, handing Eugene back the letter he'd been reading, 'The chances ain't the greatest. But they ain't the worst neither.'

Eugene pocketed his brother's missive. Hank was older by eight years but, at times like this, the gap seemed wider. The Oklahoman's parents had died during the Dust Bowl years, leaving him to run the farm, stave off foreclosure and raise his brother by himself. The task would have defeated most boys, but Hank was like a tree. He stood steady, and simply endured. He might have gathered a few gnarls and knots along the way, and he bent with the most violent of storms, but to Eugene he seemed eternal, his presence comforting. And instead of growing bitter, Hank's trials had only strengthened him and that deserved respect. Eugene often deferred to the older man with no hard feelings either way.

Eugene drained the glass and waved for the bartender. As he ordered, Hank eyed his consumption warily.

'Another, and whiskey to follow, Mac.'

'Seems to me, the worst odds are right here, in the Eighth Air Force,' Hank continued.

Eugene nodded glumly. They were still waiting for their crew to arrive and it had been good to air his worries in private before the evening's drinking. He'd not asked for or expected a resolution. Hank reached over and rested his broad hand on Eugene's shoulder. It was a familiar gesture, unconsciously done and matter-of-factly received.

'The thing you gotta do, Eugene, is concentrate on getting yourself through. No, getting *us* through. Your brother's a smart guy, and he's not going to take any risks, but you can't live his life for him. *We* need you, and *you* needs you.'

Hank took a draught of beer and gazed across the spacious room.

'Don't that British girl help none?' he asked. 'She's sure pretty.'

Eugene looked at him. Somehow he'd not have talked about her with anyone else.

'No dice.' He fell silent.

'No monkey business?' Hank was grinning. 'I kinda guessed not. Not like you though.'

There was a pause.

'How did you know it was no dice?' Eugene said finally.

'Expression on your face when you talk about her.'

Eugene nodded. 'Yeah. No monkey business. She's one of these good English girls. Nothing before marriage. Besides ...' He hesitated. Even with Hank he hesitated to say out loud what he wanted to do to her. It had taken all of his determination to resist his baser instincts, and, if he were truthful, he had no idea of why he was behaving so out of character in doing so.

'Sounds like a nice girl,' said Hank. 'A keeper.'

Eugene made no comment, but avoided his friend's eye. He had difficulty in understanding what was happening himself, much less explain it to another guy.

The beer and whisky chaser arrived.

'Sometimes,' said Eugene, supping the pint thoughtfully before downing the whiskey in one, 'sometimes, I think that what I need is not a nice girl, but a really bad one.'

Hank shot him what he called one of his old-fashioned looks, but before he could say anything more, a gaggle of familiar airmen entered the bar.

Eugene raised his hand and waved their crew over. They came, joking and baiting each other, although less jovially than when their tour began, he thought.

Billy went to sort out the drinks, and Tony walked up with Babyface, Meatball, and Karl. Ferret, the stick-thin inventor of unlikely excuses and perpetual chain-smoker, was to join them later with the others. It seemed like a lifetime ago when they formed up.

'Jeeze!' Tony was saying, 'Are we lucky to be here or what?'

A chorus of agreement came from Tony's companions.

Eugene took in the chattering crowd and his mood began to pick up in spite of himself. He loved them, though they made him feel old.

Tony continued, rattling off words like a machine gun. 'We was just crossing da apron and guess what? That freaky bastard from operations comes past on his goddam limey motorcycle and nearly wipes out the lot of us!'

'That guy should definitely be given a rank in the German Air Force,' chipped in the studious New England voice of Babyface.

There were agreeing murmurs all round.

'Yeah!'

'This Dougal they're talking about?' Eugene addressed the question to Hank, who nodded.

They both knew the guy. He was an intelligence officer who appeared at operations briefings but had never flown. He seemed to spend most off-duty hours polishing and drooling over a large black V-twin two-wheeler.

'As if it ain't enough to get it up in the air, now we's getting it on the ground. Jeeze!' Tony concluded the story with a characteristic 'you can't believe it' shake of the head.

Eugene watched the New Yorker sup his beer. There was something sly, perhaps even vaguely criminal about Tony. A rumour had gone the round he only enlisted to avoid prison, but Eugene had seen his file and wouldn't have been surprised if the rumour had been started by Tony himself. It would fit with all the other parts of his lovingly self-created myth: his prowess with women, ability with a knife as yet unproved, and his skill as a card player, which admittedly was true.

Hank's gaze fell on Meatball, who had propped himself precariously on a barstool, rested his beer on the bar and pushed the last part of a hotdog into his mouth, through which he made an incoherent reply.

Hank shook his head. The guy was always stuffing his face. It made him the butt of many jokes ('Hey, Meatball, you're the same shape as the ball turret, you know that? Round! Why don't ya take over there for a change! You'd be a perfect fit!') but he didn't seem to care.

Tony chipped in. 'He's like a goddam food-eating machine. Perhaps we should drop him on the Reich on the next trip and he could eat Hitler out of house and home. What yer think of that, Meatball, my old friend? Ha?'

Meatball made a rude gesture, sipping his lager unconcernedly. He was used to Tony's humour and took it like he took combat duty, with little comment and apparently complete calm. Providing, that was, the food supply remained unthreatened.

Eugene glanced around the chattering group as they stood around the bar, glasses of freshly poured beer chinking against each other.

At the back, well out of the mainstream, was Karl. A Pole, supposedly from a wealthy family, he'd got out, losing it all, back in '39. Practically the first thing he'd done on arriving in the States was to enlist. Unexpectedly rejected by both Infantry and Marines, he'd eventually found his way into the Air Corps, where he was now bomb-aimer in their crew. Eugene himself had lain prone in the bomb-aimer's position himself once or twice, flat on his stomach and with only Perspex between him and the ground, and the enemy guns. He had a secret admiration for the tall East European, or anyone else who could fight a war like that.

He began to relax. He felt happier when he was with the boys. Watching and listening to them was almost like living several vicarious lives at once and he welcomed the distraction their antics brought. They might not quite be a family of brothers and they didn't always see eye to eye, but they closed up rapidly if threatened from the outside, and he knew that by some magic they'd gelled into a team.

He listened as Tony related yet again the story of the motorcycle, the estimated speed having risen considerably over the course of his pint. The others were egging him on.

'Fast. Goddam fast,' he was saying. 'Fastest thing I ever saw.'

'Not as fast as that new Mustang that flies with us now.' It was Karl, his East European accent heavy and his dark eyes serious as usual. He seldom spoke and his comment drew agreeing nods from all present.

'Not as fast as the Two-Six-Two the Krauts are supposed to have either,' added Billy gloomily, turning to Eugene for confirmation. 'Ain't that right, Cap?'

Eugene had been briefed on the new ME 262's, the world's first jet fighter. Most of the details he'd kept to himself, but there was no denying its speed.

'So they say,' he said carelessly, not wanting to talk up anything the enemy had. 'They don't have many though, remember that.'

'Not as fast as their rockets or buzz-bombs either,' Karl added.

There was a consenting mumble.

'Well, I say that bike is the fastest thing on the planet. Yes, sir! Hey, Professor?'

Tony prodded Babyface encouragingly.

They all turned to the youngster when a definitive answer to anything scientific was required. The young radio operator's face was as pasty and untroubled by hair as a schoolboy's, but his abilities with science were unassailable.

'Hey, Professor,' Tony continued, 'what's da fastest thing in da world?'

'Well, it sure ain't me.' It was the Billy, the Virginian, his voice slow and deliberate as his manner.

'Nope. It sure ain't you,' came Ferret's nasally voice from the back, his arrival confirmed by a cloud of cigarette smoke which drifted across the group.

'But I git thar in th' end,' the cowboy added.

'You sure do, pardner. Cigarette?'

'Well, I don't mind if I do.'

'Let's hope we all come back,' added Babyface soberly.

'Amen to that.'

'Oh, are you here too, Father?'

For a while the banter went back and forth. There was a pause as glasses clinked in the unspoken but superstitious ritual.

'Well, Baby?' Tony had his face close to his crewmate. 'What's the answer to my question, *huh*? Da fastest thing in da world?'

'Well,' began the young man, basking in the attention of his older buddies, 'firstly I ain't your baby.'

'*Is you is or is you ain't* ...' Ferret, who had arrived at the back of the group, sang in a mock-negro voice.

'It's obvious!' Tony interrupted him. 'It's me in a bar full of dames!'

There were groans all round.

'Hey, he said fastest not daftest,' muttered Karl, pleased with himself that his growing knowledge of English was permitting him to throw a few insults.

'Or Eugene dealing cards.' It was Meatball.

This time they all nodded solemnly.

'I'm retired,' Eugene lied, to disbelieving laughter.

'Do ya want to know or not?' inquired their young educator, who was still wanting his moment of glory.

'The fastest thing fer sure is Meatball when da chow-line opens!'

'Very funny, Tony,' said Babyface.

At last, the laughter faded to an expectant pause.

'It isn't anything you've said so far.' Babyface paused for effect. 'The fastest thing, gentlemen, is light.'

There was an intake of breath and a few mumblings as if he were a wise man addressing a clutch of mediaeval villagers.

'Get outta here!' scoffed Tony, 'Light don't have no speed – it's just ... It's *just.*'

'Light? Yes, but the photons – the things that light is made of – travel at a certain speed.'

Tony recoiled. 'Oh yeah? How fast?'

'About one hundred and eighty-six thousand miles ...' he paused, 'per second.'

There were howls of derision, mumbles of disbelief as the crew considered this news.

No one was quite sure when Eugene first picked up on the other conversation: some bragging tale being told by the Captain of *Dirty Dozen*, a new outfit, sitting around a table playing cards some way off. But one after another the crew caught sight of the expression on his face and fell silent.

'So I told the guy,' came the voice, 'it ain't grunts like you is gonna win this war. Running up some strip of sand and shootin' a rifle. It's airpower that's gonna win, not raggedy-assed Marines stickin' a few of Tojo's four-eyed cousins and then taking it easy under some coconut tree.'

There was a murmur of laughter.

'Yeah. It's us that history is gonna remember, boys. But you should have seen this guy, he went goddam purple!'

'Take it easy, Eugene,' said Hank.

But it was too late.

'Dammit.' Hank set down his glass and followed his captain.

Without being asked, the crew did the same.

'I'll remember them.' Eugene spoke the words quietly.

Howard Cody had lost count of the number of drinks he'd had that evening. They were having the desired effect of suppressing the nerves he had been feeling about their first operational trip later that week. He felt strong in the kingdom where nature and the Air Force had placed him.

'Well, good for you, buddy.' Slowly his eyes focused on the man in front of him.

'My brother is a Marine.'

Cody laughed, conscious that the eyes of his crew were on him.

'Well, never mind, captain, every family has one.' He turned to his crew. 'A loser, that is.'

To Cody's surprise his crew didn't laugh. Instead, one or two of them shifted uncomfortably and one folded his cards and backed away. Kids, he thought. What did they know?

'What did you say?' Eugene moved closer until the two captains were almost touching.

Something about the man, his breaking into a perfectly good story, suddenly irritated Cody.

'You think you're heroes?' Eugene said. 'Well, let me tell you, captain, you're not. At the end of every day you got soft beds to lie in, warm food and no one trying to kill you while you sleep. When you're a Marine, you got a dirty foxhole, a couple of tins of rations, if you're lucky, and if you're unlucky, some Jap will cut you to pieces when they catch you and *mail you home to the fucking Emperor!*

His voice rose to a shout at the end. At the back of the room some guys playing dominos began to watch. The barman reached for the phone, but the receiver was quietly replaced by another flyer.

The strength of the outburst stunned Eugene's crew. No one had seen Eugene mad, even when they goofed in training.

Cody sneered, but he looked suddenly less sure of himself.

'Just get off of my cloud, captain.' Cody placed his hand on Eugene's chest and pushed him back.

Hank's reactions were just fast enough to catch Eugene's blow mid-air. Using his greater strength, he pinned Eugene's arms behind his back. The rest of the crew took a step forward.

'Easy, Cap,' came Hank's steady voice.

'*Nah, take him, take him!*' It was Tony, almost jumping up and down with excitement.

Hank was wondering how they could get out of the situation without getting themselves arrested by the MP's.

Eugene was silent, but his eyes glinted dangerously.

'Step outside, captain,' Eugene said, his voice low but steady.

But Hank pushed forward, shaking his head, and moving a restraining hand from Eugene's arms to his shoulder.

'No, you don't, Cap. We're almost done, tour's almost over. If they drop you in the pen then we're all stuck. I ain't flying with no one else.'

There was a murmur of agreement from his crew.

The new crew were young and wide-eyed, and clearly had no appetite for a fight.

The two groups stood facing each other uncertainly but neither captain was willing to give way.

'*Indian Wrestle!*' It was Tony. 'It's easy. Whoever loses has to apologise to the other guy.'

The crews considered the idea.

Babyface looked at Cody's broad shoulders and winced. 'Bad move, Tony,' he murmured quietly.

Cody grinned to his men, then stared at Eugene.

'What's the matter? Left your balls upstairs?'

'Balls? *I'll show you what balls are!*' Eugene glanced at the pot of matchsticks on the table, marking the card game's modest stake. He reached into his pocket and pulled out a wad of cash. He stuck it on the table. 'One thousand bucks.'

There was a whistle from somewhere in the crowd that had begun to gather.

Eugene took off his watch and cufflinks and added them. He looked hard at the other man.

'Twenty-one. One hand. Winner takes all, and gets an apology.'

Hank shook his head and muttered under his breath. He'd thought the gambling thing was done.

But Cody's expression had changed. 'I ain't got that much cash.'

Eugene remained silent, letting the other man sweat.

Conscious that the eyes of his crew were on him, Cody reached inside his jacket.

'But I got me this.' He placed beautiful gold pocket watch on the table. 'My grandpa's. Solid gold.'

It was a beautiful and ancient timepiece. There was an intake of breath from the assembled watchers.

He produced a wad of notes and counted five hundred, threw it on the table.

'Seems fair to me.' Eugene glanced at Tony who considered a moment and then nodded.

'Done.'

They called a nervous barman over and sat him down.

'No gambling,' he was muttering. 'You guys know the rules.'

But eventually he did as he was told, taking up the role of dealer at the table. The two players sat down opposite. The crowd pressed closer and Babyface disappeared to keep look-out.

The barman, hand unsteady, gathered the cards. Despite his nervousness, he seemed to know what he was doing.

'Hey! You know this guy?' Cody regarded the barman, a young Private First Class, with suspicion.

Eugene shook his head.

The barman shrugged in an embarrassed kind of way and, avoiding eye contact, dealt each player two cards.

Eugene picked up his hand but did not look.

'Stick.'

A murmur of astonishment went round the table.

Tony bent down, and tugged Eugene's sleeve.

'Boss,' he whispered in alarm. 'You gotta check da cards. You can't just bet blind.'

Hank coughed.

But Eugene was determined. 'Stick.'

Cody stared in disbelief, then shook his head. 'Man, you must be some mug.'

He glanced at his own cards and his eyebrows rose.

'Twist!'

The barman dealt him another card.

'Twist.'

A second murmur.

'Twist.'

'Jeeze!' Billy looked pale.

'Stick.'

Cody laid down his cards. He had a two, a three, two fives and a six.

He grinned and leant back. 'Twenty-one! I needed a spare watch!'

A couple of his men laughed nervously. He reached out for the pile of loot.

'*Woah!*' It was Tony. '*Not so fast, mister!*'

Hank had covered his eyes. 'Goddammit, Eugene,' he muttered.

With a sigh Eugene flipped his two cards onto the table. A Queen of Hearts and an Ace of Spades.

A chorus of disbelief rose from the crowd, which had meanwhile gathered.

'*Shit!*'

'*Holy Mary, Mother of God!*'

'*No way!*'

The barman, who, after a slow start seemed to have got into his stride, didn't miss a beat.

'Sudden Death, gentlemen?' he enquired.

The two nodded. The crowd had grown, some at the back were standing on tables to get a view.

Cody took a swig of his beer. 'I wanna new deck.'

Eugene nodded and the barman went and brought a fresh pack which he opened and shuffled.

'Gentlemen. Are you ready?'

The room was pin-drop quiet.

Eugene sat stony-faced, but a thin bead of sweat had broken out on Cody's brow. He swallowed and nodded.

The barman flicked a card to each player.

Hank was almost beside himself. Five hundred of the thousand he'd loaned Eugene himself only the previous day.

Cody turned first. It was a nine. He shuffled his chair closer, ran a hand though his hair, and glanced at the gold pocket watch.

Eugene banged his card down on the table.

'*Jack!*'

Uproar erupted, cheering from one side, bitter mumbling from the other.

Cody stood up, face like thunder. 'Take it.' He pushed the pile towards his opponent.

'You're forgetting something.' Eugene remined seated, his eyes steady.

Cody hesitated. Twenty pairs of expectant eyes rested on him.

'Sorry,' he mumbled before striding away and out of the room.

The place erupted in hoots and catcalls.

But Hank was staring at his captain, and he wasn't smiling.

CHAPTER 18

'You sure you want to go ahead with this?' Eugene asked, not for the first time.

Rosie glanced across the car's interior and knew from the look on Eugene's face he was still hoping she'd changed her mind. Perhaps he didn't think she would manage it, or would get scared when confronted with the reality of sitting squarely in the driver's seat of such an imposing vehicle as the huge green Air Force Packard. If so, she thought, he was in for a disappointment. She'd been looking forward to the promised driving lesson all week. Familiarity with riding on her father's motorcycle had cured her at a young age of any trepidation she might have felt and, in any case, driving was a passport to the adult world. She'd decided, as part of her plan, she had to master the car, but part of her wanted to impress Eugene and perhaps make him realise that, although she might be younger, she was still capable of independent thoughts and achievements.

She looked out over the long bonnet at the early-morning mist still clinging to the hedgerows of the country lane they had chosen for her first attempt, and felt a thrill of excitement so intense she wanted to laugh. She glanced again at her companion, expectantly raising her eyebrows.

'Well?'

He shook his head in admission of defeat, and broke into a dry smile.

'Well, first of all,' he began, noting she had already begun to examine the controls.

She was reaching underneath, there was a clunk and the bonnet of the car rose a couple of inches.

He clasped his forehead in mock exasperation. 'That would be the hood.'

She smiled. 'I know.'

Not for the first time that morning he seemed surprised.

'You do?'

Rosie nodded, and hopped out of the car. He followed and was astonished when she raised the heavy metal hood, propped it carefully open and disappeared beneath. He found her pulling out the dipstick.

'Oh,' he laughed, 'you don't have to worry about all that. That's guy's stuff in there.'

'Oh but I do,' she answered.

His eyebrows, already elevated, went up a further notch. She seemed to be checking the oil level. Most girls didn't care how a car worked so long as it was available to pick them up or take them home.

She pointed at the row of spark plugs.

'It's a six-cylinder, isn't it?'

'Uh, yeah.' He scratched his head.

'How much horsepower?' she asked.

'Uh, I, er ...' He began.

'No matter,' she said, tugging at the throttle cable. 'I bet it's a lot. It's a big motor and the carburettor is enormous.'

He could no longer hold back, and laughed out loud.

'God in heaven, girl, how'd you know that?'

She grinned back. 'I told you. My father had a motorcycle. And —'

'And you used to help … yeah, I remember. Well, I'll be goddammed.'

Back in the car, Eugene went over the controls: the pedals, the steering wheel, choke, horn and starter. With some trepidation he finally nodded and she pressed the button. The engine coughed into life and, with it rumbling at idle, Rosie depressed the clutch and pulled the column shift lever down. She could see from the corner of her eye that he was grimacing.

'Now gently…' He was about to explain the tendency of the Packard to lurch on take-off but it was too late. The pedal came up with a clunk and they were off, kangaroo-hopping down the lane like something from the Marx Brothers.

'*Eyes ahead!*' he shouted as they veered towards a hedge.

Rosie tugged the wheel hard to the right and the car came to an unceremonious halt, stalled in the middle of the road. Eugene collected himself from the under the dashboard.

'Wonderful!' she murmured, her eyes shining.

Eugene shook his head, a thin sheen of sweat formed on his rugged face.

But she'd soon get the hang of it and then he'd calm down, she thought.

She pushed the clutch pedal and reached for the starter.

Eugene glanced behind them. 'Always look behind —' he began, but it was too late and they were off again, this time more smoothly. They were driving more or less straight and on what was, in England anyway, the correct side. The only thing wrong was the engine, which was screaming in first.

'Change up!' He gestured vigorously with his hand and to his surprise she completed the manoeuvre, the car giving only the slightest shudder as the gears meshed and the vehicle accelerated.

Eugene pulled her over to the side of the road and finally laughed. They did a few practice turns at slow speed. At first she kept stalling, but when he encouraged her to give it more gas, the opposite happened and they almost ended in the hedge. But she persisted and soon it was clear she was getting the hang of it.

'Dammit, lady, you sure are determined,' he said, the admiration clear in his voice. He grinned and she beamed back.

'I don't like to be beaten by anything,' she said. 'Once I start, I'm going to finish.'

Despite her upbeat tone, Rosie felt mildly surprised at the boldness of her own words. But he seemed to have been finally convinced she was going to make a good driver.

'Oh, I noticed.' He pushed his Air Force cap back on his head and grinned.

'Let's go again!' she said.

They drove more or less randomly for half an hour. Rosie had found top gear and the car was bowling along, the hedgerows passing in a blur of green. She noticed he had wound down the window. Occasionally his eyes would close and he would exhale. The great American saloon motored through the green-and-brown patchwork of fields. Here and there along their route, smoke rose from a farmhouse chimney, and workers and machines appeared in gaps in the hedgerows. Eugene seemed lost in his thoughts. It was a strange feeling, to be the one in charge. It was as though she had been suddenly transformed from child to parent, and it was an empowering sensation. And she was glad to be able to do something positive and real for him.

Belatedly, they saw the farm cart as they rounded the corner and Rosie caught the terrified expression of the farmer who reflexively raised his hands. They were going to crash. The man would be crushed. *The brake!* She stamped down hard on the middle pedal and felt the thin cross-ply tyres squirm beneath them. Time seemed to slow, and Rosie became aware of an open field gate to the left. She tugged hard on the enormous steering wheel and at the last second the car swerved violently, passed through the gate and ran for a short distance across the stubble, before coming to rest, the bonnet buried two feet deep in a haystack.

Rosie sat, still gripping the wheel, horrified, her hands frozen. The engine shrugged and died with a faint groan.

For a few seconds there was silence save for shouting from behind and the ticking of metal from the cooling engine.

Rosie glanced at Eugene, unable to speak, a blush forming on her pale, freckled cheeks.

'You OK?' he said at last. She expected him to be angry but instead he was grinning.

'I'm sorry…' she began, still flustered.

He was touching her hair and, instead of anger, on his face was a look of odd tenderness.

'It's alright, honey. You crashed, but into the straw. You had the sense to swerve.'

They peered through the windscreen. The impact had set off the windscreen wiper, which tracked solemnly across the screen, gathering small clumps of hay at every pass.

Then a ruddy but unhappy face appeared, gesticulating and shouting.

It took a while to calm the agitated farmer, but he was eventually placated with a suitable bribe, which Eugene paid reluctantly but on

Rosie's insistence. They drove on, and recovered from the drama with a lunch and tea a roadside café. Rosie was glad Eugene had a full day's pass, something apparently due to his plane having two new engines fitted and hence being unfit to fly a mission.

That evening in the fading light, they pulled up at a spot Rosie's father used to take her on his motorcycle combination, an area of ground on the flat top of the lonely hill that overlooked the town to the west. As the motor finally died with a shudder she peered beyond the long bonnet at the fast-dissolving view. Far below, the streets were spread before them like a map and, carved into the slope just in front of the car, a gently eroding ditch and rampart was all that now remained of an ancient fort that her father had said was built by the Romans.

Rosie scooted across the bench-seat to be closer to Eugene and they sat in the cocoon of the car's cabin, watching the evening sky change colour as the sun descended from beneath the purple clouds overhead into a band of clear sky near the horizon. Eugene put his arm around her, and wound down his window. She heard at once the opening spatters of warm English rain, and as she listened they grew louder, the fat drops falling with increasing frequency until drumming on the car's metal roof. In the town far below, the cobbled streets were slowly changing their dull colours to a palette of shimmering blues and greys, until they flashed and glinted wet in the low-angled sunlight, like the scales of a fish. A shabby kind of rainbow was forming as the light filtered through the rain and she could imagine the sheets of water that must even now be flowing over her mother's slate roof, gurgling into the gutter, and barrelling down into the drains in the alley. At last, stray spots of rain began to enter the cabin and Eugene wound the window back up. He stretched over and opened the glove box, taking out a carton of Lucky Strikes, offering her a smoke. Inside the compartment lay the book of poems she'd given him.

'What did you think of the e.e. cummings?' she asked.

'I read him before, back in the States,' he answered. 'I've always remembered "The Moon's a Balloon".' He took a drag. 'Especially when flying. I liked the bit about sailing away. Away from the earth, to escape.'

'Except there's no one shooting at that particular balloon,' she said, squeezing his arm.

He smiled wryly. 'No one shooting, no.'

Below them, the town had almost been consumed by the darkness. Before the war, streetlamps would have lain like strings of bright pearls in the darkness. But in the blackout, the buildings were passing unimpeded into a deep, primal darkness. Only at the station was there a final hurrah, as the steam of a terminating train rose, catching the embers of the sun and glowing against the darkening sky like a huge orange flower.

The darkness, thought Rosie, enhanced the enclosure of the car, and with it the intimacy it created. He was so close she could feel his breathing, a powerful rising and falling. He was young, and strong, and it was impossible such a life force could be stopped, that death was real. But she knew many just like him took off every day for Germany, and never came back.

He glanced over, and she caught the same intensity in his eyes she'd seen in the Park. Part of her wanted the passion she saw, but another more cautious one was afraid. She pulled away, lying back against the seat.

'Tell me about America,' she said, at last.

There was a pause.

'America?'

He began to talk only haltingly at first, a story about his father's shipping business, founded by an immigrant grandfather, but gradually he became absorbed in his own narrative, his voice growing keener and expansive. When the war was over, he said, he'd build a house somewhere called Up State. And perhaps he'd buy a car with his discharge pay. He thought he might take a road trip – perhaps as far as Florida or Mexico, just drive and drive, for days without a map, letting the road and fate take him wherever it willed. Drive, and forget.

For her the places he described carried a sheen of glamour, almost magical when spoken aloud, like the words of a poem, or a prayer: California, San Francisco, Mexico, New York.

She'd often conjured America in her mind: the land of movie stars and bright city lights. Until Eugene, she'd had little to go on other than films and magazines, and she'd imagined it variously as a land of dusty plains, or deep canyons, perhaps cool, blue, snow-capped mountains, or at times as a place of chic, car-filled cities.

'Mexico? That's another country though, isn't it?' she asked.

He nodded. 'Yeah. About 2,300 miles from New York.'

'You'd drive two thousand miles in a car?' she asked suddenly.

'Sure. Why not? Anything's possible, kiddo.'

'Anything's possible, kiddo!' she repeated, imitating his accent.

He grinned and moved closer, looking at her intently with his warm brown eyes.

'Oh, well, why didn't you say so?'

She sensed something then, a deep and unsatisfied longing within him. He touched her hair and Rosie felt her breathing quicken and a sudden unexpected thrill run through her stomach. Her mind sensed danger but something else relished the risk, wanted it even. His hand was on her shoulder and, then, in the tangerine light of the dash, he kissed her. She closed her eyes and returned the embrace of his lips, his mouth soft as marshmallow, and yielding. She felt a rising sense of pleasure and anticipation – there could be no existence outside of themselves, and this kiss.

His hand travelled slowly up her body until it reached her breast.

His breathing was growing coarser, harder now, and she returned his kiss more firmly. His hand slid downwards, under her dress. For a moment she tensed, holding her legs together. But the kiss was intoxicatingly sweet, and a rising tide of the same simple sweetness began to well inside her. She felt her legs part, his hand hot and rough within the clasp of her cool thighs. He reached her knickers and she felt herself suddenly wet, and burning as though on fire. She moaned as his hand slid beneath the elastic, and his fingers ran like small electric shocks through her soft, downy hair.

Some madness in her urged her to throw caution to the winds, to submit to the tide and allow it to carry her away on its flood, but the unwanted alarm of some ancient fear was insistent in dragging her back. It was too much, too fast. Her body was running away with her, like a car with no brakes.

'*No!*' she was suddenly saying. '*No!*'

To her surprise the words seemed to spur him on. She became aware of his weight and strength and was suddenly afraid. He was powerful, unstoppable, rushing forward like an express train.

'*Don't,*' she was saying, '*don't do that to me!*'

Forcefully, as though she'd consented, he pushed his finger in, making her gasp with both shock and guilty pleasure.

He recoiled at the slap and she found herself with her back against the car door, hands defensively drawn across her breasts, blouse awry, skirt pushed up. He was nursing his face, his eyes tearing with frustration. She should be angry, she knew, but instead she felt a wave of sympathy. What had she done?

'*Goddam it!*'

He glared, and for a second she thought he must hate her. He jerked the handle and swung the door open, jumping out and slamming it shut behind him. Outside there was the sound of male

174

cursing followed by the metallic ching of a lighter. For a second the fluttering flame lit the car interior.

Rosie's emotions swirled uncontrollably, but refused to coalescence into clear thoughts. Had she not led him on? He was a man. And one that might die any day, and he had needs. Should she have stopped him? Yet, she had needs too, and one of them was to be respected. She could not give up all control, but she knew then she didn't want to lose him. Slowly she got out of the car and approached him. They were standing at the edge of the old hill fortress, the ground sloping steeply away into the blackness and the old town beyond. She reached out her hand, but he turned on her, his eyes blazing.

'*You stupid fool!*' he hissed. '*Why did you let me start if you wouldn't let me finish?*'

She didn't know what to say but grasped his arm. Her eyes were pleading. 'Come on.'

He hesitated, then exhaled, throwing away the cigarette, the gleaming spec tumbling away through the air as the updraft caught it, and followed her. They slammed the doors and he sat, unspeaking, whether sulky or just frustrated she didn't know. But the storm seemed at least past its peak.

To her surprise, she found herself taking the initiative.

'English girls don't …' she began.

'English girls don't what?' he snapped, glaring but with less fire than before.

She forced herself to stare him down.

'We don't do that before marriage, and … before we really know someone.'

He looked as though whatever poison it was that had been inside him was about to rupture the surface.

'*Marriage? Goddamit!*'

'I'm sorry but –' She hesitated.

'Look,' he said, seemingly to struggling to stay calm, 'how can I make plans, when … when I might not even be here tomorrow?'

She couldn't bear to acknowledge he might be right.

'I'm sorry.' Then she found herself adding, 'But you need to respect what I want too.'

'You don't seem to need, to want what I do,' he said bitterly.

'That's not true,' she heard herself say, softly.

For a time they sat in silence. At last his hand slid across the seat and grasped her own.

'You'd want to go, wouldn't you? To America? If I made it.'

Astonished, she found herself responding with an affirmation of surprising strength.

'Yes,' she said. 'I would want to go.'

He paused. 'To go to the States we would have to be … married.' He looked her in the eye. 'If we were, they'd ship you over, after the war.'

Rosie's raised her eyebrows. It was an unexpected reversal and she struggled to find words.

'Yes,' she said then, 'I suppose we would.'

'Then,' he asked, 'then … if we were?'

She found herself smiling. Her heart was beating very fast.

'Then – yes,' she heard herself say, 'I would go.'

CHAPTER 19

The front door slammed, the shock wave of the reverberations running through the thin walls and timbers of the cottage. With her mother out, it was as if the house had finally heaved a sigh of relief and it was safe to go downstairs. The simmering antagonism between them had been building like an electrical charge before a storm, creating an atmosphere toxic to the point of suffocation. They'd stopped speaking after she and Eugene had last been out to the pictures, having come home well past her mother's curfew. Since then her mother had refused to speak and instead had communicated by notes pinned around the house, a tactic so irritating it forced Rosie either out or upstairs to her room.

Free of her mother's presence, Rosie's mind could run, tumbling over the experience of mastering the car, and spontaneously lurching into memories of things Eugene had said, and more particularly, done. His fumbling attempts at sex inspired the familiar twinge of curiosity about 'It', the great mystery of what Hazel called 'You Know'. She knew she wanted a deeper connection, so why did she always feel such fear when the chance came? Perhaps her mother had been right when she'd said during one of their arguments that the American was too old, too worldly-wise for an English girl who was not yet eighteen.

Rosie made her way down to the kitchen. Since the Invasion, Eugene had been on duty more and more and she'd had several disappointments when a message had come, cancelling an agreed rendezvous. She hated the war, and the interruptions it forced in her life. The only benefit seemed that it allowed time to consider each surprising episode as it came.

Rosie filled the hexagonal coffee percolator Eugene had given her and, after it brewed, spooned two rebelliously large spoons of sugar into a tin mug, pouring the swirling, brown aromatic liquid on top and savouring the aroma.

It was the coldest June anyone could remember, and, unbelievably, the stove was on in the living room. She clicked the Bakelite knob of the wireless and, as the valves glowed, the sound of the Lena Horne hit, 'Stormy Weather', filled the air. She sipped the coffee, letting the bluesy words flow around her. The dreamy music ended all too soon, but then the news began. Since the landings, she'd listened several times a day, and now she turned up the volume.

The dignified tone of the announcer was accompanied by the faint hiss of static.

'*Allied forces have linked up across the battlefield in Normandy,*' said the plummy BBC voice. '*They now form a solid front more than fifty miles wide. At sea, the Royal Navy are gallantly covering the invasion and transporting troops across the waters of the Channel. A number of vessels have been lost.*'

Rosie sipped. Mention of the Navy reminded her of her brother. She'd been shocked when the letter from him had arrived. After reading it her mother had become distraught, and it was only when she had calmed enough to reread it they'd realised his wounds were not life-threatening. It seemed that, when D-Day arrived, he'd been sent with his fellow trainees to help with rescues and had been wounded in the process. Soon, however, he would be home, honourably discharged, but with a crushed left hand.

'*Our planes are now operating from airstrips in France,*' the announcer continued.

Rosie's heart quickened. Was that why she hadn't heard from Eugene? Was he in fact no longer even in England? A sudden chill ran through her as she became oddly aware she was listening to history unfolding.

'*The wounded are returning from Normandy, with their stories of the battle. And work has begun on building a new airport for London ... it's at a small village called Heathrow.*'

Dumbly, Rosie clicked off the receiver and wandered back through the house, into the dank backyard, taking the mug with her. She opened the hencoop, shooing the clucking birds out, where they strutted nervously, astonished at their suddenly enlarged world.

'You won't find much there,' said Rosie to a straggly old broiler with wattles that lay to one side. 'It's all cinders and brick dust is all.'

She sipped while she watched them. She wondered suddenly whether the unsettling feeling she had about Eugene and the fear that gripped her when he was away were proofs they were in love? It was certainly true she couldn't get him out of her mind. And then he'd gone and mentioned marriage. She knew they were already more than friends, but the proposal seemed to indicate he wanted it to go much further than that. The shameful thought came suddenly to her that marriage to an American would be a way out – a way out from her mother as well as from the rationed, bombed-out shell Britain was becoming. Yet, was it love, really? Being trapped in the shell of a marriage without love must be worse than not being married.

Rosie threw the chickens some peelings from the pail kept in the kitchen, and watched as they scrabbled and squawked after the fragments. The dog wandered out behind her, regarding the birds curiously with head on one side. She knelt and the familiar old animal came, wagging his thick black tail. She fondled his velvety ears and pressed his great rubber doorstop of a nose, grinning as she returned to the house, where she grabbed her coat and his lead. She shooed the chickens back into their coop and headed off for the walk she knew he was asking for.

It was afternoon before hunger drew Rosie and her four-legged companion back to the cottage. Having been away from the house and in the unrestricted open air, she walked with a lightness of step and an unselfconscious smile. Coming in, she sploshed water into the dog's bowl, and gulped down a couple of slices of indigestible grey wartime bread. There was no jam, but plain bread was preferable to the dreadful margarine her mother bought. The tap water tasted metallic, as it usually did, but she couldn't be bothered to brew a pot of tea. The living room was empty and she smiled – her mother must still be out.

She sprang lightly up the treads of the creaking narrow staircase. She would be able to lie on her bed and read in peace.

Rosie opened the thin wooden door to her room and jerked back. There, sitting on her bed, was her mother. Tatty though the room was, it was hers, and she felt a surge of anger at the invasion.

'What are you doing?'

Her mother looked up, completely unabashed. 'I'm finding out just what you've been up to, my girl.'

She said it with a degree of satisfaction. Around her were piles of paper and, with a lurch of her stomach, Rosie realised they were Eugene's letters. Her mother had one in her hand.

'*What are you doing?*' She was aware her voice was higher in pitch, but it seemed beyond her control.

'You stupid fool!' her mother said, casting a withering look at her. 'You have no idea what you're doing, 'ave you?' She sighed theatrically, threw the letter onto the floor and picked up another disdainfully with her fingertips. 'This Yank,' she waved the letter for emphasis, 'is using you, and you'll get hurt, mark my words. Men can't be trusted, least of all the Americans. Savages, the whole lot of 'em!'

'You don't know him.'

'*Hah!*' her mother shot back. 'I do, I can see it here. In these letters. Men like him just wait for a fool like you to come along.'

'Just leave!' Furious, Rosie found herself batting back tears. 'Get out of my room!'

She advanced and her mother stood. Rosie towered over her.

'*Your* room? This is *my* house, my girl!' She jabbed her daughter in the chest. 'So don't come the old "I Am" with me. I can see what's going on here.'

Rosie didn't trust herself to speak.

'Had you, has he?' her mother said, nodding knowingly.

'*What?*'

'Up the spout, are yer?' She patted Rosie's stomach.

Her daughter backed away, appalled.

'No! Of course not!'

Her mother moved to the door.

'You were trouble when you were born! Eighteen hours of labour. Nearly bloody killed me. And for what? I wanted a boy. Instead I got you, a useless creature of no use to anybody!'

Rosie choked, but at last found words. 'Why,' she managed, 'do you have to be so spiteful?'

'Spiteful? It wasn't me who twisted my husband against me,' her mother sneered. 'I shouldn't be surprised how you've turned out. A tramp, cavorting with Americans!'

It was like watching an erupting volcano, though from far away. Rosie could feel her palms sweating. She'd stay calm. She wasn't going to behave like her mother, or become like her.

'You're mad,' she said, as simply as she could. 'You need to see a doctor!'

'Mad?' her mother snorted. 'I'm not ready for the knacker's yard yet, my girl! You can't get rid of me, but I can have you sent back to that orphanage any time I like!'

Suddenly Rosie had heard enough.

'I will tell you something, Mother.' She reached down and pulled the suitcase from under her bed. 'I can *leave* any time I like, and I think I will do so right now!'

'Go on then. I'm better off without you, you ...' her mother's face was beetroot, 'you *slut!*'

'*Get out!*' Rosie heard herself shout, astonished at how loud her own voice had become. She watched, fascinated, as the water jug she must have thrown hit the wall, shattering into a shower of water and a thousand shards of ceramic shrapnel.

Her mother gave a shrill cry and retreated, stumbling down the stairs.

Rosie sat heavily on the bed and tried to regain her calm. She was trembling and a tear was trying to force its way out, though she would not allow it. As calmly as she could, she gathered the letters, smoothed and folded each one and packed them neatly into the case. There wasn't much else: a few dresses, including Mrs. B.'s evening piece and the jewellery, a picture of Eugene and his crew, magazines and toiletries. As an afterthought, she drew out the box of books and threw a small selection into the case.

She walked to the dormer and looked down at the alley and rows of untidy, slip-tiled cottages beyond. It felt odd, yet strangely right, to be seeing them for the last time. After a moment, she put on her coat and picked up her belongings. There was just the dog left. She didn't trust her mother not to take it out on him, so he'd have to escape too.

Downstairs she found him hiding wide-eyed under the dining table.

'Come on,' she said gently.

She attached his lead and the pair walked down the crunching cinder path to the gate for the last time, exiting into the alley beyond.

CHAPTER 20

For the first fevered steps Rosie rode a high tide of adrenaline, propelled by the rocket fuel of anger and pride. She'd faced down her mother and, with hindsight, it had been inevitable, something building for months. And it hadn't been about revenge. She hadn't been the one who started it, and it hadn't been the tantrum of a disloyal child. She'd acted as an adult, holding her mother to account.

Rosie turned onto the main road and began the walk to town, the dog trotting wonderingly alongside. It was cold and she turned up the collar on her mac. So she'd finally left home, and that had been right. But the awkward truth was, it had been earlier than she'd planned and, more pressingly, she had nowhere to go.

Rosie frowned. The suitcase felt suddenly heavy and, although afternoon, the sky was darkening. Clouds, bruised and pregnant with rain, were gathering. The temperature was freakishly low for June, the coldest summer for a hundred years, someone had said, and an icy wind whipped the road, disturbing cigarette ends and sending them spinning on miniature tornadoes. Far from being a heroine, her conscience unhelpfully suggested, perhaps she'd been a fool. Wanting to escape and be independent was one thing, but she had nowhere to go. Her pace slowed and she pulled the fedora she'd taken to wearing down, against the cutting wind.

As she reached the town centre, the pavements grew crowded, as if the whole place was on the move. Some of the pedestrians were soldiers, going to or from the station, but the mass were civilians hurrying about obscure, domestic errands. Manners had been thrown aside, for she was repeatedly barged into, the impacts sending her rebounding from one passer-by to another, her feet snagging occasionally on the dog's lead. Frustrated, she halted mid-flow and put down the case. It was promptly kicked by a man passing by, which caused Peter to bark loudly, but stopping worked, for people no longer knocked into her but flowed around, as though she and her dog had become islands in the stream.

Gobs of rain spattered the pavement and, as if on command, the trampling hordes deployed umbrellas in a rippling canopy of ribbed canvas. Rosie walked on and dodged between the new obstructions, but the rain soon descended in force, a cloudburst that began to run across her hat's brim and down her neck, wetting her hair and soaking cold and deep into the fabric of her clothes. She pressed determinedly on and the doubts resurfaced. She was homeless. Perhaps she hadn't acted as an adult, but as a child. She'd not kept calm after all, but in fact had thrown something at her mother. Around her the scratching, scraping umbrella forest jostled and stabbed, alternately protecting her and then deflecting cascades of cold water her way. They were being carried with the herd into the main square.

More by chance than navigation, she found herself at the red telephone box. She made a grab for the door and, finding the small brass cupped handle, yanked it open. She shook her hat and hunted for change, the air of the tiny cubicle filling quickly with the steamy scent of wet dog. She'd call Eugene. He'd know what to do. She knew the base number. She raised the handset and put the sixpence in the slot. Suddenly she stopped, replacing the receiver in the cradle. If she ran to him it would look foolish. She could make a case for leaving her mother, but it should be calm and deliberate.

Rosie drew a breath and wiped a squeaky circle in the condensation that was rapidly forming on the glass. The roads were jammed with war traffic, a line of American jeeps sitting immobile, rain bouncing off their canvas tops as the drivers peered out. Pedestrians were running everywhere, milling across the road, winding their way round the sudden obstacles. Every so often a gust of wind would send someone's umbrella inside out, and from the doorways peered a number of stranded civilians, one man with a newspaper held over his head, calculating whether or not he should run for it. Suddenly she knew what she should do. She picked up her case, opened the door and began to walk.

'She no longer lives here.'

Of Hazel's housemates Rosie remembered this one best for some reason. Her name was Diana, or was it Delilah? Then she remembered. No, it was Doreen. But they called her Droopy. Her face did have a long, petulant look.

'Hazel doesn't live here anymore?' she asked in disbelief.

Droopy peered at her and spoke slowly as though talking to an idiot.

'I have already told you. She left. Apparently some of us were not good enough for her. Though why she of all people should think so is beyond me.' She leant forward, saying with relish, 'Common as muck, if you ask me!' She had a habit of tossing her head when making a point like a bad-tempered donkey. 'Was there anything else?'

she asked petulantly. Her tone was nasal. She even sounded droopy.

'Yes,' Rosie replied. 'Where is she?'

Doreen stiffened, and looked her slowly up and down. 'I wouldn't have put you as one of her ... kind.' Acidly, she pursed her lips.

Rosie was starting to get fed up with her. She could see how she'd earned an unflattering nickname.

'Never mind all that,' she said. 'Where can I find her?'

Doreen disappeared inside for a second and came out with a small handwritten card.

'She left these behind. Frankly, my dear, we were so glad she left.' She closed the door.

Rosie glanced at the card, an address by the railway. It was odd Hazel hadn't said anything, but perhaps her departure had been sudden. She turned at the gate to see Doreen peering at her from behind the curtains.

'*Goodbye, Droopy!*' she called, as loudly and cheerfully as possible, and the figure vanished at once.

It was almost teatime when Rosie finally arrived at the pebble-dashed semi, one of many that lined the concrete road laid down a decade or two earlier. A row of flowering chestnuts grew along one side, shielding the properties from the railway line, and giving the place a leafy, suburban feel. It looked a very grown-up place to be living and for a second Rosie wondered if Droopy hadn't played a trick on her.

Hesitantly, she opened the double gate that ran from the road to the half-glazed front door. She rang the bell.

''Oo is it?' came a familiar voice.

Rosie breathed a sigh of relief. Suddenly she couldn't wait to get inside.

'*No one here but us chickens!*' she said into the letterbox.

The door flew open.

'*Rosie, love!*'

Soaked through and freezing, she was suddenly enveloped in a warm embrace. It felt good to be wanted, to have somewhere to go after all.

'Come in,' Hazel said softly, taking her case.

Rosie stood in the hall, her mac dripping tiny puddles on the linoleum. The dog had barged past, and was busy making an olfactory map of the new territory.

'Tha looks like Humphrey Bogart in that get-up!' said Hazel, nodding to where Rosie had turned her collar up against the rain.

Despite herself, Rosie laughed. 'It is man's stuff. I had no coupons and I got it second-hand from Albright's.'

Hazel helped her off with the sodden beige trench coat, now heavy with rain, hung the hat and ushered her into the lounge. She was about to turn for the kitchen when Rosie grabbed her.

Hazel turned. 'Hey, lass, whatever's the matter?'

For a moment Rosie couldn't speak. 'I've run away. I mean, I've left home.'

Hazel didn't miss a beat. 'Sit thee down by the fire.' She motioned to the grate, in which a coal fire was burning brightly. 'It's got a back-boiler,' she added, 'an' I was already jus' heating the water for a bath.'

They sat on the rug in front of the blaze, the dog between them, mugs of tea in hand.

Rosie shivered despite the fierce heat.

'Some bloody summer,' Hazel mumbled, looking out at the overcast sky. 'I do feel sorry for them boys, over there.'

There was a pause as they thought of what was happening just a few miles over the Channel.

'Tha's left the Old Bat then?'

Hazel's forthrightness kindled a wry grin in Rosie. 'Aye. I mean, yes. Left the Old Bat.'

Hazel laughed. 'Tha should be celebrating then, I reckon.'

Rosie shook her head. 'I just feel sad. And guilty, if I'm honest. What a mess!'

Hazel remained silent.

'I got angry at her,' Rosie explained.

'Aye, I reckon!'

'No, not ordinary angry. I went mad. I threw a water jug at her and it smashed.'

Her friend's jaw dropped. 'Bloody 'ell!'

'Yes. And it had been in the family for ages.' Suddenly she remembered. 'It was my grandmother's. It was a lovely old thing. It was an antique, you know.'

'And thy mother,' Hazel enquired. 'How did it start?'

'Years ago,' Rosie replied reflectively. 'It's been coming for a long time'

'But what 'appened today like?'

Rosie continued as if she hadn't heard. 'I didn't want it to end like that. We had a blazing row. I mean, blazing like the fires of Hell. I caught her reading my letters.'

Hazel, who was stoking the fire, suddenly dropped a large piece of coal. Her eyebrows rose.

'I tried to keep calm,' Rosie continued. 'I wanted her to know what a miserable person she is and what she had done. I thought I was being a grown-up. But my temper got the better of me and in the end I feel ashamed.'

Hazel patted her on the shoulder and shook her head. 'Most people would want revenge, I reckon. Mother or not. What she did was just plain wrong. Don't be so hard on thyself.'

Rosie shook her head. 'But that's not how I want to live – being angry, I mean. My father taught me to live and let live. Now I've let him down. Now it's almost like my mother's dead too, and I really am an orphan.'

'Tha didn't hit her with that jug?' said Hazel, suddenly wondering.

'No, no. She's alive, but I feel I've lost the last thread I had holding me anywhere. I've nowhere to go.' Rosie sniffed. She wasn't going to let herself give way to tears no matter what. Once you gave in to weakness there was no knowing where it would end. She wiped her face and took a gulp of tea.

'I had a row with Droopy,' Hazel volunteered. 'I expect she let you know. We all did, as a matter of fact. She'll moving out soon as her parents come and get her.'

'She said it was you that started it.'

Hazel laughed. 'Maybe I did. I got fed up of her. It were politics, that's all. Anyroad, I had my eye on this place. It's one of Morelli's.' She gestured around the sparsely furnished room.

'Morelli's?'

'Aye. He's got several in the town. I went to see him, and we had us a chat about this and that.' She put a finger to her lips. 'Least said soonest mended,' she said with grin. 'Anyroad, he had this one up on the board. Was going to rent it to one of his pals, but I took it.'

'But how will you afford it?'

'I'm a supervisor, lass, as of Friday.' She winked. 'And, besides, I shall have to get me a housemate.'

Hazel looked at Rosie and beamed.

CHAPTER 21

The crewmen, loaded with parachutes and sheepskins, waddled from the overworked jeep that had brought them bumping roughly over the grass to *Luck of the Devil,* their ship for nineteen missions.

Eugene scanned the faces. His gaze came to rest on Hank. The great barndoor of a man was leaning against the port undercarriage, as if he didn't have a care in the world. Eugene watched the boys dismounting, noisily shouting banter to each other.

The captain checked his watch. Perhaps, he reflected, the social glue of fear was a more effective adhesive than discipline. When all was said and done, the crew didn't fight for Uncle Sam, nor because they hated the enemy; they weren't there because they wanted to follow their captain nor did they give a damn about the colonel, who would, even now, be watching them from the tower through those binoculars of his. They fought to earn the right to go home.

As a rule, Eugene chose what he had to say carefully and didn't raise his voice. But today his temper was fraying. He felt jagged, mind abraded by fatigue and the bright, unconvincing alertness of Benzedrine. He counted the heads. One missing.

'Where the hell is Rick?' He was surprised at his own sharpness.

Someone coughed. 'He's, *uh,* in his room, Cap – seems he's ill or somethin'.'

'Yeah, like hell he is.' It was Tony, louder than the rest as usual. 'He's chicken. Why don't ya just say it, fer god sakes? The guy's been on the sauce since midnight. If ya ask me, we're need a new ball-turret gunner, and permanently.'

'This true?' Eugene asked sharply.

No one met his eye.

'Look, boss …' It was Billy. 'Rick's had a hard time at home, we all know that. He was real cut up about his dad passing. So, the dude's having a bad day. We only got to call the tower and get a replacement.'

'A bad day?' asked Tony, incredulously.

Eugene cursed quietly. Inside, he felt like quitting, and if everyone else started feeling the same way as he felt deep down inside, he didn't know if he could hold himself together. Abruptly he turned the anxiety into action, striding stiffly back towards dispersal, catching up with a passing fuel truck, grabbing the rail and hitching a ride.

'Someone's in for trouble,' said Babyface, gazing knowingly towards the barracks, where they could just make out their captain entering the building, its steel door closing rapidly behind him.

Hank stared thoughtfully after him before snapping out of it and motioning the crew to get aboard.

Inside the crew quarters, Eugene found the missing gunner.

'Rick?'

A pair of wide brown eyes beneath blonde lashes looked up from under a grubby baseball cap. Rick shifted uncomfortably on his bunk. He was wearing a flying suit, but not his Mae West.

'I can't find Donald.' The young man looked searchingly around.

'What?'

'I can't go without Donald, Cap, honest I can't. I know I'll never come back.'

Eugene drew in his breath. He hadn't understood the obsession with talismans that gripped so many airmen until he'd felt compelled to bring on board the picture he'd taken of the English girl.

'What's that in your pocket?'

'Oh this, ah, it's just a little bit of help.' The young man looked down. 'I need help these days.'

Eugene swiped the metal flask from his hand. It was almost empty. Drinking before a flight was one of the only pre-flight taboos they actually stuck to.

'*Goddam it, Rick!* This is the last time you are going to do this to me! We're all scared, OK? But we don't let each other down. How you gonna hit anything after this?' Eugene shook the flask demonstratively. 'What if we get attacked from below and it's your call?' He threw the small metal container on the bed. 'Now get your goddam kit.'

'But I can't, Captain,' the young man sobbed, suddenly moved to tears, 'I gotta have that duck. He's my lucky charm. He's kept me safe all this time.'

For a moment Eugene felt like grabbing the youngster and dragging him bodily to the plane. But he knew all too well how Rick was feeling. Instead he drew a breath and looked around the room; the neatly made beds, personal lockers, the larger wardrobes. The wardrobes. He'd caught the rest of the crew teasing Rick the night before, throwing his Donald Duck mascot around like a football. Striding over, he ran his hand along the top of the nearest wardrobe and felt something soft.

He pulled it down.

'This it?'

'Oh, thank God!'

Rick grinned as he caught the toy and held it to his chest.

'Thanks, Cap.'

Eugene nodded impatiently. 'Now get your kit and get moving.'

Rick hesitated.

'I mean it. If you don't get on the plane, Rick, the guys and me, we'll make sure you regret it. Get me?'

The young man met his eyes and rose, grabbing his life vest and following him meekly from the building.

Eugene returned to find everyone but the co-pilot aboard. Hank was wandering around doing a final check, wringing the last bit of flavour from his tobacco. As he saw Eugene, he spat the plug, wiped his mouth on his sleeve and clambered into the belly, patting the picture of Eugene's latest pretty girl that adorned the entrance. It had become a ritual they all observed. All three boarded.

Hank and Eugene synchronised watches and settled into their seats, clipping on oxygen and intercom.

Eugene could feel his hands tremble. It didn't help that today's was also a 'Maximum Effort' job, a complex operation to a deep penetration target. The last time they'd done that sixty-nine of six hundred planes had failed to return.

'*Call in!*'

The crew recognised Eugene's voice, clipped with tension but steady enough.

One by one the crew answered.

'*Tail-gunner checking in.*'

'*Left waist-gunner checking in.*'

There was a pause. Eugene pressed his mike.

'*Tony. Right-waist gunner, you there?*'

'*Right waist-gunner here, boss. I was just getting Rick into the ball turret. He*' *was a bit upset that he didn't get to pat the picture.'*

Hank and Rick exchanged glances.

'Good Lord preserve us!' Hank muttered.

'Upper turret, checking in.'

'Radio operator, checking in.'

Seconds after the roll call was completed, far across the field a white flare popped, arcing lazily into the grey overcast.

Hank glanced at Eugene.

'You good for this, Gene?'

Eugene nodded. 'Today I'm good, Hank.'

It wasn't true, but from somewhere he found just enough strength to hang on.

He gave the order.

'Pre-start check complete. Start engines.'

Hank switched on the fuel pumps and pressed the starter and 'mesh' buttons for each engine, and one by one the four huge Pratt & Whitney radials spluttered into life, their thrumming filling the cabin with a sound like a billion angry bees, making the instrument panel tremble and rendering conversation without their throat microphones impossible.

The take-off was uneventful, the lumbering bomber, its belly full of explosives, rising grudgingly into the air barely a hundred feet before the fence. It took an hour to claw their way to altitude and form up, and by then they were over the great North Sea, a flock of giant metal birds filling the sky from horizon to horizon as the friendly coast of England fell behind.

Before they were ordered to tighten up the formation, Eugene gave the order to test the guns, and to the harsh rattle of gunfire was soon added the whiff of cordite which percolated throughout the aircraft in a light grey fug.

Eugene was about to run through his instrument checks one more time when he heard something like music, but a way off. He pressed his throat mike.

'*Captain to waist-gunners, what's that?*'

There was a pause, then Tony's voice came crackling over the intercom.

'*It's that goddam chicken we got as a ball-gunner, boss – the sonofabitch is singing. I tried kicking on his turret lid but the critter won't shut up.*'

Straining his ears, Eugene could just make out what sounded like 'Chattanooga Choo-Choo'.

Suddenly Hank cut in.

'*Rick, goddam it. This is Hank. Shut that noise. We're about to enter enemy airspace. And keep your eyes peeled.*'

Eugene looked at his co-pilot, surprised.

Hank shook his head. 'Sorry, Eugene, but you gotta get a grip on that fella. He's getting to be a danger to us all, and he ain't gonna hit any Germans either, not if he's high.'

Behind his oxygen mask, Eugene blushed at the rebuke.

The fleet droned on, breaking through the clouds and into the perpetual sunshine. Brilliant white vapour trails streamed out behind, pointing to their location like thin, accusing fingers against the shrill blue sky. An hour later, they were passing the wave-line of the enemy coast, each man's pulse increasing as he found his own way of dealing with the rising tension. Hank checked his instruments, Billy hummed some cowboy song to himself, while Babyface simply drew the curtain on his window. Ammunition was checked for the fourth time, weapons cocked and uncocked. Gloved hands closed and unclosed around thin metal triggers as eyes strained, scanning the sky. Some stamped their feet or wrung their hands mechanically. It was hard to concentrate when the temperature was minus thirty and falling.

'*My god!*' It was Rick again on the intercom, his voice high-pitched in alarm. *'They're leaving us! The fighters are goddam leaving us!'*

They could hear the whirr of the motors as Rick's ball-turret rotated. The captain glanced up at the lighter contrails of the fighters. A sudden flurry of tiny black falling objects showed the Mustangs had jettisoned drop tanks, and were diving.

'Shut up, Rick, or so help me God, I'm gonna prise you outta that tin can and kick your miserable behind out into space!' It was Tony, more anxious than exasperated.

Eugene broke in to settle them down, his voice as level and calm as he could make it.

'Listen up, all of you. The fighters are leaving to sweep ahead. You'd have heard it at the briefing, if you were awake. They'll pick us up after the target. Now shut up and stay sharp.'

A moment later the singing started again. This time It was 'Don't Sit under the Apple Tree.'

'God dammit, Rick!' came Tony's Bronx voice.

There was a clang as a hand-wielded wrench made contact with the top of the ball-turret. Hank shifted in his seat, flexing a gloved hand.

'Want me to go shut him up?'

Eugene glanced at the co-pilot. It struck him that without his friend in the next seat he'd feel almost naked with vulnerability.

'No, Hank. We're almost at the target.' He cut into the intercom. *'Rick, this is Eugene. You got to keep quiet, OK? And Tony, just cool it.'*

Later, no one remembered whether Rick or Tony had answered.

'Eugene!'

Eugene barely recognised the screaming voice as Hank's.

His vison snapped back just in time to see the angry Fw 190 fighter in front of them, barely three hundred yards away and closing at five hundred miles an hour.

'Goddam it!'

He could hear the stutter of fifty-calibre fire from the upper turret. The fighter was still coming, its stubby wings expanding to fill their field of vision, the whirling black-and-white spinner on its nose oddly hypnotic. Would it be the last thing they saw? His brain slowed, and so did the world. He knew with an overwhelming certainty there was nothing he could do to save them. There was no time and the fortress, though strong, was slow to turn. He closed his eyes and hoped there would be no time for pain.

Seconds passed. But no hail of cannon shells came splintering through the fragile glass. Disbelieving, he opened his eyes. The engines were running, the gauges correct. Had he dreamt it? Was he hallucinating?

Then with a shudder and sound like a passing train, the Focke-Wulf was gone, diving away, disappearing below. It had been no dream.

'*God! His guns must have jammed! How freaking lucky is that?*' It was Hank, the big man's voice suddenly shrill like a schoolboy. He face was distorted into a mad grin. '*Ha-ha!*'

'*Too close! Goddam it!*' chided Babyface over the intercom. He'd seen the shadow of the Focke-Wulf pass narrowly in front of his curtain.

'*Fighters!*' Eugene heard himself yell. '*Call them out!*'

All over the ship anxious eyes scanned the sky.

'Oh Lord!' It was Hank again. This time his voice was unusually weak.

'What is it?' Eugene glanced at his co-pilot.

'He's collided with *Love and Liberty*. Cut their tail clean off. Oh my God, those poor boys!'

Eugene peered to the right. Far below, the doomed enemy fighter and disintegrating fortress rotated around each other in a perverse flaming ballet, whirring downwards like seeds from a sycamore tree.

He could see the fortress coming apart under the G-forces, fragments of aluminium and steel scattering over the sky. The laws of Karma had balanced out: one piece of good luck exchanged for one bad.

Eugene had Babyface switch him to the squadron radio.

'*This is Luck of the Devil. Any one see chutes from Love and Liberty?*' he asked, surprised at how tense he sounded.

There was a squeal of static and a few seconds later the reply came back.

'*No chutes.*'

He recognised the voice over the squadron net as Jake from '*You'll Remember Us*'.

'No chutes,' muttered Hank, 'Poor bastards.'

'*Two miles to target.*' Babyface's steady voice came over the intercom.

Eugene felt sick. He grabbed his co-pilot's arm.

'Hank, get ready to take the plane if I get hit.'

For a brief second their eyes met.

'Roger, captain. You'll be fine. Uh, I think we're drifting a bit.'

'Yeah.' Eugene made the necessary correction with the rudder. Keeping a tight formation was vital to ensuring a tight bombing pattern and minimising collateral damage. Today they were bombing rail yards and acres of civilian housing were just outside the target area.

'*Keep your eyes skinned, everyone, we're approaching the IP,*' he instructed.

'*I am ready down here, my captain.*'

Eugene recognized the strong Polish accent of Karl the bomb-aimer.

Suddenly the plane shook and along the metal outer skin something rattled like a pebble skipping over a tin roof. Simultaneously, ahead of the formation, dark black spots appeared in the sky, like inkblots flicked into water: tight and dark, but rapidly dispersing. Each one was an exploding flack shell, its hot metal shards now flying through space, seeking a target. Of metal. Or flesh. The flack was edging closer. The innocent-looking puffs crawling into the formation as the radar-guided guns zeroed in. Today the bursts seemed particularly numerous.

'*Well, I'll be doggone.*' It was the still lazy voice of Billy, in the waist-gunner's position.

'*Jus' how many guns they got down thar? It's sure getting might-tee thick.*'

'*It's crazy today!*' chipped in the Meatball. '*I ain't never seen so many guns.*'

'*About two hundred guns, according to the briefing. Radar Guided. Some in the city, some either side of our track,*' Eugene said.

'*What?*' It was Tony. '*Two goddam hundred? Hell, Cap, it's so thick, why dontcha just drop the gear and we'll go land on it?*'

There were a couple of laughs.

'*All crewed by Hitler Youth, Tony,*' Eugene came back, repeating a line from the briefing that neither he nor Hank believed. '*We'll be fine.*'

'*You tellin' me we're getting shot at by a bunch of lousy German boy scouts?*' Tony said.

An explosion beneath and in front of the aircraft caused the plane to shake and rise a dozen feet in the air. Everyone grabbed for something cling to.

'*Shit! You bastards! I don't care if you're schoolkids or not, take this!*'

They could hear the sound of Tony loosing off a burst of fifty-calibre fire at the ground.

'*Tom and Jerry's been hit,*' announced a voice.

'*Going down?*'

'*Negative. His number three's on fire though.*'

'*Shee-it, this stuff's getting personal.*' Another burst of fire from came from Tony. '*Bastards!*'

Shouts broke out again from all sides, becoming so numerous they merged into a tense melee of sound. The plane rose as if a giant hand had picked it up. High-pitched screaming came over the intercom.

'*Go away! Go away from me!*'

It was Rick. They could hear the shudder of the ball-turret's twin fifties firing. Then came a violent thud, followed by an ominous quiet.

The intercom crackled. Another voice came through.

'*Eugene. I think Rick's been hit. I'm going to get him out.*' It was Tony.

Eugene had no time to reply.

Babyface's voice came over the system again, clear and steady.

'*We're at the IP, captain. Begin the bomb run.*'

An amber light illuminated on the panel in front of Eugene and he heard Karl's precise Slavic accent.

'*Bomb-aimer to my captain. On bombing run.*'

'*Roger.*' Eugene flicked the amber switch. Beneath him in the nose, he could almost see Karl kneeling at the bombsight, staring at the ground beneath passing below through the glass floor. Now, thanks to the famous Norden bombsight, the Pole would be flying the plane as well as aiming the bombs.

'*You have the aircraft.*'

'*Roger, my captain. I am having the aircraft.*'

Seconds later they felt the heavy clunk as the bomb doors opened. Around them the flak groped closer, seeking their plane, now flying straight and level on its run-in, two hundred miles an hour suddenly felt like crawling along. Below them the streets and parks of the enemy city were unfolding like a tourist map. With nothing to do but wait, Eugene's fear reappeared. Now he and Hank were passengers, completely helpless, while below hundreds of Germans tried their best to send them to a fiery grave and the bomb-aimer tried to do the same to them.

'*Goddamit!*' he whispered to himself.

As the plane's engines hummed their remorseless tune, the seconds seemed to drag like hours. He glanced at Hank. The big man wasn't saying anything, but his body was hunched forward. He looked as tense as a rattlesnake curled up ready to strike.

'Come on, Karl, come on, for God's sake! Drop them why don't you?'

Still nothing happened. There was no relieving whistle of departing bombs, no upward surge as the weight was gone. Something inside him broke. He had to do something, anything.

'Hank, take over,' he announced abruptly. 'I'm going to see Rick.'

Clambering through the fuselage, Eugene found Rick on an ammunition box, back against the side of the plane. His face was a mass of blood and pulpy flesh, the contents of a first-aid kit were strewn around and Tony was trying to stem the copious red flow with cotton wound-patches. In his hand Rick clutched the singed remains of his Donald Duck mascot.

Eugene felt a stab of guilt. He'd forced the lad to fly.

'He's got flack splinters just about everywhere,' Tony informed him glumly.

Eugene knelt on the floor. Another flack round detonated outside and they all involuntarily ducked.

Eugene forced himself to seem strong. 'How are you, kid? Don't worry, we'll be on our way home soon, son.'

Eugene took off his gloves and felt the young man's pulse at the neck.

The kid tried to smile, but his eyes flickered. The pulse was dangerously weak.

CHAPTER 22

Rosie was glad Hazel had rung Morelli's from the red telephone box at the end of the street to get them the following day off. They'd slept late and spent the whole afternoon and on into the evening talking, the conversation flowing eccentrically between Hazel's past, surviving the experience of her father's death and growing up among five apparently brutish brothers, to Rosie's time at the orphanage. And, as they talked, Hazel seemed slowly to relinquish the role of the plain-speaking and the worldly wise. She was affectionate, and knew how to touch a person's heart. But she made Rosie feel respected too, her deepest thoughts prized. It was intoxicating to open herself this way, and to be encouraged to do so, like falling willingly under a spell.

It was true that Hazel would gently steer the conversation away from Eugene, on the occasions he stole into the dialogue, and Rosie had the vague idea that despite Hazel's increasing openness there was still something on her side, a dark or painful secret, that her friend was not revealing. But, compared with Eugene, how different it was to her talks with him! With the airman she felt she was sometimes putting on a performance, saying what she thought she should say, to impress or please. And, sometimes, when she'd think they were getting close, he'd withdraw, shutting himself inside an invisible shell she couldn't break through. True conversation with him, anything personal, was sporadic, like snatches of a voice emerging from a haze of static on the radio or bursts of sunlight on a squally English day. But that afternoon, the conversation with Hazel was more like a private line to the soul, and she felt herself bonding with the other woman with a speed so rapid it was like falling in love.

Eventually, the mundane need to feed their bodies, announced by the rumbling of their stomachs, burst through the dream, sending Hazel to the kitchen and Rosie upstairs for a bath.

Feeling tired but oddly complete, Rosie gratefully climbed the stairs.

'*End of corridor on left!*' Hazel shouted from below.

Rosie approached the enamel bath, put in the plug and cautiously turned the knobs. There was a hiss, and she watched in wonder as clean, scalding liquid began to fill the roll-top. She'd only ever bathed in a tin tub, never seen water running hot from a tap. Spotting a jar of green salts on the windowsill she opened it curiously and sniffed. It smelt pleasantly of pine, and without really knowing if it was the right thing to do, she tipped some into the rapidly filling bath and watched the water foam, kneeling and stirring it absently with her hands. The anticipation of slipping into the soft, hot water became a deep longing.

Clouds of swirling steam rose from the water's surface, filling the room, sheathing the mirror above the sink in a fine layer of condensation. Rosie undressed and clambered in, reclined with a sigh and let her body relax. Atop the water floated bergs of white foam which she pushed dreamily to and fro, and she exhaled, letting the cocooning embrace of the hot water seep into her bones as it freed her from the burden of gravity.

'*Is tha going to be in t'bath all bloody day?*' called a querulous voice.

Rosie's mind jarred back into consciousness.

'*Sorry, Hazel!*' she called. '*I'll be out in a minute!*'

'*Aye, well, don't forget to leave me some water!*'

Rosie dragged herself reluctantly out, feeling at once the pitiless downward force of the earth and the comparative chill of the air. She dried herself with a coarse white towel, wrapped her hair in another, and put on a bathrobe that was hanging on the back of the door.

Gathering up her clothes, she made her way down the corridor, yelling down the bath's availability. In the bedroom, she found that the satin curtains and blackout sheets had already been drawn, shutting out the outside world. The walls were covered with pink flock paper and there was some basic furniture: a veneered wardrobe, a bedside cabinet, and an ornate iron bed. After the awful row with her mother it was a haven, clean and safe. She dressed in the pyjamas Hazel had set so kindly on the pillow and sank into the well-upholstered double bed. Rosie's body tingled and she felt lightheaded as she spread out, luxuriating in the novel experience of space, and freedom. She focused her thoughts. She'd left home, and part of her was surprised at her own strength in having finally done it. She had survived the row, and, amid a pool of conflicting emotions, a wave of guilty triumph rippled briefly through her mind.

She heard Hazel go into the bathroom. Sometime later she emerged and Rosie could hear her pad down the thickly carpeted stairs.

She lay a while staring at the ceiling. Her life had entered a new phase, not as she'd planned but she was moving at last, onwards and hopefully upwards. She caught the welcome aroma of something cooking, and the alarm bell of hunger rang again, more insistent this time. Rosie got up and, finding a man's dressing gown on the back of the door, put it on, just in time to hear Hazel calling from downstairs.

Their feast turned out to be bowls of some tinned stew and potato, set out in the dining room with a grinning Hazel behind one of them. From the kitchen came the unmistakable *schlopp*ing sounds that suggested Peter was already enjoying his.

She sat opposite Hazel at the small square oak dining table and from bottles in the middle, Hazel poured them glasses of Rum and Coca-Cola, with very generous measures of rum. Even though there was still light in the sky, she'd drawn the curtains and even lit tall red candles. It seemed to go with the general madness of the day, and the pyjamas and dressing gowns they were both wearing. The flickering light danced on the table in yellow pools, where swirls in the wood reflected back the gentle flames. The morning's storm was returning with a vengeance, and the wind whistled hollowly down the chimney behind the ornate tiled fireplace. The gale slung raindrops viciously against the windows like lashes from a whip. Little wonder people were calling it the worst summer for a hundred years. It was good to be indoors, especially with Hazel.

'*Cheers!*' Hazel lifted a glass.

Rosie grinned and took a gulp, the sweet aromatic liquid warming the back of her throat like the cough medicine her father gave her as a child. For a second she could hardly speak. 'This is strong stuff to be drinking in your pyjamas!' she managed at last.

They laughed, ate, drank and talked, speculating noisily and disrespectfully between mouthfuls about the family that had lived in the house before the war, their lives, loves and even the manner of their deaths, for it seemed the former tenants had both been killed in a raid, ironically while in a municipal shelter in Coveringham.

Rosie looked around. 'It feels odd, not having parents upstairs … or someone at least,' she said.

'Aye. This can be our own little house. You will stay, won't you?'

Rosie swallowed a mouthful of potato and nodded. 'If you'll have me.'

'Of course I will!' Hazel replied, grinning her infectious grin. 'Home sweet home!' She reached over and took Rosie's hand. 'Thank you, lass, for being my best friend.'

'It's me that needs a best friend,' Rosie replied truthfully, 'and I do need a home.' She felt the deepening sense of gratitude that only someone in real need ever knows.

'We all do, pet.'

Hazel's green eyes seemed to be positively glowing and Rosie noticed how beautiful they were, and at this moment strangely hypnotic.

'I wonder,' said Rosie suddenly, 'can you be best friends with a man?'

Hazel inhaled deeply. 'Doubt it, but I suppose it depends on the man,' she replied, tucking a generous forkful of the stew and potato into her mouth.

Rosie considered. 'Doesn't the …' she paused, 'the sex thing get in the way?' She couldn't stop a giggle and put a hand over her mouth. '*Oops!* Dirty word. I shouldn't say it. I should say what my mother says: S.E.X. She spells it out, letter by letter!'

'Nay?'

'Aye! S.E.X. – sex!'

They both dissolved in laughter.

'Speaking of S.E.X.,' said Rosie, suddenly serious. 'Eugene … he …'

'He's tried it on?'

Rosie nodded. She'd been wanting to share the experience.

Hazel paused, spoon halfway to her mouth.

Rosie went on. 'Yes, but I … I wasn't ready. It wasn't just that there could be consequences ... I wasn't sure enough of him. Part of me wanted to have "You Know" ... but part was just afraid. It just seemed ... overwhelming. And he seemed so driven, so ... urgent. I wasn't sure it was me he wanted or just the thing itself.'

'S.E.X. Aye.' Hazel's eyes seemed to have grown larger, rounder. A fuller, richer green.

'He was so ... blind,' Rosie continued. 'Are men all like that? So one-tracked ... thinking in straight lines, and short-term, for what they want at the moment?' Her father, for one, seemed to offer a contradiction.

Hazel nodded. 'Aye. Most are. I never understood 'em, truth to tell. But this thing in all of them, this desire to push on – they have to, what's the word ... strive. It's not a choice even, and it does makes 'em blind. They just go right for the goal and miss all else. Screwing women or building empires. It's the same thing. *Allus pushing on. Pushing on.*'

Rosie's eyebrows rose, surprised at the sudden venom in her friend's voice.

Hazel continued. 'I saw it in the pits, in the digging for coal. Burrowing like animals in the earth. Deeper, always pushing forward, blind like. It's there in the war an' all – the same. Invadin', pushin', destroyin'. 'Tis their nature. They see only what they want, an' they must 'ave it. They don't think of t'consequences.' She paused, swallowing another spoonful of stew. 'An' after a lifetime of it, or when they're spent, when all energy's gone, they seem to just give up and die.'

It seemed to Rosie a grim view to hold of men, and life.

'And what are we women then?' The drink was seeping into her bones, and her flesh tingled.

Hazel gulped a mouthful and carried on. 'We're meant to hope, m'dear. Oh, an' deny ourselves. Always go without. Give up what we want for the man, and his children. We persuade, we plan, we leap at chances. An' we take our smaller pleasures where we find 'em. Like eating t'leftovers, or what fall's from the man's table.'

Rosie raised her eyebrows. 'And that's ... it?'

'It's what men 'ave left us. There's nothing else, unless tha wants to be a rebel. An' an outcast. Or, perhaps, unless tha's rich an' can afford an education. 'Tis different if tha has money. Everthin's different then.'

'But having children is a kind of power, isn't it, and a kind of ... wealth? And men can't do that.'

'That's what they want you to think,' Hazel replied grimly. 'But what about living your life as your own? Not through children or husband, but as who you really are? As who you were born to be?' Hazel's eyes were burning, her conviction real and passionate as though a deep nerve had been struck. 'Any ole fool can 'ave a child, but I want summat as will last for longer than a 'uman life.'

Rosie stared. 'Like what?'

'Like a new bloomin' world. A better world.'

'A socialist one?'

'Tha's learnin'. Hazel held up the empty rum bottle. '*Bugger!*'

The alcohol was clearly getting to her, her softer manner of the afternoon slipping back into the coarser, more gritty girl Rosie nevertheless admired.

Hazel stood before swaying gently out to the kitchen, returning rapidly with a fresh bottle. In her other hand was a large plate on which rested two oranges which she placed in front of Rosie.

She sat back down and topped up the glasses with the golden-brown rum.

'Drink up!' she said.

Rosie closed her eyes and took a gulp. This time the drink stunned her throat rather less and she was able to follow the first gulp rapidly with a second. It seemed suddenly funny to sit drinking in the afternoon. Like a man, and of the worst kind.

'Oranges!' she exclaimed, gazing in surprise at the impossible fruit.

'I got them from some spiv in town. Same place I got the rum.' Hazel took a slug of rum. 'You was talkin' about thy feller tryin' it on?'

Rosie re-adjusted her mind. Her thoughts were getting harder to grasp but it felt pleasant, like the feeling of sitting on a swing and soaring up into the air. 'Yes. He did.'

'But, tha hasn't?' Her words were a little slurred.

Rosie shook her head. 'No. Of course not.'

Hazel looked relieved. She nodded at the oranges. 'Had to pay through the nose for these. I can never peel them. Can tha?'

She peered quizzically at Rosie, who nodded. Her mother had, in one of her saner moments, taught her how to remove the peel with her nails, keeping it in one long piece.

The brightly coloured fruits seemed suddenly very beautiful. Rosie took one and ran her hands over the surface. 'Smooth, but not smooth,' she found herself saying, almost to herself.' She giggled. 'Slippery, but not slippery.'

'What is tha talkin' about?'

'The orange!' Rosie, who could feel the alcohol furring her brain, replied with the air of someone who had discovered a truth about the universe and was explaining it in the simplest possible language. 'It's smooth, you see, but has fine little bumps all over it. And it seems slippery, almost oily but, you see, it's dry.' Suddenly the texture seemed vitally important.

With an effort, Hazel picked up an orange and using her nails began to pry off the skin.

'I'd rather eat the bugger than talk about it,' she said, belching suddenly. 'Oh, pardon me, m'dear.' She leant across the table and topped up Rosie's glass.

Shedding the peel, they teased apart the naked fruits, splitting them into halves and segments. Sweet glistening juice ran from their fingers as they gorged. To Rosie eating them held a hint of the forbidden, the black market; a faint suggestion of danger, made stronger by the conspiratorial glow of candlelight.

Rosie's eyelids closed, and for a moment her consciousness was gripped with pleasure, devoted to the single task of absorbing and remembering the texture and the flavour she'd stored from years earlier.

When she looked again she found a pair of huge green eyes very close, looking steadily back at her. They were like jewels in the candlelight and in the irises Rosie became aware of flecks of amber and brown. Hazel's skin glowed, shining as though illuminated from inside. Her mouth remained fixed in a kind of wrestling match between the fruit, her lips and tongue, yet her attention was on Rosie. There was a faraway look in those eyes, as though she too was remembering something pleasant from a long time ago. Among the many things the look suggested was mischief.

Finishing the orange, she spoke: 'Has tha seen upstairs? Four bedrooms an' every one has a double bed in.'

'Every room?'

'Aye. No kids' beds, just doubles. Bit odd, in't it?' She popped a final segment of orange into her mouth. 'Seen a lot of action, I expect!'

'Hazel!' The exclamation was just a reflex. Rosie found she wasn't shocked. She heard herself laugh. 'What sort of action?'

'Tha knows. Sex. S.E.X. Having relations.' She paused. 'Fucking.'

Rosie found herself pleasantly shocked, a curious thrill running inside her belly at the use of the most forbidden word. The 'F' word.

'Well, I suppose ...'

'Aye. Men and women.' Hazel paused. 'Men and men and women and women, too, I wouldn't wonder.'

Rosie's eyebrows shot up. 'Men and men?' Her mind reeled as it tried to calculate the possibilities. 'But women and women. I mean, a woman can't ...'

They giggled.

'No?' said Hazel thoughtfully. She leaned forward and cupped Rosie's face in her hand. 'If it were possible for one woman to love another ... I mean, as one ...' she sought for the words ... 'as one soul loves another, I would love you, Rosie.'

It seemed so matter of fact, reasonable even said aloud, that Rosie found herself agreeing. It was enough to keep feelings under wraps when in public, but there was no denying here with Hazel how much she wanted, and needed, to be loved. She dropped her spoon, and covered her tearing eyes with her hand.

Hazel reached over and with her napkin dabbed the juice from Rosie's mouth and chin, and the tear from her cheek.

Rosie looked at her friend and she was struck by just how much a face can say without words. Here was someone who wanted her, and needed her.

'I'll not hurt thee,' Hazel said. 'Not like a man can hurt thee.' She reached out and touched Rosie's hair, then leant across the modest table and somehow it came as no surprise to Rosie when she felt her kiss, first on her cheek and then on the lips.

Later she would not remember how she came to be in Hazel's room. She simply found herself lying in a winged chair, a hand lolling off the arm, head propped on a soft cushion. Her pyjama top was lying on the floor, with only the bottoms remaining. The room was in semi-darkness, lit only by a shaft of light from the landing, which penetrated the gloom with a narrow yellow beam.

Hazel, with her back towards her, was standing by the mahogany bed, silently shedding her own nightwear. As she unbuttoned the pyjama top, dim rays of light illuminated her strong arms, and broad shoulders. Rosie could just make out moles in the centre of her back, near to the spine. They formed a straight line running downwards, like the three stars in Orion's sword. He'd been a hunter, had Orion, she remembered, strong and swift, and it seemed appropriate that Hazel's back should bear his mark.

The dim light glowed briefly on the globe of Hazel's short golden hair as she cast the pyjama top to the floor. Next to go were the pyjama bottoms, revealing a small, pert behind clad in ivory satin knickers.

Hazel turned and smiled, letting her knickers fall to the floor. Somewhat to her surprise, Rosie didn't feel embarrassed. Instead, the sense of intimate connection she'd felt earlier, when they'd been merely talking, returned with even greater strength. Her friend's figure, Rosie noticed, was slender, yet finely curved, something an artist might admire. She was slim, the modest swellings of her breasts matching the outward curve of her hip, a womanliness that had until then had been almost concealed behind the trousers and overalls Hazel so often wore. Her skin was radiant, almost golden in the reduced light, which was nevertheless strong enough to cast intriguing blueish shadows into her hollows.

Hazel smiled and turned a full circle, displaying her nakedness in the intimacy of the room's dim glow. She was completely unashamed of her body, as though sharing it with another was the most natural thing in the world. Rosie knew, even though the fuzziness of the rum, that the mood was sliding inexorably into something different, but she felt disinclined to deny the new warmth in her stomach and the curious aching longing in her thighs. She'd left home, and what she did now seemed no one's business but her own, a rightful fruit of independence. She had a vague sense she was being steered, perhaps even manipulated into a kind of submission, yet she went knowingly, and freely.

Hazel drew closer, and Rosie stood. She let Hazel tug down her pyjama bottoms and stepped out of them as they hit the floor. Facing, their naked bodies were almost touching. There was no sound in the empty house, except the ticking of the hall clock and the faint crackle of the fire downstairs.

'*My love*,' Hazel said, cupping Rosie's face in her hands, her deep green eyes slowly closing.

'*Hazel*,' Rosie heard herself say.

Hazel's lips touched her own, a caress so soft it seemed scarcely more than the brush of a butterfly's wing. The sensation was pleasant, and instinctively Rosie let her own eyes close. The lips withdrew momentarily, so that for one delicious moment Rosie could feel her friend's warm rummy breath while the kiss she now wanted with increasing desire hovered just out of reach. The lips returned, firmer this time, yet still with an underlying tenderness, as though this were an enquiry, or reconnaissance, rather than a conquest, or penetration.

Hazel pushed forward, their wet lips sliding over and around each other until they finally clamped harder together. As their tongues met, Rosie felt herself falling, and melting.

Hazel had been right about a woman's kiss.

Hazel's fingers were running through her hair and caressing her neck. She opened her eyes to find herself gazing into Hazel's own.

'*I love thee,*' Hazel whispered.

Her breath was hot and smelled of rum and, when Rosie kissed her again, she tasted of the drink more clearly, mixed this time with lipstick. Their lips met and parted, a thin line of drool still joining them. They kissed, again and again, Hazel's mouth slipping onto her face, brushing Rosie's eyes, her brow, her nose before biting gently at her neck.

'*I want thee, Rosie Haskell. I want thee.*'

Despite the kiss, it came as a surprise when Hazel's fingers slid gently between her legs and she heard herself gasp, her body arching and stiffening before slowly relaxing again. The kiss had been beautiful, but she felt a surge of guilt for allowing Hazel to invade, however gently, the most private part of her. Yet the sensation was so glorious, so sweetly intense she couldn't make herself stop her. She realised that Hazel must have wanted this from the moment they'd met.

There was a rising urgency to Hazel's motions, but it was more like the swelling of the sea than a forceful stream. And the sense of mounting pleasure between Rosie's legs was becoming insistent. She could hear herself moaning. Hazel kissed her again, her strong arms sliding firmly around Rosie's slim body, the embrace tightening. Rosie closed her eyes, and they slid against each other, arms entwining in a motion that flowed sinuously as though they were two liquids, one being poured into the other. Their bellies collided, the soft marshmallow mounds kissing, sending a sharp frisson of electricity flashing like stark, aching lightning that made them both gasp.

Hazel led her to the bed and they half fell, landing side by side. There was a longing, an expectancy and desire in Rosie's belly. She wanted to be touched. She felt her hands grasping Hazel's back, pulling her closer. Their legs were entwining. Then Hazel's warm fingers slid between her legs and she moaned. She'd become suddenly taken over by instinct, her fingers gripping Hazel's shoulders as pleasure coursed through her body. The tempo of Hazel's fingers increased and the explosion when it came caught her by surprise. She heard herself cry out, as her back arched and she came loudly, in a shuddering flood so powerful she lay afterwards, panting and breathless.

CHAPTER 23

Eugene sipped his now-cold coffee and looked distractedly around the utilitarian Quonset hut office he shared on an informal rota with the other captains of his flight. He put the small bundle of scented, unopened letters bearing US stamps back in his pocket. They represented a part of his past he'd rather forget. They could wait. He had more important things on his mind.

He couldn't get the last half hour of their last trip out of his head. He'd been kneeling in the fuselage, near the gaping hole of the waist-gun position, the kid lying on one side and Tony on the other.

'I'm sorry, Cap, sorry I let you down.'

Eugene had to bend close to hear Rick's thin voice above the roar of the engines.

Rick held up a bloody hand, still holding his Donald Duck, which Eugene reached out to clasp. 'I guess old Donald must have been sleeping today, *huh*?' He tried to grin. With difficulty he continued, 'I sure feel like having a sleep myself, Cap. Can I, would it be OK?'

'*No!*'

The bleeding was getting worse, thin rivulets of it seeping out at the zippered joints in the flight suit, before freezing in the extreme cold. If they were on the ground they could have torn the suit off and dressed the wounds, but up here he'd freeze.

'Listen, Rick!'

The boy's eyes were getting misty, but they rotated slowly to come to rest on Eugene's face.

'You gotta try and stay awake until we get back to base. It's not long now.' Reaching out, Eugene took the felt toy and held it up, the fabric torn and scorched brown by red-hot steel shell splinters. 'I guess it'll be two Purple Heart's today,' he joked. 'One for you and one for Donald.'

Rick smiled back, but the grin stayed oddly frozen on his face. To his horror Eugene saw the boy's pupils widen, becoming almost entirely black.

'Rick!' He shook the young man, but there was no response.

Eugene felt Tony's hand on his shoulder. Then Tony reached forward and gently closed Rick's now sightless eyes.

Eugene didn't know how long he stayed there on the floor. He then heard Tony speaking, his Bronx accent cutting through the noise of rushing wind and droning engines.

'I'm going back on the guns, Cap. The flack's stopped. The fighters will be back soon.'

Eugene nodded, before rising and swaying back to the cockpit, just in time to hear the bomb-aimer declare 'Bombs gone!' The plane gave an abrupt upward heave as six thousand pounds of weight fell away, and around them the air was alive with the demonic whistling of tumbling ordnance. The bombs fell shrieking in lines, each stacked one above the other, like bullets in the magazine of a pistol.

Sliding into the pilot's seat, Eugene clipped on his lines and nodded to Hank.

'*I have the aircraft.*' He said the words into the intercom, surprised at his own calmness when faced with a reassuringly familiar task.

'*You has the aircraft, my captain,*' crackled Karl's deadpan East-European voice.

'Let's get out of here.' It was Hank, his brow furrowed as he glanced warily out of the cockpit.

Eugene didn't need any second bidding.

'Yeah. Let's, and fast.'

He pushed the throttles forward and the plane surged towards those that had already bombed and were exiting the target. The formation was making a gracefully slow turn to port. Everywhere anxious eyes were scanning the sky.

'*Fighters, 12 o'clock, high!*' This time it was the mid-upper gunner.

There followed the shudder of twin fifties firing.

'*I see 'em!*' Meatball yelled from the tail.

For a few moments the B17 shook with the vibration of fifty-calibre guns, their shuddering and barking making the plane tremble, and filling the fuselage with the bitter tang of gun smoke and tumbling showers of brass cartridge cases. Then, without warning, it was suddenly quiet again. Only the mechanical throb of the engines could be heard, steady and harmonious.

'*Where'd they go?*' It was Meatball.

His question went unanswered. As often happened, the sky which had been so full of whirling machines was suddenly empty, the great vault of blue stretching above like a heavenly dome, so serene it was as though nothing untoward ever happened there. The faithful radial engines droned obliviously on as the formation headed home.

Hank usually flew the plane back to base, so Eugene went back into the fuselage and lowered himself into the ball turret, clipped on the safety line and plugged in his suit. He was too big for the space and had to bring his knees into his chest to fit, his boots skidding on a slippery ooze of blood. He shut the lid behind him. Cocooned in the tiny capsule, he used the levers to move the turret on its electric motors. Through splayed feet he could see the central pane of glass had been cracked by the flak. Outside the wind howled past at 200 mph, an icy stream that made him glad he was wearing fur-lined boots.

He rotated the turret and scanned the formation. Here and there a hole had appeared in a fuselage or tail, and one plane had a smoky engine, but most of the flight seemed to be there.

Eugene walked from his desk to the window of the base office. In the typewriter the sheet of headed paper still sat, accusingly blank after half an hour's thought. It was his fault. If he hadn't bullied the kid, he'd still be alive. They could have picked up a reserve gunner easily enough, as the crew had suggested. Absently he flicked through the small box of personal belongings on the desk. A packet of cigarettes, a baseball glove, a wallet and a few letters and photographs from home. He turned the pictures upside down so he wouldn't have to look at the accusing faces.

Perhaps, he thought, if he'd carried out the pre-flight checks he'd skipped that day, they might have arrived over the target a minute later, and missed the shell that had flown the five miles up from the ground to strike them. Perhaps if he'd used a more exaggerated pattern for weaving the aircraft, they might have dodged it. A little bit to the right or left. He'd consumed more than a bottle of whiskey the night after their return, and now he had the DTs, his hands shaking as he lit a cigarette. Reluctantly he began to type one-fingered on the stiff clacking keyboard.

'Dear Mr. and Mrs. McGraw,' he began. **'It is my painful duty to enclose the personal effects of your son, Rick.'**

He took a long drag on the Lucky Strike and glanced at the crib sheet that another pilot from the squadron had given him. It had been doing the rounds, full of standard platitudes and short, soothing but euphemistic phrases. Most of the captains used it when it was necessary to write a condolence. He pushed it aside. He was going to make himself do it without help.

'As you know,' he continued, **'Rick was a ball-turret gunner in our plane, an important position but one he undertook well and without complaint.'** He gulped. **'It is no exaggeration to say that Rick saved us on many occasions from enemy fighters. He was an excellent shot and a fine airman. Most of all, he was one of us, the crew of a B17, and we will miss him like we would miss a brother.'**

Eugene rose restlessly and went to the window. Over at the main building green army lorries were unloading a batch of new recruits. Like chicks emerging from beneath the wings of their mother, they came blinking innocently into the sunlight, looking around with awe, and pointing. He shook his head and went back to the desk. He added a couple more feeble paragraphs before finishing, extracting the paper, carbon and air-force copy and signing it. He wondered what some other officer might write about him if he bought it, and winced. If they knew him, really knew him, not much of it would be good. The Air Force was supposed to have been his new start, but any day now he could screw that up, another in the long list of screw-ups from the car crash that had put his brother in the Pacific to the woman whose name could hardly bring himself to utter, but who even now was somewhere back in the States probably scheming his downfall. And now there was Rick.

Eugene folded the letter, placed it in the out-tray and tried to think about Rosie. She was refreshing, young and untainted by knowledge of either his past, or the war. And she seemed, if not to hang on his every word, then at least be willing to listen. If only he'd met her first, when he was young. An impossible thought.

Outside the office a group of women – British WAAFs – were being noisily shown around by an overly enthusiastic officer from the unit's press corps. They were fresh-complexioned English girls, pristine in their blue uniforms. He couldn't help automatically undressing them, imagining each with a different outfit of lingerie. God! He needed relief. Despairingly he stood and mentally shook himself like a dog dispelling water.

He thought of Rosie, how beautiful she was, how unspoiled, fresh and clean. So different from the cynical, precocious girls back home. She didn't deserve a bum like him. In the cooler part of his mind there were times he actually admired her for defending her virginity. But not when the mood gripped him, which it did nowadays with obsessive frequency. Her denial of his needs might be morally right, but it tested the limits of his patience and he knew he wouldn't be able to restrain himself much longer from a far worse outburst.

The redhead at the M.O's office, on the other hand, had signalled loud and clear that she was available, her tight white uniform barely concealing a curvaceous body that, in his worst fantasies he longed to possess and subdue. The woman herself was, of course, what his mother would have called 'the worst kind': calculating, without morals and, if the rumours were true, wildly promiscuous. Damn, this was getting to be a problem. But he couldn't stop the thought of her ample breasts exposed to him and waiting for him to touch. Or kiss. She would have the sly knowing look, the one she often bestowed on him, that seemed proof of both illicit knowledge and bad intentions.

Whenever they'd meet, which was often in the confines of the base, she always managed to brush against him, accidentally or on purpose.

Eugene exhaled and drew another cigarette from the rapidly depleting pack. He had to get her out of his head. Like a pilgrim reaching for a relic, he fumbled for the picture of Rosie. He'd had it taken that day they'd spent hopping from café to café to keep out of the endless British rain, and it was a duplicate of the one that now adorned *Luck of the Devil.* She was the kind of girl you'd dream about, or even, in an ideal world, marry. A fine soul, far beyond the sordid business of war, of killing and being killed. Even the crew had seen something they imagined was pure and even saintly about her, an idealist and probably imaginary fixation but one that that had turned her into some kind of holy icon the ship carried to ward off evil, and German bullets.

CHAPTER 24

It was only weeks after her arrival at Hazel's house but even in that short time, Rosie reflected as she washed her face at the bathroom sink, she'd learned more about her friend than she'd have done in years as things were before. What passed between them in the bedroom no longer caused her the twinge of guilt she'd felt the morning after the first night, but what Hazel assured her would be the world's reaction to their relationship most certainly disturbed her.

Rosie finished her ablutions and made her way downstairs, following the yelled call summoning her to the back door.

The world seemed so irrationally hostile to the idea of two women loving each other, and Hazel had been insistent on impressing that fact on her over and over, so much so that Rosie began to wonder whether it reflected some dark event in Hazel's past. She'd been stunned at the cruel names people could apparently give to women who happened to love other women: 'queers', 'dykes' or 'inverts', and sensed a vague threat of violence also existed. So she'd done her part, going in to work and leaving separately, being careful of where they were seen together, and of what she said to others by way of their friendship when Hazel wasn't around. But the lie was suffocating, and unnatural, and seemed to threaten the very happiness they'd found.

Their social life, of course, had shrunk to zero, except the new trips to the Labour Party talks that Hazel seemed to enjoy so much, especially when there was a female speaker. It intrigued Rosie that among these gatherings there seemed to be a number of other strong, confident women, not unlike Hazel. Rosie, however, would prefer to talk in a quiet lounge bar, or walk through the town. But Hazel refused to go to her old haunts there, as if somehow the regulars would know, or guess the relationship between them. Naturally, they lacked a car or the petrol coupons to run one but, had they had a vehicle, Hazel would have insisted on driving it as far away as possible.

The contradiction between their lives at home and in public began to grate and Rosie was growing to resent a world that demanded her life be rigidly compartmentalised. She couldn't turn her affections on and off, like a switch, and it stung her that she was forced to do so. She longed to be open and matter of fact, to share the new affection she'd found, except of course with Eugene. She needed time to think what to do about him, and them. And then there was the sex thing. Her upbringing urged shame, and guilt, but she rejected both. It had been an experience of tenderness, of joy, and the physical pleasure opened an entirely new and beautiful world. She would *not* regret it. Yet Hazel's drive for sexual touch, for bed, seemed insatiable, even obsessive and more like the kind of men she purported to despise.

Rosie sighed. She'd begun to learn their differences, and well as their coincidences.

'*Coom on!*'

Rosie reached the foot of the stairs to find her friend waiting impatiently. She followed her out to the garage, where Hazel opened the doors.

'*God, Hazel! It's enormous!*' Rosie stared at the hulking metal machine her friend had somehow sneaked into the garage.

Sunlight was falling through the doorway, hitting the chrome handlebars which gleamed temptingly. The motorcycle was over six feet from end to end, and had both rider and pillion seats. The masculine protrusion of the engine stuck out beneath the black frame, while the bulbous red tank bore a pad for the rider's knee and the words '*Royal Enfield*' in shiny gold lettering.

'Taken prisoner by the Japs, the feller that owned it.' Hazel didn't take her eyes off her new possession. 'An 'is wife let me have it fer thirty quid. It's a five hundred and right scary quick.'

'A five hundred ? How on earth did you get it here?' Rosie asked, taking hold of the grab-rail and sensing the bike's weight.

'I rode the bloody thing, how else?'

Rosie laughed. 'What? But, how did you, I mean, who taught you?'

She'd seen riding as a dark art, something which only men like her father were capable of.

'Behold!' said Hazel pulling out a paper manual with a flourish. 'T'instruction book.'

Rosie gasped. 'You never rode it just by reading the instructions?'

'I only bloody well did. It's not hard when tha gets the hang of it. Starting the bloomin' thing is the only buggeration. Help me push the old girl out.' Then she stopped and turned, as if compelled by a sudden burst of honesty. 'I did fall off 'er once or twice.'

They pushed the heavy bike out onto the drive and Rosie closed the garage door behind them. The machine smelt agreeably of oil and sweet, dizzy petrol. Hazel bent over it and sniffed.

'Lovely!' she grinned. 'I love the smell of machines. Something sexy about 'em.'

Rosie shook her head. Her friend had a fondness for the sensual –

sensations of touch, smell, taste.

'Thy bum goes here,' Hazel was saying, patting the pillion seat. She bent and sniffed the seat and looked wickedly at her friend. 'Lovely smell of leather.'

She was outrageous, thought Rosie, but grinned.

'And my bum goes here.' She patted the rider's seat, gazing thoughtfully at Rosie.

Rosie shook her her head and laughed, slipping on the pair of goggles and the cap Hazel had bought for her. Hazel donned the helmet she'd got for herself and they looked at each other.

'You look like George Formby in '*No Limit!*' Rosie laughed, her anxieties forgotten. 'Only prettier,' she added, noting Hazel's mock-offended expression.

Hazel grinned and mounted the bike, which was still partly supported by its side stand, grunting at the weight as she lifted it upright.

'Are we going out on it now?' asked Rosie, who had only just begun to take in what the bike meant for them, the freedom and fun it held. She thought of her father and it suddenly struck her that for the first time she was able to smile at his memory and not feel sad.

'Aye, why not?' Hazel grinned. 'Tha's not chicken, is tha? Besides she needs some oil.'

Hazel pushed the kick start to the bottom of the stroke, and let it rise. Abruptly she raised her foot and kicked hard. The rather lopsided technique worked. The engine coughed, a thumping tick-over turning into a roar as she twisted the grip.

'*Where did you get the petrol?*' asked Rosie above the noise, astonished that someone the size of Hazel would have the courage to do something she'd only seen her father do before.

'*Tank were full, and I reckon I can get the necessary on the Q.T. I know 'ow.*'

Hazel pulled on what looked like an old leather flying jacket.

It came as no surprise that Hazel should be acquainted with the black market. She took the pullover Hazel held out for her and tugged it over her head, before closing the house door and clambering aboard.

'*Put yer arms around my waist!*' Hazel shouted over her shoulder. '*Sit yer arse on the seat and hold on!*'

Grinning, Rosie obediently clambered aboard. It seemed strange but somehow fitting she should be on a motorcycle again, and with someone who loved her.

With a jolt they were off, the gravel drive slipping away rapidly beneath them until they reached the smoother surface of the road. There was a brief wobble as they turned right and then they were away, the bike accelerating so fast Rosie felt herself being pushed backwards, making her shriek with laughter and tighten her arms around Hazel's waist. A draught of cool air hit Rosie's face, the scent of hot oil blending with the tang of suburban gardens: fresh cut grass, clipped privet and the bark of cedars, drying like spices in the sun. Faster and faster the bike went, the verges flying past in a matted blur of green and brown.

Suddenly they were entering a curve, but they were carrying too much speed. The bike leant further and further over, drifting dangerously close to the road's edge, their knees and even elbows getting awfully close to the rushing black tarmac. She closed her eyes and waited for the crash. But suddenly they were upright again, the road straightening, the bend receding and above the noise came Hazel's demented laughter, which Rosie heard herself joining in. They hit the dual carriageway and the road widened, the machine still accelerating, the pressure of the wind growing intense so it became hard to breathe. Beneath them sharp, tingling vibrations ran up from the throbbing engine through the seat and into their bodies. There seemed like nowhere they couldn't go and nothing they couldn't do. The old excitement was back. It was wild and free and she grinned like a maniac.

But all too soon the by-pass petrol station loomed on the near side ahead. Hazel must have been late in spotting it, for the front of the machine dived suddenly under heavy braking, and Rosie felt the rear tyre wriggling disconcerting beneath them. There was the smell of burning rubber, the bike flicked briefly left then right in a short skid, and they were off the main road, shooting up an exit ramp and coming to an unsteady halt on the forecourt, at which point the machine fell one way and the girls the other, Hazel on top of Rosie.

Observing the scene, an old man in greasy blue overalls wandered slowly towards the solitary pump. He had the air of an old war horse, one who has seen battle many a time before.

'I reckon you'll be needing some assistance.' He peered at the riders as they tugged off their goggles. 'Ladies.' He reached over and switched off the engine.

Rosie wriggled her way out from underneath Hazel, whose mind was apparently far away, gazing at the bike with a look approaching religious adoration.

'I think we could do with some oil,' Rosie said lamely.

The man effortlessly lifted the machine upright before deftly kicking out the side stand.

'Righto.'

He seemed to be trying hard not to laugh.

'There's some lemonade in the shop if you like,' he added consolingly.

A younger man came out and there was an exchange of words before the junior pushed the bike into the shade of the workshop and began to check it over, the old man following, mopping his brow with a handkerchief in the unusual warmth.

Hazel promptly disappeared into the shop and emerged carrying two bottles of lemonade. They sat on the wall, sipping the sharp but refreshing drink and swinging their legs freely.

'Bloody hell!' said Hazel at last, grinning at her friend, her face was flushed and her eyes bright.

Rosie, who could feel a febrile tingling in arms and hands, was just experiencing a realisation of how close they'd come to crashing.

'Bloody hell!' she echoed.

Spontaneously, they both laughed.

'Hazel, you're a maniac!'

'Aye and tha loved it!' Hazel leant over and kissed Rosie on the cheek. 'Makes me all ... well, "You Know" ...'

'You know?' Rosie caught the suggestive look in her friend's eye which seemed to be imagining her breasts beneath the pullover, and laughed. 'Oh, you mean "You Know"! Hazel, you're terrible!'

But Rosie could feel the same unsteady thrill of the ride that made her friend's eyes gleam even brighter than usual, there was something in its power and madness that was like 'You Know' after all. Hazel had removed her cap and was running her hands through her short blonde hair, the sun catching the outer layers and making them glow. Her upturned nose and boyish manner was irresistibly attractive and Rosie had a sudden urge to kiss her.

A 'ping!' of the garage bell announced the arrival of a glossy black Ford Model A, which pulled onto the forecourt with a squeal of brakes and a dying rumble of the engine. From the front two seats a pair of respectable-looking middle-aged men in city pinstripes got out. One strode up and down, stretching his legs, while the other fumbled in a pocket, presumably for coupons.

The younger garage-hand emerged, they exchanged cursory greetings and he began to fill the car, the pointer on the pump dial rotating slowly, clanging once every cycle. Rosie sat back and sighed. Once again the world had come between them. It seemed so wrong on a day made for being young, for loving and being loved, that they could not just be free. The fact that half the world was presently trying to kill the other half seemed to add insult to injury. If there was more love then perhaps there would be fewer wars in the first place.

She decided to ignore the intruders. She wiggled closer to her friend who was staring at the men and coughed discreetly.

'You ... want me?' she said, trying to imitate the suggestive, knowing look Hazel often gave her. She placed her hand on Hazel's thigh.

'Aye. You know I want thee,' Hazel replied, her eyes not shifting from the men, one of whom seemed to be staring at them.

'Are you ...' Rosie sought the phrase her friend had recently used and lowered her voice to what she hoped was a more husky and suggestive tone. 'Are you "on fire", my love?'

She giggled but Hazel remained immobile and irritatingly stony-faced.

Rosie persisted. 'You're so quick to ...' she hesitating teasingly, 'ignite!'

But there was still no response and Rosie frowned. It was silly and vexing that Hazel maintained such a cold outward front, even in the presence of strangers whom they'd never met and would never see again.

Impulsively Rosie leaned over and kissed Hazel on the cheek. She'd meant it to be a lingering kiss, a V-sign to those watching, but Hazel pulled away, cutting the soft, moist contact short.

'Is tha daft?' she hissed, 'Not 'ere, not in front of them buggers!' She inched firmly away.

Rosie could hear the men with the Ford talking. They were staring over at her and Hazel and exchanging words with each other. They were too far away to catch their words, but it was clear they were unfriendly.

'*Disgusting!*' one of them then said loudly.

The other replied and Rosie caught the two words. '*Bloody dykes!*'

Hazel, for all her anti-establishment, anti-men bravado looked ominous – whether from anger or embarrassment it was hard to tell. There was no point in continuing and Rosie withdrew her hand from Hazel's thigh and looked away.

The attendant finished fuelling the car, and the driver got back in. The passenger threw the two young women a hostile glance, spat venomously on the tarmac and also climbed aboard, slamming the door behind. The Ford coughed roughly into life, and pulled onto the highway with a roar.

Hazel's face had flushed dark pink, but Rosie was defiant.

'I don't bloody well care!' she announced, flicking a defiant V-sign at the departing vehicle. 'It none of their bloody business!'

Hazel turned at last, apparently surprised at her friend's vehemence and uncharacteristic use of bad language.

The lad at the pump cast the girls a curious glance and headed back to the workshop, Rosie avoiding his eye, her pulse racing.

For a while they sat in silence, sipping their lemonade and letting the peace of the summer day gradually return. The local jackdaws, whose home the garage was, wheeled, descended and began to strut about in a proprietorial fashion, peering quizzically at the new arrivals. At length there was a rumble from the road, and a long convoy of camouflaged trucks and guns began to pass noisily by. After a few minutes they were gone, leaving behind only the scent of burnt fuel and dry, flinty dust.

'Looks like it'll all be over by Christmas,' Rosie remarked, trying to rekindle conversation.

'I think someone 'as said that afore,' replied Hazel. 'More than once. But tha sounds sad about it. It 'ud be a good thing, would it not, to have all t'killin' and the dyin' over?'

Rosie sighed. 'Aye, I mean, yes. Of course.'

The war was horrible, but she couldn't help but want it to continue. Being loved and wanted by two people was such an affirmation of living. She didn't want it to stop, and even less did she want to choose between them.

'Mind you,' Hazel began, apparently relaxing once more, 'it'll be no good thing to be a woman in peacetime, tha knows.'

Rosie raised her eyebrows. She didn't want another of Hazel's political monologues, but she was intrigued in spite of herself. Hazel was passionate about her beliefs and Rosie admired her for them, even if there was little room for disagreement. Nowadays such chats could easily become one-sided, a world away from the meeting of minds when it all began.

Hazel looked at her younger friend sagely. 'Don't you see what's going to happen when t'war's over? The war's not like any time before, and it won't be the same after, neither. It's a special time, one of a kind. There'll be no more well-paid factory jobs for the likes of thee and me. No more women working their way up the ladder. It'll be reet back to the kitchen sink, cryin' babies, dinner on the table and just you be bloody grateful, my girl. The only hope, and it's not a great one, is that we get a labour government.'

'Well, I suppose the jobs will go.' Rosie hadn't thought about it.

'Aye. The truth is that this war has been bad for men, but not bad for women. We've had women bus drivers, managers in factories, even flying Spitfires.' A faraway look came over her face. 'Imagine that. Four hundred miles a bloody hour! Magic!' She took a noisy slurp of lemonade.

Rosie by now had no difficulty seeing Hazel in a Spitfire. And it would be the worse for the Luftwaffe if she ever managed it.

'Some girls have travelled halfway around the world, tha knows,' Hazel continued. 'Fat chance of that in peacetime.' She paused to light a pair of Woodbines, then glancing at the pump thought better of it, tucking them back into the packet. 'Aye, when they needed us they called us, and they can send us back again.' She exhaled forcefully. 'Bloody men!'

'You don't like them much, do you?' Rosie said, half-teasing.

'They're all right if you need somethin' heavy shifting,' said Hazel, grinning, 'but no, frankly, my dear, I don't. They are our natural sworn enemies. Like the upper class, as I told thee.'

Rosie raised her eyebrows. Not for the first time she thought friend's views extreme.

'And Eugene,' she asked, 'is he my enemy?'

Hazel leant forward and grabbed her hand. 'He's a man, Rosie – a Yank – and he's got a readymade way out if it goes wrong. Not to mention that they all find it difficult to keep their hands on just one woman.'

Rosie felt a twinge of irritation. 'You're jealous!'

Hazel looked directly in her eye. 'Aye. Of course I am.'

For the last few weeks Rosie had staved off thinking about the conflict that might lie between Hazel and any future she might have with Eugene. She'd almost convinced herself that what had happened was simply different, and not either-or. Why did she have to choose? It was so good just to be wanted. The present was marvellous, and the future could take care of itself.

But Hazel looked set to force the issue.

'What'll 'appen when the war's over?' Hazel looked directly at her. 'I mean, with thee and the Yank?'

The question was so like her, direct to the point of bluntness. But Rosie liked even that.

'Oh, I don't know. Perhaps I'll marry him.'

She threw the statement out carelessly, not daring to add that Eugene had already spoken of a wedding and had almost finished his tour.

Hazel recoiled slightly but her face remained composed, if tense. 'An' tha loves 'im?'

Rosie drew a deep breath. 'Honestly, I don't know. It's hard to explain. He's become ...' she hesitated, 'like gravity. I feel drawn to him. Like it's not me making the decision. There's something in me that responds, something beyond my mind. An instinct, perhaps?'

'Dangerous things, instincts.'

'Are they?' Rosie considered it. 'I'm not switching my mind off, if that's what you think.' She paused. 'It's just that there's friendship and laughter, and he cares. That's all real, and it's fun with him.' There was no easy way to say it. 'And he can offer me so much: security, a home, perhaps a fresh start.'

There was a pregnant pause.

'And us? That what 'appens between us?' Hazel's voice seemed huskier than normal. 'Ain't that love?'

Rosie looked around. 'Hazel, you know I love you,' she said quietly.

The sun had risen almost to its height and the day was gloriously warm. The scent of wildflowers and sweet hay drifted from the nearby fields, mingling with the odours of petrol, oil and warm tarmac. It was a day for riding endless winding lanes, feeling the rough tussling of the wind in your hair, and the sun, for so long absent, on your face. Rosie glanced at her friend and longed to be on the road again, with only the sounds of the rushing air and engine to listen to. She didn't want to talk.

But Hazel pressed doggedly on. 'Then tha would trade love for a home and security and all that, with a Yank?'

Rosie felt a twinge, if not of anger then of frustration. 'You don't understand. It's not that I simply want those things, I need them. And I don't want to sacrifice anything. It's just that I don't want to be lonely ever again, and I don't want to be poor. I want to be safe and secure and ...' She tailed off. 'I want to escape. And be free. And be loved. And never go back to how things were before I met you.'

'Tha wouldn't be free if tha married,' Hazel countered. 'And tha might not be loved, neither. But we two could mek a go of it, over 'ere, I reckon.' She looked longingly at Rosie and put her hand on her knee. 'And tha would be loved.'

Rosie put her head in her hands. It had begun with such a lovely morning, an uncomplicated day of sunshine and birdsong, seemingly made for being young, and loved, and free and rejoicing in the newness of it all.

'But how?' she asked. 'If the good jobs for us end when the war does, as you say, then a woman will need a man just to survive.'

Hazel fell silent and, seeing her dejection, Rosie took her hand and squeezed firmly. 'And then there's people, like those men in the Ford. They frighten me. It frightens me that anyone can be like that about something ... something that doesn't seem to matter at all, in the greater scheme of things.'

Hazel snorted. 'To 'ell with them. I don't care.'

Rosie gazed sorrowfully at her friend. 'But I do,' she said slowly. 'Hazel, I do. I want to live in the open and not hide my love away, like some awful secret.' She sighed. 'The world's just not ready for two women to live openly together – in that way.'

From the workshop came the sound of the motorcycle being started and revved up. After a while the revving stopped, the motor died and the faint sound of tools clattering on the ground reached them. On the forecourt the jackdaws had wandered closer and were now strutting around, peering up at the two young women again, apparently looking for scraps.

'What about ...' Hazel hesitated. '"You Know"? With 'im, like?'

Rosie turned to her friend. 'Sex?' she said it quietly, careful they were not overheard.

'Aye. Meking love. Like we did. Has tha done that with 'im yet?'

Rosie recoiled. 'No! Of course not! I'd tell you, anyway ... But he wants to, I know he does, and I ...'

'Aye?'

'I'm curious, and part of me wants to. He's ...' she blushed slightly, 'he's keen!'

Hazel snorted. 'Aye, them Americans are known fer that.'

Rosie glanced at her. 'You sound like my mother,' she observed wryly, amused at the irony in spite of herself.

Hazel had been picking a few daisies that grew in the sand of a fire bucket.

'Present,' she said, holding them out.

'You're always picking flowers for me.' Rosie took the offering and laughed gently. They usually came from someone's front garden, but at least the thought was there.

Hazel shrugged. 'You're going to go on seeing him, then?'

'*Hmm-mm*,' Rosie responded warily.

Hazel had a temper, as she'd discovered during an argument that had erupted only the week before. That had been about the airman too.

'Then you'll do the "You Know" with him one day. Won't you?' Hazel continued.

It seemed safer to make no reply.

'I don't want to share thee.'

Hazel said it with such determination that Rosie's heart lurched.

'Or be seen touching in public,' Rosie replied tartly. 'Besides,' she added, 'I haven't decided anything yet!'

Turning, Rosie saw with relief that the lad had finished with the bike and was wheeling it out. He arrived, mopped his brow with an oily handkerchief and presented the machine to Hazel with a cursory nod.

There was something in his look, and it wasn't the covert interest of a young man in two pretty girls. He looked them up and down and, while it could have been her imagination, Rosie thought she detected a faint hint of disgust.

Hazel paid him without comment and he left.

Rosie pulled on her goggles and cap. 'Let's not talk about the future today, Hazel,' she said. 'There's still a war on and no one knows even if we'll still be alive when it's all over. And it's so beautiful today, for once.'

Hazel looked up at the clear blue sky, nodded resignedly and stood. She stretched, pushing her breasts out, stretching the jumper she wore inside her leather jacket.

'I can't help it.' She said it openly and without hushing her voice. 'I do love thee, and I want thee.'

Rosie looked at Hazel. She was strong and handsome. And there really was no way of telling how things would work out. No way at all.

CHAPTER 25

The enormous B17 rolled to a quivering halt for the final time. Only three of its four engines were turning, an uneven rhythm that made the aircraft's frame tremble even more than usual. From the fourth motor, silent and caked in soot, dribbled a thin trail of smoke and on the wing behind, scorch-marks bore witness to the white heat of fire. In the tail, Meatball was wonderingly examining a pattern of holes that had shattered the cabin all around him while leaving him miraculously uninjured.

Slowly the crew emerged, dropping from hatches onto the runway. One knelt and kissed the tarmac, another grasped a blade of grass from the field and stared at it as though looking at a rare flower.

'*Guys!*' Eugene dumped his parachute on the ground. He was gazing up at the tail.

'*Shit!*' said Hank.

To his expletive was added a chorus of others.

'*Holy Moly!*'

'*There's a lot not there that should be there, that's fer sure!*'

Eugene scratched his head and hoped no one would notice the

tremor in his arm. There was so much adrenaline in his body that he wanted to scream. It was hard to stand still, to play the part of captain. Was this really it? Had they truly made their last trip or would it prove to be some kind of sick joke? There were rumours they would be forced to do a second tour. If so, they'd need a new ship for sure, and even then he didn't know if his crew would obey the order. Across the field ground crew were racing towards them, trailing a cloud of dust.

Eugene walked along the plane. All over its battered green body the bomber bore fresh scars. The top of the tail fin was gone, as though it had been simply sawn off two feet down, and both the elevators bore fist-sized holes. The protruding guns of the rear turret were bent upwards by exploding cannon shells and the ball turret was dented like it had been attacked by a maniac with a sledgehammer. Everywhere bullet holes ran in neat, stitched lines over the aluminium, and on the wing, behind the engine, several yards of skin had been burned off, revealing the skeleton of ribs and spars.

The group stood, silenced.

'How the hell did that thing still fly?' Hank said at last.

'Beats me.'

'Down to you, Cap.' It was Babyface, breathing on his glasses and polishing them before looking again.

Eugene turned away. He coughed and spoke without turning around. 'They build 'em well,' was all he could say. He recovered. 'Anyone got any rounds left?'

A chorus of no's or 'you must be goddam joking' confirmed what he suspected.

Eugene drew a deep breath. The journey in had been fine, flak over the approaches had been light, almost disorganised. He'd thought the advance force that had gone on ahead as arranged had knocked out German radar-guided guns. And perhaps the diversionary raid fifty miles away had helped too, confusing the air defence controllers. But *Luck of The Devil* had barely dropped her bombs and begun leaving the target area when the sky, which should have been full of waiting escort planes, suddenly yawned wide and empty. Loud chattering broke out over the net. Everyone could see someone had screwed up. A few minutes late in taking off, a degree out in navigation. It didn't matter. They were on their own, and without a fighter escort they were sitting ducks.

From the innocent blue sky the attack came, and it was brutal. The whirling yellow-nosed German fighters, a ragtag of battered ME 109's and FW 190's, dived in from two sides at once, splitting the bombers' massed defence. Two Messerschmitts and a Focke-Wulf had been sent to earth by the Americans' barrage of fifty-calibre guns, but the remainder had hit at least a dozen forts and downed four. *Apple Pie*, with its cheerful, all-southern crew, all under twenty-one, had exploded in a bright yellow fireball, sickeningly clear for all to see. And there had been no 'chutes.

Standing on the solid ground of the airbase, it was hard to believe now what had happened 'upstairs'.

Eugene walked slowly along *Luck of The Devil,* running his hand gently over the fuselage, like a man running his hands down the flanks of an old and loyal warhorse. She'd been a good plane and had got them through. As long as no one tried to make them sign up for another tour, they were going home. Not for the first time he said a silent prayer to Boeing, grateful for a machine as rugged as the B17. It seemed a miracle that this collection of half a million steel and aluminium parts had survived all the Germans had thrown at her. But she had.

Everyone aboard had heard the 20mm cannon shells smashing into the rear and exploding along the fuselage. After that the ship wanted to dive and turn, and both Eugene and Hank had to pull hard on the columns to keep her straight and level. They had damage to the control surfaces somewhere. On the port wing, number two engine had begun vibrating and Hank had shut her down. As the propeller came to a stop, they were astonished to see the blades had been shredded, like wood chewed to splinters by some giant dog.

Back on the ground, Eugene shuddered and completed his inspection, patting the plane's flanks one last time with a gloved hand. Unable to stop the tremor of his arm, he thrust the hand into his trouser pocket and turned away.

'Captain?'

It was Blakey, the ruddy-faced Crew Chief, standing on the grass before them, looking nervous.

Eugene returned from his thoughts and looked at the engineer. He'd chewed him out so often he felt embarrassed. But for once he could think of nothing to say.

The chief was gazing at the plane.

'*Gee!*'

His guys were all smiling at first, but the grins rapidly faded when they caught sight of the expressions of the survivors. Wyatt, the top-turret gunner, was sitting on the ground with the thousand-yard-stare, and next to him Joe, the radio operator, was being sick as unobtrusively as possible behind the right landing gear.

'Catch you later, captain.'

The experienced engineer began to marshal his guys to tend to the wounded aircraft. He had worked with the squadron long enough to know what the crew had been through, and when they needed space.

Eugene tapped Meatball on the shoulder.

'Sure you're OK?' he asked, marvelling that the tail-gunner was not only alive but relatively uninjured. The rear turret had been shredded.

Meatball, who was picking shards of Plexiglass from his left hand, nodded but said nothing. None of them, thought Eugene, were a picture of happiness, not like you might expect guys to be who'd just completed a tour, earning the right to go home. Perhaps, like him, they had heard the rumours about the compulsory second tours.

The tired, dishevelled group walked out over the field, following their captain. Eugene, still trying to stop his hands from trembling, grasped them behind his back. At last he halted and automatically they gathered around him. He looked over their expectant faces, one at a time. He was closer to them than anyone, closer even than to his brother. And this moment would never come again. But before he could say what was on his mind he had a duty to perform. Perhaps they guessed, for they looked at him curiously.

'The Colonel …' he began.

There was a groan from his audience, which did not bode well.

'The Colonel has asked me to ask you whether, at this auspicious moment …' Eugene halted.

There had been too much bullshit in the war and he was tired of it.

'Suspicious what?' whispered Tony.

'Auspicious. He means an important moment in our lives,' Babyface mumbled back.

'Oh, I get it, a moment in our lives while we still have them.'

'Guys,' Eugene said, 'I'll give it you straight.'

'Yeah.' It was Tony again. 'Why dontcha, Cap? The old man never does.'

A murmur of agreement rippled through the crew.

'The Colonel wants to know if we'll sign for another tour. The Invasion is on and they need crews. There's a signing bonus.'

In the silence that followed each avoided the others' eyes. Some of the crew scanned the sky or found something interesting in the grass at their feet.

Tony spoke up. 'Ah, would this be in the way of like, ah, an order or is he just asking?'

The others all looked up.

Eugene drew a deep breath. His training and rank demanded he do one thing, while his humanity and instincts another. Something inside of him snapped.

'The rumour is that this is a request first, and if we say no then it becomes an order. Without,' he added, 'the bonus.'

There was a murmur of curses and dark, whispered words.

Eugene straightened himself. 'Well, I might as well say where I am on this. I'm not going again. Request or order.'

His crew gazed at him, a mixture of astonishment and relief on their faces.

Tony's cigarette fell smouldering from his mouth. '*Jeeze!*'

Eugene coughed. 'It's just my view of it, boys. I say we've done enough and it's time for someone else to take over.'

An audible ripple of relief came from the assembled young men. '*Yeah!*'

'Goddam right!'

'They can't jail all of us!'

'I just don't think,' Eugene continued, 'it's fair to change the rules halfway through the game.'

'*Good for you, Cap!*' Tony suddenly stuck his hand out and Eugene was surprised to find his own being grasped in a vice-like handshake. '*Way to go, Cap! I'm with you!*'

The chorus of agreement ran through the group.

Only Babyface looked doubtful. 'But if ... if they order us, then ... I mean, won't we be in trouble or something?'

'Listen, sweetheart,' said Tony, grasping the youngster around the face, 'I don't goddam-well care!' He kissed the lad firmly on the lips.

Babyface fell spluttering backwards.

Tony turned to the rest of the group and began to dance. Grabbing first one then the other, he waltzed over the grass.

'*I'm going home! Home sweet home!*' he shouted. '*New York, New York!*'

Eugene let his gaze pass over the ragtag group. In a couple of years they'd gone from strangers to something like family. And it felt longer than two years, more like as if they had always known each other. Now their futures would also be inseparable, joined by some invisible thread no matter how far apart in space they became. Some part of them would belong to the crew, and the war would define them.

As they walked back to the field, Eugene found himself surrounded by jubilant airmen, each grasping his hand in turn and pumping his arm so much it soon grew sore. Although moved to see the relief on the faces of the boys, inside his guts were churning. It was weird how he always felt worse after a mission than during it.

At Eugene's side strode Hank, gazing up into the sky, a piece of rye grass stuck between his teeth, hands tucked into his belt as if he were looking at a field of corn, contemplating a cut. He was grinning.

Then the big Oklahoman stopped and placed a gigantic arm on Eugene's shoulder.

'You did good.'

'Did I? Deciding to refuse orders, you mean?'

'Hell, no! In getting us all through this.'

Eugene shook his head. 'I was just the bus driver. You know that, Hank, and besides I shared even that job. With you.'

Ahead of them Tony was chasing Wyatt, trying to kick his behind, while Babyface and Karl seemed deep in some post-mission argument. Billy was strolling along by himself behind a group of the others, playing on the short tin-whistle he kept in his pocket. It was their victory, this group of boys, and he'd been little more than a passenger, or, yes, perhaps the bus driver. They'd all gambled their lives, and won, but by luck, not his judgement.

And now he would have to go up against the Colonel and fight one more battle. If he lost, the crew's celebrations would be premature. He forced an unsteady grin.

CHAPTER 26

The sign above the once grand entrance was peeling and windblown, and it was clear the Royal Hotel had seen better days. The white-painted building was a provincial interpretation of the solid English classical style he'd come to admire, nicely proportioned sash windows punctuating the white, stuccoed façade. The grand double door, framed by a pediment and four thick Doric columns, marked it off from other, more mundane buildings nearby.

Eugene glanced around. He'd never been to the small and ancient city of Coveringham, some thirty miles from the base, until now. But the petite and curvaceous redhead had been insistent, and somewhere in her otherwise seductive intonation he'd detected the faint hint of blackmail.

There was no doorman to greet him as he walked in, passing quickly through the plywood partitioned lobby, presumably erected to preserve the blackout. Once through the utilitarian barrier, the grandeur of the place was more apparent: deep red Turkish carpets running down the centre of the marble hallway to reception and beyond to the bar the nurse had dictated as their rendezvous. As he walked down the passage, he noted the walls on either side were decorated by paintings in oils and here and there a card table held a carefully placed classical bust.

Eugene passed the reception desk and became aware of the icy gaze of the cadaverous old man behind the desk. He stilled a fresh twinge of guilt at the secret meeting, one he'd kept not only from Rosie but also from his crew. He didn't want to think why he'd really agreed to make the journey, telling himself he was going out of curiosity, or perhaps to clear up any misunderstanding, though this would of course have been a lie. And there was the matter of the medication, the beautiful high she'd withheld that afternoon.

'The bar is to the left of the dining room.'

The guy behind the desk, who possessed that old limey air of superiority, had anticipated his unspoken question.

Eugene pushed open the frosted doors to the lounge bar, and he had to admit it was the most impressive place he'd seen outside London. Everywhere polished wood competed with marble and gleaming brass. Paintings decorated the oak-panelled walls, while above the guests, gleaming Art Deco globes illuminated the scene. Conversation among the well-heeled inhabitants was audible, but pitched politely at a discreet Anglo-American rumble.

He stood at the bar to be served, but he didn't have long to wait for company.

'Well, hello, flyer-boy.'

She'd sidled up behind him silently, like a snake approaching its prey.

He turned and observed her. He couldn't help but notice her small upturned nose and the delicate whiteness of her neck. She was a fine-looking woman. Delicately, she perched her shapely bottom on a barstool and shot him a sly look as she lit a Player's.

'What can I get you to drink?' he asked, feeling he was moving even further down a slippery slope.

'Gin and lemonade.' She fixed him with a penetrating gaze. Her lips, bright with a lurid red lipstick, parted as she laughed.

He ordered a gin and lemonade and a large gin and tonic.

He met her gaze. Was she mocking him? He could smell her perfume and his eyes seemed pulled by some hidden magnetism to the prominent outline of her breasts beneath her dress.

For ten minutes after the drinks had arrived, she danced carefully around the purpose of her invitation, fending off persistent questions and diverting him on to other things she knew would catch his attention. It seemed that she had her finger on more than the pulse of her patients, because there was one piece of news that he'd been completely unaware of.

'Hang on there.' He could hardly believe what she'd just said. 'Say that again.'

The redhead leaned forward and grabbed him by the tie, pulling him closer. She grinned.

'Your war's over, baby. That rumour about second tours? Well, it's all off. Volunteers only required now, baby.' She leant back on her barstool and laughed. 'You look kinda shocked, honey. Aren't you pleased little old Ginger found that out for you?'

'Uh, yeah.' His mind reeled and he hardly noticed when she ordered a second round, the drink slipping down his throat rapidly as he processed the information. It really was over. He'd never have to feel that sick dread again. When the men heard the news they'd probably assume he'd spoken with the Colonel and think him a hero.

He moved like an automaton to the table she'd booked in the dining room and mechanically ate the meal she ordered. He'd lost count of the glasses of wine the snotty English waiters delivered, but when the food was finished and they'd both lit up, he made an attempt to get to the bottom of whatever it was that was happening.

'Look, Ginger,' he leaned across the table, his vision blurring, 'what's this all about?'

The redhead regarding him closely. There was something so slutty yet appealing about her face. He didn't know if he wanted to slap it or kiss it. She didn't reply.

'What do you want?' he said finally. He wanted her but doing so made him despise himself, even more than he'd begun to hate her.

She just smiled and blew a delicate smoke ring with affected elegance.

'Can't you guess?' She leant towards him, her firm round breasts bulging forward.

Eugene caught the look in her eye and knew exactly where he stood.

'Ginger, I ...' he began, but she was already walking away from the table towards the door.

He stood unsteadily and, after a pause, followed.

They collided in the hallway. She pulled him into a small alcove and he felt her arms snake around him. His breathing quickened involuntarily. He needed release. She kissed him, a slow wonderful wet kiss, her tongue gently probing his mouth. The pressure he'd been nursing for months suddenly peeled open, like a dam bursting.

'Ginger ...'

She broke away, grabbing his hand.

They found themselves at the reception desk.

'My husband and I,' she was saying, 'would like a room.'

The old man looked at Eugene, His face was haughty and his eyebrows raised.

'No luggage, sir?'

'No luggage,' Ginger cut in. 'Just give us the key, buster.'

She scribbled something in the register and, throwing a glance that might have killed, swiped the key from the man's knobbly old hand.

Eugene avoided the receptionist's eye. His body was like a train running out of control, careering down a mountain without brakes.

The room was in darkness. She moved swiftly over the plush red carpet to pull the blackout curtains before snapping on the bedside lamp. He watched in the pale golden light as she removed her clothes down to her black lace underwear, her eyes never leaving him. On the wall behind, her giant shadow danced, its very size seeming to amplify their crime. She reclined on the bed, beckoning to him, the black of her suspenders stark against her skin.

Losing his trousers on the floor, he crawled on all fours across the quaking bed. She held up a hypodermic which had appeared as if by magic, as though demonstrating its use to a class, and placed it carefully on the bedside cabinet.

'Dessert,' she said, grinning wickedly.

He smelt the drink on her breath, mixing headily with the perfume and the musk of feminine perspiration, and reached to touch her breasts, just as her cool hand slid between his legs. She was slow, teasing but not fully touching, starting a fire but not letting it roar. Her ability to play with sex, to toy with him, was remarkable, and he wondered dimly how she'd learnt. She pulled his shirt back over his shoulders, unclipped her brassiere and throwing it to the floor. She lay on top, their flesh contacting in a smooth electric ooze. Nothing outside the room, outside the moment existed. He forgot where he was, even perhaps who he was. He must have responded too eagerly to her gentle caresses, because she retreated, holding him off and sliding to his side. Their tongues slid slowly around each other, and he moved his hand between her legs, hearing her breathing abruptly catch.

Then she mounted him, swinging her leg over until she sat astride. He closed his eyes and felt her take him in her hand. Arching her back, she fed him slowly inside her. He groaned, his head recoiling into the pillow and his breathing accelerating. She was moving slightly, up and down. Tormented, he tried to thrust into her but again she resisted, still teasing. He was sweating, his breath short. He reached up and held her breasts, squeezing her nipples between his fingers. She moaned but still would not increase the rhythm.

At last he could bear it no more. Like a beast he rose, pushing her onto her back. The redhead laughed, amused by the fever she was causing in him. She gritted her teeth and looked him in the eye as her long red nails dug into his back. He thrust forward and, as he re-entered her, felt pain – she was pulling on his hair, her hands scrabbling among the dark roots. Her body flexed against the sheets and she was grunting as her nails again flailed his back. She was biting him, her teeth chewing into his shoulder, alternately clamping and unclamping.

'*Now!*' she was saying. '*Now! Harder!*'

But with her beneath him, control had been transferred. Now it was he who held back, the flat of his hand holding her down, his thrusts shallow and slow until her breathing became short and harsh.

'*Goddamit, now!*' she screamed, the words reverberating inside his head as he finally drove fully into her.

He felt strong, limitlessly powerful, infinitely capable. They collided rhythmically and he wondered distantly whether the other guests would hear. He felt the connection with the world, the room and even with the woman fading, becoming conscious only of the motion and the relentless thrusting. His energy flowed out and into her, dark and strong, impaling her repeatedly. It went on and on, each thrust more violent than the last. He stared into her eyes like a madman, looking but not seeing. He was wild and beyond himself. His motion was not simply his own, but a force of nature, like the power of the sea.

She was spluttering, gasping, and he suddenly realised he had one hand on her neck. For a few seconds he did not release the pressure around her throat, but retained it, watching her face grow redder as her climax approached. Then he was gushing into her, a tide of white light and heat that coursed from his loins into her body, stopping at last with a short, final cry. His hand released and she gasped, panting breathlessly. Like a wounded animal, his chest heaving and his body glistening with sweat, he threw himself off, rolling onto his back.

He lay there staring at the ceiling, the sweet flood of endorphins cascading through his body as his chest heaved and the breath left in short, coarse gasps. She was, save for the rapid rising and falling of her breasts, unusually quiet. He could not bear to look at her, and stared mutely upwards. A jagged crack ran from the ornate central rose to the wall and at its junction a house spider was building a web.

He felt his eyes growing heavy as post-sexual coma hit him with an extraordinary intensity. Ginger's hand was on his arm.

'*Bastard!*' She hissed the words from between clenched teeth and a thin drool of spittle dripped from her mouth. She had the hypodermic in her hand. Her face was flushed but her look was almost demonic. She stabbed his thigh hard and he felt the instantaneous rush: a rolling wave of golden warmth, spreading through his consciousness, lifting and destroying him.

'Ginger ...'

She seemed to be bending over him, pulling on her dress.

'*You're one sick bastard, you know that?*' she spat.

Dimly he heard the click of the door opening and for a second the departing woman was silhouetted against the light from the hall. Then he was alone, tumbling like an autumn leaf, headlong into a deep and glorious darkness.

CHAPTER 27

The bulbous nose of the Air Force Packard slowed to a crawl at the base gate, before being waved brusquely through by the sentry. Eugene pointed the dull green-painted car towards town and accelerated through the gears, the rising and falling snarl of the engine a satisfying accompaniment to liberation. It felt good that the thing with Ginger was over, and the DTs from withdrawal of the drugs had faded.

As the vehicle sped rapidly through the countryside Eugene rejoiced too in the thought that he'd never have to fly a goddam plane again in his life. There was a brief period of leave and then the temporary assignment he'd begged from the Colonel before anything happened in terms of shipping out to the States. He felt calmer than in years. Dance music was playing over the car radio, and he tapped out the beat on the wheel. Even the annoying tic in his left eye had gone.

He'd done of a lot of thinking in the short time since their last mission, and, now that the worst was over, felt a growing sense of shame. He'd survived by luck, not courage or skill, and the things he'd had to do to stop from going crazy seemed shabby now they were no longer needed. Eugene stubbed the Lucky Strike out into the car's ashtray. The drugs, the booze and the women had had a part to play, but they were unworthy. The English girl was different, and it was to her the greatest debt was owed. She'd been more than a feminine balm to soothe his nerves, more than the other distractions. For him and the crew, she'd been a kind of symbol, of hope, and innocence, something from the world they'd left behind. He, and the boys, they all owed her.

But he'd found a path, some small way to a redemption. It wasn't the powder-blue women's suit with black velvet collar he had on the back seat. They'd all kicked in for that. No. His way back, to get to like himself again, had to be something of a much greater order. He had to save her life as she'd saved his. Nothing else would do. And he'd finally he'd figured out a way. A quick trip to see the Colonel and another into the local limey town, and it was all set. Eugene switched off the radio.

He caught sight of her waiting at the usual place outside the Morelli factory gates, grinning at the approaching car. He shelved a twinge of guilt and pulled up, beaming back what he hoped was an innocent 'please-to-see-you' smile.

She got in and he pressed the accelerator.

'What's that?' She'd seen the box.

'*Ah-ha!*' he said and grinned. 'Later.'

Rosie smiled. 'Where are we going?'

Her pretty face seemed to be positively glowing tonight. She must have had her hair done and she regarded him curiously with those wide, slate-blue eyes. He felt suddenly, expansively generous.

'Your choice,' he replied. He'd been so elated he'd not had time to plan anything.

'Oh!' Rosie paused. 'Do you know the Royal Hotel in Coveringham? It's a bit of a drive, but I've heard it's fabulous.'

Inwardly shocked, he glanced sideways at her as coolly as he could manage. The same hotel? Could she possibly know? He tried to concentrate on the road and feigned disinterest. It might be best to admit he'd been. Someone there might recognise him.

'I've been once or twice.' He tried not to sound too enthusiastic. Or familiar.

'Oh, good! Let's go there!' She beamed at him.

Keeping a straight face, he took the turning at the ring road and headed north.

He drove slowly, trying to think, stretching the journey from the usual thirty to forty minutes. As they entered the suburbs, he began to think of how he'd deal with the hotel staff if they recognised him. He glanced at Rosie again. She was so light-hearted she *couldn't* know. She'd wound down the window and was carelessly tapping her fingers on the sill.

'*Oh!*' she exclaimed, her eyes suddenly gripped by the view ahead.

They'd reached the city outskirts, the sign bearing its name standing on a pile of rubble marking the junction of two major roads, and he nodded at her exclamation. The ancient mediaeval city had been the target of several raids earlier in the war, and, although fitful rebuilding was underway, the damage was apocalyptic.

Waved across the junction by a policeman, the car jinked over slippery tram tracks into the dark urban heart, motoring past gloomy shops, dusty workshops and dark, forbidding churches. They neared the centre and the traffic increased, but so did the devastation: rubble and bricks bulldozed into mountainous heaps, buildings torn open like dolls' houses and part-sheathed with tarpaulins, a few with repairs under way.

Eugene slowed, peering into the blackout barely illuminated by the feeble glow of the shuttered headlamps. At last, after several diversions, the grand white building of the Royal Hotel appeared.

She'd insisted on taking a peek in the box, letting out a squeal of delight at the unimaginable luxury of the new outfit. Even though he told her the crew had chipped in, he still felt like hell when she'd thrown her arms around him and planted a kiss on his cheek … but it was a start.

Inside, the opulence seemed to stun the girl. She kept staring, from the crimson carpet to the cascading chandeliers overhead, which sprinkled their luminance onto the diners seated at the numerous white-clothed tables. Perhaps, he thought, her early life had been tougher than she'd said, though what she had said had been bad enough.

He gestured to a waiter who wore a disdainful expression and they were shown to their place, and presented with menus. Before the waiter left, Eugene ordered wine and when he returned they watched as he poured the clear, yellow liquid into the heavy crystal glasses. Eugene watched his companion weigh the heavy crystal in her hand before sipping curiously at the cool liquid. Despite himself, or perhaps his old self, the feelings he had for this girl were shifting from mere attraction into something like love.

Rosie talked and he let her. She seemed relish being out of the factory, her words pouring out in a pleasant stream that passed around him. He was half-listening, nodding appropriately at what seemed like key points, but not taking it all in. Now his war was almost over, he could suddenly see what she'd done for him. It had not just been the companionship or the fun he'd had kissing her. She'd been a lifeline, something decent and good to set against the horror and the loss. He wanted more than anything to do something to repay her. He felt inside his pocket. The trip he'd made into town the previous day seemed more justified than ever.

'It can't go on much longer, can it, the war?' she asked conversationally.

He drew in his breath, coming back to earth with a bump.

'I hope not. But the Germans ...' He paused.

'What do you know?'

She was learning to read his face, he thought.

'The Germans aren't easy to beat,' he replied guardedly. 'They may have a trick up their sleeves.' There were limits to what he could say.

'But we are going to win, aren't we?' she asked, concerned. 'After everything, all the people killed ... it has to end.'

He knew she was seeking comfort and there was no harm in providing it. It was true enough if the post-raid photos of German cities the rest of the squadron were levelling were anything to go by.

'Of course. It will be over soon, and there's no doubt we'll win.'

She was looking more beautiful than he remembered. There was a gleaming necklace around her pale white throat, and for a second he wondered if someone so innocent could have other admirers. Perhaps it was a family heirloom.

He raised a glass. '*To the end of the war!*'

Their glasses clinked together.

'*And the end of my tour!*' he added, grinning.

She almost choked, the wine catching in her throat and making her splutter.

'Really? You've heard?'

He nodded, his mouth widening into a huge grin. It felt good to share the news with her. She was getting it first, before his folks. Before anyone. She reached across the table and their hands met. A few other diners stared but he ignored them.

Her eyes were captivating, such an unusual shade of blue, and so large, like a child's. Her lipstick was a dark red, a new shade, and contrasted sharply with pale, faintly freckled skin. He couldn't help but think about the beds upstairs.

'Can I have my hand back?'

He hadn't realised the strength of his grip. He laughed it off and released her. The food, when it arrived was wholesome if less impressive than the architecture, consisting of mutton in a brown sauce with carrots, peas and potatoes.

When the question came it caught him off guard.

'What happens when the war is over?' she asked. She had the courage to look him in the eye, although it as clear the wine was also having an effect. He finished his mouthful and took a sip himself. He was glad he had an answer for her, but he would wait until the right moment.

'I've agreed to do some other work, in intelligence, at least for a couple of months. After that, I don't know.'

He noticed the relief, so clear on her young face, and smiled to himself.

'Hazel says that the country will change,' Rosie said, hurrying on, her face flushed. 'She says it has to, after all everyone has been through. She says there's no going back. She says it's high time too.'

She put a large forkful of the dinner in her mouth and ate with apparent relish.

'Hazel — isn't she a communist?' he asked, faintly amused at her unselfconscious affection for her friend.

Rosie laughed. 'No. I told you before, if she's anything she's what I suppose you'd call a socialist.'

'There's a difference?' he queried.

'In Hazel's case, yes. She wants to build a better world, not live under Stalin. Many people here, and not just working people, feel the same as she does.'

He nodded, and was surprised to find he'd extended his hand across the table towards her while she'd been talking.

Rosie glanced around the dining room. A gentleman at a nearby table was staring at them again. She grinned back unashamedly.

'I'm not like Hazel.' she went on, adding reflectively, 'in many ways. Britain seems … just … broken. Not only the buildings. The country. It was broken before, anyway. There are divisions, between people – into classes and more – and so many hidden rules. The war's brought us all together, but I don't think that will last long.'

She took a large gulp of wine. Her enthusiasm was amusing and engaging. He let her carry on.

'English people like dividing,' she continued, 'categorising – you know, different types of people into groups, or pigeon holes. And these groups must not mix. No. And you can do this, but can't do that. For no reason! And the rules seem designed to keep most of the people down, doing what they are told. I suppose it's not patriotic to say so, but I just don't feel I belong in a place like that. It seems wrong. Hazel thinks in time ordinary people could change it, but I don't.'

When they'd finished the meal, she emptied her glass and smiled at him over the rim, a little unsteadily, he thought. How impossibly beautiful she was. And not only physically. Despite the troubles she'd had with her family there was no bitterness in her, only hope. Some would have called it a foolish kind of innocence, but she was too intelligent for that. It seemed like the plain old goodness of a decent soul.

'You could do what you wanted in your apartment, I suppose? In New York?' she asked.

He smiled, caught off-guard. Was she talking about sex?

'Yeah, I suppose.'

She leant forward and tugged at his sleeve. 'What's it like?'

'Oh, the apartment?' He coughed. 'You know. Big, modern.'

She nodded and put down the glass with elaborate care.

'There are lots of rooms in this hotel,' she said suddenly. 'The sort of place you could have your wicked way with someone … Someone you'd treated to a fabulous meal, and a swanky new outfit!'

He halted, fork halfway to his mouth while his heart lurched inside him.

'You don't know what I want,' he murmured at last.

CHAPTER 28

She kept pace as they strolled from the hotel to the river, her strides almost two to his one. Despite the wonderful meal and the wine, she sensed an odd turmoil in him and for a while they walked in silence. At the river they found a path, sheltered from the steep drop to the water by a parapet that centuries of rain and wind had rendered crumbly as cake. Overhead, a thin moon yielded barely enough light to guide their feet. Rosie paused and looked down to the black, fast-flowing water. The current had eaten away at the bank creating a rocky beach where a few ducks squatted; most sleeping, a few preening or dabbling. One, a large silver-and-green drake, suddenly gave vent to a loud quacking, a long drawn-out noise that echoed off the bridge into the darkness. It was as if the bird were laughing.

'I wonder what he's saying.' Rosie turned to Eugene and grinned.

He seemed to have made a decision for he approached and she felt his arms slide around her waist.

'He says "Kiss Rosie".'

Their lips met, the warm wetness of it a sensual contrast to the chill night. She felt her breasts flatten against the hardness of his chest.

She began to laugh through the kiss, breaking off.

'He says "Kiss Rosie"! What are you like, Eugene?'

He joined in the laughter.

'Not my best line,' he admitted.

Soon they were walking again.

'How many kinds of love are there, do you think?' she asked. She looked at his raised eyebrows – it gave him an almost comical look, and she giggled.

'Well … I don't know … Love of country? Love of a mother and father? Love of a child.'

'Yes?'

He turned to her. 'Love of a woman.'

She laughed, adding, 'Or a man.'

'Thank you.' He smiled.

The drink had made Rosie giddy but was boosting her courage.

'But can't people love each other as they are, no matter who they are?' She could see he didn't understand.

'I love Hazel,' she announced suddenly.

'*Uh-huh*,' he responded, his tone flat and uncomprehending.

'Do you love your crew – like, what's his name, Hank?

'Well, I guess so. I suppose, like a brother?'

She paused. 'Well, I love Hazel. Does that bother you?'

He laughed. 'Nope.'

Rosie smiled quietly to herself and they walked on.

Soon they reached a bombsite, a scar gouged in the earth, stretching from the river, a rubble-strewn tear. Rosie began to wonder what kind of building could have left such mighty remains and then she saw the spire. They were standing on the edge of a graveyard, a once peaceful green space. The church that had been smashed had been old, perhaps the conduit of prayers for almost a millennia.

'Come on,' she said suddenly, ducking under the ineffectual cordon. Shaking his head, he followed.

'You're one kooky woman if you go in there, you know that?' he said into the darkness.

In the upturned earth tombstones lay, scattered and at odd angles.

Rosie squatted unsteadily by one.

'Do you have a lighter?'

He exhaled heavily but passed her the small device. 'You're going to get us arrested, you know that?'

'*Shh!* Look!' Rosie replied in a loud whisper.

He squatted down.

'*Eileen Smythe, departed this life 2nd May 1878,*' he read.

'May – there would have been blossom on these trees.' She could almost see them, trembling in an early summer breeze.

She left him behind while she drifted like a curious spirit. Across the graveyard, here and there a sudden burst of light flared, lingering like a firefly and then going out. Every so often she'd make an exclamation as though discovering treasure.

'*Come here!*' she called to him at last.

Shaking his head, he approached over a layer of churned mud and splintered stone.

She flicked the lighter, splashing a small puddle of light.

'Look. "*John and Edith Honeysett. Beloved husband and wife. Died December 24th, 1815.*"'

He peered at the stone. 'Christmas Eve,' he said thoughtfully.

'Yes, and both together, on the same day!' She stood, slipped her hand into his. 'In a way, that's perfect. Isn't it? Neither would have to live without the other.'

He seemed to be regarding her strangely. He looked as though he was about to say something.

The wail of a siren suddenly split the still night air, making them jump. The single note began as a moan, but rose rapidly, reaching a blood-chilling howl. The device must be on a rooftop – the volume was deafening.

'A raid?' she said. 'But I thought …' A look of horror appeared on her face. 'Oh my God! I must have attracted them with the lighter! Eugene, I've brought the Luftwaffe down on us!'

He grabbed her hand and headed for the remains of the church.

In the side of the remaining wall, a dark hole promised shelter. Pushing against the chewed remnants of an ancient door, they blundered inside.

'Did I do it, Eugene?' she asked, panic-stricken.

He slid his arm around her, practised eyes scanning the sky.

'I doubt it, honey.'

Rosie glanced around. In the pale starlight they saw stone steps corkscrewing into the belly of the earth. They must be at the entrance to the crypt.

He took her hand. 'Come on.'

But she pulled him back. 'I don't want to go down there.'

The darkness of the stairs seemed final. And if it collapsed they would be buried. No one would think of looking for anyone in that place.

Above them the sky was dissected by probing searchlights.

'We'll be alright here, won't we?' she asked, staring up.

Eugene nodded, but he too was looking anxiously at the sky, scanning with what must be a reflex action. In the distance, orange puffs glowed and faded, followed by the hollow boom of exploding ack-ack.

The throbbing vibration of engines didn't materialise. Instead, from the direction of the flashes, a spluttering trail of sparks arced towards them like a meteor.

'*They got one!*' shouted Rosie '*He's hit!*'

Then came an odd mechanical droning, like Hazel's motorcycle out of tune. The noise stopped, and the night was silent. The red ball of fire dipped, falling towards the ground, trailing blobs of sharp, spluttering embers.

'*Down!*' Eugene shouted.

She had no time to scream. He'd grabbed her and she suddenly found herself under him. There was a brilliant flash, followed by the roar of a detonation that made their ears pop. A couple of seconds later, debris rained down, pieces of wood and stone smashing into the ground all around them like deadly hailstones.

When it stopped, they surveyed each other. Lying on the cold stone floor they were covered in a thin film of flinty dust.

He coughed. '*Holy Moly!*'

'What was that?' Rosie asked, eyes wide.

'A flying bomb, I think.'

'A Doodlebug? This far north?'

He nodded. 'Yeah. They just started air-launching them.'

'Air ... you mean from a plane?'

'Yeah.'

'My God.' Rosie looked out at the sky, which seemed to be lit from the town with a new red glow. 'What a world!'

To the south, two more red trails could be seen heading away, accompanied by the guttural spluttering of their strange jet motors.

The two of them sat up, propping themselves against the wall as they recovered from the shock of near-annihilation. Somewhere in the direction of the town they heard the ringing of a fire engine's bell. She looked at him and saw something new in his face. She'd caught glimpses of it all evening.

'We talked about the States,' he said.

'To which you will be returning someday,' she replied, avoiding his gaze.

He fumbled for a moment in his pocket.

Thinking he was looking for his cigarettes, Rosie reached for her own.

'Rosie?'

'*Hmm?*' she responded, still searching.

'Will you marry me, really?'

'Marry you?' she said, a grin forming, 'Marry you and live in New York?'

From his pocket he produced a small leather case which he opened. Inside gleamed a diamond engagement ring.

'Yes.' His smile was clear and his deep-brown eyes sincere.

Rosie paused. The moment of decision had come far sooner than she'd expected. For a second she wanted to tell him about what had passed between herself and Hazel, of the feelings she had for the young woman who had become more than her best friend. But she sensed the enormity of the occasion, its importance in her life, and steeled herself to respond. A few weeks earlier it would have been harder, but recently Hazel's dominance in the house had been growing stronger. And two days earlier they'd had the first of what she assumed could be called a 'lovers' tiff'. The argument had been about Eugene, and how much time she'd been spending with him. It had reinforced vague doubts about the future, and especially about living together. Reluctantly she'd had to admit to herself how impossible this would be. All her life, it seemed, she'd been longing for freedom, an escape, but a future with Hazel would mean perpetual secrecy, and a public denial of feelings that seemed the very opposite of freedom.

He was looking at her expectantly, head on one side. Something had changed in him too, now the end of his war was coming. She had sensed a greater closeness than before, and the closeness of their escape minutes earlier seemed to confirm it. He coughed. She had to choose. She gazed out towards the city, now lit from somewhere by a strange orange glow.

'Yes,' she heard herself reply.

Eugene kissed her gently on the forehead.

She coughed. 'There's just one problem,' she said hesitatingly.

He raised an eyebrow.

'I'm only seventeen.'

She watched with a mixture of apprehension and humour as the airman lay back and laughed.

'I had no idea! I thought ...'

'The problem is ... well, there's a rule, you see ... if you're under eighteen ...'

He looked suddenly shocked. 'Have we been breaking any laws? I mean if you gotta get permission at seventeen to marry, how old do you have to be to, *uh* ...'

'Oh.' She could see him only dimly but heard the embarrassment in his voice. 'That's sixteen. But we haven't. Have we? Yet.'

He shook his head. 'No. But, then, what's this rule?'

'Well ... because of my age ... you'll have to get my mother's permission.'

She saw his face drop.

'Oh my God,' he mumbled.

She walked with him back to the car. As they rounded the corner of the street, they were brought to an abrupt halt. The hotel had taken a direct hit. It was as though someone had cut a huge slice from the middle of it, exposing the floors, together with trashed rooms, plaster-covered beds, hanging pipes and wires. Here and there a grimly twisted shape, perhaps a human body, was visible. Stunned, they made their way across the approach road, feet crunching on broken slate and splintered glass. A tongue of flame erupted in the building, blasting into the sky with a '*whump!*' By its brilliant hissing light they saw a line of figures had been already laid on the ground.

Rosie grasped Eugene's hand. 'We were ...' she began, then recalled what she'd said about him having his way with her. If he had, they'd both be dead, and buried under the rubble.

'Easy.' He said it absently, as though calming a frightened horse, or perhaps himself. 'Easy.'

The Air Force Packard, when they found it, stood one-eyed and looking sorry for itself, covered in plaster and pieces of debris. Here and there a patch of stickiness adhered to its flanks and the windscreen was covered with bright red streaks. She watched Eugene wrench the door open and clear the debris with his foot. He brushed off the seat and eased himself inside, pressing the starter. The engine roared and she climbed in from the other side. It was only when they were finally bumping over the firehoses that had spread everywhere like bulbous red roots, that she remembered the two red trails in the sky.

She turned to him. 'Those other bombs ... the ones that kept going ... they were heading south.'

'South?' he queried, peering through the damaged windscreen as he tried to find a way back to the main road.

'Towards the factory,' she replied, her voice suddenly urgent. 'Hazel's there, working an extra shift.'

He nodded, realisation dawning on his face. '*Shoot!* Hang on, honey.'

They'd reached the road out of town. As the wheels bumped finally onto sound tarmac, he floored the accelerator.

CHAPTER 29

Rosie watched Eugene's face as he drove. He was focused on the road, his whole being dedicated to getting them to the factory as fast as possible, and she felt a surge of gratitude. It was as though, having been two separate people until tonight, they were truly bonding together as a team. God alone knew if she was doing the right thing about the marriage, and she didn't want to think of the effect it would have on Hazel. Hazel, who might even now have been caught in the same raid.

It took twenty nail-biting minutes before they reached Rosie's home town, the green Packard roaring gallantly through the unlit streets. On the outskirts of town they dodged an ambulance slewing into the turning to the industrial estate, the manic trilling of the emergency bell quickly fading behind. Eugene kept the car in low gear, making the transmission whine, rough tarmac flying beneath the dim pools of light of the wartime headlamps. They'd gone only a further hundred yards when out of the gloom Rosie saw the glowing taillights of a speeding fire engine heading in the same direction.

'Please God, let it not be Morelli's!' she said, aloud. 'And if it is, not Hazel!'

The fire engine swerved left then right, the crew clinging to the outside, hanging on grimly as their driver took the turns fast. There was a glow in the sky ahead. It must be Morelli's after all.

'*Oh God, please let Hazel be alright!*' Rosie was surprised to find her hands together as if praying.

At last they slid to a gritty halt on the factory apron, its surface littered with debris and twisted shards of metal. The firemen disembarked, uncoiling hoses and shouting as they hastily sought the main.

Rosie opened the door and stepped straight into the searing heat of an oven. Less than fifty feet in front of them was a lake of fire, balls of boiling flame and smoke billowing up seemingly from underneath the ground. Beyond the huge hole sagged a mass of girders and half-collapsed trusses, wires sprouting like tendrils, small fires like bright little flowers. The air was heavy with dust, causing them to cough and their eyes to stream, and to the noise of the fire-engine bell was added the jet-roar of conflagration and the crackle of tiny explosions.

'We must get back,' Eugene was saying, pulling her arm.

But she broke away, transfixed, fear as well as the flames reflected in her eyes. It seemed impossible that something as solid as the factory could be gone. Had anyone got into the shelter?

She approached the remains of the machine shop, a heap of masonry and metal, draped with cables, fragments of machinery and spewing mains, the pipes disinterred from below ground like dug-up tree roots. In a far corner, what must have been the canteen glowed with the light of ruptured gas, pipes hissing flames at weird angles, filling the dark with an eerie glow, like an old painting of Hell. Behind, the lab was on fire, chemical green flames spitting like a firework, and above the shouts of the fireman could be heard the shattering of glass, as one by one the windows blew out.

271

'*Move away, please!*'

Rosie looked to see the owner of the gruff voice, a man in overalls, wearing a black '*Heavy Rescue*' helmet.

'*There was a shift working!*' she shouted above the noise.

The man nodded. '*I know,*' he shouted back. '*We're waiting for a crane – the roof of the workshop came down on them. We can't go in because of risk of collapse and we need to get the fires out.*'

Rosie had to do something. Before Eugene could try and stop her she took off running, the acidic fumes tickling her throat as the heat from the enveloping fire seared her lungs. Behind, the shouts of the *Heavy Rescue* man receded and were lost in the roar. She kept going, stumbling down a sheer slope of rubble and with difficulty clambering up the other side. She slipped and fell, cutting her knee. She must be near the washroom because there were pieces of water pipe and on top of a mound of bricks stood a complete WC, perched like an absurd throne in the ruins.

Suddenly, amid the mangled jigsaw of stone, metal and glass she recognised a familiar shape: a hand sticking from a hole, almost covered by a metal sheet. The steel was hot, but she tugged it, cursing her weakness. Prising it up and away, she saw him at last, face up, one lens cracked and the other missing and filled with dark soil, so for one awful moment it looked as if he were a pirate, wearing an eyepatch.

'*Clarence!*'

It was the factory boy.

'*No! Not you!*'

She began to dig frantically, scooping the dirt from around him. He must be alive. He had to be. He was just a kid, and much too young to die.

'*Clarence!*'

She grabbed his tank-top and shook him. The boy's head moved with a sickening loose backwards and forwards motion but there was no response. His face, although covered with dirt, bore an expression of serenity and the eyes were closed as if he were sleeping.

A large hand came to rest on her shoulder, and she found herself looking again into the face of the *Heavy Rescue* man. He was breathing heavily and his skin was red, stretched tight with heat. Rivulets of sweat ran down his brow and onto his face, leaving marks in the grime like tears.

'We'll take it from here, miss,' he said gently.

Rosie slumped down, squatting on the rubble, watching as the man and a companion lifted the boy's lifeless body and carried it away.

She wondered if she were dreaming, but a sudden pain suggested reality. There was glass in her knee. She tugged out the splinter and watched fascinated as a tiny rivulet of blood followed. Time seemed to have slowed down, and she began to feel dizzy. Absurdly, all she could think of was who would have Clarence's shiny red works bicycle. She remembered his tuneless whistling, his childish jokes and the ringing of the bell as he arrived, always early, for work.

The shouts of the rescue team dragged Rosie into the present, forcing her to move from the encroaching flames. She stumbled clumsily towards the voices across the burning debris, arriving spluttering near the car.

'Where have you been?'

It was Eugene, his uniform covered in mud, and an odd mixture of fear and relief on his face. He was perspiring heavily, face stained with soot.

'Holy smokes! I was worried about you.'

He pulled her close. For a few moments he held her tightly, rocking her back and forth. She could feel something like distress in him, his body shaking and chest heaving.

They broke apart.

'I'm so sorry.' His eyes welled with moisture.

'What?' He looked horribly awkward and a sudden chill ran through her body.

'I've been helping them,' he said. 'They lifted part of a wall. Come with me.'

He led her across the yard.

He stopped and she could see at his feet a row of bundled shapes lying on the ground. With a shock she realised they must be bodies, hastily covered by blankets. She drew level and Eugene grabbed her hand.

'I tried, I really did,' he said, looking urgently into her eyes, as if willing her to understand.

There was something familiar about the shape of the bundle on the ground. It was slender and long, and from under the blanket protruded a lock of blonde hair. Rosie braced herself and pulled back the sheet.

Hazel lay quietly, eyes closed.

'I found her under a piece of metal,' Eugene was saying, 'I thought it had saved her, but … I'm sorry.' His voice petered out.

To the right of Hazel's temple the hair was matted with a dark clot of blood and a livid blue bruise marked her forehead and neck. It was impossible that she could be gone.

Rosie wanted to scream, but the pain was beyond any sound she could make.

Eugene bent down and touched Hazel's cheek.

Suddenly he recoiled.

'*Hazel?*' he said.

'What is it?' Rosie said, leaning forward.

The eyes of the corpse opened slowly, and they heard a faint cracked voice.

'Clara?'

'My God!' Eugene muttered.

'*Hazel!*'

Disbelief mixing with joy, Rosie kissed her friend's cheek.

Hazel tried to sit up but failed. She focused with difficulty on Rosie.

'Well, you took your bloody time,' she managed at last.

'I'm sorry!' Rosie was half laughing, half crying.

The ambulance man arrived, astonishment on his broad face.

'*Oh my God! Stretcher!*' he bellowed.

'Got a gob on him, hasn't he?' said the undead Hazel, trying again to sit up.

She looked at the HR man, then at Eugene who looked like someone who has witnessed a miracle.

'Would you keep down the noise?' she said croakily, closing her eyes. 'Some of us is restin'.' She lay back in a fit of coughing.

A stretcher arrived and she was soon in an ambulance.

The *Heavy Rescue* man was standing awkwardly, a notepad in hand, looking at Rosie.

'Ah, no.' Eugene moved towards him, guessing his unasked question.

Rosie interrupted. 'It's alright, Eugene. I know what he wants. It's OK.'

'You're from the factory, miss?' the man enquired. 'I was wondering …' He was clearly embarrassed.

Rosie nodded. 'I'll help … identify…' She couldn't finish the sentence, but stooped, lifting the next blanket.

She forced herself to look beneath. It was Mr. Bland, the caretaker. There wasn't a scar on him, but his face held a surprised look as though he hadn't expected his life to be over so soon. She gasped, wanting to cry, to release the grief building inside her, but no tears would come.

'Miss?' It was the HR man. He had a bundle of what looked like luggage tags.

'This one,' she said, 'is Mr. Bland, the caretaker.'

The HR man scribbled on a tag and attached it to an exposed toe. They moved grimly along.

Eugene lifted another covering.

Rosie gulped. 'This one is Mercer ... she is ... she was a cook, in the canteen.'

'This one ... this is Clarence Greenstreet. He was the office boy.'

She sighed and couldn't stop herself from reaching out to touch him. His body lay motionless, pale.

'Clarence?'

She found herself grabbing Clarence's shoulders but the body was empty, the force that had given it life and personality gone. She saw once again that the body of a person was just a shell, a vehicle by which the personality and soul was transported. All that had made him who he was had gone: thoughts, memories, everything he had learned or seen. A torrent of tears poured down her face, running through the grime, cutting clear pink lines in the dirt. It wasn't only Clarence she was grieving for, but for all those lost, for all the pain and suffering, for herself, for her father.

'It's OK, miss,' the HR man was saying, discomforted, 'we can manage.'

Rosie shook her head. 'No, I'll finish.' Crawling to the next body she identified it, and the next, driving herself on.

She reached the end of the line and knelt by the last body.

Rosie took a deep breath as Eugene pulled back the cover. The dark-brown hair had been stained almost black with burned blood, rivulets of it streaking the young woman's pale face. The eyes, once glinting and fiery, stared blankly at the sky, pupils dilated like holes leading to nowhere. Rosie pulled back and, after a moment's silence, the HR man coughed.

'You knew her, miss?

Rosie nodded dumbly. 'Clara Clampitt,' she managed at last. She felt a sudden connection with the dead woman. Their past conflict seemed petty and she was ashamed.

Eugene tugged the tarpaulin back into place.

'The other one,' the HR man nodded in the direction of the ambulance, 'the young blonde lady – she went back in and tried to get this one out. They were coming back over that pile of rubble when the wall came down on them. It caught this one,' he gestured downward, 'on the head. She didn't stand a chance.'

Eugene and Rosie went back to the car. They clambered in and silently she felt his hand quietly enclose her own. It was large and comforting.

'The wedding,' she said, staring ahead.

For a moment he seemed to struggle to keep up.

'Oh yes. The wedding.'

'It will have to be soon, won't it? I mean you'll ...'

He sighed. 'Be going home soon. Yes.'

She looked at him. His brown eyes were full of emotion, fear, hope. This one night had changed them both.

She pressed on, suddenly determined. 'I want it as soon as possible.'

He leant over and with unusual tenderness ran his hand through her hair. It was as though he too had come to a decision.

'Sure thing, kiddo,' he said.

CHAPTER 30

She'd climbed as high as she dared, but the outer branches of the veteran tree were getting precariously thin. The last fruits looked the most perfect, but were suspended from a sub-branch that ran near the canopy's edge, where strong wood thinned until barely more than a twig. Rosie edged slowly along the limb, but a loud crack forced her rapidly back. She descended the tree, reluctantly leaving the last of the bounty unpicked. At the base of the lichen-encrusted trunk a wooden crate stood, half-filled with crisp Russet apples, ready to go to the garage and join those already there.

Rosie dropped the final few feet to the ground.

'Tha'll do thyself a mischief one of these days.'

Hazel was observing her with shaded eyes from the wingback chair Rosie had dragged into the garden for her. She shook her enamel mug.

''Tis thirsty work, this supervisin'.'

Hazel's smile was lopsided, the right side of her face bruised and still healing after the final removal of the stiches that ran from halfway up her cheek to her skull. She'd been lucky, for the visible wound was relatively light and the cut not too deep. Besides, while a scar on most women might have seemed like a violation of beauty, on Hazel it might even add to her tough, boyish character. If anyone could wear it, it would be her.

Rosie took the mug and walked slowly back to the house. It wasn't only the external wounds she'd had to deal with. The days since Hazel had been home had proved there were others, unseen.

The kitchen was littered with the sweet-smelling but rough-skinned Russets. Rosie filled the kettle and placed it on the hob.

Hazel's changed mood since the Doodlebug was weighing on her. She'd expected her friend to be upset about Clara, but the reaction to her death was extreme. She almost gave up speaking, slept continually and refused food except when Rosie became insistent. It became suddenly clear that the bond between Hazel and Clara was a deep one, far deeper than Rosie had ever imagined. But it was only when she recalled the intensity of the passion between Hazel and Clara during their fight in the factory that the penny finally dropped. With an odd sense of disappointment she had realised she was not the first of Hazel's lovers.

Hazel had seemed at first to recover, but her changed moods looked to be a more permanent state of affairs. Rosie glanced out of the kitchen door down the path to where her friend sat. It was as though the battered young woman who sat there, surrounded by butterflies and meandering bumblebees, was not the same person at all. She could be suddenly argumentative, had a patchy memory and would withdraw into herself for long periods, only to resurface and want to talk about the event over and over again.

When the tea brewed, Rosie poured the bright, reddish liquid through the strainer into their enamel mugs, added milk and kicked open the back door. Overhead a flight of B17's buzzed past on their way to the American field. Above them a pair of fighters wheeled and circled still higher in the blue. Rosie stared at them for a moment. The sun was glinting on the Plexiglass of the cockpits, and she felt a wave of gladness that Eugene, who was now flying a desk in Intelligence could not possibly be up there. Since the night of the bomb, she'd felt closer to him and oddly protective.

Hazel's injury though, and the stark reality of the deaths of Clara, Clarence and the others had left an odd sense of guilt hanging in the air. Rosie often found herself wondering why she'd survived and was herself gripped by an unease that came and went like a fog bank, paralysing her thinking. She wasn't sure she had a right to be breathing when so many others were dead. Perhaps that was what ailed Hazel too, though if it was it seemed she had a worse dose of it.

Rosie reached her friend, upended a wooden crate with her foot and put the mugs on it.

Hazel had been reading one of her political magazines but it was left, unusually half-finished, on the grass.

In the street on the far side of the house, a motorcycle went by, growling and backfiring. Hazel stiffened, but the sound moved quickly away, rising and falling as the rider pushed the machine through the gears, and she slowly relaxed.

'For a moment I thought it was one of them bloody things,' she muttered darkly.

'A Doodlebug?' Rosie nodded. 'It sounded like that, didn't it? Like the one that horrible night.' She patted her friend on the shoulder and shivered.

'I never saw owt,' said Hazel into her tea, as if she hadn't repeatedly said this before. 'Just some gert flash then I couldn't breathe and all the lights were out. I remember finding Clara then, next thing I were looking up at that bloody Yank, and after that your ugly mug.' She paused. 'Then I knew for sure – I were in Hell.' She began to laugh, grimaced in pain and raised a hand to her face.

Rosie reached out and touched her friend's scar.

'Bloody freak I am,' said Hazel.

Rosie shook her head. 'Don't exaggerate. You'll be fine. You just have to let it heal. It'll look worse before it gets better.' She recalled awkwardly that that particular hopeless saying was one her mother used. 'Budge up!'

Rosie sat on the wide padded arm of the armchair.

'I *hate* that bloody Hitler,' she said with feeling. 'Not just for the bombs, not just for those freakish flying robot things, but for all he stands for – for his hatred, and his strutting about, for the pain he's spread across the world like some kind of sickness.'

Hazel nodded glumly. 'Aye. Bloody right. He'd have us making babies for his army if he ever got in here.'

Morelli had been generous in allowing them paid time off and the lack of occupation had given Rosie time to think.

'What I mean is,' she went on, 'this war is just ... different. There's something ... else, something evil about it, with all the women and children killed.' She grimaced. 'If I could get my hands on his scrawny throat, I'd strangle him myself!' she declared, making a violent gesture with her hands.

Hazel turned and looked at her. 'Bloody 'ell, that doesn't sound like thee!'

'I'm changing.' Rosie picked an apple from the ground and regarded it, 'I've felt it for a long time now. I'm getting stronger, and it feels good.' It was true. Despite all that had happened during the Night of The Bomb, as she had taken to calling it, leaving home, working, dating Eugene and making love with Hazel had combined to lift her onto a new level.

For a while there was silence. They sat and watched as the local blackbird determinedly tugged a large worm from the grass.

'Tha don't have to go back to factory for a week or so?'

There was a note of pleading in Hazel's voice.

Rosie took her hand. 'You know that. I'm here till they get the temporary factory up and then I'm on part-shifts. Morelli's been kind. He knows I'm looking after you.'

'Oh.' Like many things Hazel had been told since the flying bomb, this seemed to be another one she'd forgotten.

Rosie had a sudden idea and jumped to her feet.

'Just a minute!'

She ran back to the house, emerging a few minutes later with a hairbrush. She brandished it with a smile.

'This'll cheer you up!' She stood behind Hazel and began to run the bristles gently through the still-tangled hair. The left side was growing out of the bob, towards the shoulder. But the right side had been partially shaved, with fresh growth only just appearing to cover the scar. Rosie had washed it for her that morning, removing the last of the dried blood.

'I'm not a bloody dog!' Hazel said as she picked up the magazine again.

Her face wore a scowl and it wasn't easy to tell if she was joking.

Rosie dropped the brush into her apron pocket. She'd nursed Hazel since she'd been back from hospital, but she'd been a far from easy patient. She would wake every couple of hours through the night with sickly nightmares that she'd relate at once in gory detail, and her bursts of temper had become more frequent as her body began to heal.

Rosie had to insist on having a bed to herself and that hadn't gone down well either, but her sleep had suffered and she needed the rest.

Rosie felt a brief flicker of irritation and on impulse decided to tell Hazel about Eugene. She had to know sometime and the strain of keeping it from her was becoming unbearable.

'Eugene has asked me to marry him.'

The truth was out, and in the silence came the rumble of traffic from the main road.

'What did tha tell 'im?'

Having started it, Rosie's courage wavered.

'I said I might,' she lied.

Another pause.

Hazel tossed the magazine onto the grass. 'Well, that's that.' She put her head in her hands.

'I've put off answering him,' Rosie lied again, suddenly panicking that Hazel might break down. She didn't feel up to dealing with that. 'But he wants me to give him an answer. He has to go back soon, back to America.'

Hazel turned to her. A tear was running down the left side of her face. Curiously, the right eye remained dry.

'Why?'

Rosie felt flustered. 'Why what?'

'Why say tha might?'

Rosie paused. There was no easy way to say it. 'He asked, and we're closer now. I don't know … I'm flattered. Besides … oh, Hazel, he's offering a new life!'

'In America?'

Rosie nodded.

Hazel stood unsteadily.

'And tha believes him?'

Rosie felt the green eyes observing her keenly.

'Yes, of course I do. I think he has some problems he doesn't talk about, maybe because of the war. Plenty of pilots have that, and soldiers and sailors too, I gather. But I think I can help him, change him, and I believe he will help me.'

'Dead romantic you are!' Hazel retorted. 'An' a fool. Tha cannot change a leopard's spots. Tha knows that. He's a man, Rosie. And a Yank.' She shook her head in exasperation. 'An' what about me? Does tha want me to be noble? And accept it all? Does tha? Well, I won't. I'm selfish, Rosie. Bloody selfish.' She'd begun to cry. 'I'm afraid if you leave me.'

'I'm not leaving you.'

'Tha will if tha goes to America. What does tha expect me to do, rush out and get me a Yank and tag along? They'll not want me like this. Like bloody Frankenstein.'

She sobbed, covering her face with her hands.

Distressed, Rosie rushed forward and embraced her. 'I'm sorry, Hazel. So sorry.'

For a while Hazel cried, then Rosie pulled away.

'I'm not going anywhere now, Hazel,' she said as reassuringly as she could. 'Not just like that. And we'll work something out. But I will marry him. I'll never have the chance again.'

Hazel said nothing but rested her head on Rosie's shoulder.

Rosie carried on. 'I'm going to go through with it. I don't know if it's the right thing or not. But, anyway, it'll be a year before they ship us GI Brides out – so they say.'

'A year?' There was suddenly a glint in Hazel's eyes.

'Yes. There's thousands of us, apparently. So, for a while, it'll just be you and me. Then we can decide.'

Hazel looked her in the eye. 'Promise?'

'Aye. I mean, yes. I promise.'

Hazel nodded. She broke off and shuffled away, back to the house.

Rosie felt as though she were being ripped in two, dragged in opposite directions by the two of them.

CHAPTER 31

31st July 1944

It was supposed, Rosie reminded herself, gazing contemplatively at her reflection in the gilded mirror in the hotel's Ladies Room, to be the happiest day of a woman's life. But instead she felt an odd, dream-like sense of detachment, even confusion, as though she were the star in a play in which only everyone else seemed to know the lines. She'd had the most outrageously expensive hair-do, managed to procure some elusive pre-war make-up and had almost cried when Mrs. Barton presented her the week before with an Edwardian country dress in the most beautiful cream-coloured silk. Yet she had the odd feeling of being in a dream, witnessing something that was either not real, or that was happening to someone else.

Rosie gazed at the dress, absently caressing the small red and blue silk flowers sewn into the neckline that matched the larger paper ones Mrs. B. had later tucked, like a crown, into her hair. She couldn't help but think that the off-white colour, for which her old friend had been unnecessarily apologetic, was, given what happened with Hazel, more appropriate than anyone knew. And yet, despite that earlier experience, the thought of what was going to happen that evening, with Eugene, filled her not only with excitement, but also unexpectedly a sense of fear.

She checked her hair again for the fifth time and bent to blot her lipstick on her handkerchief. The wedding ceremony itself had gone flawlessly, but had taken place in a rather gloomy registry office. She'd expected something solemn and meaningful, given the event was intended to shape the rest of their lives together, but it turned out to be a rather brief and informal thing, rather like anything else you might do at the local council offices, like complain about the drains or register for the ARP.

And Eugene had turned up late. He'd looked wonderfully glamorous in his full dress uniform, but seemed oddly harassed, even distant. He'd come from the base, so perhaps something was up.

But it had at least gone smoothly, none of her pre-imagined disasters taking place. Her brother, home from the Navy and somewhat the worse for rum, stepped in to give her away, while Eugene's huge friend and co-pilot Hank was the genial and endearingly emotional best man.

Her mother did attend in the end but, although she remained icy cold and aloof in a space of her own at the back of the Registry Office, at least there'd been no scene, unless that is you counted her odd choice of a funereal black dress and bonnet, which did cause some whispering among the guests.

Hazel didn't appear which, though regrettable, might have been for the best. She'd prayed for no disaster and had, after all, been granted her wish. The hymn, 'Amazing Grace', one of her father's favourites, had been sung heartily if a bit tunelessly by Eugene's crew. The only truly awful moment had been when Eugene hesitated for what seemed like an absolute age before signing the register, although this seemed to have gone unnoticed by everyone else.

Rosie gave the mirror one more glance, adjusted her hair yet again, and walked through the door into the hotel lobby as boldly and carelessly as she could manage. To her surprise, she was greeted by a welcoming murmur from the swell of guests which had materialised out of nowhere. With no family to speak of, and with Eugene's overseas, she'd been worried that there would be only a few people there, but she hadn't counted on the innate hospitality of the Americans. Crew, sweethearts and it seemed half the Air Force had turned up to celebrate her day, and she felt a surge of relief. They'd even brought a band, a number of brightly coloured flags which had been draped on the walls, and the glitter-ball from their first dance which was now suspended, somewhat incongruously, from the hotel's low ceiling.

Her spirits began to lift as she recognised the tall Air Force padre, and a couple of the senior officers from the ceremony earlier, but many of the other smartly dressed young men and women, in and out of uniform, were complete if welcome strangers.

As she moved through the friendly throng, she was greeted by other familiar faces. Mrs. B., of course, was there, looking splendid in a gorgeous dress, while from the factory both Mr. Morelli senior and his son had arrived, both raising glasses in salute from the bar, where her brother seemed to be entertaining a group of Yank airmen with some loud and humorous story or other. Here and there, it seemed like hesitant new liaisons were being made between local girls and airmen while somewhere in the background the band was playing 'Sentimental Journey'.

Behind a scrum of young men in a corner, she could make out Eugene, and was surprised to see him taking a generous top-up of champagne. She knew the wine that everyone seemed to prize so much had come from captured Luftwaffe stocks in France, brought over by a reconnaissance plane at the airbase. But somehow she'd expected him to wait for her and drink the first glass together. And from the look of him, it seemed this wasn't his first drink. She was about to approach when she caught sight of a figure sitting in an alcove on a *chaise-longue* and rather incongruously sipping a dimpled pint glass of dark English beer. At first glance she'd took it to be an unknown young man, but with a shock she realised it was a woman, and someone she knew only too well.

'Hazel!'

As she approached Rosie saw her friend was wearing a pair of slacks with a tweed waistcoat and jacket, topped with a hat at a rakish angle. A pink rose protruded from a buttonhole and she wore a pair of men's brogues. Her hair had been ruthlessly cut short, like a boy. It gave her the look of a handsome youth, or perhaps one of those educated women you saw in posh magazines. At a push she could almost have been one of Virginia Woolf's hangers-on. Rosie sighed. It was rebellion of course, a statement against her, the wedding but also society at large, daring them to criticise so they could be subject to a lecture on natural justice, or women's rights. Or far worse, her prior claim to the bride.

Rosie had begged her to come, leaving her much the worse for drink the night before, when she'd accepted Mrs. B.'s unexpected invitation to stay over so she could help with the dress and make-up the next morning. She'd gone directly from there to the hotel in an Air Force car driven by a Polish guy from Eugene's crew and had not seen her friend in almost 36 hours. It looked as though she'd not been sober since.

Other guests were staring at the oddly attired visitor, but Rosie wouldn't make the mistake of losing her cool.

'You didn't come to the Registry Office,' she said, dropping down next to her friend on the *chaise-longue* and regarding her sadly.

'I'm 'ere now, ain't I?'

Hazel swayed slightly. She really was drunk.

Rosie glanced uneasily at the other guests.

'How many have you had?' Rosie nodded at the remains of the pint, which Hazel raised and drained in one, the contents embarrassingly leaking out from the sides of her mouth and running down her chin.

'Not enough,' she said, glancing blearily at the bar.

Rosie grabbed Hazel's sleeve. 'I'm glad you came. Truly. But ...'

'Don't make a scene?'

Rosie nodded. 'Please, it's been a strange enough day already.'

'Oh, aye?' her friend enquired, looking suddenly more interested.

Rosie drew a breath. She wasn't for the life of her going to let Hazel think it had been a flop. 'Only because I've never been married before!' she joked weakly. Everything is just so ...' she looked around, 'grand, and there are so many guests I don't even know.'

Hazel peered at her over her pint, eagerly searching for some deceit.

A figure materialised out of the crowd.

'I'll be going now, my dear.'

The aged voice belonged to Mrs. B. She nodded at Hazel.

Hazel belched uncontrollably and wiped her mouth on her sleeve. 'Pardon me, I'm sure.'

Mrs. B. exchanged glances with Rosie.

'What a lovely outfit, Hazel,' Mrs. B. managed before turning to Rosie. 'I have to be going. Old Mr. Morelli has offered to give me a lift in his smart auto and I've accepted'. There was a bright twinkle in her eye. 'It's been a lovely day, Rosie. I'm so proud of you.'

The old lady kissed Rosie on the head, nodded uncertainly to Hazel and was gone, heading for the door where a dapper and apparently keen Mr. Morelli waited, hat in hand.

Rosie turned to Hazel who was now standing very close, swaying gently.

'Tha knows I couldn't have borne it to be there, girl.'

'Hazel …please …'

'I'm not well, tha knows.'

Rosie looked her over. Suddenly she caught sight of a thin trickle of blood, slowly making its way from under her friend's hat.

'*Hazel!*'

Hazel reached up and touched the blood, examining her reddened fingers with exaggerated care.

Rosie looked round. To her embarrassment, a few of the lads from Eugene's crew were looking their way.

'Nay, lass. Not that old thing,' Hazel was saying. ''Tis my heart that's broken.'

As if to emphasise her point, a fat tear made its slowly way down her cheek.

'Hazel, you know I had to do this. I just had to. You know that.'

'But tha doesn't love 'im, does tha?'

Rosie drew in her breath. 'I'm not sure I know what love is, Hazel.' Then she added, hoping to placate her, 'Not with a man.' She reached out, putting an arm around her emotional friend.

'I love thee,' Hazel announced, rather too loudly, and before Rosie could say any more she planted a lingering, damp kiss on her cheek.

Rosie accepted her kiss. Whatever anyone else might think, she did still love Hazel, and it was easier just to play along. In any case, the sight of her friend's tears had pricked her conscience.

'I must go,' she said then. 'I've hardly spoken with Eugene since the ceremony.'

'Tha'll have ter rush then,' Hazel announced, nodding past her to the door. 'Looks like 'ee's got what yer might call urgent business elsewhere.'

Rosie whirled round. Eugene was being escorted calmly but firmly from the hotel by two armed MPs. In one corner she glimpsed another Military Policeman holding back some members of Eugene's crew who seemed to be none too happy about the proceedings.

'Rosie.'

'Hank!'

It was a relief to see Eugene's bear-like co-pilot. The American nodded after her departing husband.

'Don't worry, Rosie. It's nothing we can't sort out. I'll get him back, I promise.' He disappeared rapidly, shouting after the disappearing group. 'Hey!'

Her face flushed pink, Rosie turned to Hazel who gave her what her father would have called an old-fashioned look, and seemed about to say something.

Rosie raised her finger to her lips. The day seemed not so much to be slipping as running away from her. 'Don't you dare say a word!'

Hazel coughed, and extracted what Rosie, to her horror, saw was a pipe from her pocket. She lit it with a flourish.

'I'm sayin' nothin'.' She nodded at the bar where a crowd of questioning faces were looking their way. 'But tha better get back to thy guests.'

By the time Rosie turned back again, her friend was sauntering, in a particularly infuriating and masculine way, out of the door, trailing a cloud of blue smoke, the pipe stuck jauntily in her mouth.

Rosie forced herself to stay for at least the first half of the evening, being what she imagined a good hostess would be, absorbing the countless reassurances from the guests and trying to seem as calm and nonchalant as a heroine from some patriotic war picture. Mercifully, the bar served food at eight, by which time the murmur of voices had in any case recovered from its earlier deathly hush and was now a raucous but reassuring babble, punctuated by singing which ranged through the fug of smoke and clink of glasses. The meal was something the Americans called a cold buffet: dishes of meats, salads, sandwiches, potato crisps and cakes, the like of which, while seemingly taken for granted by the Americans, made the eyes of the English guests almost pop out of their heads. A crowd several deep soon formed as people queued to be served by waiters from the hotel.

For an hour more Rosie forced herself to stay on, drifting to the door every so often to check for Eugene's reappearance. There was no sign of Hank and she was too embarrassed to approach any others of the crew.

By ten she noticed she was getting glances from the other guests, so, a little awkwardly she said her goodbyes and her thank-you's and made her way upstairs to the double room she'd seen briefly earlier. She reached the top of the stairs and turned, giving one last look for Eugene. Despite the long day, her mind darted about restlessly, as though confused at the signals her body was sending. It was typical of the Air Force to have pulled him away. Neither it nor The War gave a damn about two young people getting married and a sense of grievance, smouldering into anger, began to form in Rosie's mind.

Inside the bedroom, she put the bath on to run and while she waited for it to fill gently teased the flowers from her hair. Rebelliously, she ran the bath three times the regulation five inches deep before stripping and plonking herself down in the comforting warm water. There were no foaming bath salts, just the hotel's bar of hard, unperfumed soap to clean herself with. She scrubbed herself clean, a self-flagellation that seemed to be more about wiping off the frustrations and disappointments of the day than becoming clean. When she had finished, she lingered a while before pulling the plug and watching the water swirl away down the belching drain.

Rosie dried herself on one of the large white towels before she donned the blue satin nightdress, a wedding gift from Eugene. It slipped smoothly over her head, cascading down her slender body until it came to a halt some ten inches from the floor. She let down her hair and sat in front of the dressing-table mirror, brushing it while she gazed in some confusion at the young woman the glass reflected back.

Downstairs the reception showed no sign of quietening down, the guests perhaps waiting, like her, for the groom's return.

Looking around the small room with its cracked plaster ceiling and heavy blackout curtains, Rosie wished there was a radio to fill the time while she waited. She threw herself on the double bed, rifled through the cabinet, but found only a copy of *Woman and Home*. She lay on her back and half-heartedly tried to read. The cover showed a deliriously happy woman cutting a wedding cake. Inside were advertisements for prams, articles about gardening and a pattern for a cardigan. It was mundane, and Rosie wondered why magazines didn't include articles about subjects that were important, like difficult mothers, marriage, or even sex. Perhaps one day they would.

Downstairs a man, not Eugene, made what sounded like a speech, and the piano struck up again. The hotel resonated with singing. A tide of hot irritation mixed with disappointment began to rise in her. But everyone had to put up with bad things in a war, she reminded herself. Perhaps this was not so bad. She sighed, covering her ears with the pillow. She tried humming to block out the noise, then lying face down, head buried in pillow, but the absurdity of it was too much and she sat up again. As if on cue, gales of laughter suddenly echoed loudly up the stairwell.

Her patience suddenly snapped sending Rosie for the door, but pausing when her hand closed on the brass knob. There she halted, perplexed with feverish second thoughts. If Eugene were still not back, she would look foolish reappearing to look for him. But it would be even more embarrassing if he was there and it was obvious she'd only come to drag an apparently reluctant husband to their wedding bed. People would stare, or snigger.

Restlessly she moved to the window and glanced out. There was no sign of him in the driveway. She sat down on the bed.

'What the hell are you doing?' she asked the floor, imagining Eugene below. She felt angry, furious even, but knew that if he walked in the feeling would evaporate.

With agonising slowness, the leaden hours ticked by. According to the smart new watch he'd bought her, it was after one in the morning when she rose from the bed and took hold of the champagne bottle which was by now swimming in a slushy pool of glacially cool melt-water. After a brief struggle with the cork there was a satisfying pop. White spume immediately surged out, surprising her with its force, dripping to the floor and spattering the front of her nightdress. Disregarding it, she put the bottle to her lips, and coughed as the gaseous liquid expanded, tingling in nose and throat. The music was still loud, but then she supposed it could be. There were no other guests, for the Americans had invaded the hotel much as her mother had insisted they'd invaded the country, taking over every room. She began to sway, dancing gently by herself. By the time the spent container clunked to the floor, she was more drunk than she'd ever been in her life.

'Ha!' she said. 'I hope you heard that!'

Raising two fingers, she made a rude gesture at the floor, switched off the light and walked as haughtily as possible to the window. She tugged back the heavy blackout curtain and opened the casement, climbing unsteadily out to sit on the sill. The moon was rising, turning the stream that ran through the hotel into a ribbon of mercury and rendering the trees and shrubs in the grounds in shades of silver and grey. It was much cooler outside and the fresh air quickly reacted with the champagne, sending a thrill of bitter-sweet euphoria surging through her.

Rosie belched, giggled at her own rudeness, and swung her bare legs back and forth, bumping them against the wall. She gazed into the void, leant forward, wavering over the edge, swaying close to the point of no return. Some way off she heard the gruff rumble of a motor vehicle, and closer the high-pitched clicks of swooping bats.

She must have sat there for hours, listening to the sounds of the night, for when she thought of returning inside she was shivering with the cold and the hotel was eerily quiet. Clambering through the casement, she almost fell back into the room, staggered to the bed, covered herself with the blankets and sank immediately and unexpectedly into a deep and irresistibly seductive sleep.

CHAPTER 32

It was the rude early morning light that prodded Rosie into a state of consciousness. Momentarily forgetting where she was, she opened her eyes and sat up. Then, with a sinking feeling, she remembered. The wedding. The hotel. Eugene. It had been real. She checked the bed next to her and found the other half still unslept in. Her eye caught sight of something pushed beneath the door.

Dizzily she crossed the room and picked up the large plain envelope. Fuzzy-headed, she tore it open. Inside was a thick piece of paper which turned out to be a marriage certificate, informing her in stark black letters she was now the wife of Captain Eugene Flynn. A piece of notepaper fell onto the floor, which she stooped to retrieve before sitting at the dressing table. The paper bore the letterhead of the Eighth Army Air Force. She took a sip from the glass of water left there and began to read.

Dear Rosie,
You are probably wondering where I got to last night.
I can't tell you much about the emergency I was called away for, but it's do

with the Invasion, which as you know has gotten bogged down now we're so much further into France. Anyway, they need everyone who can fly, and although I hoped all that was over, I was 'persuaded' to go.

I didn't want to do it, and of course I refused. But you may as well know by now that a certain person made certain allegations against me concerning the use of drugs when I was flying, and I was given a choice – to go on the mission or lose my rank and everything that goes with it. I wanted to say goodbye last night, but the M.P.'s had their orders and were most insistent. I tried to avoid what you British call 'a scene'.

So, I'm writing this in case I don't come back, and because, even if I do, it's unlikely they will let us meet again before you come to America. The Colonel says that you will be sent your papers in due course, but it seems that I'll be on a plane bound for the US not long after I get back to base.

I can't imagine how disappointed you must be. A wedding night is a special thing, I know. But I'm going to ask you to be strong and understand that it was not my fault. We will meet again, in the States, and then everything will become clear.

But, for now, I want you to know that you, Rosie, have kept me sane during my tour, and without you I don't know if I would have made it. I grew close to you not only because you are beautiful and funny, but also because I saw a brave soul battling against the world. No matter what the world has done to you, you did not become bitter, did not return evil for evil, and I respect you for that. You are a much better human being than I could ever be.

I know that the best place for you is not England, but America. It's a place where the lights are still on and the buildings still standing, a land of better opportunities, of hope. I wanted to give that to you for all you have done for me. I know I have been distracted sometimes, because of the war, but I realised that 'night of the flying bombs' just what I owed you, and what I wanted to give.

So, speak to the Colonel and get your papers. Come to America, and then at least something good will have come out of this terrible war.

Your husband

Eugene

Rosie put down the letter, her mind spinning with disbelief. He wasn't coming. She felt sick and moved to the sink where her stomach heaved, spewing its contents violently into the white porcelain. Wiping her mouth, she sat back down at the dressing table and looked at herself in the mirror. Her hair was a mess, her face blotchy where she'd been crying and dirty tracks of mascara ran down her cheeks like the painted tears of a clown. It wasn't the face of a newly married woman, but that of a humiliated girl. She felt herself beginning to tremble and at the back of her eyes came the hot pricking of fresh tears. She shook herself. No matter what had happened, she wasn't going to just give in.

She read the letter again, but the more she went over the words, the odder they seemed. And the drugs! What could he mean? They had landed him in some kind of trouble with the Air Force but how could you be in trouble for taking medicine? Were they drugs he was not supposed to have, meant perhaps for someone else? Had he stolen them? Perhaps he needed them to cope with the missions? It didn't sound like something to be ashamed of. Her heart sank. They'd seemed to be getting closer each time they met but and now it was as though she didn't know the tall American at all.

Rosie poured a glass of water from the jug on the table. Images of their short time together ran helter-skelter through her mind like frames from a movie stuck together at random. The night of the flying bomb remained strongest. They'd been close then, and it had seemed so real. They'd connected. She'd thought she'd seen into his soul, and what she'd seen there was loving, self-sacrificing, true. Had she been wrong about him all along?

Staring at herself in the mirror, she made a snap decision. No matter what happened, she decided, she was not going to be crushed. She wouldn't give up her plan of escape and freedom, even if it meant going to America and finding herself alone when she got there. It was as though she'd suddenly reached the bottom of a deep well into which she'd been falling and now the only way out was up. She would survive.

Rosie took another sip of water and began to tidy her hair. A few minutes later she was putting on the powder-blue jacket and skirt hanging on the back of the door. She picked up her suitcase and walked downstairs and out of the hotel. It was five miles to town, but she needed the time to clear her mind. The way was rocky and rough for a woman in heels, and from time to time she stumbled. But her feet were running on autopilot, and knew where they were going.

The hedgerows, scented with sweet summer hawthorn and damp woody soil, thinned until they were replaced at last by the creosoted palisades and plain brick walls that marked the outskirts of town. Weeds were growing through the cracks in the pavements, and here and there pieces of litter scurried, blown haphazardly by the wind. She gazed at the rows of mock-Tudor suburban houses as she passed, one or two still covered with tarpaulins after raids earlier in the war.

At last Rosie stood on the corner of the great west road, a wide ribbon of tarmac that skirted the inner town. The day was beginning and the inhabitants stirring, smoke rising from a thousand breakfast stoves. She would get to the bottom of whatever had happened to Eugene, but for now she was exhausted, and there was only one way to go.

Turning east, she walked towards the sun; the new road taking her away from the old back-to-backs and towards the modern house she still shared with Hazel. All around her the townsfolk, oblivious to her inner turmoil, were moving, the cool morning air torn by the metallic clattering of trams, sprinkled with the notes of garden robins and alive with the coarser chatter of streetwise, urban sparrows.

Eighteen Months Later

CHAPTER 33

Christmas 1946

There was no Christmas tree in the old front room but on the floor lay the same Chinese rug, worn by decades of trespassing feet and pock-marked by fallen embers. Around them the yellowing wallpaper peeled as though the house was trying to shed its skin, and outside dry, splintery snow was falling. Her glum-faced brother seated opposite did nothing to raise Rosie's spirits. The place had been warm once, and full of life, but it was hard to believe that the two young adults now facing each other had been the children that had crawled on the same floors, wrestling for presents and asking their father to referee. Gripped by an uncharacteristic melancholy Rosie suddenly thought of another house, icy cold and similarly bare, across town by the railway where she would be spending the night, alone. The soullessness of that house too seemed to reinforce the sense of loss and, to an extent, the failure of 1946.

And yet it had been a mercy when Hazel finally did quit their shared house to go back 'Up North', their conflicting needs having finally torn the friendship in half. An odd, cheerless letter had come from her earlier in the week, but it had been hard reading and Rosie had left it unfinished, putting it off until she'd gone through the ordeal of meeting her brother. Now she sat, the steaming coffee pot positioned defensively between them. Despite the stark emotions of the past week, she could find no connection with Roger, and had seized on the task of brewing the drink as a means of keeping busy while she worked out what to say.

'I can't believe she's gone,' Roger said at last, looking around the room.

It was indeed unreal and, despite having organised the funeral herself, Rosie half expected the grumpy woman to come growling in from the kitchen at any moment. She recalled the sight of her mother's face, worn down to the soul it seemed, as she lay in the fine mahogany coffin, and her own sense of peace that came when she finally realised that behind the enmity, beyond the insults and the belittling, even past the banishment to the orphanage, had lain a well of pain.

Rosie sighed and glanced at the condolence cards on the mantelpiece. She'd been surprised at the number, and even more so at the crowd that came to their mother's funeral. It had been a simple, chilly affair in the stony little church where her father had been laid to rest.

'She had a good send-off,' said Roger.

'Yes.'

Rosie got up and knelt by the Parkray, opening the door and stoking the coal before adding more. Roger seemed to find it easier to speak when he was not looking her in the face.

'To survive Hitler and die from something as simple as flu,' he said. 'I can't believe they are both gone, Mum and Dad.'

He reached for the coffee and poured, then produced a small hip flask and added a stiff tot of rum.

'What will you do now, Rosie?' he asked offhandedly as if he hadn't been wanting to ask it all along. 'Married but husband three thousand miles away? If that isn't a world upside down, don't know what is.'

His eyes hunted for an answer and it was Rosie's turn to struggle for words. She hadn't told anyone but Hazel about her wedding night, so he must think all was well.

'Yes. I'm married.' It was technically true. She searched for the right expression. 'I don't know. He writes, but the Air Force says it will a while before they can start shipping war brides over. It's all very slow.'

'*War Bride*,' Roger mulled over the words. 'Is that what they're calling you?' He attempted a chuckle but it sounded more like a sigh. 'But you'll go?' His voice had sharpened.

'Yes.' Rosie nodded. 'It's all I have left really. Hazel's gone too now.'

Her brother seemed satisfied. He pulled a small striped hatbox up onto the table, opening it and pushing it towards her.

Mystified, Rosie dipped in a hesitating hand and pulled out a few documents. It looked like the family archive. She could make out what looked like certificates of birth, death and marriage, small bundles of letters tied with ribbon, a few faded photographs.

'Been reading through this,' he said. 'And I think you should too.'

For a few moments there was silence between them.

'Our mother had a whole graveyard of skeletons in the cupboard, Rosie.'

His sister shook her head and flipped through the contents absently.

The Napoleon on the mantelpiece whirred and slowly, as if on the verge of expiring, intoned ten.

'It's getting late,' Rosie said, patting her brother's hand. 'I'm going to give Mrs. B. her present before she goes to bed. Her lights will be off soon.'

Even though there was no more blackout, it still seemed strange to be talking about lights being on.

Roger looked suddenly startled.

'Shall I come too?'

He asked the question dutifully, Rosie thought. His connection with the old woman had never been strong as hers.

'No.' She surprised herself with the firmness of her words. 'I'd rather go alone, if you don't mind.'

'Not at all, Rosie.' He peered at the watch which sat on the wrist of the still gloved hand. 'I expect I'll just pop down to the Dog and Duck for a late pint.'

As he pulled on his duffle coat and scarf and headed out, she turned back to the table and tipped all the papers out of the box.

Rosie hadn't expected to see the house lit, nor a motor-car outside, its wheel-marks inexorably filling with snow. From inside the old lady's house came voices, and she hesitated. Before she could change her mind, a face bobbed at the diamond-shaped pane and then the door opened.

Rosie stood, exposed in a sudden fan of light.

'Hello,' said a warm, sherry-filled male voice. 'Not singing on your own, are you?'

The man smiled and seemed about to reach into his pocket for a shilling. He was dressed in buff corduroy trousers, shirt and a red cardigan and his kindly, ruddy face was creased from exposure to the weather.

'Oh no,' she said hurriedly. 'I just came to give Mrs. B., I mean Mrs. Barton, this.'

She proffered the small parcel.

The man smiled. 'You'd better come in. I'm Lionel, Elizabeth's younger brother, and the noise you can hear are my supposedly grown-up children. You must be Rosie.'

She followed him warily, feeling vaguely tainted by association with the funeral. The house was warm and the air redolent of spices. Mrs. Barton appeared, wearing a brown-and-cream dress, beamed a smile of welcome and they went into the parlour.

In the bay window a tree stood, decked with candles and wooden birds, while on the walls were swags of mistletoe and pine. An open fire was burning.

'I'm so sorry about your mother,' Mrs. B. was saying sympathetically, 'especially at this time of year.'

She looked faintly embarrassed at the cheerfulness of their surroundings as they sat down opposite each other.

'It must have been a blow.'

Rosie nodded.

'I thought it all went well, the funeral though,' Mrs B. added, carefully. 'And your brother made such a good speech. He looked smart in his uniform.'

From the kitchen flowed a cocktail of exuberant voices jingling with laughter. The old lady waved her hand in the direction of the back of the house.

'As you can hear, my brother's here for Christmas. He's brought his family back from Nova Scotia and they're going to be staying on. He's got a job at Morelli's. They're switching to producing those new television things. I'm so pleased!' She looked suddenly awkward as though she shouldn't have spoken of good news.

Rosie handed over the present shyly.

The old lady, with the modesty that was so typical of her, seemed surprised to have received it.

'Rosie, you are kind! Shall I open it or wait for the day?'

'You can open it,' Rosie decided.

After a brief fumble with the wrapping paper, the box of 78's emerged.

'*Oh!*' Mrs. B. exclaimed, opening the lid and sorting through the half dozen records inside. She came to the last one and paused.

'*Chanson Bohemien,*' Rosie said simply.

She glanced around the room, and caught sight of the photograph of the French officer she'd noticed before. He was dashing, in a *Beau Geste* sort of way, with a proud waxed moustache and a stiff military cap. The image had acquired the sepia tint of age, but the silver frame gleamed as if it had been recently polished.

Mrs. B. caught her gaze and as Rosie turned back they exchanged glances. It could have been the light, but the old lady's eyes seemed moister than before.

The old lady hurriedly cleared her throat and said, 'You've decided to go, haven't you, to your American?'

'Yes.' It had been easier to say than she thought. 'I'll be going by boat, so they tell me, though it might take up to a year to arrange. All the soldiers and airmen have to go home first, I think.'

'Are you excited?'

'Afraid,' said Rosie truthfully. She could only have said it to the old lady.

Mrs. B. nodded.

'It's been so long,' Rosie continued. 'The truth is, I can hardly remember him. But I'll go ... especially now that Hazel, my friend, has gone.'

Mrs. B. nodded. 'Ah, young Hazel, yes, you were close to her.'

Rosie felt herself blushing. There was something uncanny about the old woman's perception.

'Yes.'

'I remember Hazel, a fine hardworking young woman,' Mrs. B. continued hastily. 'The country will need more of her kind.' She paused. 'And you must survive, move on.'

Rosie looked at the older woman in surprise. How could she understand so much?

'Auntie Lizzie?' It was a girl, a few years younger than Rosie, sticking her head around the door. 'Would you and your visitor like some coffee and mince pies?'

'My mince pies?'

The girl laughed. It was a lovely bright sound, like water tinkling over the rocks in a stream.

'Yes, Auntie.'

'That would be lovely, Jane.'

The girl disappeared.

'It seems like yesterday,' Mrs. B. said, 'when you arrived back from the, *er*,' she trod carefully, 'the Special School. A little mouse, though perhaps with a gleam in her eye.'

Rosie smiled. 'Yes. I'm not the same as when I … when I started work.'

'If you were my daughter, I would be proud.'

Rosie gulped and briefly looked away. Her relationship with the old woman was the only tie of any strength left.

'Thank you,' she managed. 'But I'm not sure I've achieved much. And the price. The price seems to have been high.'

Mrs. B. nodded. 'It hasn't been easy for you. And it seems to me you've done a lot more than find a career, and a husband. You've begun to find yourself.'

Rosie raised her eyebrows. She'd spent the last few nights sitting alone in the house by the railway, staring into the hissing coals of the fire, trying to make sense of it all. The determination to travel to the

States had waxed and waned, before finally strengthening on the death of her mother.

She found herself gazing again at the photograph of the French officer.

Mrs. B., noting the direction of her gaze, said, 'And did you find love, Rosie?'

'I found friendship. And love. Of a sort. But …'

'It wasn't how you expected?'

'No.' Exposing the thoughts, even to Mrs. B., was like removing her clothes, an embarrassing but somehow necessary act. 'I found people were … weaker than I hoped. I …'

She wanted to tell her about Eugene, about doubts and still unanswered questions but couldn't find the words.

For a moment there was silence between them.

Rosie looked at the old lady. 'Do you remember my father?' she asked.

'Leonard? Of course.' Her smile held the warmth of cherished memory.

'He gave me a kind of optimism, a belief in goodness. He always said that, no matter how dark things got, goodness would always win in the end. He said it about Hitler, and the war, and he was right. He had this … faith, a conviction that reason and love would triumph. I believed it too, and it got me through some of the worst times. So I'm clinging to that.'

'He was a very,' Mrs. B. hesitated, 'intuitive man.'

Jane reappeared, carrying a tray with a plate of mince pies and coffee. She grinned and left them, closing the door quietly behind her. Mrs. B. poured the coffee into two tiny porcelain cups, on the side of each of which was emblazoned a small French Tricolour edged in gold.

'I can't afford it very often,' she confessed, gesturing to the expensive beverage, 'but I get a gift of it every year. From France.' She caressed her cup gently and took a contemplative sip.

For a while they sat, ate and drank and gazed into the fire. The heat seemed to be penetrating more than Rosie's bones. She'd anticipated there would be some emotion in their meeting but inside she was struggling to maintain control. She shook herself and sipped the hot coffee. It was rich and dark.

'Would you like some advice from an old woman?'

Rosie smiled. 'I think I could do with some.'

'Go, and don't be afraid. Fear is your enemy, it holds you back, stops you doing things.' She hesitated. 'It stops you having the life you really should have. Whatever happens between the two of you, you're young and capable. America is such an opportunity. You and that country were made for each other.'

Rosie grinned. 'I never really belonged here.'

The old lady nodded and smiled. 'No, perhaps not.' She paused. 'To tell you the truth, I think now that perhaps I never did either.'

She topped up the coffee cups, and they sipped for a moment in silence.

'I wanted to ask you ...' Rosie said and hesitated. 'Roger has said a few odd things since he's been back home about my mother ... that she had skeletons in the cupboard among other things.'

The old lady picked up the poker and broke the crust forming on the coal. A shower of sparks shot up the chimney swiftly, riding the wave of rising heat, and were gone.

'Bad things, I think,' Rosie added.

Mrs. B. looked at her thoughtfully. She seemed to have made a decision.

'It's time you know the truth. At least what little I know of it.' She drew a deep breath, and looked directly at the young woman. 'Your grandfather, I'm sorry to say, was given to the drink. He'd beat your grandmother.' She paused. 'Then when your mother was born he seemed to calm down, became almost normal. Until the daughter – that's your mother, I mean – got to be ten or eleven.' She coughed. 'Then people started to notice him ... touching her. She started missing school and there was a big kerfuffle. I don't recall everything but the police were called and it was all most unpleasant. It's not unknown, of course, fathers and daughters. Do you understand what I'm saying, Rosie?'

Rosie nodded. 'Yes.' She looked away. She'd not known her grandfather, but it was a horrible thing to hear. And her mother's odd preoccupations suddenly made sense.

Mrs. B. hurried on, 'I think it was that problem in her early life that affected her mind.' Her eyes rested on the suddenly uncomfortable young woman before her. 'Your father knew, but he married her just the same. He loved her, you see. Anyway, her problems got worse, but he stuck with her. There were those that said he should put her in an asylum, but he wouldn't do it. For him "in sickness and in health" meant just that.'

There was a knock on the front door and outside they could hear a group of the local youth hacking their way remorselessly through what had once been a Christmas carol. Out in the hall Lionel was opening the door. For a few seconds they listened to the well-meant but spectacularly tuneless offering.

'Speaking of your brother,' Mrs. Barton said suddenly, 'did Roger show you the box?'

Rosie was startled. How could Mrs Barton know about that when she herself had only just seen it?

'Yes,' she said, curious.

'He spoke to me about it,' Mrs. B. explained, 'though I knew about it before he found it, wherever it was your father had hidden it.'

'You did?'

'When you were still very young, I used to help your father out with your mother. When she got, so to say, really bad. He confided in me.'

'Oh.' Rosie blushed. She still found it awkward to deal with anything to do with her mother, especially in such detail.

'So you saw the will?'

'The will?'

'It was in the box. It's on blue paper with a red seal. Quite distinctive. Didn't you see it?' Seeing Rosie's blank look, Mrs. Barton continued. 'Your father left the house to you, Rosie. I know because he asked me to witness it. It's the last will, because your mother, well, she just wasn't capable, you know.'

Rosie felt as though she had suddenly become frozen to the chair.

'Roger didn't say anything?'

Rosie shook her head. She'd only scanned through the documents quickly, but she was positive there was nothing in there that might have been the will Mrs. Barton had described.

'Ah.' The old lady took out a handkerchief and blew her nose. There was a long pause.

'I'm glad you were honest with me,' said Rosie.

From within the kitchen could be heard the chink of glasses and the sounds of voices. Rosie stood. Suddenly she needed to be alone.

'I must go and leave you to your guests.'

Mrs. B. got to her feet. 'Rosie ...'

For a moment they stood close and Rosie was relieved when Mrs. Barton embraced her.

'Say goodbye to me before you go. To America.'

'I will. Of course.'

The old woman raised a hand. 'Just one more thing.'

She rose and fetched a small brown volume from near the top of her bookcase.

'This is for you.'

Rosie accepted the gift and glanced at the spine. **'A French Affair – Eliza Lavigne'**, it read.

Her eyebrows rose, and she glanced at her friend.

The old lady's face cracked into a smile. 'My nom de plume,' she said bashfully.

Rosie re-entered their cottage, leaving a trail of mushy footprints in the snow-covered yard. In the warmth of the house, the flakes on her coat were soon melting. She brewed a pot of tea, and took it to the table. She sorted quickly through the documents. There was no will or anything like the document Mrs. B. had described.

She sighed and, deep in thought, went to sit by the fire. She'd not been there long when the front door opened and Roger entered and set his snowy coat on the hook.

Rosie looked at her brother sadly. Now she knew what had been on his mind.

'I'm going to have an early night, Roger.'

'Ah.'

He'd never been good at hiding his feelings. He was swaying slightly and she could smell the hoppy tang of beer.

'But I wanted to tell you, I am going,' she said. 'To America. Definitely.'

'Ah,' he said again and, while he was smiling, there was an unspoken question on his face.

Rosie gave a weak, humourless smile. 'Don't worry, Roger. You can have the house. I'm not going to turn you out of your home.'

He looked suddenly embarrassed, but not wanting to talk.

Rosie walked to the front door, opened it and looked around one last time. It was not the house she had grown up in, the happy house of her father's time. All that remained was the husk of a building, and its very deadness repelled her.

She paused before pulling the door to.

'Merry Christmas,' she said.

One Year Later

CHAPTER 34

February 1947

The line of Air Force coaches crawled along the windswept English highway in the opaque February afternoon, their windows encrusted with snow. They followed each other ponderously, like a line of elephants, each clutching the tail of the one in front, drivers taking care to stay within the tracks of the preceding vehicle. Rosie, her suitcase stowed by Sam their black coachman, sat behind him in the first row of seats, across the aisle from the only other female on the bus, an American Air Force sergeant by the name of Arleen.

Whether the twenty of so American servicemen were glad to be starting their journey home, or simply welcomed the chance to flirt, they'd been kind, gifting the women candy bars, and insisting they take all of the blankets kept on the vehicle for cold weather. The Yanks, noisy at first, had settled down after the few hours, but Rosie could still hear the odd twang of their accents and the uplift in the voices.

Then there was the coachman.

'Damn you, girl, git on!'

Sam's rambling one-sided conversation had begun miles back. He'd chatted to Rosie before they left, before the snow had begun to descend like a swirling curtain, though she noticed he didn't speak to the white passengers, nor they to him. Now that the roads were disappearing beneath snowdrifts, he'd fallen almost silent, gripping the wheel in rigid concentration.

Most English people, Rosie thought, would have described Arleen as 'forward' or even 'nosey', but she rather liked her. They'd been sitting on opposite sides of the aisle for barely two minutes before the American woman had leaned over and, bracing herself on the seat's chromed grab-handle, begun the conversation. After another fifteen minutes Rosie knew her companion came from a small town in the Mid-West, her family were farmers and she was going home, supposedly to marry her sweetheart. Although she'd heard rumours that he'd been less than faithful while she was away, she was keeping her mind open, for now. She looked ominously determined.

'Honey, if I find out he's been a flannel-mouthed rat while I been gone,' she confided eventually, with blithe American candour, 'I'm going to tan his hide, and hang it on the shed!'

Rosie couldn't help but laugh, but wondered if, perhaps, the young woman might actually mean it.

'Then I'm going to find me another feller, and it won't be no cowpoke neither.'

Arleen's shoulders were strong and Rosie had no trouble in believing she'd get to the bottom of any misdeeds before she'd wear a ring. American women, like American men, seemed refreshingly different to their English counterparts.

'And yours?' The female sergeant said it as though discussing a piece of farm machinery or perhaps a horse.

'Oh. Eugene.' Rosie paused.

Mention of his name caused a knot to clench briefly in her stomach. She'd been trying not to think too deeply about him. Since the wedding she'd received letters, apologising, even humble but, she noticed, growing shorter over time. Eugene dodged questions she'd sent in reply and the sense of confusion and a gnawing doubt she could barely admit even to herself, remained.

Arleen's troubles reminded her of Hazel's warning about men in general. Yet the cold and noisy bus didn't seem the right place to discuss such things with a stranger, even one as empathetic as Arleen.

'It's complicated,' Rosie said to her travelling companion with a thin smile.

'*Uh-huh*. Ain't it always, sugar?' the American replied with the air of a woman who'd been disappointed one time too many.

Rosie turned to look at the passing scenery. Thin fingers of frigid air were slipping through the door seals, grasping remorselessly for her ankles and forcing her to pull the coach-blanket down defensively, finally wrapping it around her feet. Outside, the white-blanketed countryside was slipping by, spikey dark fragments of hedgerows interspersed with black, spidery trees peeking up through the snow. For a second it seemed it was the scenery that was moving, while she was staying still, watching England, and all she had known of it, pass by the window from her present, and on into the past.

As Rosie's mind stilled, random memories fluttered like leaves through her mind: walking with her father in the park in the years before the orphanage, and his death. Drinking tea with Mrs. Barton, or Mrs. Morelli as she was now. Rosie smiled to herself. It was warming to think of the old lady finding such unexpected happiness, and so late in life. It was even better she'd been the agent of their chance meeting at her wedding. But of all the ties that claimed to bind her still to England, only one caused her pain.

She hadn't seen Hazel now for almost a year. They wrote but only patchily, for her old friend seemed to have found some work with the

315

Labour Party, and was apparently busy helping to build the socialist world she'd often preached about. She even had a new 'close friend', a girl a year younger than Rosie called Anne. A lump rose in Rosie's throat.

She glanced over at Arlene, but she seemed engrossed in the view from her own window on the other side of the coach.

Rosie reached into her bag and pulled out the writing pad she'd bought at the post office together with a pen and envelopes. Making sure she wasn't overlooked, she rested the pad on the book she'd tucked into her bag at the last minute and began.

Dear Hazel,

I'm sitting here on this bus, surrounded by 'Them Yanks' as you used to call them, heading to Southampton. I'm finally on my way, bound for the ship that will take me to America. If you can't believe that, then neither can I. I never really thought it would happen, except perhaps at the beginning, and even then it was still just a silly dream.

But here I am. And'

Rosie paused and glanced around. Shielding the paper from curious eyes she resumed.

'I miss you. More than anyone or anything. We were more than friends. Sisters perhaps.'

She crossed out the last two words. She could be honest, finally. There was no war on and letters were no longer checked, or censored.

'We were lovers.'

Rosie looked at what she'd written. Just reading it made her heart beat faster. Hurriedly she turned over the top of the letter so no one would be able to read the name of its intended recipient. If anyone saw it they'd think she was writing to a man.

'You may not believe this, as you will no doubt think I chose Eugene over you, but the truth is I don't regret one second of what we did or said. And I still love

you. I always will. You were, after all, The First. I think of you whenever I am about to do anything new, wondering what you would have said, for you were often very wise. And sometimes, when I'm alone in my bed, I think of you there too, the precise sound of your voice, the feeling of your breathing or the beating of your strong heart. I can smell the soap you used to wash with, just by closing my eyes.

The more I think about how our love broke apart, the more I think that it was not about you or me, or about Eugene, but just about the way things are. The way people are, and England is. And I think now that I was changed very much by the orphanage. I have this terrible need now, not to be alone, and an even greater one for safety, and security. I don't want to ever lose my home again. This is why I accepted Eugene, and why, despite what happened on the wedding night, I must go through with it.'

Rosie cast a sideways glance at Arleen. The American was quietly reading a paperback, her head against the seat. What would she say if she could see her thoughts, written above her head like the speech balloons in a comic? There would be more than raised eyebrows, that was for sure. She returned to the letter. If she was going to be honest about her feelings, she decided, she had to be honest about everything.

'I could have loved you, and stayed with you, but the world of 1944 was not ready for two women living together 'as man and wife'. Perhaps one day they will be, but not now, and not in our lifetimes. 'Leave for somewhere fine and warm, just find a ship and go,' you said. Do you remember?! Then in some foreign land I could teach English and you could get work fixing motorcycles. You were, as always, so practical! But it would not have worked. And in your heart you must know. And, in the end, it was you who walked out on me.

I won't forget the talks we had, the sitting up all night by the fire we'd stoke up with broken pallets from the factory. As it hissed and spat on that poor fuel we put the world to rights. If only people would have listened to us the whole world would be able to live in peace and happiness. Or so we thought. And dreamed.

Well, those were good thoughts and good dreams and I don't regret a single one. But Eugene's offer was real, in a way they couldn't be. How would we have managed as two women? Apart from the things people would say, neither of us have a School Certificate and the jobs we could get in peacetime would never have paid enough to keep a roof over our heads. Now the men are back, everyone wants to give them the jobs. You were right about that. Now the war's over they want all the women to take off their uniforms and put on their aprons once again.'

The coach had turned off onto a smaller, more bumpy road. It was getting harder to write. Somewhere at the back a buzz of conversation had started and she could smell coffee. There was more she had to say and she hurried on. She must say what needed to be said, to clear the air, even if it was too late.

'And you changed after the Doodlebug. You kept drinking and grew so bossy. Honestly, you became so very unlike the happy, bouncy person I met on my first day at Morelli's. Sometimes you could be so cruel then we would row —goodness knows how much crockery we got through. But "It", the possibility of our living together, finally ended for me when we had the fight. You shouldn't have broken down my bedroom door. I thought I was safe in my room. It made me frightened of you. And when you left that broke my heart too. I can still see you stomping away towards the railway station struggling with your suitcase, taking Peter with you, which, although it was probably right in the end, was a cruel thing to do.'

Her companion across the aisle was coughing. Looking up, Rosie saw the proffered cup of steaming coffee, which she took gratefully. There seemed to be a supply of it coming from metal flasks which the soldiers were passing around.

'Oh. Thanks.'

'No problem, toots!' The American drained her cup and passed it and the flask back to the row behind. 'Always drink upstream of the herd.'

She laughed as though she'd made a particularly clever joke, but it was lost on Rosie.

Americans would have called the metal the flasks were made from '*aloominum*', not aluminium. Soon she'd be surrounded by people like Arleen, and would probably end up talking like them. Whenever an Americanism drifted past, she'd add it to her growing store-cupboard of words to learn, and use. Their vocabulary seemed so modern, and attractive. She'd begun to treasure the words and sayings: '*Baby-doll*', '*Say-what?*' or '*See-you later, alligator.*' It would be good to be surrounded by people who spoke in a bright new way, unstained by British pessimism or stuffiness.

Arleen seemed to want to talk again and Rosie put away the letter, intending to finish it later.

Arleen was holding out something.

'Like some gum?'

Rosie took the packet and took a piece of gum, but when she tried to hand the packet back, Arleen raised her hand.

'Keep it.'

Rosie laughed. The generosity of the Americans was reassuring. She might need all the generosity she could get.

'You don't want it?'

'Nope. Can't stand it. A Yank that don't like gum, like a Britisher that don't like tea! The gum comes with the rations and I take it to trade.'

'Oh. Perhaps I should give you something?' Rosie said, worried she might have broken some odd transatlantic rule. Her pockets she knew were empty except for a last fluff-encrusted barley sugar.

'No! Don't you worry none, honey. You're welcome.'

For a while they chatted about Arleen's experience and how she'd come to be with the Air Force in England. She was being sent home but, after being three years enlisted, was facing her first ever flight in a plane and was surprisingly afraid. She was careful to explain how kind her hosts had been and how much she'd enjoyed England.

'Though the weather's dang awful.'

Half an hour later Rosie detected a change in the coach's atmosphere. Glancing down the aisle she saw some of the airmen reaching up into the lockers. She peered forward again and felt a sudden shock as a sentry post loomed ahead. They had arrived and her heart lurched. The coach was slowing and she could make out the striped black-and-white barrier of what must, at last, be the base they were heading for.

The heavy vehicle halted, engine running noisily, and a guard emerged from a hut, puffs of breath drifting on the icy air. After a brief exchange with the driver and an examination of papers, the barrier rose, and the vehicle crunched forward. With the back wheels spinning and sliding, they left the road and crossed onto the tarmac of the base, a transit of territory that seemed symbolic.

'*Welcome to USAAF 117*,' Arleen intoned like an announcer at some mainline railway. 'Or perhaps I should be sayin', your own RAF Bagley-Benton.'

Outside a row of planes were parked along the edge of the field. A distant tower rose over a mass of snow-clad, jagged-roofed buildings contained within a vast, chain-link fence. The bus stopped next to one of the semi-circular Quonset huts, hydraulic brakes hissing as it slid finally to rest. The passengers noisily disembarked, boots ringing dully on the metal steps. Arleen hoisted a green canvas bag on her arm and waited until the last of the G.I.s from the back of the bus had passed. She held out her hand and Rosie took it, unsurprised when the handshake proved to be firm.

'Good luck, honey,' Arleen said.

'And you. I hope your man's not a – *er*, a rat.' It felt funny to say.

Arleen laughed. 'Well, if'n I find he ain't on the level, sugar, I'm gonna get madder than a swarm of bees. But after I've done that I will just go my own sweet way,' she added with a wink. 'Just cos trouble comes a-calling don't mean you have to give it a place to sit down.'

She turned and joined the queue and Rosie followed, impressed with the woman's forthrightness and grit, and wondering if all American women were like her.

Having acknowledged the soldiers' goodbyes, Rosie examined the scene. The snow was falling heavily, soft, fat flakes whirling down as though someone above had ripped a vast pillow and let the feathers drift down at random to earth. It blew impishly in odd flurries, into the faces and down the necks of those waiting to check their papers. She suddenly remembered one of the lines of poetry Eugene liked – 'The snow doesn't give a soft white damn whom it touches' – and she smiled and joined the queue, waiting to be told what to do next.

Under Rosie's feet the white carpet crushed with a satisfying crunch, and she felt a sudden childish urge to run in it, or make a ball of it and throw it. Perhaps Hazel was doing that, right now, with Peter. She stomped her feet vigorously up and down. Outside of the coach, and without the blankets, it was freezing. Beyond the Quonset, she could make out dim rows of similar buildings, their curved roofs sitting in the landscape like snow-quilted mounds. Some of the huts sported sooty stove pipes, and between them the boots of inhabitants left dot-and-dash tracks, like messages written on the pristine whiteness in Morse.

Rosie reached the front of the queue, where she presented her papers to an American officer wearing a priest's collar as well as his green uniform, and thin, gold-wire glasses. He was a thin, mild-faced man and seemed genuinely welcoming.

He smiled. 'Guess you're the only one so far.'

She looked at him in surprise.

'The only one?'

'The only Approved Alien. All the other camps are full, and this is an overflow. Can I help you with your case?'

Rosie followed the officer-priest as he trekked through the snow towards what seemed like the furthest hut, barely visible except as a grey shadow in the gloom.

'*I told a lie!*' he shouted back over his shoulder. '*There's one other wife here, she came yesterday, I believe. I forgot, I'm sorry! We're expecting more of you any day now!*'

They arrived and he set down her case, scraping the snow away from the door with a heavy boot.

'Come to the Reception Centre,' he pointed to a large steaming building, 'first thing tomorrow, and we'll start to sort out your papers.'

He smiled benevolently and turned, stomping energetically towards the tower like a missionary bound for the North Pole.

Rosie opened the icy steel door and walked into the sparse utilitarian interior, a regimented space lit by regularly placed electric bulbs in metal shades. Down the sides were metal-framed beds, rigidly made with an identical steel locker and wardrobe adjacent. The floor was linoleum and in the centre a cast-iron stove shot a black pipe to the roof. In front knelt a thin young woman wearing a fur coat. She glanced up.

'*Bloody thing!* Know anythin' about stoves, do ya?'

The accent was clearly identifiable as coming from London's East End. A puff of smoke blew out of the stove, causing the woman to cough violently.

'*Bastard!*' she yelled suddenly, as though the device might be intimidated into working by sheer bad language.

Rosie couldn't stop a wry smile – the woman's bad language and feisty temper reminded her of someone. She dropped her case, squatted and examined the fire. After a few minutes of riddling the

322

handle, adding kindling and opening the vent, she had the coal inside spitting and flaming.

'Thank gawd for that,' said the woman gratefully, rubbing her hands and shivering. 'I'm Stella Chaney.'

She held out a grimy hand and they shook.

'Rosie Hask–' She began again, 'Rosie Flynn. So we're the only ones here?'

'Bloody well looks like it, dunnit? Mind you, that vicar fella said something 'bout a coachload comin' tomorrow.'

Stella's dyed platinum hair and gold-plated earrings were as brash as her voice, but she had a tiny nose and bright attractive eyes like a bird. She was cheeky, like a robin, and something about her was instantly appealing. She smelled overpoweringly of cheap floral scent and Rosie's mother would have called her 'vulgar', or 'common', but that only added to her attraction.

'There's nosh over at the main building, if yer fancy it?' Stella informed Rosie, raising her eyebrows enquiringly.

Rosie grinned and nodded, relieved. The last thing she wanted was to be alone in the cold and empty Air Force hut, and after the long journey she was utterly starving.

CHAPTER 35

'*She's so grand!*' yelled the lean-faced young woman, her fur coat buttoned tight against the biting cold, a Russian ushanka on her head. The cockney voice was more raucous than usual and the fur made Stella look like a small brown bear.

'She?'

Rosie's voice was absent, distracted, her fingers gripping the ship's rail, slippery with February rime. Her eyes scanned the crowds on the dock, but her mind was detached, as though observing events one step removed, in a film. From her position on the Sun Deck, seventy feet above the water, the features of those waving and shouting goodbye melded into an overwhelming pink-and-grey mass.

'*The ship!*' bawled Stella, struggling to make herself heard above the screams of the women and children and the blaring resonance of ships' horns. '*We're on the bloody Queen Mary! The biggest bloody ship in the whole bloody world!*'

Rosie grinned. It had been a relief to have had Stella for company at the camp, and now here on the ship where they were sharing a cabin.

Being processed ashore had been a bizarre and dehumanising experience. Two days of interviews, and forms, embarrassing medicals and painful vaccinations. The oddest things were the probing political questionnaire and the taking of fingerprints, a surreal process that left thousands of pairs of female hands inky black and their owners feeling vaguely criminal.

Rosie looked down, past her new friend, beyond the wood-capped rail to which she clung, over the black-painted side of the liner. A thousand or so feet long, the ship tapered at the front to a gigantic arrow-headed bow, while the white superstructure above and behind them was crowned with three gigantic red funnels, each as tall as a church tower. On the quay far below, she could see dockers busy preparing for departure. The cacophony of their shouting joined that of the spectators and well-wishers, the deafening sound washing around them in waves, like the roar of a storm, or a cup-final crowd, making it hard to think.

Beneath the feet of the young women, the cold flanks of the steel behemoth trembled, and, thirty feet under Southampton harbour's greasy-green water four thirty-ton bronze propellers began slowly to turn.

Stella shrieked and redoubled her waving as the great ship inched serenely out of the dock, rope lines splashing one after another into the harbour, while on the tugs oilskinned crews scurried around their grimy craft like frantic black beetles. Magnificently, and with grace, the great steel bow finally nudged out into the Solent and, as though waking itself from sleep, the *Queen* shuddered, gently putting on speed before making her way blithely towards the open sea. On board three thousand young Englishwomen, bound for lives in a land unseen except on cinema screens or magazines, cheered and cried, laughed and sometimes prayed.

Later in the cramped cabin they shared, Rosie hung up her coat and settled thankfully into her bunk's squeaky metal frame, one of the last troop beds to be removed as the ship was restored to pre-war glory. Stella had fallen into conversation with a couple of over-friendly sailors, and Rosie had excused herself, though arranging to meet later to eagerly sample what the grand dining room had to offer.

She glanced around. It was unreal, a working-class girl on board the *Queen Mary*, the '*Ship of Dreams*' as the newspapers had christened her. But they were finally on board and heading for America.

Rosie pulled off her gloves, let them drop to the floor and looked at the wedding ring she seldom wore. It was hard to believe that the event it signified was more than two years in the past. Two years since she'd seen Eugene, or heard his voice. There were times she struggled to remember the exact colour of his eyes or the way he laughed, but in a few short days they'd stand face to face, and be expected to build a life together. There was nothing for her in England, nothing that would enable her plan of building herself a life that was stable and secure. But, her main hope had been to do this through love. Of all the elements of her plan, this was the most important, and apparently the hardest to achieve. Her head had insisted on making the voyage but her heart was afraid.

Rosie had looked forward to the peace and quiet of the cabin, hoping to gather her thoughts there, perhaps complete her letter to Hazel, or just snooze. But now she was lying in the comfortable bunk, her body seemed unwilling to lie still, wriggling and squirming, either unable or unwilling to get comfortable. At last she resignedly got up, donned her thin mac and opened the cabin door. Outside a white-jacketed boy, struggling with bags almost as big as himself, eased past in the narrow featureless passageway, while in the opposite direction a waiter, balancing a tray of teacups swayed along precariously.

Trying to accustom herself to the gentle rolling of the liner, Rosie embarked on her first look around. At the end of the passage she climbed a modest staircase to the next deck up. She followed a far wider passageway that ran from the open foyer into which she'd emerged, past a bright, elegant café, where gaggles of women stood smoking, chatting loudly in doughnut-shaped groups – competing, she thought, subtly with each other. She wandered on, observing the passengers playing noisy games of cards or hanging over the rails, and numerous children running about, drinking in the novelty of motion, pointing, exclaiming and asking endless questions.

My God, she thought, noting the sheer number of small faces, they're everywhere!

The cries of the tiny humans echoed down every passageway and their sleeping or toddling figures were to be found on all decks. The presence of so much life, all crammed onto a single ship, made her think of Noah's Ark.

After several more steep staircases, Rosie finally reached the Promenade Deck, a wide teak-floored avenue, enclosed by glass on the seaward side and a steel roof overhead. Here and there were steamer chairs and a few benches, mostly empty.

A solitary cooing mother was holding her baby up to the window to catch a glimpse of the sea. Rosie followed the child's glaze. Outside, a capricious wind flecked the marbled surface into thin white tops, while the winter sun speckled dazzling sparks of late afternoon light onto the water. It was a beautiful sight and she wondered idly whether the baby would remember. The mother surely would.

She walked on. There was an hour before diner would be served in the Grand Salon, a huge high-ceilinged room she'd glimpsed in passing. Perhaps she could read a book. There'd been hundreds in the ship's library two decks down. Then she remembered, somewhere in her bag was the novel given her by Mrs. B. She found an empty steamer chair and opened the book's dark-red cover. Despite the radiators placed under the benches, the space was cool and she shuffled her shoes on the deck to keep warm.

'**A French Affair,**' said the flyleaf. '**By Eliza de Lavigne.**'

It was a new sensation to be reading something by an author she knew and, before turning the page, Rosie mentally prepared herself for what would follow. She recalled the aunt-like figure of her childhood and her latter-day old friend. It would, she thought, be a tale of gallant heroes and beautiful, tragic heroines. Chivalrous and fantastical. She noticed that the corner of one page in particular had been folded and it was there that the book fell naturally open.

'*No, Jean-Claude. Don't, please!*' the book read.

He was hurting her, her frail wrists held tight in his powerful, masculine hands as he thrust her back onto the firm chaise-longue.

Rosie's eyebrows elevated. She suppressed a faint laugh, and continued, disbelieving.

'*I mean to have you, Brown Eyes!*'

'*No, Jean. That's all over now. I'm engaged to Arthur!*' *she protested. But deep inside her he had roused powerful, primitive emotions. She could feel the hot, strong weight of him lying on her pale young body, barely concealed beneath her silk slip.*

Rosie laughed aloud this time, causing a pair of women pushing prams to look at her curiously. She glanced away and buttoned her coat up further against the encroaching cold, before turning back to the book.

'*A mere boy!*' *he sneered, as his warm, sensual lips found hers.*

And then she knew. She could never belong to cold, money-obsessed Arthur; she was the woman of Jean Claude Laval, his woman to do with as he wanted.

'*Yes!*' *she heard herself cry. '*Yes, Jean! Oui, oui!*'

The waves of passion closed over her as she submitted to her desires, free, naked and unashamed. His rough military shirt fell to the floor to join her shimmering slip.

Far below on the bare rocks of the island, the surf pounded on and on, relentless and without mercy.

Rosie was still laughing quietly when she heard his voice.

'Pardon me, but you might like to borrow this?'

The accent had a civilised American twang. She turned and looked into the face of a young man a little taller and not much older than herself. He had the most unusual piercing green eyes behind heavy-framed glasses, and his unruly dark hair fell naturally forward. He was wearing the uniform of a White Star officer and was holding out a blanket invitingly.

'I thought I saw you shiver, ma'am.'

She wasn't used to being waited on and the gesture seemed extravagantly gentlemanly, even chivalrous.

'Oh, thank you,' she said, taking the heavy grey woollen cover in one hand and allowing him to drape the rest over her knees.

He smiled and she noticed that his face was kindly, with a charming and inviting smile. There was something else, however – perhaps the indefinable mark of experience, for somewhere along with the happiness she thought she detected sorrow. She must have shivered at the cold for his high brow furrowed suddenly in concern.

'You know, it's much warmer inside,' he suggested. He glanced over his shoulder and hurriedly went on. 'But it's a beautiful view outside and I can see why anyone would want to stay here.'

She should have simply smiled and nodded her thanks but she heard herself reply, 'I prefer to be alone, when I'm reading.'

She hadn't meant it as a dismissal, just a statement as to why she was there, perhaps even as a conversation-opener. But he seemed to have been rebuffed and moved back smartly.

'Oh, I am sorry, ma'am.' He nodded at the novel. 'Enjoy your book.' He smiled broadly and with that turned and, opening a steel door in the superstructure marked **'Crew Only'**, disappeared.

Rosie pulled the blanket around her and stared regretfully after the young officer. She hadn't meant to rebuke him and a sudden feeling of disappointment at his going served to emphasise her need for company. She'd closed herself off to most social interaction after the wedding, concentrating instead on work, building up her savings, and was clumsy and out of practice when it came to socialising. But she needed to begin again, in preparation for the Great Adventure that was coming.

She walked to the rail. They were heading west, just a little south of the setting sun. The great orange disc glowed brilliantly, descending rapidly into a cushion of vermillion and gold that fanned out along the horizon in a dazzling display of colour. Rosie screwed up her eyes as the light hit the water, enveloping the ship in a funnel of dancing fragments of gold and orange that seemed to play around her and the ship like a shower of sparks. Behind, the towering superstructure of the great vessel stood erect, bathed garishly pink in the glow as it continued impassively and unstoppably on its course.

CHAPTER 36

The next night the breeze dropped and in the enormous blue-blackness above the ship, the fragile skein of the Milky Way glowed silently. Beneath, the liner steamed its lonely course across the ocean, its mile-long wake glimmering faintly in the starlight. Either side of the diagonal mist of stars, a sprinkle of brighter, more brittle lights winked and gleamed like jewels in the crisp, cool air.

Restless again, and denied Stella's company thanks to two attentive sailors, Rosie put on the mac, before heading to the Promenade Deck, which seemed to be becoming her regular haunt. Her footfall rang hollowly against the teak as she walked the two-hundred yards from their staircase to the stern where she stepped out from the protection of the glass enclosure and felt at once the coolness of the night. She glanced out and up. Beyond the rail, the darkness of the sky was an impenetrable inky black, the stars cool and somehow removed from humans and their troubles. Against the awesome emptiness of the universe, she suddenly felt small, and alone.

But, here and there along the rail of the gently vibrating ship, the pulsing glow of a cigarette indicated that she was not alone, and the muffled rumble of muted conversation soon reached her. Looking over the stern, she gripped the rail tightly, staring down at the lathering wake unfolding behind like a frayed white ribbon more than sixty feet below. Some way off to the right, against the glimmering horizon, she thought she saw the silhouette of an iceberg – nemesis of another, equally famous ship that had passed this way a generation earlier. Rosie glanced down again at the black, glistening water. It seemed sinister, its embrace as cold as the grave, and she shivered at the thought of ending life in such a frigid, lonely place.

It was some minutes before Rosie became aware of a man standing in an alcove in the superstructure a few yards away, quietly smoking. He was wearing a Navy duffel coat and looked up briefly and nodded, before resuming his gaze at the passing ocean. Without warning, something suddenly flashed across the sky, dragging a bright tail of sparks behind and both figures recoiled slightly.

'What on earth was that?'

She must have said the words aloud, for he moved closer.

'It was a very bright one,' he replied, 'but just a meteor. I guess it must have broken up when it hit the atmosphere.'

She peered more closely at him. 'Oh, it's you!' she said in recognition 'The kind man with the blanket!'

She wasn't going to let him think again she'd been ungrateful.

He grinned, pointing to a small circle of burn marks on the deck around the sheltered alcove he'd been standing in.

'Unofficial crew smoking spot!'

'Oh!' She searched for something to say. 'I often look at the stars.' The words seemed to come out of their own accord.

He nodded. 'Me too, I have a map of constellations on the wall of my cabin.'

Rosie laughed and he looked perplexed.

'Did I say something funny?'

'Oh no! It's nothing, really. It's just that that sounds rather like "Come up and see my etchings"!'

He backed away. 'Oh, I'm so sorry. It's my duty to look after you. I wouldn't want you to think …'

Seeing him in the light spilling from the glass windows of the Promenade Deck, she thought that he looked a little like a younger Gregory Peck.

'It's alright,' she said. 'You're very kind, and I'm sure you're a gentleman. It's just me. I'm in an odd mood. I'm glad of company, as it happens.'

He seemed to relax and pulled out a cigarette case bearing the Cunard White Star flag. She took one of the proffered white sticks and leant closer as he shielded her hand, using a lighter that appeared as though by magic from nowhere. For a moment they drew on the glowing tips.

'So, you're heading to a new life, ma'am?'

Despite his initial confidence, he appeared a little awkward, she thought.

'I am going to a new life, but,' she fished for the right words, 'I don't know what I'll find when I get there.' The doubt she had been nursing privately had slipped out, and to a perfect stranger. She heard herself continue, 'An old life is ending, and a new one's beginning. Some people say I'm at the start of a big adventure. But I don't feel it.'

Why was she unburdening herself to this unknown man?

To her surprise, he nodded understandingly. She saw he was one of those people whose eyes looked right at you. It gave the impression that when you spoke you were the only person in the world.

'The trouble with big adventures,' he said, drawing on his cigarette, the slipstream sucking away a few sparks into darkness, 'is that they only feel like big adventures when they're over, and you're safely tucked up at home.'

Despite herself, Rosie smiled. He seemed to have an odd, deadpan humour.

'You think so?'

'Yes. Adventures tend to be a bit more alarming at the time. Take me, for instance, I ran away to sea when I was seventeen. It only seems like a fine adventure now, in retrospect. Now it's safe to laugh, but at the time I was scared enough.'

Running away to sea sounded like something from a nineteenth-century novel. She couldn't help but smile.

'You ran away to sea? Isn't that a bit like running away to join the circus?'

He grinned. 'Just like a circus if you mean my first boat. But our captain was a rather mangy, sick old ringmaster, and didn't stay the course.'

He had an intriguing way of describing things.

'At first,' he said, 'I thought I was an adventurer – a hero – but then I felt terrified, and after that just plain foolish.' He laughed dryly and paused. 'But I found another ship and, before I knew it, four years had just flown on by. I had adventures, if you can call them that, some good, some bad, but now the war's over, now everything's over, it feels right to do something new.'

'Yes!' She beamed. He'd said out loud the essence of her thoughts. The world did seem open to new things, to fresh starts and new beginnings. She blushed, suddenly wondering if she was being too forward.

He regarded her with a trace of what she thought was amusement.

'I fell out with my father when I was in my teens,' he confessed, apparently not afraid of sharing personal things about himself. 'He ran a shipping business out of Maine and as I grew up we had different ideas. So, I upped and packed my bag and started walking. At Cape Cod I ran out of land and, as I can't walk on water, it seemed a good idea to find a boat.' He paused. 'Then, the war came. I wanted to join up, of course, but all they would offer me was the Marines. There were plenty of shipping lines taking on staff, and so, a lot of water and a lot of exams later, here I am.' He tugged at the gold braid on his sleeve.

'I expect you were glad to be out of the fighting.' She winced inwardly at her own clumsiness with words. 'I mean ...'

'It's alright!' he said with a laugh. 'I know what you mean. But the Merchant Marine was no picnic, as it happens.'

She shivered involuntarily and he indicated the glass-shielded Promenade Deck.

'We should go back inside.'

She noted he had said 'we'.

They walked to the steel door which he held open for her. Inside they found a bench.

'And what about you?' he was asking.

'Oh,' said Rosie, 'nothing so dramatic.' She laughed self-consciously. 'I worked in a radio factory and, now, I'm here.'

'Having met one of my countrymen.'

'Yes.'

Rosie smiled awkwardly, finding herself curiously unwilling to talk about Eugene. She searched her mind for a change of subject.

'I lost my father – some years ago.'

She wondered where in her subconscious the statement had come from. It seemed to be a very intimate a thing to be discussing with a stranger. But then the war had changed so many things.

'I'm sorry.' His face creased into lines of genuine concern. He paused, sighed. 'Me too, as it happens.' He saw her surprised expression, and continued. 'He had a heart attack and that's one of the reasons I'm on this trip. It's time to go home.' He shrugged and continued, his voice oddly flat. 'I leave the ship in New York and then I'm going home. First time in four years.'

She stared at him. 'I'm sorry,' she said.

Their words of comfort to each other were banal, yet the sense of shared experience of grim reality resonated, and both could feel it.

A couple of girls smothered in furs passed, a rude cloud of cigarette smoke and chatter trailing behind. For reasons she could not fathom, Rosie found herself waiting until their footfall had died before going on. She looked out over the small dark channel of water visible at the side in the ship's lights.

'Were you on the convoys?'

For a moment he didn't speak, as though the question had wrong-footed him. 'Yes, the North Atlantic. Liverpool to Nova Scotia, Southampton to Boston. Mostly troop ships. Some of your guys going over and then us Yanks coming the other way.'

'Gosh. Did you ever get, you know ...'

'Torpedoed? Yes, and bombed once.' He said it abruptly in a way that did not invite further enquiry, before adding quickly, 'Not on the Queen, of course, she's too fast. I've only come aboard for this trip. Do you know she has guns?'

Rosie shook her head. She realised that despite her brother being in the Navy, she knew little about the war at sea. She felt a twinge of embarrassment in case she'd trespassed upon a difficult memory.

'What's the read?' He gestured to Rosie's pocket where the top of a book protruded.

'Oh.' She pulled it out. 'I bought it in the ticket-hall at Southampton.'

She had decided to keep Mrs. B.'s book for when she got to America and had reverted to something more appropriate for a voyage at sea.

He looked at the cover and his face lit up with recognition.

'Ah, *Wreck of the Titan*!' He laughed. 'You're a brave soul reading that on board, aren't you? The story of a great liner striking an iceberg?'

She nodded. 'It doesn't bother me. But, you know, I assumed it was about the *Titanic*.'

'A lot of folks think so, but strangely it was written a dozen or so years before *Titanic* ever sailed. The plot is exactly what happened to *Titanic*, just written in advance. Weird, huh?'

Rosie raised her eyebrows and looked at the cover.

'I didn't know. I feel so sorry for them, all those poor souls.'

He nodded. 'Yes, indeed. A terrible way to go. It's not good to be in the water.'

'Are we,' she asked hesitantly, 'I mean, is our course the same as the *Titanic*?'

He smiled faintly. 'Similar to *Titanic*, but we sail a little further south – where there are fewer 'bergs.'

'I suppose you're going to tell me our ship is safer than *Titanic* and can't sink?

She wondered, remembering the lifeboat drill the wives had been forced to participate in earlier in the day.

He looked at her for a moment. 'If it floats,' he said at length, 'and it's made by man, it can sink.'

Then he seemed far away again, and for a moment they sat in silence.

'Do you read?' She found she wanted to keep the conversation alive. His knowledge about the novella had made her curious.

The quiet smile played again around his lips. 'I most certainly do, ma'am. I'm rather in love with books.'

There was a look of self-deprecation, as though the admission were a weakness. Further away in the darkness they could hear raised voices. He glanced at her.

'My leave was always in England,' he said, 'and I got it into my head that I should read as many English authors as I could: Shakespeare, Hardy, Austin, and also some of the modern ones like Forster. No idea why, we have them in America, it just became something to do.'

He'd become animated, as though on the trail of something important.

A short way along the deck a steel door opened and a head wearing an officer's cap bobbed. The indistinct face peered in their direction.

'Miller?'

Suddenly he looked like a schoolboy, caught out of bounds.

'It's our Second Officer.' Looking at her, he grasped her hand briefly. 'We seem to have told each other rather a lot. I'm sorry, I'm a terrible one for going on. I shouldn't have bored you. I gotta go, or they'll have me walking the plank. I sure hope we'll meet again.'

He turned in the direction of a voice and she could hear him answer. 'Coming, sir.'

Rosie looked towards the door where he had vanished. The air seemed suddenly colder, the night emptier, and she sank into her coat. Below her the eighty-thousand-ton hull of the great ship ploughed steadily on, trailing her great white furrow, as the steel bow sliced the water and the bronze propellers chewed hungrily at the deep green breast of the ocean.

CHAPTER 37

Late the following evening the wind strengthened and shifted to the north, a gale blasting directly across the course of the ploughing liner. Outside, the wild, streaming air whipped the wave tops, capping them white, and flinging foam hissing onto the decks. In the rigging of the radio-mast the wires, adorned with tiny daggers of ice, whistled mournfully. The sea's complexion had shifted from blue-green to muddy green, marbled with veins of spume, while an earlier swell had grown into what was now an uninterrupted range of vertiginous peaks and steep, dark troughs.

The vessel, despite its enormous size, was alternately lifted up and plunged swiftly down, as though its eighty thousand tons counted for nothing. Inside, the lights glowed brightly, and passengers relaxed as best they could in the unstable interior. Some braved the staircases to reach the upper lounges, while others clung biliously in the main salons or made their way, green-faced, to the cabins.

Despite the weather a boisterous and enthusiastic crowd had assembled in the ballroom as the ship's band competed with the storm, determinedly thumping out the latest American tunes. Every so often the great *Queen* would roll, causing the dancers to hop and skip from one side to the other. Some steadied themselves on the columns, as the chandeliers swayed gently overhead, while others collided in a plethora of laughter and excuse-me's. Most on board had by now heard about the infamous *Queen Mary* Roll, but those that hadn't now found out for themselves. Rosie, for her own part, was unfazed by the ship's motion. From her seat adjacent to the dance floor, she wondered only about the absurdity of her being on a ship so grand. The polished glamour of the *Queen* was a hundred worlds away from the orphanage.

Among the waves of dancers there bobbed not only the white uniforms of civilian crew, but also the dark blue of the Royal Navy. Where partners were in short supply some women danced with each other. A grinning Stella whirled past in the arms of a man, laughing. She must have been dancing for hours, and had enveloped herself in a palpable cloud of cheap, flowery scent. Rosie was still smiling when she heard the voice.

'Ma'am?'

It was familiar and American. She turned, and saw the officer she'd met at the rail. He was wearing a white tuxedo, and his green eyes twinkled invitingly.

'Hello again.'

He smiled. He looked oddly uncomfortable in evening dress, like a boy who'd borrowed his father's suit. Steadying himself against a column, he stood there smiling at her.

'Not on duty tonight?' she asked.

'I traded with another guy and, as it's my last trip,' he grinned, 'he was OK with it. I like music.' He nodded at the band.

Before Rosie could speak, the ship chose that moment to plunge steeply into a trough and for a second she felt weightless. In an instant he'd grabbed her waist, and with an odd sense of inevitability they fell into the revolving swirl of dancers. The floor rose again and the sudden feeling of increased gravity made her dizzy.

'Shall we?' he asked, grinning, his hand already finding hers.

She hadn't been thinking of dancing but here they were, moving into the centre of the throng.

'OK?' he asked.

'I'm fine,' she heard herself respond with a nod.

He seemed to sense her inexperience on the floor, and kept his movements delicate. He braced them against the ship's roll so they occasionally paused, but did not fall. It was easy to tell he was used to being at sea and on a dance floor.

They managed a slow, if necessarily drunken waltz. At first she was stiff, tense at being in the arms of a man who was almost a stranger. Her mother would have called her a scarlet woman, to be on her way to her husband yet so close to another man. But her mother was gone. So was England. Even the war was over. The man was young, and attractive, and the past year had often been lonely and cold. They gathered confidence in moving together, and Rosie soon found herself laughing. The faster they rotated, the clearer her mind and body became. Dancing left no room for thought. There was only movement, the music, the swirling smiling faces and simply being.

Eventually the band broke for drinks and Rosie hesitated, wondering if he would ask her to stay. She baulked at the risks of alcohol, but dreaded going back to an empty cabin. He was speaking, holding her hand, as they swayed back and forth, supporting each other.

'I'm Third-Officer Theodore Miller. But people just call me Theo.' He smiled. He seemed relieved to have the chance of introducing himself properly and inclined his head in a small bow.

'Any relation to Glenn?'

'Sadly not,' he replied, laughing dutifully at what must be for him an old joke.

'I'm Rosie Haskell.' She surprised herself by using her maiden name.

'I see. Well, would Rosie Haskell care for a drink?'

Flushed with the excitement of the dance, she found her spirits suddenly soaring.

'She would.'

They left the dance floor and moved to the gleaming mahogany bar, settling at her wish with Rum and Coca-Cola. Their conversation was mainly about the ship, of which he offered a tour later in the voyage. But every so often she thought she sensed an attempt to dig deeper, as he planted an odd remark in otherwise carefully phrased sentences.

He became most alive when they talked of books. Of American literature she loved Jack London's *Call of The Wild* and he was enthusiastic about the story, having been to the Yukon with his father.

'I had to leave my dog in England,' she said, with a sudden pang of sadness, remembering Peter and his lugubrious but loving face.

'Ah, a domesticated wolf?'

She laughed, thinking of Peter's puppy-like nature.

'Not really. He was a Labrador, soppy as anything. But,' she paused, 'he had a kind of survival instinct. He hung on when things were tough. And he was loyal. He used to remind me of Buck in that way.'

'Probably couldn't pull a sled though.'

'No.' She grinned. 'But he'd grow more wild if he was kidnapped and sold to a sled team.'

'So would I. I'd be furious!'

She laughed.

'He'd be better at it than my family's dog,' he said.

'Oh?'

'A poodle. It was my mother's.'

They laughed again.

'That wouldn't get you far,' she said, adding, 'It would be like that film with Bing Crosby and Bob Hope.'

'Ah, *The Road to Utopia.*'

'Yes, that was it.'

'I laughed until I cried!' he said, remembering, his face creasing into a smile. It was hard to imagine a British man crying with laughter, or Eugene for that matter.

His eyes were really twinkling now.

'I used to go to Radio City when I was a kid,' he enthused. 'Radio City Music Hall, that is. Midtown Manhattan. It's on 6th Avenue. A terrific cinema.'

Her wide eyes regarded him steadily. It was like listening to someone who'd visited the moon.

'A wonderful building, Art Deco – this ship reminds me of it. It's the largest auditorium in the world, but it's still somehow friendly and intimate. I used to go when I could – especially in the daytime.'

'I love the pictures in the daytime!' she exclaimed, struck that someone else should have the same odd inclination as herself. Eugene had gone when she'd suggested it, but preferred the evening shows.

'Me too. I love shutting out the world and getting immersed. Surrendering to the story.'

'Like a spell.'

'Yes.'

He smiled, and she thought that for a second he looked at her oddly.

He continued. 'And afterwards I'd find somewhere to eat and take a cab to the Empire State.'

'You've been inside the Empire State Building?' She found it hard to think of the famous landmark without the figure of King Kong hanging from the side and Fay Wray screaming from the top.

'Tallest Building in the World? Sure. You can ride the lift, and way above the city there are observation decks with telescopes. It's quite a view.'

Rosie was almost dreaming, immersed in the images he was presenting, mixed with memories of her own and boosted by the encouragement of the rum.

'I love films,' she said. Over the last year they'd been a relief from the monotony of being on her own, and just waiting. She began to realise how much of just living she'd missed.

'And books too, I think,' he replied. 'I've seen you a couple of times, always with a book, or poking around the library.'

Rosie raised her eyebrows. She'd not realised she'd been observed. But saw no harm in confessing.

'Reading's always been something I've loved. And you, are you reading anything?' Prodding him for his choice of book seemed forward, but she might find out more about him.

'Oh, I'm trying something from one of your countrymen, a certain Mr D. H. Lawrence.'

'Lawrence? Yes, I've heard of him. Wasn't he sent to jail or something?'

'Or something. He's had a book banned.' A brief shadow of something like embarrassment passed over him, 'But I like him. Delicacy and precision, yet passionate, and flowing, and ... such ...' he paused, 'beauty. Although ...'

'Although?'

'Oh, nothing. You should read it yourself.'

Rosie was intrigued. She'd have to search the library. The last person to have recommended a book had been her father, and that seemed almost a lifetime ago. And he, of course, had one of Lawrence's books on his forbidden top shelf.

The waiter brought more Rum and Coca-Colas and they sipped the sweet icy liquid together. He seemed too practical and outgoing to be called bookish, but he was clearly well educated, and intelligent. Perhaps some of the former came from schooling, and some from experience of the world. She searched for something intelligent to say, lest she embarrass herself.

'What will you do when you get home?' She could have bitten her lip. It seemed too intimate, and presumptuous.

He gazed at her and she glimpsed something troubled in his eyes.

'I'm going to take over the business,' he said. 'We've got a place on Martha's Vineyard.'

'Boats in a vineyard?' she queried

'It's just the name of an island. I'm thinking of what I guess you'd call tourism. It's a beautiful place, not far from New York. I figure folks are going to want to go there for vacation. I could have two boats first, then four, then eight. I could have a yard for repairs and a chandlery.' He looked momentarily crestfallen. 'But I'd need a partner.'

Rosie could picture the boatyard, a sloping concrete slipway down to a tranquil harbour where sailboats plied under a clear blue sky. Was it a line he was shooting? But he seemed too young and guileless to lie. There was no hint, as there had been with Eugene, of things concealed.

'And you?' he asked, brushing an imaginary spec from his immaculate uniform. 'What will you do, in your new life?'

She fell silent. Protocol demanded she be a loyal wife, but she couldn't bring herself to lie to this man.

'I'm not sure about anything anymore.' It was a relief to tell the truth. 'So much has changed. And I've seen things ...' She thought of the deaths, her father, mother, Clarence and Clara. 'Things that make me realise how precious life is, and yet how difficult. To make the right choices. How winning or losing is a game of chance. Nothing turns out as you think it will.'

'*The swift do not have the race, nor the strong the battle … but time and chance overtake them all.* A wise man once said that.' He nodded.

'Life is mostly a matter of luck, isn't it?' she agreed. 'Not virtue, or having got what you earned, or deserve. Just blind chance. As if the universe is … indifferent.'

To her surprise he suddenly leaned closer, grabbing her wrist.

'No.' His eyes were suddenly bright, urgent with conviction, like an old world preacher. 'No. It's not just blind chance. I don't believe that we can't make a difference, that we're helpless. And I can't believe the universe is indifferent. Look at how beautiful the world is. How diverse, so perfect, as though it's deliberately made just for us.' He released her wrist, and added more quietly, 'I think that the universe is always just waiting for us to take the first step.'

She smiled. He was so young, so keen, yet the wisdom and feeling behind the words was older, like something her father would have said.

A pair of women came to the bar and cast sideways glances at them.

'*To peace!*' said Rosie loudly, raising her glass.

As the drinks clinked together their hands touched briefly.

Rosie straightened. She should bring down the temperature.

'The band was good,' she said randomly.

His eyes didn't deviate from her as he spoke. He seemed to be having trouble forming words.

'Yes. There's a dance tomorrow. Tuxedos, ties and all that jazz.'

She regarded him with new interest. Every time she tried to

maintain some sense of social respectability he surprised her, pulling her back in towards the candid and intimate.

He paused before blurting out the question. 'Will you come?'

'Yes. I'd like that,' she heard herself answer.

He looked pleased and smiled as he checked his watch.

'Good. I must go.'

Then the young officer was gone, leaving her mind to wrestle with a hundred conflicting thoughts.

CHAPTER 38

The sleek Art Deco clock showed well past one when Rosie looked into the Grand Salon the following day. Lunch was being served and a stream of voices seeped out into the passageway where she stood. She glanced at the huge automated map that formed a magnificent two-dimensional display on the wall. She could make out the bronze model representing the ship, and was dismayed to see it seemed to have moved with unwanted speed, being now almost halfway across, between the shores of Ireland and America. There could only be two or three days of the voyage remaining.

Rosie turned away. Oddly, she had no appetite and, finding the grand staircase, began to climb towards the open Sun Deck. As she emerged into the pale winter sunshine, she found knots of women had gathered there, some with babies in prams or cradled in arms, others nursing bumps and clutching backs, some cooing or staring appreciatively, or anxiously, anticipating their turn. She'd had a restless night and slept until late, telling herself the previous night's talk with Theo had been just something to pass the time. But no matter how hard she focused on the goal of meeting Eugene, thoughts of Theo, his ambitious plans and bright, youthful optimism, intruded. Somewhere in the back of her mind it was as though a quiet but insistent bell was ringing.

The weather had cleared, leaving only streaks of dirty yellow cloud remaining close to the horizon. Below her, the ocean was a jade green expanse, the colour reminding Rosie of Theo's eyes. Frustrated at not being able to expel the sailor from her mind, she stopped opposite a group of women, hoping to discreetly eavesdrop on their conversation as she gazed firmly in the opposite direction, out to sea.

'I'm so desperate to see him!' chirped one.

She must have been holding a photograph for Rosie could hear an appreciative chorus.

'It's been months,' she continued wistfully. 'He was wounded and I want to be there to nurse him, I don't want some other woman doing it. After all he's gone through. As I see it, that's my duty.'

A muted accompaniment of agreements and 'there-there's' followed and Rosie could imagine the sympathetic feminine embraces.

Rosie reached into her coat pocket, guilty fingers connecting with the cool metal of her wedding ring. She knew what the women behind her would have said about her unaccompanied meeting with Theo, however platonic. She hardly knew herself why she'd been so forward with him, or even why, before setting out for the evening, she'd removed the ring. Whatever Eugene's limitations, whatever his sins, didn't these have to be set against the bizarre context of war? There were examples of people doing the right thing, like the women behind her, quiet everyday heroes that just got on with things. And, perhaps, devoid of the pressures of flying, he might have changed.

She felt a pang, if not of remorse, then perhaps something like duty. Perhaps she shouldn't see the officer again, however friendly. On a ship of married women, she shouldn't be the one to break ranks and, so it suddenly seemed, let the side down. She turned and walked away, joining the slow procession around the deck. She should be discreet, she thought, and not look for trouble. Perhaps she could even hide for the rest of the trip – it would only be for a couple of days. If she didn't see him she should be strong enough to do what fate demanded: to meet her husband. It was what the world demanded of her. She nodded to herself. She would try.

Back within the cabin's restraining walls, the afternoon soon began to drag. At first Rosie tried to doze but when this proved impossible, pulled out the novella. Her mind insisted on wandering, however, and soon she put the book down, trying instead to reread Eugene's letters. She paused after each related episode to close her eyes and remember, trying to conjure up the details, and when some proved harder to grasp than she wished, filled them in using her imagination. Finally, she even rubbed the paper, trying to recreate a feeling of intimacy from any scent it might contain, but there was only the empty, everyday odour of ink and paper.

At last, she could no longer resist the impulse to escape. She got up, threw on her powder-blue jacket and matching skirt, and went up two decks to the on-board salon, where she surprised herself by paying for a perm. After the lengthy and sometimes excruciating procedure she returned to the cabin and examined the result, beholding a transformation so sweeping she felt a rush of embarrassment at the immaculate creature staring back. She smiled and lay down on her back, taking care not to crush the expensive creation. She tried again to summon the image of her husband, their first meeting, their first kiss, but the swirling mass of dancers at the base resolved repeatedly into the crowd on board, including someone with startling green eyes.

She must have fallen asleep, for she awoke with a start to find Stella leaning over the sink, attending to her make-up in the mirror.

350

'Gor blimey, you been out like a bloomin' light you 'ave!' The young Londoner blotted her lipstick and squinted at her new friend. 'Ain't yer going out tonight?' She checked her final cosmetic preparations. 'Yer should, y'know. Be good for yer, like.'

But before Rosie could reply, Stella grabbed her bag. She could obviously hardly wait, and seemed determined to have as much fun as possible before she met her husband.

'Well, I'm off. A nice young sailor man 'as invited me for a drink!' Stella patted a still-befuddled Rosie on the shoulder and seconds later the cabin door shut behind her with a click, without waiting for a reply.

Rosie stood and swayed unsteadily to the mirror over the cabin's sink and regarded herself. She looked how she felt, tired and drowsy with ill-timed sleep. She splashed water on her face and, patting it dry with one of the smart monogrammed towels, suddenly felt thirsty. She decided to get a cup of tea in one of the cafés. Then she could go to the library, a secluded place to spend a safe and solitary evening.

CHAPTER 39

Rosie found the library thankfully empty, and for a while wandered up and down the deserted aisles, grazing the shelves, pulling out books and reading at random, digesting a bite or two of knowledge and moving on. She found herself at the Encyclopaedias, the beautiful red-leather tomes lettered in gold, and selected 'A-C'. She sat down and began to read. It was new and, as she turned the pages, the sharp scent of printer's ink rose from the paper.

She found '**America, Geography**' and began to read: '**The land area of the United States is 3,794,000 square miles.**'

On an impulse she got the volume 'S-U' and checked under the entry for UK, which informed her that its territory was a more humble 95,960. Basic mental arithmetic proved America to be forty times bigger. That didn't take account of the British Empire of course, but even so.

Soon half a dozen huge volumes were laid one on top of the other as her curiosity led randomly from one interest to another. Eventually she settled on 'L-M': **Literature, American**. Some of the names and books she recognised: Melville's *Moby Dick* – others like Henry James

The Wings of the Dove, or F. Scott Fitzgerald's *Tender Is the Night*, she did not. From the encyclopaedias she moved on, finding a novel written by a woman, something called *The History of Eliza Wharton* by Hannah Webster Foster. She became absorbed in story, a tale of a female seduced and abandoned. The heroine was courted by two different men, a clergyman and a less respectable character. She skipped to the end, where it seemed that unable to choose between them, the female protagonist found herself alone, while both men were happily married to other, less fussy partners.

'When you didn't show, I thought I might find you in here.'

It was that same soft yet strong voice, like the voice of a man who could calm wild horses, and have them obey him, not through fear but by some instinct.

Shocked, she looked up.

'Oh!' She hesitated. 'I'm glad to see you,' she heard herself say, her own admission immediately making her blush.

Theo craned his neck to see what Rosie was reading.

'Ah, *Eliza Wharton*. We don't have many American women writers.' He smiled. 'Which is a shame.'

She remained frozen. He had tracked her down and now she was failing to send him away.

'Now that you're an American, perhaps you'll put that right,' he added.

She was not used to being called an American. And he was flattering her.

'You're being silly.' She managed to keep her voice neutral.

'Not necessarily.' He sat on the edge of a nearby table and smiled. Seeing she did not move or reply he continued. 'Perhaps it's because I was raised by my mother, an independent lady. She was a suffragette, you know, campaigned until women got the vote. She had a career as a pianist before my father came along, and she only agreed to marry him if he allowed her to keep her job and her interests. I grew up thinking a woman should want to make something of herself.'

He kept on intriguing her. She had no idea of where her next question came from.

'And you think a woman today could just start out on her own, in America?'

'Sure, a woman could get an apartment, and there's work, so why not?' He grinned, gesturing. 'You look different. Quite a transformation.'

'Oh,' She hoped he wouldn't think she'd done it on his account. 'I had it permed.'

'A bit of American pizazz meets old-e English charm. Not that you're old-e.' He added, pronouncing the 'e' deliberately. His eyes twinkled but his mouth remained undecipherable. There was another moment's silence.

'I've spent a long time in here, one way and another,' he confessed, looking around.

'My father used to read to me,' she blurted out and was surprised at the banality of the statement, quickly adding, 'And I found I could just lose myself in books.'

'My mother used to read to me.' He grinned. 'That's how I started collecting books. Now I'm an addict. I've nowhere to put them. Boxes and boxes. Another reason to get back on land and buy somewhere to settle down. A place with many shelves.' He raised his eyebrows in a comical fashion and went on, 'The problem is that the more I learn, the more I'm aware of what I don't know. One question leads to another. I can't stop buying and reading. And I bore all the guys on board with my questions.'

He glanced again at the book. She had put it on the table, but it was still open, vulnerable to his gaze.

'Love is the question, isn't it?' he said.

His eyes were on her and she felt herself staring back. Was this a practised line? It seemed so direct.

He continued smoothly, explaining with a modest laugh, 'I mean, it's central to what you're reading. *Eliza Wharton*, that it. Whether there can be real love, between men and women, or whether it's impossible.'

She thought frantically of something, anything to say. Something not romantic but from the encyclopaedias, but all that came to mind were the industrial products of the Great Lakes.

'Literature's full of that question, in one form or another, don't you think?' he continued, clearly not put off by her lack of reply. 'Can there be more to love than just physical attraction? A meeting of minds ...'

She admired his confidence in talking openly about something intimate, and to a stranger. But the illicitness of it raised the hairs on her neck. Finally she found a voice.

'Perhaps in books and films things are perfect but ... perhaps to compensate for how they really are in life.'

He hesitated. 'I wouldn't have put you down as a cynic.'

'I'm not.' Opening herself to someone, to exchange thoughts, was so wonderful – she'd not had anything like it since Hazel. Suddenly the awful thought came to her: she wanted to kiss him.

Clearly off-duty, he was wearing an old sports jacket, and from the pocket she could see a thin, rather worn book protruding from a pocket. He followed her gaze.

'Oh, the book.' Suddenly he seemed embarrassed. 'Oh, I don't think you'd be interested in that.' He tried to bring the subject back to what they'd been discussing. 'The question is interesting though, about the nature of love, what is and isn't possible.' He picked up a random book and began to thumb through the pages. 'And, even if it's impossibly rare, it must be possible, to have a love that's perfect, don't you think? We can't just be clever animals, can we? I know it sounds naïve, but I want to believe there's something grand and beautiful, even if only to balance out the bad.'

Rosie was astonished. She'd thought the idea of balancing out evil with good was simple, probably foolish, but her own.

Their eyes met but he broke the connection quickly. She felt her breathing grow perceptibly faster and laughed nervously, opening the leaves of an encyclopaedia, letting them flutter gently against her fingers.

'What a conversation we are having!' she said, almost to herself. What he was saying was just a common-sense observation. Probably.

'Comes from talking in a library, I guess.' He waved around. 'Plenty of inspiration.'

He had a natural, blunt sort of humour that underlined his apparent honesty.

Perhaps she had been staring at him for he suddenly grinned, got up and wandered a short way along one of the shelves before returning. He walked with a certain natural grace, she thought, and when he spoke his manner was gentle, precise, like a doctor or some other well-educated man. But there the clinical element stopped, for he was also warm, with a ready smile.

He sat down beside her, but at a discreet distance, and resumed the conversation, a discussion about literature, with nods to politics, England, and America, and unavoidable references to the war. She tried to keep her responses short, to listen but avoid being drawn in, yet he had an uncanny knack of summarising in a few words things she had been wrestling with within herself for years. Whether life was pre-ordained, or whether the individual had choice, the existence or otherwise of pure evil and the possibilities for women in England or the United States.

Rosie pretended to read. It wasn't his looks, but the conversation that was the most dangerous. It wasn't even that it seemed to have a tendency to drift close to the limits of what was acceptable between a young man and a married woman, but the depth of thought and freedom of expression it contained could probably become addictive. She realised how lonely the last two years had been, and how hungry her mind was to meet another like it.

She decided to press him about his book. He looked embarrassed, but eventually relented, tugging it out.

'It's the D.H. Lawrence book I mentioned – the one banned in your country and mine.'

'Oh yes. I used to think he was the other one, you know.'

'Of Arabia?'

'Yes. But that's T.E. – I know that now.' She paused. 'Isn't it futile, to ban a book?' She had spoken the thought out loud.

He looked at her, intrigued.

She blushed slightly. 'As though you can ban a thought, or suppress an idea.'

He nodded and smiled. 'Yes. I think it is. It's futile.'

She examined the book. '*Lady Chatterley's Lover.*' She smiled in recognition. 'Ah, yes!'

'You know it?' He looked surprised.

She nodded. 'I know of it. It was one of the titles on my father's top shelf. Where did you get it? My father seemed quite proud of his as though it was rare.'

'It is. I got it from someone on the Mediterranean Route. Lawrence had it printed in Italy when his publisher couldn't get it done in England.' He still looked awkward. 'I should probably not show it to you. We don't know each other well. We shouldn't discuss it really.' He hesitated. 'But I found it ... life-affirming. Especially if you want to believe in a complete love, and against the odds.'

He paused and seemed to be gathering his thoughts before he continued.

'It was banned because of its passion,' he said, 'its language, and the nature of the relationship ... between people of different social classes ...'

She knew the book contained forbidden things. She should tell him to stop.

He continued hesitantly. 'This is quite adult material. Some say obscene. Are you sure ...'

'Yes,' she heard herself reply.

He adjusted his collar nervously and carried on. 'Alright. If you're sure.' He coughed. 'Well, If I understand it right, Lawrence says the only complete relationship is one of both the mind and the body... It's hard to achieve but, crucially, not impossible. It can be found in unlikely places, and it should be seized and valued, no matter what the cost. In a sense, that is the mission, or purpose of man. Or woman.'

She tried to appear nonchalant as if she discussed erotic fiction in libraries every day of the week. 'The mind and the body?'

'A relationship of ideas and understanding, but also ... of ... of physical love.'

She could not avoid the blush now. She should leave, politely. But her legs would not obey.

'I'll read it to you,' he said impulsively. The statement was harmless, yet it was as though he'd said he was going to undress her. But then he smiled nervously. 'No, really, perhaps it's a book you should read yourself.'

'No,' she heard herself say, with satisfying coolness. 'It's alright. You can read it.'

Still he hesitated. 'It really is quite ... passionate.'

'But it is only a book.'

He nodded, inhaled and opened a page folded at the top corner.

'The story is a love affair between a lady and her gamekeeper. Her husband is an intellectual man, but has been injured and is no longer ... physical with her. The gamekeeper on the other hand, is ... physical, but he's intelligent too.'

She thought she could detect a sheen of perspiration on his brow. They had both been carried along on a current of feeling, but Theo looked oddly vulnerable and exposed.

'Read it.' Her voice was steady.

'The intelligent part or the passionate?'

She saw his face colour slightly. 'Choose,' she commanded.

He flicked the book and it stopped open. He smiled awkwardly.

'Remember, you asked for this.' Then, in a soft yet clear voice he began to read.

'And it seemed she was like the sea, nothing but dark waves rising and heaving, heaving with a great swell, so that slowly her whole darkness was in motion, and she was Ocean rolling its dark, dumb mass. Oh, and far down inside her the deeps parted and rolled asunder, in long, fair-travelling billows, and ever, at the quick of her, the depths parted and rolled asunder, from the centre of soft plunging, as the plunger went deeper and deeper, touching lower, and she was deeper and deeper and deeper disclosed, the heavier the billows of her rolled away to some shore, uncovering her, and closer and closer plunged the palpable unknown, and further and further rolled the waves of herself away from herself leaving her, till suddenly, in a soft, shuddering convulsion, the quick of all her plasm was touched, she knew herself touched, the consummation was upon her, and she was gone. She was gone, she was not, and she was born: a woman.'

He looked at her and was surprised to see her eyes brimming. He reached out, but she retreated.

'No. Just read.'

Something wonderful was happening. There was intimacy of a new kind. And she felt in control. There was long-supressed desire, but her mind too was opening.

Theo unbuttoned his collar, thumbed the pages and then continued, his voice a touch hoarser.

'She felt, now, she had come to the real bed-rock of her nature, and was essentially shameless. She was her sensual self, naked and unashamed. She felt a triumph, almost a vainglory. So! That was how it was! That was life! That was how oneself really was! There was nothing left to disguise or be ashamed of. She shared her ultimate nakedness with a man, another being.'

His tone was low, but carried power, and his accent had that glamorous American twang. She found herself closing her eyes, slipping into the feeling rather than the sense of the words and being carried along like a twig on a stream. Then he was close, gazing intently. It was as though the world had stopped. Neither could feel the rolling of the ship and even the air was still. Perhaps they were the only two people alive in the world. She became aware of his chest rising and falling. And of his scent, a mixture of musk and soap. Unbidden, her mind made a comparison with Eugene, and she realised the intensity of what she felt was unlike anything she had experienced with him.

She went willingly from the library. Theo led her down plush-carpeted passageways, reaching at last a small steel door bearing the words **'Crew Only'**. Casting a glance up and down the corridor he opened it and, as the door closed behind them, she realised they were standing on a landing atop a metal staircase.

'You first,' he said.

'No, you first.' She stepped behind him and held onto his shoulder.

Gingerly she followed him down the flight of steps until they came to another landing. Several times the ship swayed, and she found herself suddenly close, her breath on his neck.

'Steady.'

She wondered whether he was talking to her or the ship.

The windowless passageway ran rabbit warren-like, left and right, and she found herself hoping they didn't meet anyone, or they would be forced into an intimate squeezing-by and she might have an insane desire to laugh. They turned left and at last a steel door creaked open to reveal a small cabin with a neatly made bed. He closed the door behind them.

Inside the cabin, his face was open, and something indefinable crackled in his deep-green eyes. She sensed his breath quickening. Without a word, he placed both hands on her shoulders and drew her gently to him, allowing his lips to slowly brush against hers, so that she pushed forward to meet his teasing. Her pulse quickened, and she had the delicious aching sensation of anticipated intimacy. But without warning he withdrew, the kiss postponed. He seemed suddenly nervous, opening a small cabinet, withdrawing a bottle of rum and two glasses, his hand trembling.

They sat on the narrow bed, a surprising distance apart, and she regarded him curiously. He said nothing but raised a glass full of the dark tea-brown liquid. She took it, and savoured the strong, burning rum. Its sweet, spicy intensity scorched her throat on the way down, but ended in a pool of expanding warmth in her stomach. With Eugene she had been a junior partner, and with Hazel the submissive one. But with Theo, the roles seemed more equal.

'It's good of you to ...' he paused, 'come here with me.'

'Or very bad,' she mused aloud, marvelling at her own coolness.

He helped himself to more rum and seemed to be wrestling with something. She sipped from her glass and he topped them up. She noticed the surprising softness of his skin and the clear definition of features: a strong brow and nose, small pink ears and a freckled face tinged pink by the wind. His eyes although green, included tiny flecks of amber. His body was slim, more lightly built than Eugene's, and he looked at her with an astonishing, almost schoolboy earnestness. He stood, and paced the cabin, looking faintly ridiculous in the tiny, low-ceilinged room.

'What do you do?' he asked awkwardly.

'Do?' she asked, suppressing a giggle.

'Well, I mean, what will you be doing when you reach the States?' He blushed and sat down again, even further away.

'I'm supposed to be married.' She looked down at her ring, which she had put on that morning as a defence, now failed.

'Supposed?'

'It's hard to explain,' she said, thinking how true it was. She wanted him to come closer so she took off her jacket, kicked off her shoes and slid behind him to lie back on the bed. 'It's not a marriage in the sense you might think.'

Theo's eyes widened.

'It's not?'

She hid a smile at his interest behind her glass, sipping the rum and holding the tingly fluid in her mouth before releasing its warmth to trickle down her throat.

She'd closed the door on her conscience when the cabin door had shut. What they were doing might be wrong, but her body and perhaps her mind too wouldn't be denied any longer. He was talking of something, but the words were indistinct. She realised a response was expected.

'*Hmmm*,' she said, 'I see. Perhaps you'd better come here.'

'I don't think it wrong,' he was saying, getting up before kneeling at the top end of the bed, his face now close to hers. 'to believe in a dream, even to follow it. The prize seems worth it to me.'

'Oh yes,' she said, leaning against him. 'I know all about dreams.'

She wished he would stop talking. He was saying his family lived in a suburb of Princeton, which apparently was in New Jersey.

'It's like Old England.'

'In America?' she asked, deflected.

'Not all of it. But it looks English.'

'You talk a lot for a man,' she said, as the euphoric tide of the alcohol overwhelmed her.

'I know.' For a moment the man looked like a lost child.

She reached out and touched his face. Although the skin was soft, on his jaw was a faint scratchy stubble.

'I like it when you talk. You have a nice voice,' she said, smiling.

'If you want to go,' he said suddenly, 'I mean, I don't want you to think I'm the kind of guy who would just lure a woman down here and ...'

'And?'

'Well, you know ...'

'Oh,' she said as if the realisation had just dawned on her. 'You mean, this.'

Cupping his head in one hand she kissed him, firmly, lingeringly.

He made some faint sound.

'I think,' she said, his breath hot on her face, 'you'd better turn out the light.'

CHAPTER 40

'But who is this scarlet woman?' someone asked.

Stella had dragged Rosie, along with her posse of new friends, to one of the chic cafés, where aproned waiters plied deftly between tables. Rosie was only half listening. Caroline, whom Rosie recognised from their first lunch in the Grand Salon as the elegant, well-spoken one, removed her cigarette holder and paused, relishing the suspense.

'As you know,' she said slowly, letting the tension build, 'she's one of us.'

'One of us?' Stella looked around, grinning lasciviously.

'Oh,' Caroline shook her head, 'a G.I. Bride, but present company is of course excepted. She's the wife of some Air Force pilot, so I have heard.'

Rosie's ears pricked.

She and Theo had woken at four and talked for an hour – a sharing of memories, hopes and dreams. He'd finally had to leave at six to go on duty. Half of her mind was still with him, going over what had been said. It had finally happened, the great thing everyone talked about, the thing that inspired poets and artists, the thing that obsessed every man. She had expected an intimate meeting of two souls, the physical expression of oneness, the joining of two as partners together in life, or crime. Instead there had been a sharp physical pain followed by a growing tide of pleasure that climbed inexorably to a peak.

After he'd gone she'd lain back, wanting to luxuriate in the sheets that bore witness-marks to what they'd done, surprising herself by glorying in it. She'd rolled, lying face down, inhaling the faint memory of him.

'My mother always said, never gossip, it's bad for the soul.'

It was Violet, the small religious one. But her bright mousey eyes were gleaming with intrigue.

'What pray would she have said about a Martini before lunch, *hmm*?' Caroline smiled a crocodile smile and the other girls giggled.

Violet went quiet and sipped her drink. They all knew she'd never drunk a thing before she came on board, and her taking to it with enthusiasm had struck a chord of humour among her more experienced fellow passengers.

'I saw them.'

It was Joan, the short-haired blonde, whom Rosie at first glance found more thoughtful and amenable than the rest. Rosie was grateful Joan avoided eye contact.

'Really?' chorused a number of voices.

Joan nodded, adding quickly, 'From a distance. They were going along some hallway towards the crew quarters.'

'No!' From the tone of her voice, Stella was fascinated, or amused.

Joan nodded but didn't elaborate.

'Well, I say it's disgusting.' The voice came from a large-boned girl in a pale yellow cardigan twinset, pearls and earrings.

'She's a married woman,' she said. 'Carrying on like that, when her husband waits over there.' She nodded to a random horizon. 'I hope she gets caught out.'

There was a murmur of agreement.

But both Stella and Joan kept quiet.

After a pause during which they sipped their aperitifs, Yellow Cardigan carried on.

'I hear they've been, you know, "at it" since we left port.'

Another murmur and a few gasps.

'In the lifeboats too, would you believe!' Yellow Cardigan was warming, somewhat creatively, to her theme.

'In the lifeboats?' Rosie was surprised to hear her own voice. 'I don't think they went in there.'

'Oh?' said Caroline, swivelling around to gaze at Rosie. 'Did you see them? Rosie, isn't it? Were you there? Do tell.'

Rosie blushed. 'Well, I mean, how would they get in there – they're all up on rope-things, aren't they?' They were staring at her and she couldn't help blushing. 'I heard she was actually his sister, and there was nothing to it.' She added the last as carelessly as she could.

Yellow Cardigan laughed loudly, unwilling to let the story lose any of its juiciness. 'You so naïve, my dear!' she said, snorting with derision.

Rosie wondered whether it would look suspicious if she made an excuse to leave.

'Your husband is a pilot, isn't he?' Caroline had turned to her.

Rosie picked up her coffee and sipped the beverage, trying to appear as casual as possible.

'Navy,' she managed. 'He's in the Navy.' She hoped Stella wouldn't give away the lie and her luck held, although barely, as the Londoner, who had already detected the romance, could barely hide a grin.

Eventually Rosie finished her coffee, made an excuse and left. Alone, she wandered aimlessly. She passed the Grand Salon again. The model ship was, alarmingly, two-thirds across the make-believe ocean. That meant another day and two more nights to go. The possibilities of the nights suggested themselves. She couldn't deny it, she had a longing for him. She wanted the feel of him, the sound of his voice and the scent of his body. The more wrong it was, the more attractive it became.

Even saying his name quietly to herself was an odd, clandestine thrill. She'd experienced true intimacy: a sensation of yielding innermost privateness that exceeded anything that had gone before. It felt as though she and the man were bound together by it: culpable, like partners in crime. It could just be her imagination, but since she had lain with him everything in life seemed sharper, more acutely defined. Colours were brighter, sounds richer and more complex and she had become aware of the sheer intensity of beauty in the most unlikely of places. In the details of a carving, the stiches in her new leather handbag, or the smile of a gurgling child. It was as though overnight her senses had all been supercharged.

She reached the promenade deck and gazed out over the passing blue-green ocean. Beams of sunlight were breaking over the stern, landing on the ocean and settling as balls of light where they appeared to bob randomly, like recklessly cast pearls. Restlessly, shielding her eyes, she noticed a great white bird with enormous wings and a keen eye, trailing effortlessly, following the wake. He seemed to be watching her alone, turning his head every so often but maintaining a steady course and distance. They must be closer to land, she thought. It was not a welcome realisation and the creature suddenly irritated her. Her emotions were tumbling wildly over each other, and she needed time. She walked away from the bird's relentless gaze, wondering to herself whether ships like the *Queen Mary* ever broke down.

Rosie walked restlessly for several minutes, her feet ringing off the tough teak deck. Women and babies were everywhere, and as she passed she smiled absently at them, listening to snippets of conversation as they speculated about their lives to come in America. Taking the stairs to the Sun Deck, an open platform, unlike the lower Promenade Deck, she passed beneath one of the lifeboats and to the side of a pair of naval officers, her ears detecting a characteristic Yankee twang. She thought of Eugene and felt a twinge of anger. It was his weakness that had created the fatal flaw, a fracture that had allowed sin to enter. Had their wedding night proceeded as normal she would not have responded as she did to Theo. Her British-trained conscience immediately corrected the thought. Two wrongs didn't make a right.

'Been looking for you,' he said, making her jump.

How did he keep appearing like that? He was light on his feet, but even so it was uncanny, and suddenly he irritated her.

Theo's face glimmered with a shy smile.

'Hullo,' he said, grinning.

She felt confused and angry.

'Hullo.' She said it flatly, even coldly.

'You're looking lovely today,' he persisted. He must have realised how clumsy he sounded, for his expression changed to one of awkwardness.

For a few moments neither spoke.

Rosie turned to the young officer.

'I'm married, Theo.' She did not mean to be so blunt. But she needed to provoke, to throw in a pebble to make the pond ripple. What was he thinking?

His face grew downcast. 'I know.' He paused. 'I feel rotten.' He hesitated, perhaps mulling over his words. 'But, you know, you just didn't seem like a bride. Not over the moon. And I thought you were thinking ...'

'*You don't know what I was thinking!*' The words had come out with more force than intended, and she saw hurt in his expression. 'I'm sorry. But ...'

The sentence was left hanging. She struggled, wanting him to take charge. He seemed to sense it for he spoke calmly.

'You're right. Of course I don't know what you think, but I'd like to understand.'

There was a directness, an earnestness, that had been missing in Eugene. And his refusal to be deflected by her rudeness seemed to confirm the depth of feeling part of her longed for. Theo looked out over the passing ocean. His voice was soft, but carried strength.

'Last night. I know we shouldn't have ... But, Rosie, I thought I'd never feel love like that. How can something that feels so right be wrong?'

She shook her head. But he would not be stopped.

'You're radiant,' he continued. 'I could say I feel this because you're pretty, and I could say it's because I ...' he paused as if plucking up courage, 'I want you. And these things would be true. But there's something else, something much better than that, something a lot harder to find.' He halted, as if searching for words. 'I think I love you, Rosie. I truly do, and something tells me if we just part I'll never find the like of you again.'

Something inside her suddenly snapped. The depth of his feeling was obvious, but the intensity seemed to make things worse not better. Why had they met now, when it seemed too late? When it would brand her a social outcast, an adulteress?

It was not too late for her plan to be ruined.

'No!' The words were blurred beneath sudden tears. 'No, Theo. I just can't.' Rosie turned and almost ran along the deck, into the first doorway she found, leaving him standing alone.

CHAPTER 41

She'd taken herself as far away from the ballroom as possible, that evening. It was a dangerous place, to be avoided. Not only might he look for her there, but the music and the spell it could weave might break her will to resist, overturning her decision as quickly as she'd made it. Even getting into an evening dress seemed risky and instead she put on something even her mother would have thought sensible, a warm tweed skirt and Fair Isle twinset. At first she'd wandered the Promenade Deck, comfortable to lose herself among the dozens of other women. She ran briefly into Stella, and chatted with her until her attention and eventually her company were seized by the gang of new friends she spent much of her time with.

Rosie excused herself and found a relatively sheltered spot behind a steel beam that supported the roof, forming the end of one of the huge windows in the ship's side. There she could lurk unseen and while away some time gazing out at the emerging stars. It was a fine and oddly calm evening with very little apparent motion. The cold dark sky, with its flecks of early stars was as clear and beautiful as a painting.

She was still thinking dreamily of the stories her father used to tell her about the same twinkling lights in the sky when she first heard the commotion, a babble of raised childish voices, and the thumping of tiny feet on the deck boards. She resisted the temptation to turn around but allowed the procession to pass by behind her. And it was then she heard his voice, the smooth baritone unmistakable among the many high trebles. Covertly Rosie peered after the now departing horde. He was there among them, leading the small troupe like a uniformed Pied Piper, winding his tiny charges carefully between the strolling adult passengers. Behind the group followed a bunch of mothers and a pair of stewards in their smart white uniforms, pushing a large brass contraption on a wheeled carriage.

For a few moments Rosie struggled with her resolve, but the question of what Theo was doing seemed suddenly important, the answer imperative, so she waited for them to almost disappear into the throng before following at a discreet distance. After a few dozen yards Theo led his troupe through a door she knew led to the stairs to the Sun Deck. Making a shrewd guess, she imagined they must be heading for the Observation Lounge, the only large public space at the very front of the vessel, just below the higher deck of the bridge. It was an odd room she rather liked, completely semi-circular, with wraparound windows at the front and a recessed bar along both sides and at the rear. There was only one entrance other than the main one and that was the one for staff that Theo himself had shown her. Quietly she slipped through the next door marked '**Crew**', closed it carefully behind her and climbed the narrow steel steps.

Within a few moments she appeared behind the bar, surprising a young steward. Whispering an order for Rum and Coca-Cola to him and before he could reply holding a finger to her lips, she slipped past the break in the bar and took a stool on the other side. It was a good position, almost concealed from the excited little group at the front by a carved mahogany column. They were noisily considering a large brass telescope. And it was then that the penny dropped. Theo had said he watched the stars, and even had a chart of them.

Rosie paid the barman with some of the bright American coins and settled onto her barstool. Occasionally she would look up into the mirror behind the bar, from where she could make out Theo, surrounded by young women and some of the older children. Finally the lights dimmed and the front glass door was opened a crack. One by one, his diminutive audience climbed onto a stool to peer through the great brass instrument, their mothers bracing them against the now barely perceptible motion of the ship. The ocean had calmed dramatically that afternoon, and now there was only the slightest of pitching as the *Queen*'s eighty thousand tons cut smoothly through the water. Rosie could just catch his voice over the ruffle of cool air blowing through the room. Patiently he was explaining the stars and the planets with a gentleness that soon put his young charges at ease.

Rosie hunched further over her glass which seemed to have suddenly become empty. The steward, who'd been watching the show while polishing a glass, was the soul of discretion, merely raising his eyebrows enquiringly. She nodded, accepting another drink.

Theo's voice meanwhile filled the room, his mellow American tone accompanied by an orchestra of exclaiming youngsters.

'The bright one is Venus, isn't she beautiful?' he was saying, 'She's almost a twin of the Earth, but over thirty-eight million miles away. She's named after the goddess of love. Can you fly there? Well, perhaps one day.'

Like the children, she felt herself slipping, sliding, as though being tugged by an invisible but inexorable gravity into his orbit.

She'd finished her rum and, judging by the chorus of young voices, the lesson in astronomy was over. She peered around. People were leaving but she could still see Theo, lifting a blonde, curly-haired child onto the stool. The girl began to cry but he spoke calmly to her and, after a few moments, the youngster smiled and peered into the eyepiece. A few minutes later she could hear the last of the children leaving.

That's enough! She said the words silently to herself. She needed to leave.

She slid off the barstool, but then she heard his voice again, this time much closer.

'Rum and Coca-Cola, please.'

He was at the bar and almost jumped with surprise when he caught sight of her. He probably hadn't recognised her in the outfit which she'd not worn before on the ship.

For a few seconds they regarded each other.

'In hiding?' he managed finally, with an uncertain smile.

'Yes.' Rosie couldn't stop herself responding with a smile of her own.

For a moment he said nothing more, but she could see him wrestling with his thoughts. Perhaps it was the same clash of guilt and desire that tormented her. In either case, he seemed unable to drag his eyes away.

They drank and talked, offhandedly at first, but slipping inexorably down a slope of ever-increasing confidence, and intimacy. Again there was that indefinable sense of calm that radiated from his voice, some kind of certainty, as though somewhere inside of him was a compass no one else could see, so that he alone knew what direction to take. There was a directness and honesty too, in his eyes, the way they looked so directly into hers, stripping away the layers of formality, so that she felt more of a collision of souls than the mere meeting of minds. She knew with a sudden certainty she could tell him everything, things she'd never said to Eugene, or Hazel, things about her father, the orphanage, even perhaps the night at the lake.

Others began to join them at the bar but when Theo invited her back to his cabin, she accepted. They needed to talk, she told herself. They would have a civilised, adult conversation and then she would leave.

As they walked, she noticed his occasional, covert glances. They were intense, as though trying to fix her image like a photograph. She could tell by his manner that he was agitated, brimming with emotion. Suddenly he came to a complete halt. They were under one of the lifeboats, its distended grooved belly hanging protectively over them. He pulled her to him.

His presence, so close, made any denial of her own feelings impossible. Instead, she reached out, deflecting a lock of hair that had fallen forward over his face. Behind them were the davits for the lifeboat, and she could not stop a smile when she remembered Yellow Cardigan's allegations.

Theo kissed her, a gentle caressing kiss followed by a more urgent embrace.

'Rosie,' he said at last, 'what happened between us ...'

'Was lovely.' She felt the giddy release of desire suppressing her conscience. 'It was the first time for me.'

He nodded. 'I know.' He coughed and avoided her eye. 'I was wondering about that because ...'

'I'm married?'

He nodded and suddenly she wanted to tell him everything.

'We need to talk, Theo.'

Her hands caressed his face, pink with the burning kiss of sea air. She could smell him and wanted to wallow is his scent, to bury her face in his hair. With an effort she pulled away.

'Come on,' she said.

Inside his cabin, they sat on the bed and she took his hand, examining the whorls of fingerprints, the life, heart and fate lines and, just at the edge of the palm, the white indentation of an old scar. She felt like an explorer examining a map, and found herself trying to commit every line to memory. She raised the hand and held it close to her face.

'What will we do, Theo?'

She could feel his warm breath on her face. Part of her wanted him to decide, take the burden of guilt away from her.

'We can't go back,' he responded. 'I mean to before we met. I mean, I can't.'

'No.'

He pulled away and sighed. 'With your husband, why ...'

Rosie paused, struggling to explain what had happened on her wedding night.

'It's alright,' he said, taking her hand, 'if it's too painful to talk about ...'

Rosie shook her head. 'No, it's not that. It's just that I still don't really understand myself. He ... he had to leave suddenly on our wedding day, and then he was shipped back to the States. I haven't seen him since.'

Theo pulled away from her, incomprehension on his face. 'He had to leave? Just like that? On the very day?'

Rosie coughed. 'I understand he was in trouble with the Air Force.'

'But,' he scratched his head, 'didn't he write, and explain it all?'

Rosie put her back against the cabin wall.

'He left a letter,' she said slowly, 'but I still don't really know what the story is.'

'But you came – I mean, you're going to America.'

Rosie nodded. 'I know. I thought about not going for a long time.

375

But the truth is, there is nothing left for me in England. The Universe, as you might say, well, something just wanted me to make the first move.'

She grimaced, sure he wouldn't understand. But to her surprise he came forward and slipped his arms around her.

'I get it. A lot of crazy things happen in wartime. It makes sense to come, no matter what. A woman like you has a lot better chance of finding happiness in the States.'

'A woman like me?'

He bent and kissed her lightly on the cheek.

'Someone wicked, and immoral and foolish?' she said.

'Someone bright, and smart, and hopeful,' he replied.

Rosie laughed. 'I don't know about bright or smart!'

'Yeah, you do,' he said encouragingly. 'You told me a little about your past, remember, the morning after ...'

'The morning after ...' She repeated the words, remembering.

'Yeah. You pulled yourself up by the boot straps, lady. Got yourself an education.'

'Of sorts.'

'Good enough by all accounts.'

'Good enough for what though?'

'Good enough for America. And good enough for me.'

He bent and kissed her full on the lips.

She could feel herself trembling.

He felt her agitation and going to the slim cabin wardrobe, removed a bottle of rum and two glasses. He poured two stiff tots and handed one to her. They sat side by side and sipped the precious warming liquid.

'What will we do?' Rosie repeated. 'When we get to New York?'

Theo took her hand, a mixture of love and empathy in his eyes. 'Where your husband will be waiting.'

Rosie nodded. She couldn't look at him directly. 'My husband!' She gave a dry laugh. 'It seems strange now, that Eugene could be that. I don't feel like a wife. It's you I feel close to, and a wife should feel close to her husband, shouldn't she, inseparable in fact?' She didn't wait for him to reply. 'But I don't. It's you I am close to.'

She threw her arms around him. It had been sudden, but unlike with Eugene there was a depth and certainty to the feeling that frightened as well as thrilled her.

'*Yes!*' He said it with an answering passion and his grip became so tight she felt the breath being squeezed out of her. 'We are close! Far closer than most people ever get!'

'But Eugene ...' She drew a breath. She could suddenly imagine the tall America airman, standing there in the port, waiting. 'I couldn't just run away and not turn up.'

Theo took a deep breath and pulled away, looking her straight in the eyes.

His answer surprised her.

'No. That wouldn't be right.' He paused. 'You will have to meet him, and tell him.'

Rosie gulped. 'What would I tell him, Theo? That I've met a man, slept with him and that I'm eloping? That I'm an adulteress and, he'd probably say, a common tart, or a whore?'

He grabbed her suddenly. '*Don't ever speak like that! That's not what you are. Never!*' He relaxed, recovering himself. 'You're a young woman who has found love. It's not your fault that it happened. It has happened all over the world. People get separated, mixed up and then things just happen. Amid all the killing and the dying, and the grieving, loving doesn't seem like such a crime to me.'

'So we blame it on the war?'

'No one is to blame. It's not about blame.'

Rosie paused. The truth of what lay ahead was becoming clearer. 'I would feel guilty. And ashamed. Wouldn't you? Can we live with that?'

She expected him to deny the guilt, but he did not.

'Yes. You're right. There will be guilt. Worse for you, but I will feel it too. But the question is: can either of us walk away now? What would be worse, the guilt, or never seeing each other again?'

She knew the answer, even before he'd finished speaking.

'I can't leave you.' She said the words, knowing that they were true. 'But you know, Theo, the guilt might ruin things between us – later?'

He shook his head. 'No. What we have would rise above and beyond that. It's not about sin, or sex. It's about love, and I can't leave what I've found here.' He squeezed her hand. 'I just can't.'

She fell silent.

'You would have to get a divorce,' he said.

'A divorce,' she said, almost to herself. It sounded terrible. In England divorcees were considered little better than sluts, social outcasts.

'America is different,' he said, as though reading her thoughts. 'It's not the same there. People just take you as you are. There's less stigma. Anyway, why would anyone need to know?'

'I'd know. We'd know.'

Theo held her and the distress, the churning inside of her seemed to lessen. Perhaps with him by her side she could cope, even with the guilt of leaving Eugene.

'I can hardly remember him,' she confessed, trying to bolster her courage. 'And I always had a sense of … distance, as though …'

'You were younger too. You must have been very young.'

'Yes, I was.'

'Meet him in New York. Tell him. Explain that you have to …'

'Get divorced?'

'Yes. Your marriage was a mistake. We can be together. I will be inheriting the house, and the company.' He smiled and it was like the sun peering out from behind clouds. 'You can help me make my dream come true!'

'The boating business?' She laughed.

'Don't laugh. It's a dream, but I'm going to make it happen. We could build it together.'

'You make it all sound so easy. I think it wouldn't be though. Nothing is.'

For a while they were silent. With Theo she'd found someone she both desired and could talk to as an equal. Someone she could build a life with, not living in their shade, but as a full partner.

'I will do it,' she announced, finally. The pitch was low, but her voice held conviction.

'You will?'

She nodded, not breaking her gaze. 'Yes, I will.'

A brilliant smile lit up his handsome face, making his green eyes sparkle.

'But I meant it, about the guilt,' she continued. 'Without Eugene, I wouldn't even be here. I'm taking advantage of him. Those thoughts might ruin us, damn us.' She paused. 'And I haven't met him yet.' But even as she spoke the words, she felt like a moth, circling a seductive but possibly lethal flame.

'I'd rather be damned with you than saved,' he said.

She smiled. It sounded like something poetical, such as her father might say. 'Would you?'

He nodded, reached out and ran his fingers though her hair.

She felt it like an electric shock.

'Yes,' he said.

Gently he kissed her neck, her ears and then her cheek. When he reached her mouth Rosie's eyes were closed. She felt the gentle brush of his lips, and the soft penetration of his tongue. She heard herself moan gently. Inside she felt the warm stirring she'd been trying to suppress all day, a quivering ache of desire. Swiftly, decisively, she leaned into him, kissing him back harder, more urgently. His mouth opened and she explored it gently, her tongue finding his, wrestling as they explored every angle of the kiss. He broke off and began once more to kiss her neck, nibbling her ear and sending a sharp breath-catching thrill through her body.

'It's wrong!' she panted, her breath coming in short gasps.

He moved lower, nuzzling her neck, his hands nudging aside her cardigan, cupping her breasts through the thinner wool of the twinset pullover.

'Yes.'

She guided his hand under her slip, until it found the space between her legs, the skirt riding up as his hand brushed on past the tops of her silk stockings.

'I can't help it.' His voice was breathless, and hoarse.

'No, we can't help it. We can't stop it. I don't want to stop it.' She was almost breathless as she wriggled out of her cardigan.

His hand was moving rhythmically between her legs, occasionally snagging in her suspender belt. The contact between his fingers and the fragile material of her silk cami-knickers was magical. She felt him fumble with the buttons on her suspenders and gasped, closing her eyes.

For a few moments she let him continue, the sensation a rising wave, displacing doubt like a morning sun burns off the night's mist. Occasionally he would slow into a rhythm that was firmer, more circular and she would gasp. He had removed his trousers and she reached out, grasping the burning stiffness that filled her hand. It felt gloriously obscene, rude and powerful. Tightening her grip she felt him moan. She couldn't bear the delay any longer.

'No, no,' she whispered, pushing his hand away.

Misunderstanding, he paused.

'No,' she managed. 'My skirt.'

He understood, allowing her to wriggle out of it, shedding his shirt and pants.

'Quickly!' she begged. 'Please.'

He tugged at her slip, pulling it over her head and for a second she was trapped in the funnel of it, making her giggle.

Then she was free, and their eyes met. The connection was intense and she felt the hair rising on the back of her neck. She'd never felt she belonged anywhere as much as she did in this place, and this moment in time. He smiled his infectious smile and gently kissed her, his hands reaching around and uncoupling her brassiere. She lay back, allowing him to pin her wrists down, hard against to the mattress. She felt deliciously vulnerable, outrageously brazen, at his mercy, and she wanted him inside her. His body shone in the cabin light: broad shoulders above, and below a body from which individual ribs marked the pale surface lightly, tapering at the waist below. Here and there ran the thin white lines of old scars.

They looked into each other's eyes as she slid out of her knickers, the thought of losing the final barrier causing her pulse to quicken even further. His was a dreaming look, his eyes ripe, as green and deep as jade. She felt his kiss on her breast, sighing involuntarily as his mouth closed over a nipple. Slowly he moved lower, kissing her quivering belly until his face was between her legs. Her breath came raggedly now, currents of intense pleasure flooding across her mind in bright febrile waves.

'I want you, Rosie.' He paused, reappearing and nuzzling her face. She kissed him hungrily.

'Have me, have me,' she murmured.

She felt the shaft enter her smoothly and without pain, continuing until he was fully inside her. She felt a shudder and longed for him to withdraw. No sooner had he done so that she craved him inside again, her body rising to meet the rhythm of his thrusts. He impaled her, driving himself deeper and she felt the pleasure inside her rise until it felt as though she would burst. Her hand reached round and she grasped his small behind, pulling him deeper.

She felt him climax before a burst of pleasure ripped through her like a sunburst, a convulsion on mind and body that left her shaking.

He lay beside her, panting, and she reached over, running her fingers though his hair, a sensation of floating buffering her body against the crisp sheets. They lay together, bathed in the afterglow, slipping in an out of a half dream, a blurry reflection of their pink bodies shimmering in the swirling flames of the mahogany cabin wall.

Rosie tried to stay awake, to burn the memory of the moment deep into her mind, but could feel herself being pulled inexorably down into the deep, feathery bed of sleep. Her breathing slowing, she began to dream, a dream in which she heard Eugene's footsteps in the corridor, the odour of his cologne filling the room. She wanted him to open the door, to discover what she'd done, for a fire had been lit inside her and she wanted it to burn, even if it consumed all of them. The footsteps paused, and then moved on, their sound quickly subsumed beneath the rumble of the *Queen*'s great vibrating engines.

CHAPTER 42

Rosie woke in her own bed, having retreated again to the sanctuary of her cabin when Theo rose for his shift. Her bleary eyes opened. She'd dreamt of him. She'd been holding him, but with the casual oddness of dreams, he'd changed into a child. The image seemed to be of significance, but the more she tried to focus and bring it back, the faster it evaporated. She was jolted fully awake by a sudden noise and cast a glance at Stella's slumbering shape. The noise clarified into the excited voices of young women coming from the passageway. There was an uplift in their words, a sense of haste in their footsteps. Then she remembered: this was the last day at sea. The proximity of her fate and the moment of confrontation loomed, and in her stomach she felt a sudden plummeting freefall of pure dread.

She dressed and left quietly, pushing her fears temporarily aside. In the dining room she drank coffee but left the French toast half-eaten, making her way to the deck, where she joined the daily circular parade of women, crew and off-duty sailors around the ship. The sky was clear, the air cool, and she wished she'd brought her coat. In lieu of its warmth she increased speed. Finally, near the bow, she stopped.

She gazed across the furrowed sea moodily, and felt a growing frustration mingled with indignation. How, despite her good intentions had she ended up here, travelling to meet a man she could hardly remember, while on the very ship lived and breathed someone, who …? Rosie stopped the train of thought.

The great white bird was flying alongside again, its unblinking baleful eye watching her.

'I'm still here,' it seemed to say. 'And I know what you're doing.'

The bird opened its beak momentarily as though laughing. She cursed it, turned and began walking, pushing her way through the gathering crowds. She collided with a group of women, but shoved on, ignoring their indignant exclamations. Inside her, anxiety tinged with anger blazed and there seemed no escape from its heat, except perhaps to throw herself into the sea.

Rosie caught sight of Stella in the Observation Lounge. The young Londoner was chatting with other wives, but her companions were leaving. Rosie entered and, giving a brief wave of recognition, ordered two coffees before making her way over. For a while she forced herself to be merely sociable and they sat people-watching, chatting.

'Only a day now,' Stella was saying, looking critically at her nails. Her gaze followed the young barman and, as he bent to retrieve a bottle, she craned her neck slightly.

'Yes,' Rosie replied mechanically, her voice flat. 'What do you think it will be like?'

'America?'

'No. Marriage.'

'Alright, I expect. So long as you don't expect too much.' She gave Rosie a knowing look. She lit a cigarette. 'Course, what 'appens afterwards is anyone's guess. If it don't work out, I can always get on Shank's Pony and get right out of it. I'll be in then, an' there's plenty of fish in that particular sea.'

Stella was so in control, Rosie thought, but also unbearably hard. But perhaps the hardness was just a way of protecting her mind.

'You think I'm being a cow?' Stella asked, looking intently into Rosie's face.

Rosie was about to say no when Stella continued.

'I don't know much about you, Rosie, but where I came from things was tough.' She paused. 'I 'ad four brothers and I was always last, for food, for clothes, for everyfing. I thought I was unhappy till one night during the Blitz. Then sudden like, it were all over. Even the little that I 'ad were gone. Then I knew what unhappiness was alright. An' loneliness an' all.'

She fumbled for a cigarette. Beneath her brittle outer shell, the pain was clear enough.

'I'm sorry.' Rosie found a lighter and lit her up.

'Ta.' She inhaled and continued. 'But sorry don't do it, does it? Being sorry wouldn't have got me off the pile of bricks that was left. I knew I had to fight. Fight! Fer meself, and grab every bit of 'appiness, live every day to the full cos you never know when your time's up. I had ter do it, not only for me but for them that didn't make it. Is that daft?'

'No.'

Rosie admired Stella's strength, and her determination to make things work for her. She'd seen the flame of female determination and independence lit a thousand times in the war, when the men were away and women worked. They'd produced the weapons, driven the busses, even flown some of the planes. Yet she couldn't quite wholeheartedly embrace the kind of selfishness her friend seemed to be advocating.

Rosie looked over the sea. The wind was stirring the wave-tops into creamy white ridges. She couldn't be as cold as her companion, but she would look after herself.

For a while they sat without talking, contemplating what lay ahead.

'Why did you get married?' Rosie asked. 'Not just for survival, surely?'

It was a bald question, but the ocean was slipping past at an alarming rate. There was no time to be delicate.

Stella looked at her. 'If you mean, was I in love, or am I now? Then no.'

Rosie nodded. 'So ...'

'I fancied 'im. That's all. He weren't shy and I needed cheerin' up.' She laughed. 'An' he was as fit, fit as a butcher's dog! Drop-dead gorgeous, in fact.' Stella's gaze was straight and untroubled. Rosie's surprise at her nonchalance must have showed for she went on. 'Look. He were a Yank, yeah? He had all the charm, and a drop-dead lovely body, muscles hard as rock, and a hairy chest like a bloomin' bear. So 'ee made me life worth goin' on with. But,' she added, shaking her head, 'I kept my bloody 'ed screwed on, alright. I knew that I 'ad to nail 'im down with a ring.'

Rosie gave a faint laugh, but Stella was unabashed.

'I know what you're thinkin'. An' you're right. 'e was my meal ticket.'

Rosie blushed. Had she not done the same? Less cynically perhaps, but still.

'Not just out of Blighty when it were all over, but out of bein' poor. So I took what I wanted. I didn't have much time to find out whether he's the love of me life, but if it turns out that he's not, or if he treats me bad, I'll just move along. I'm not so bad-lookin'.'

Rosie's eyebrows shot up. 'Wow!'

'That's the way it is. Like it or lump it,' her small friend said defiantly.

Stella's advice could have been what she wanted to hear, a justification for freedom, at any price and without guilt. But the creed seemed less a plea for independence and more a licence to do what you liked; not a moral argument but a statement of self-interest, however justified by events. She'd liked Eugene, and wanted it to grow into love, whereas Stella's attitude seemed somehow colder. Yet still she felt a thin chill of guilt.

It was Stella who spotted the telegraphist's cap first. It had become a familiar sight as the passengers discovered their ability to send and receive messages from the radio room.

'*Flynn!*' he was calling. '*Telegram for Mrs Flynn!*'

At first Rosie's mind didn't register, and it was Stella who tugged on her sleeve.

'One for you, I reckon.'

'Oh!'

She raised her hand and the young man came to the table, handing over the thin blue-and-white form and taking a signature. Then he left with a nod.

'*Mrs Curtis! Telegram for Mrs Curtis!*'

Stella gave her a knowing look.

'Time I was off,' she announced. 'There's a very nice young sailor as said he'd show me round the engine rooms!'

Rosie looked at the form for a second, before tearing open the paper.

'**Hope you are Having a Fine Trip + Stop + See You in New York! + Stop + Eugene + Stop.**'

Swallowing hard, Rosie put the message on the table. Her pulse was racing and she felt suddenly sick. She'd been wondering, perhaps hoping, that he mightn't even turn up, but here was the confirmation she did not want.

At that moment she glimpsed the young, bearded officer she'd seen occasionally around the boat before, always at the edge of a gathering, unable to dance, and always with a dressing over one eye. Today he was accompanied, as he usually was, by a young woman in her twenties, with long brown hair and in an attractive floral dress almost hidden beneath a fur. They were making slow progress along the deck, the officer walking with the aid of a cane. She must be his wife, though she looked like a nurse, for her devotion to his wellbeing was all too obvious.

CHAPTER 43

It was well after dinner and pitch-dark when they met on the last night. Rosie ran her hand along the heavy passenger rail, the mahogany moulding still scored deeply with the penknifed initials of G.I.s, and gazed at Theo without speaking. Behind the pair, the ship's wake was unravelling slowly to the horizon, a trail that shone and glimmered in the moonlight like the track of a huge marine snail. Rosie fidgeted, wrestling unsuccessfully with her feelings.

'Tomorrow ...' he said, not daring to complete the sentence.

She said it for him. 'Tomorrow we'll be in the Big City. In New York.'

Her face was open, but on her brow there was the ghost of a frown. He spoke again.

'There's so little time.' He looked out over the ocean. 'I wish this voyage could go on forever and just never reach land. Don't you?'

How could she explain to him when half of herself disagreed with the decision she'd made?

Theo was looking at her closely.

'Do you still feel the same?' he asked, his voice quavering slightly.

She looked away. Her reply was strangely hollow. 'I'll do what we agreed.'

She could almost feel the relief radiate from him, though his face remained composed.

'I know it won't be easy,' he said.

'Do you?'

For a moment he said nothing but in the silence he took out his cigarette case and proffered a smoke. She shook her head and he lit up.

'When you've seen him …' he began, hesitating when she turned to him. 'Afterwards,' he continued quickly, 'we'll need to meet – somewhere.'

Rosie nodded. She felt oddly captive to her inner will, and to him. What had passed between them had welded them together with an arc of heat and light that still bound them. Yet she also felt a terrible apprehension, a fear of confrontation perhaps, and the sneaking guilt of betrayal.

He stretched out his hand and reflexively she responded. He placed something on her outstretched palm, a book of matches. The picture on the front was of a skyscraper, and it bore the inscription, '*Empire State Building 20, West 34th Street.*' Rosie flipped it open absently. Inside was a picture of a city view and the words '*86th Floor Observation Deck.*'

'There. On the Observation Deck.' He smiled weakly. 'Like King Kong and Fay Wray.'

She didn't smile at the silly joke.

'I'll wait there until midnight the day we land.' He glanced at his watch and raised his eyebrows. 'But now I have to run. Duty calls.'

She glanced at his uniform. He looked smart, dashing even, and there was still that trace of depth that Eugene had lacked. She felt her heart lurch.

'Goodbye,' she managed, feeling oddly doomed.

'I'll see you there,' he said, his voice calm, yet his deep green eyes betraying doubt, and perhaps a hint of fear.

CHAPTER 44

Not long after the grey morning light began to sneak through the porthole, Rosie was jolted awake by a deafening thump on the cabin door. In her sleep she'd already sensed a change in the ship's rhythm, vibrations from the engine reducing, the rolling of the sea slackening to a perceptibly more gentle wallow. Now an excited voice, barely muffled by the mahogany, confirmed it.

'*New York! New York!*'

Rapid footsteps receded before the excited call was repeated. Rosie sat up. She had spent an almost sleepless night, had bathed and dressed and been lying on her bunk since three. She must have finally dozed off.

Now her heart was in her throat and she experienced a wave of nausea. She must be strong and do what was right for Theo, even if paradoxically it meant doing what was wrong to Eugene. Theo was the only honest future possible, while marriage to Eugene could no longer be true, or kind.

Stella had long gone, presumably to catch sight of land as soon as humanly possible. Rosie splashed some water onto her face and, still only half-awake, emerged from the cabin. She was immediately pushed aside by a surging current of women. They were streaming from opened cabins to the upper decks. Allowing the door to click shut behind her, Rosie stepped out and let herself be carried along. She soon arrived at the grand staircase, streaming with jabbering women, all moving the same way, upward, like a waterfall in reverse. The current was strong and moments later Rosie found herself abruptly disgorged into the blinding light of the Sun Deck. Looking around, she finally spotted Stella at the rail.

'*Come on!*' Stella mouthed, beckoning to Rosie with one hand and waving at the shore with the other.

Rosie pushed through the crowd and at last arrived at her companion's side. She caught her breath. On their left, the colossal blue-green Statue of Liberty reared up towards the sky like an American Boadicea, holding aloft a torch from the massive stone plinth on which she stood. The hairs prickled the back of Rosie's neck as she stared in wonder at the famous landmark. She really was in New York. After all the delay, and waiting. She'd arrived.

Everywhere, a fleet of tugs fussed like attentive cygnets around a maternal black swan, the air thick with the hooting of horns and the shouting of voices. A couple of larger boats were spraying water from hoses into the air, and smaller sailing craft were circling haphazardly like water-skimmers on a pond. Everyone was waving, and below on one of the skidding yachts an excited terrier wearing a Union Jack scarf was barking furiously.

'*This way!*' bawled Stella, almost disappearing into the crowd, barely audible above the babble of voices, shouts and cries of women and fast-wheeling gulls.

They pushed their way forward. To the front and right of the ship a vast parade of skyscrapers was drifting past. The panorama was angular, geometric, sprouting up from the streets like a strange mass of living grey crystal.

A woman in the crowd was shouting frantically and pointing: *'Empire State! Empire State!'*

Rosie's heart skipped a beat. And there it was, the classic stepped shape of the towering skyscraper, the antenna on the top pointing accusingly at the sky.

There was so much to see, she forced herself to look away.

Below, and much closer than the sky-punching monoliths, almost touching the flanks of the great liner, row upon row of timber berths and mossy piers, clinging to the river bank like an accumulation of living growth, passed slowly astern. On the dockside, crates stamped for foreign shores stood, and here and there a nodding crane dutifully hoisted cargo aboard a waiting vessel. Further ashore, glass glinted from hundreds upon hundreds of windows. There were no sooty gaps, no cratered scars and Rosie could imagine that at night the skyline would be peppered with bright lights, all so unlike any wartime British city.

As though fatigued by the effort of her journey, the *Queen* came to a halt in the middle of the channel, the last ripples of movement radiating outward from her bow. Within minutes, tugs were bumping alongside, nudging the great ship nose-first into the berth as the passengers craned their necks from above. Three thousand brides had just arrived in a new and foreign world, and above them the ship's horn blared a single, reverberating note of triumph.

After a pause, the ship's steel gangways clanged down onto the stone dock, and untidy lines of girls, babies, luggage and trolleys immediately began the chaotic process of disembarkation.

'No point in hurrying.' Stella gestured at the numbers now queuing for the stairs down to the departure deck.

'No,' Rosie replied. 'But ...' She paused, making a sudden decision. 'I'm going to say goodbye.'

She left Stella with a mystified expression on her face, and began squeezing through the hard-pressing crowd, dodging anxious passengers where she could and at last making her way to the Off-Duty Staircase, an alternative crew-only way of traversing decks. Stella wouldn't understand her need to linger, to say goodbye to the ship that had carried them across the ocean, through calm and storm, and that had been witness to personal storms of her own. Perhaps it was true that part of her simply wanted to delay, to cling like a child unwilling to let go of a playground swing. But she had an odd affection for the ship. In some way, leaving the *Queen* was like leaving England all over again. It was the last tangible vestige of home, and soon it would be gone.

The narrow, windowless passageways were empty of passengers now, and the crew were preparing for the next voyage, evidenced everywhere in untidy mountains of linen piled at random. Her fingers trailing along the teak-panelled walls, Rosie went swiftly to the Grand Salon. There on the wall, the ship stood at the end of its journey, bow finally touching the shoreline of the North American continent. The Salon was the heart of the *Queen*, an appropriate place for goodbyes and so, quietly, she whispered hers, caressing the cold marble of one of the columns as a crew of overalled men, busy in their work, cast curious sideways glances.

Ten minutes later, Rosie found Stella waiting anxiously in the Disembarkation Lounge. Limply she followed her towards the gaping portal in the ship's side, out onto the creaking metal gangway and down to the dock. Halfway there was a small landing where the ramp turned through ninety degrees, and Rosie halted. She put down her case and wrestled with a crazy impulse to run back up the gangway, back through the labyrinth of passageways.

Suddenly she saw a man, standing on the great white bridge, silhouetted against the sky, dark hair blowing in the wind. And he was waving.

'What yer doing, girl?' Stella was pulling at Rosie's sleeve.

'Saying goodbye!' was all she could say. She turned back and pointed, but where the sailor had been was now only empty sky.

'Come on!' said Stella, 'You're 'olding everyone up! It's too late for all that now.'

Clutching her case, Rosie dumbly followed the young Londoner, tramping mechanically down the flexing steel gangway to the waiting dock. She'd anticipated the moment in daydreams, but it had not been like this, every footstep leaden and unwilling.

At last she stood on the concrete dock, surrounded by a cacophony of sound. As well as the mechanical hum of cranes, the yelled conversations of the dockers, and the murmuring of the women themselves, the air was rich with the bass rumble of engines. A few vociferous arm-banded women were marshalling the new arrivals into queues for a fleet of waiting yellow buses.

Helplessly Rosie followed Stella onto the sturdy yellow vehicle. It had an odd smell, as if it had been recently cleaned with disinfectant, which only served to emphasise the alien world they had arrived in, and Rosie's growing sense of unreality. They sat together and after a few moments, amid the vivid chatter of voices, the doors closed with a hiss, and the bus growled and bumped across the steel rails of the dock. Finally it turned through the gates and out onto the bustling, grid-iron streets of Manhattan to a chorus of exclamations and forest of craned necks. Stella had her compact out and was making last-minute adjustments to her make-up and, in front, a pair of women were helping each other with their hair.

Feeling sick, Rosie closed her eyes. It didn't matter what she looked like. She wasn't going to make the man waiting for her happy. She was the bearer of bad news, a villain who had only to speak her lines and leave. Her stomach suddenly cramped and for one awful moment she thought she was going to vomit. But she concentrated on her breathing, keeping it slow and calm, and the urge passed. To distract herself she glanced around the bus. The bubbling excitement so evident among its passengers passed over and around her without touching, leaving her irretrievably removed from the final scramble. Her mind was full only of loneliness and separation: from England, from the ship, and from Theo.

The coach ground on, crunching gears, growling angrily with its gruff engine, seemingly using its sheer size to bully a way through the mass of jockeying cars and lumbering trucks, a passage punctuated by sudden accelerations and tyre-screeching stops, the combative blaring of horns and interminable waits at traffic lights. The time had almost arrived, and the air was full of perfume and the faint choking must of powder. Just when she thought the journey would never end, they arrived at a dirty, nine-storey, red-brick warehouse.

The bus pulled up, and the passengers were able to read the sign in the second-floor windows which said simply, 'Reception Centre for Aliens'.

'That's us,' nodded Stella. 'Aliens. Can you bloody believe it? And more queues, more forms, I'll bet.'

Slowly the passengers disgorged, and the rubber-necking women squeezed into the open maw of the building in ragged, chattering, complaining streams. Waiting her turn, Rosie inhaled. The city air had a distinct tang, unreferenced in memory, not unlike a railway station but with hints of half-burnt petrol and the stale acridity of spent cigarettes. It was a man-made smell, metallic and distinctly metropolitan, belonging with the constant rumble of cars, and the sheer dominance of concrete, steel and glass.

They'd entered in the building, arriving in a great hall with a high ceiling.

'Look!' Stella stood on tiptoe to point around a woman and her glugging baby. 'They're labelling us! Like bloody parcels!'

Ahead was a row of desks and, as each woman left, they could see she wore a large brown label, like lost luggage.

'*Bloomin' cheek!*' Stella squawked indignantly.

Slowly they inched on, Rosie shuffling her feet reluctantly forwards on the dusty concrete floor from which the sounds of a thousand other pairs of shoes likewise rebounded. Everywhere were lines of luggage and nervously mumbling women, the air stirring with their muted conversations and echoing with the shrill cries of babies, while, from unseen desks ahead came the staccato thump of rubber stamps. As Rosie arrived at the first desk, her name and passport were taken, she was labelled, the label stamped and then directed on to a further row. Behind them she could see three further lines, each straddling the room from wall to wall like a fence in a steeplechase or, she thought, a defence against the unwanted, and the unworthy.

Feeling numb, Rosie awaited her fate. She was abruptly confronted by an officious lady, who checked her marriage certificate. The document were subjected to another stuttering rubber stamp, handed back and she was given a green form, marked I-151.

'Whatever you do,' said the lady, 'you must not lose that one.' Rosie must have looked confused for she added, 'It's your right of residency. You are now a legal resident of the United States. Congratulations, ma'am. Next!'

It was almost half an hour later that Rosie's queue drew towards the last row of desks. Her legs were tired and her head ached. Her feet had developed a mind of their own, dragging as though unwilling to obey commands. From the next room she suddenly heard screams of recognition, and her blood momentarily froze. He must be here, she thought, somewhere in the same building, just through the open doors in the room beyond.

Reaching a young man with a large exercise book, Rosie's overloaded mind was swimming and she struggled to answer his questions.

'Thank you, Mrs. Flynn.'

The gentleman was speaking to her. She wanted to correct him, to tell him her name was not Flynn, but Haskell.

'Welcome to the United States!' the man said, this time gesturing toward the doors.

Before Rosie could think any further, she was caught in a flowing eddy of women, pressed forward, its momentum carrying her out of the room and through the doors. She looked for Stella, but her friend was gone, and Rosie suddenly panicked. She couldn't do it, couldn't go through the door. She must have stopped abruptly for a scrum of women soon began to build up behind the obstruction she'd created. Her heart thumped wildly. It seemed to have moved from her chest to her throat where it was vainly trying to claw its way out of her body. Behind her, others were pressing, some barging past and grumbling at the unexpected delay she'd created.

Through the doors came shrieks of excitement, the murmur of deeper male voices and the ominous shuffling of leather-clad feet, all rebounding from the floor and reverberating around the high-ceilinged room.

Soon she would meet Eugene again. Would she really be able to deny him to his face? It had been over two years – would she even recognise him? When she'd married him she was just a child, and so much had happened since then. But now she must walk through the door, and face him.

Rosie reached the door and the view widened to reveal an even bigger hall; something like a railway station, uncarpeted, without furniture. At the far side almost fifty feet away, stood the young men, a football-crowd of grey suits, tweedy coats, fedoras, homburgs and scarves, enveloped in a haze of smoke and barely held back by a thin cordon of officials. The men were craning their necks, as nervous and excited as any of the women. Rosie gulped. Suddenly a flashbulb popped nearby and for a second she was stung by the light. Then, clutching her case as though it was a life-preserver, she was through.

CHAPTER 45

The café was small, intimate and Italian. Two rows of booths ran from near the door to a bar at the rear, each with facing bench seats and a central table bearing a red-and-white cloth. The walls were decorated with what looked like frescoes of the Italian countryside, and on each table sat an empty wine bottle, sporting a bright red candle, the lower half covered with woven straw. They'd been served coffee by a sly, gum-chewing waitress who'd retreated to the bar but was nevertheless, Rosie noticed, keeping a curiously hawkish eye on them. So far her own conversation with Eugene had been cool, almost mechanical, the social niceties more like the meeting of long-separated friends than the reunion of husband and wife.

The coffee was served, Rosie and her husband finally gazed at each other, neither speaking. He looked so much older, Rosie thought, the grey hair having spread so that among the black locks the occasional silver strand gleamed under the electric lights. He'd put on weight too, his face and his neck heavier set, without the former tone of youth. The grey flannel suit he was wearing was tight on his expanding form, and the homburg he'd worn to the restaurant had given him a shady air, like a spy or perhaps a private detective. On his hand was a gold wedding ring, which was odd as he hadn't mentioned in any of his letters he was wearing one. Only his brown eyes were the same, impossibly deep, and with a gaze that gave no clue as to his thoughts.

Rosie gulped. It was going to be every bit as hard as she imagined. For any faults he might have, he was still a good man. She suddenly remembered her father's stress on truth in everything, not only with others, but in dealing with yourself. From that she drew a thin infusion of courage. She would just come right out with it.

'Eugene,' Rosie said, cringing inwardly, 'I cannot be your wife. I am so, so sorry ...'

She'd hardly begun the well-rehearsed, apologetic declaration when his smooth voice cut over hers.

'I know.'

She looked at him, astonished.

'You ... do?'

He knew about Theo, she thought? How? Had someone on the boat telegrammed him? No, that was ridiculous.

He took a sip of coffee. He seemed surprisingly calm as he put down his cup.

'I have something to say too. But you go first.'

Momentarily put onto the back foot, Rosie struggled to find words. She'd just have to say it plainly.

'I met someone on the ship coming over,' she said, 'and I fell in love. His name is Theo and he's an American too.' Her voice sounded stressed, high-pitched. 'I want to marry him.'

Eugene nodded. 'I understand.'

'You do?'

'Yes. When we met you were a kid, and I was at war. A whole lot of water has flowed under a whole lot of bridges since then.' He grimaced. 'And then there was the matter of our wedding night.' He avoided her eye.

He shuffled awkwardly in his seat before reaching for a packet of cigarettes. He offered one to Rosie before lighting up himself.

'There's a lot you don't know about me, Rosie. I'm not the man I pretended to be.'

He hesitated, as though he was summoning his own courage.

'When the war started I was gung-ho,' he said. 'I thought I'd win it on my own, you know, typical big-headed Yank, right? But war ain't like in the movies, and, to cut a sorry story short, I found I wasn't the hero I hoped I was.' He opened his palms in a gesture that was more defensive than expansive. 'I got through but … I needed help. Three things kept me going, and one of them was you.'

Suddenly Rosie couldn't look him in the face. She sipped her coffee as he carried on.

'One of the other things was drugs. One was something called Benzedrine. I think the medical name for it is Amphetamine. Believe it or not, the Air Force gave us those. They kept us going on long missions, but there were side effects. I got jittery and I admit I nearly funked. But I found someone in the medical corps who supplied something to bring me down, and that was morphine.' He looked at her. 'I'm not proud of it, but I guess I did what I had to do.' He sipped his coffee and coughed.

Rosie's mind was racing. The possibility of drugs had frightened her at first. A few things had come to light about the war since then, discussed quietly in newspaper articles, but not even whispered on the radio. To seek relief from fear, to escape the horrors he'd seen didn't seem like much of a crime, or even a weakness. Rather than making her task easier, mention of them stirred the same, almost maternal love she'd once felt for him. Desperately she searched her memory.

Then she found something. His weakness had ruined what was supposed to be the best night of her life.

'There were consequences though, Eugene.' She found she could look at him directly now. 'I waited for you. On our wedding night ...'

It was his turn to hang his head.

'Yeah. I know. I'm sorry. That was rotten.'

'*Rotten?*' She was surprised at the sudden flash of anger the words evoked. '*It was utter hell.*'

He shrank before her words, body language as much as tone telling her the repentance was genuine. His hands were clenching and unclenching, he was struggling to speak. She scanned his face, detecting the presence of further revelations. Finally she sat back.

'There's something else, isn't there?' she said.

Eugene nodded.

'I said I wasn't the good man you thought I was. I'm going to let you know it all, the whole truth. It's something I have to do.' He drew a deep breath. 'What you don't know is that before our wedding I was unfaithful to you.'

Rosie felt her spine straighten. There had been no hint before about another woman.

'Unfaithful?'

He nodded. 'There was a nurse. It was near the end of the tour ... you were, you wanted to keep yourself for after we were married, but I couldn't wait ...'

The full meaning dawned on Rosie.

'You ... you slept with someone else?'

The words must have come out loudly, because the waitress stirred and scrutinised them even more closely.

Eugene blushed. He nodded, hanging his head.

Rosie recoiled, her mind suddenly incoherent with shock. The last filament of trust linking her with Eugene was gone.

'There's more,' he said, miserably.

Words failed Rosie and she raised her eyebrows.

'I'm afraid so,' he added, seeing her expression.

Their coffee cups were empty and Eugene waved for the waitress. She came slowly and slopped in more of the dark aromatic liquid, shooting a lingering sideways glance at Rosie. When she retreated, he began again.

'Before the Air Force,' he said, 'I was a foolish young guy. I was my dad's favourite, and you know the story about Frank. But there are things you don't know.' He shifted uncomfortably in his chair. 'I met a girl.'

Rosie's eyebrows rose.

'Her father was a friend of the family and both families wanted a marriage. So …'

Rosie's eyes suddenly widened. She had guessed there must have been girls before her, but a terrible new possibility suddenly presented itself.

'When we … *you were already married?*'

'Yes. But you have to understand we'd separated before I joined up.'

Rosie's jaw dropped. 'But we took vows … Eugene, we broke the law.'

He could only nod, miserably. 'I know. But I thought it was all in the past. She used to send letters, one a year, but I never opened them. I just wanted it to be over and being overseas it all seemed a long way away.'

Rosie recoiled, the anger suddenly returning. 'But you must have realised it would get found out, if I came to America,' she said. 'And what's my position now?' Nightmarish scenarios flashed though her head. Having finally made it, would she now be deported?

He reassured her. 'No. You'll be fine. You got your Green Card. And nobody here knows.' He was struggling for words. 'Rosie, you must understand why. You did so much for me. You were a ray of sunshine when my world was dark. You were hope, and youth, and life, things I'd had before it all began. I didn't know what would happen when you got to the States, but I figured we'd work it out.' He grabbed her wrist. 'The important thing was to get you out of there, a place that had been full of unhappiness. To give you this,' he gestured around, 'a new start in America. You belong in the light, Rosie.'

Rosie considered it all, her head spinning. She took a sip of coffee. It was acrid and unpleasant.

'But what do we do now?'

He passed her something over the table. It was the business card of a New York lawyer. 'It's alright.' He spoke calmly, bending his head and forcing her to look into his eyes. 'It's OK. It really is. We can get a formal divorce and the lawyers will sort it all out. I'll pay and they need never know I'm already married.' He sighed, the faint smile back on his face. 'After that, you can do what you want. You can marry this ...'

'Theo.'

'Is he a good man?'

Rosie nodded. 'Yes.'

'And he'll treat you well?'

'Yes, I believe so.'

'And money, you're going to be –'

She interrupted him. 'Yes. We'll be fine for money.'

He sat back, regarding her. He seemed to be waiting for a response, perhaps even an explosion. But, although feelings were tumbling through Rosie's mind like leaves in a breeze, she felt a rising sense, not of anger but of freedom. Her mind ran to Theo, standing on the

Observation Deck on the 86th floor of the tallest building in the world. Through his revelations Eugene had finally set her free.

'There's one more thing I want you to see.'

Eugene was gesturing to the waitress.

Rosie regarded her. How was the slovenly woman involved? A sudden alarm gripped her and she looked at Eugene. For a moment he looked puzzled at her expression, then he smiled and shook his head.

'No, not her.'

The waitress disappeared momentarily into the back of the premises. When she reappeared there was a small boy, about seven years old, at her side. They approached the table.

'Thanks.' Eugene nodded to the waitress, who retreated reluctantly, chewing her gum.

The child was dark-haired, oval-faced with a small upturned nose and had the same brown eyes as his father.

'Danny,' Eugene said, turning to the boy, 'this is your ... Auntie Rosie.'

'Hullo, Auntie Rosie.' The child said the words as if reciting his lines, but his smile was infectious and brimmed with shy warmth.

'Hello, Danny,' she said and, overcoming her state of shock, proceeded to make a fuss of the child.

A little while later, the waitress took him back into the depths of the café.

'So, you had a son ...' Rosie said.

Eugene nodded. 'Cheryl, that's, *ah*, that's his mother ... Well, she wrote me every year on his birthday, but I never opened them until I got back over here. I had no idea. And if I had ...' his hands were open in a gesture of frankness, 'we would never have happened. I never knew I had a son.'